Andrew J. Davis

Morning Lectures

twenty discourses, delivered before the friends of progress in the city of New York

in the winter and spring of 1863

Andrew J. Davis

Morning Lectures
twenty discourses, delivered before the friends of progress in the city of New York in the winter and spring of 1863

ISBN/EAN: 9783337255374

Printed in Europe, USA, Canada, Australia, Japan

Cover: Foto ©Andreas Hilbeck / pixelio.de

More available books at **www.hansebooks.com**

MORNING LECTURES.

TWENTY DISCOURSES,

DELIVERED BEFORE THE

𝕱𝖗𝖎𝖊𝖓𝖉𝖘 𝖔𝖋 𝕻𝖗𝖔𝖌𝖗𝖊𝖘𝖘 𝖎𝖓 𝖙𝖍𝖊 𝕮𝖎𝖙𝖞 𝖔𝖋 𝕹𝖊𝖜 𝖄𝖔𝖗𝖐,

IN THE WINTER AND SPRING OF 1863.

BY ANDREW JACKSON DAVIS,

Author of several volumes on the Harmonial Philosophy.

NEW YORK:

C. M. PLUMB & CO., PUBLISHERS,

274 CANAL STREET.

LONDON: J. BURNS, CAMBERWELL.

1865.

" FRIEND OF PROGRESS " PRINT,
274 Canal St., New York.

PREFACE.

The Lectures of which this volume is composed, were delivered Sunday mornings before the Friends of Progress in the city of New York, during the Winter and Spring of 1863. The subject matter of the discourses, and the language in which they are clothed, were drawn from the inspiration given during the moments allotted to their delivery—sometimes, indeed, the speaker had not chosen either his theme, or the line of argument to be pursued, until he arose to address the congregation. This fact will amply account for both the defects and excellences which may be found sprinkled through the following pages. Doubtless the author would have given more time to the selection of themes and the construction of arguments—which is ever to be recommended—if his thoughts and time had not been so entirely devoted to many and various labors wholly disconnected with this course of Lectures. And yet, in the light of his experience, it is questionable whether the contents of this volume would have been improved. If all scripture "given by inspiration is profitable," why may not the same rule apply to Morning Lectures, given under the quickening power of the same universal principle ?

That this volume may be a friend to the lonely, a guide to the wanderer, and a ray of light to those in darkness, is the sincere prayer of

NEW YORK, June 1, 1864.   A. J. D.

CONTENTS.

MORNING LECTURES.

DEFEATS AND VICTORIES.

"Many a foe is a friend in disguise ;
Many a trouble a blessing most true."

I have for years observed that the earth is full of downcast, melancholy persons, or of indifferent, stoical, lukewarm, shipwrecked characters—both the logical consequences of this over-spun popular but dogmatic theology, which is the plague of the world in general and the private sorrow of the millions of Americans in particular. Atheism is a beautiful belief, honest and soul-saving, compared with that desperate, godless, devil-full theology, which gives such splendor to the physical churches and such despair to the congregations of believing millions who support them. Mankind must obtain a new conception of the world in order to drive out this theological disease, which has been communicated to almost every sensitive, religious, spiritual, and poetic mind. It has sickened and blighted every soul that has unfortunately come under the sable wings of this dismal, desperate dream of the Oriental world. Hebrew mythology is the basis of the theology of America this very hour. Only where there happens to be a meeting Quakers, of Unitarians or Universalists,

of Spiritual Reformers or of Progressive Friends—
only in such places is there any living protest to the
prevalence of the abominable miasma which has gone
abroad like the plagues of Egypt, filtering itself
through all human institutions, not even excepting
science, literature, and the arts.

Now I find myself called upon to speak in emphatic
words against the desperate, dismal disease-promoting,
despair-propagating tendency of Hebrew mythology,
which is the accredited theology and petted religion of
Christendom. And it seems to me that, if there be
vouchsafed enough light and strength at this time, we
may do something towards augmenting the force of this
protest by considering the question of "Defeats and
Victories."

There are two propositions which stand before my
mind as incontrovertible, and as necessary to a distinct
and full comprehension of the subject:

First: That forms, vehicles, mediums, organizations, institutions, equipments, agents, attorneys, are
transient, while that which they convey is PERMANENT
and ETERNAL—and, therefore, that even what are called
"Accidents," are but the conductors or viaducts of
laws that are just as full of the wisdom of Deity as the
most delicious blessings that ever hugged your heart.

Second: That all great immutable scientific principles, and the eternal spiritual truths, have been conveyed to mankind by means of blood, fires, dungeons,
racks, gibbets, guillotines, governments, revolutions,
convulsions, spasms, fits, earthquakes, and hysterics.

These two propositions stand before my mind with
as much distinctness and significance as does any person's countenance in this room. To recognize the

Divinity in the accident, to see Good in dire disaster, to be strong enough to overcome evil in your oppressive misfortunes, to be pure enough to conquer the vice that is within you, or just touching you, is to give evidence of your complete and *practical* recognition of that sublime truth in the first proposition which is essential to every person's success and happiness in society, in business, in death, in resurrection. The most beautiful success is the most desperate disaster to him who is not wise enough to accept God as much in cloud as in sunshine.

Now, I am looking at and speaking to the world to-day from these propositions and principles. The whole universe appears to me to be regulated by a system of immutable, divine, benign, heavenly principles, which ooze perpetually forth and declare themselves even through our direst defeats, through our misfortunes, our failings and faults, and through those various and numerous accidents which occur in the history of human experience.

Rightly looked at, Adam fell *up stairs!* (I am speaking now of the accepted story in Hebrew mythology with reference to the first human defeat— perhaps the best, most full of wisdom, most searching in its spiritual lessons.) This Hebrew myth, at basis a beautiful truth, teaches that *Adam fell upward and onward*—out of his ephemeral, butterfly, useless existence, into manly health and laborious progression. He was born into luxury; *this* was the primal cause of his first defeat. He was physically and spiritually successful from the beginning; *that* caused his downfall and expulsion. Born from the skies, inheriting an incalcu-

lable fortune—never having earned a penny of it, not
having acquired an item of the powers and truths
which were slumbering in his possession—consequently
he had no appreciation of either, and like all other
superficial riches and unmerited success, his advantages
took unto themselves wings and fled, dropping him in
one of the open fields which were longing for a Man!
He met multiform obstacles on every side; but they
were his best friends. If the first man Adam had early
met a little hill of gold, not more than six inches high
and ten inches in diameter, I fear he would never have
successfully surmounted it. Undoubtedly he had sufficient of the "Yankee" in him to have influenced his
mind to bow to "the golden image and worship it." But
instead, he met only thistles, thorns, tempests, hurricanes, earthquakes and fits; but they sternly and honestly befriended him.

Do you not pity those feeble forest trees that must
grow where the winds never blow with tempestuous
fury? You never find a great, beautiful oak, never
a grand, well-developed pine, never thrifty fruit-
trees, nor a great variety of wild flowers, where the
winds are not permitted to work with great energy.
Instead, you find swamps of stagnation and cesspools
pervaded with deadly miasma; also you find subterranean beasts there—repulsive creatures, unfit to live
above ground, crawling and wriggling in the undisturbed sinks of nastiness.

Again, do you not pity a Brother man who is so well
fed in body that he has grown exceedingly lean and
mean in his spirit? General Banks (who now occupies a very prominent office, probably standing on the

threshold of the most important movement about to
connect the East inseparably with the great States and
Territories west of the Mississippi,) graduated from one
of New England's cotton-mills, and not from some high
temple of learning, not from the fostering caresses and
enfeebling attentions of very rich parents. No!
Master-men are the productions of those energetic
principles in Nature which produce and regulate all
accidents ; in the midst of apparent confusion developing the most orderly ends and guiding events to perfect
purposes.

I accept the doctrine that man is the ultimate image
of " a divine plan," and that he is destined to be sym-
metrically developed in body and caused to ripen in
spirit. These ends are accomplished by means of outward agents and spiritual influences—by mistakes and
personal faults—and not altogether by means of riches
and idleness, worldly success and bodily happiness. I
do not know of a single remarkable instance where a
man, made suddenly rich or popular, continues committed to the noble truths and large-sympathies which
distinguished him before his great success. But I do
know a man who was very poor from his birth, but
who became gradually rich and victorious in the midst
of disasters and misfortunes. He never lost his interest
in the struggling poor of the world, but gave, and still
gives, wisely of both wisdom and wealth.

The English Commissioner of Revenue near a hundred years ago undertook to gather exorbitant taxes
from the American people. He was obliged to depart
without the tax-money, and he sought his personal
safety out of Boston. The people would not submit to

1*

tyranny that came over the free ocean. The tea was thrown over in the harbor. Americans would no longer be willing slaves to the requisitions and impositions of their trans-Atlantic masters. What was the result? All history of this country is resplendently begemmed with the consequences. 1776 is referred to in all the school-books, and by all loyal persons, both in song and in story, as the commencement of "an era" of Freedom in the political and religious history of the American. England's great defeat was justice and success to her. It drove her snugly home, concentrated her upon the properties of her own kingdom and commerce, and she has ever since been nationally prosperous and self-possessed. But when she arrogantly came over here, dressed in red-coats, marching to rich and costly music, she found that victory was destined to be on the side of her opponents.

But this same victory of ours brought us a mighty defeat. We earned our "independence," but found, alas! that we were masters of England not only, but also of millions of slaves. And that sad success was the germ of our present full-orbed defeats. As a nation we have gone on with this terrible success until it has put an extinguisher upon the effulgent light of our Union. Almost are we gone nationally down into the martyr's sepulcher! Almost are hearth-stone enemies ready to roll a great stone against its mouth! But America dead and in the martyr's tomb, with the stone of adversity rolled against its mouth, is more mighty and more triumphant than when tea went overboard in Boston.

As a nation we must be forced into court and arbi-

trarily condemned. The cross of sorrow must be put
on the Northern shoulder, and the whole country must
be led up to the summit of Calvary! All are now slowly
going thither. We shall be nailed to the cross, and
two thieves will be executed with us. (There will be
no difficulty in finding a couple.) Then we shall be
taken down, and the countries of Europe about the
foot of our cross will say: "We told you so—we
expected it. We have argued it and written it for the
last half century, that such a Republic as yours, such a
loosely constituted democracy, could not and would not
long exist." Then we shall be carried away, placed in
the earth—*only for a day!* Then will angel-princi-
ples roll away this vast political obstruction, which
keeps the people in the darkness of Hades and the
misery of Gehenna. Behold we shall come forth! And
then the nations of the world, like the old officers of
Rome, will be struck with blindness and paralysis.
America will come forth—clad in white—purified,
redeemed, transformed, free! Our greatest national
success—which gave us the power to overthrow the
mastery of England—gave us also mastery over millions of Africans. That success is to-day teaching us
an expensive and desperate lesson, and we are slow in
learning it.

God, the greatest central good in the Universe, is
giving us our best development and our highest victories through disappointments, military defeats, and
political adversities. Minds, not perceiving this truth,
are cast down. They walk sadly in the vale of tears.
They live daily in bondage to a fearful, soul-sickening
sorrow. Oh, I pity those sightless editors of innu-

merable papers—those atheistic men who move and
float along in and with the rough world "just as they
find it"—minds that see nothing higher and·feel nothing
better than the hum-drum of diurnal events. I do not
wonder that they oppose and decry the Government,
and set themselves against the administration of the
Government. All the atheistic criticisms of our coun-
trymen are so many moral stumbling-blocks in the
pathway toward perdition. Banking men contemplate
the demolition of their capital. Churches and colleges,
and the institutions of common education, are wrapped
up with the nation's commercial machinery. The
important men, who support these institutions, are not
lifted by their faith in Christianity high enough above
circumstances to see that America is destined to go
down through the Gulf Stream, then put out into the
cold water, and at last outsail all the storms of capes
and gulfs, and finally reach the clear open sea of
boundless liberty. They do not believe in God, and
they are accordingly cast down. And yet they go to
their churches, they hear beautiful music, utter formal
prayers, listen to expensive orthodox sermons that
are filled with grammar and rhetoric, and with very
beautiful allusions to the Savior and his exemplary
life; but when they go home from their carpeted
churches, they are the same cast-down, hopeless, athe-
istical persons they were before they assembled for
worship. A hopeful, buoyant, and honorable man or
woman is so in spite of his or her religious creed.

Look at mankind's defeats and successes in Science.
We have a beautiful science of anatomy—a knowledge
of all the bones that enter into the framework of the

human being, or of the lower organizations. Do you suppose that a healthy man would ever have concerned himself with the items of his structure? Never! Perfect success in health would have kept the world in total ignorance of its anatomy and physiology. Disease has been our blessing! It strikes at the bone. Then comes the surgeon with his scalpel, separating parts and revealing structure, and thus he becomes a learned man; next he teaches anatomy to the classes, and then the classes go out, and thus a true education finally filters through the interstices of all human experience. And to-day almost every person knows that he has 247 bones in his body, and that woman is constituted precisely the same; and that the doctrine that man lost a rib originally is just as true as any other ancient myth—that is to say, in its external sense, not true at all.

Then came the beautiful knowledge of physiology. This science is now one of the useful ornaments of a gentleman's education. Ladies, also, have begun to acquire great riches in the direction of organs and functions. Disease has been the world's great teacher. People just begin to discover that there are such things as *nerves!* They have been long told by physicians that there were such conductors; but now they know the thrilling fact. Old sturdy Britons and Northern lords knew nothing of nerves. Read their books, and you will find scarcely an allusion to such impressible structures. A nation had to become sick—the whole people had to be cast down in sorrow—before man's mind could be moved to seek out knowledge of that mysterious system which connects his brain with all his senses, and the senses with the whole universe without.

Insanity, too, had to exist before phrenology could be practically developed and demonstrated. Mental diseases had to abound, and crime in its most mischievous forms also, before phrenology became the world's absolute necessity. The science is the child of research and misfortune, and for this reason phrenology has conquered much ignorance, and has given men practical knowledge of themselves.

Again, mankind were obliged to be afflicted and defeated with sickness in the spirit, moral prostrations, vices, and discords. There had to be swearing, profanity of various kinds, and licentiousness also, before men would seek out the great developments of music, art, religion—those higher blessings which enter into the spiritual education and happiness of the world. It was necessary that the world should suffer from its ignorance and defeats before men could be induced to inquire concerning the spiritual laws and inner principles of their existence. Men who had never seen or experienced any such evils as larceny, incendiarism, or murder, would never have concerned themselves with virtue, with truth, and with legal agents and instrumentalities by which virtue and truth are advocated, vindicated, and developed. Great saving constructive truths would never have appeared to the human mind were it not for the discords of society and the dire diseases of individuals.

The best knowledge in the world is attributable to the world's ignorance. Misfortune is esteemed by Divinity of as much value as success. Defeat is just as truly a part of God's great system as victory. Vice is a portion of the system—it is not an accident—for it brings victories as well as virtues. I verily believe this country's salvation is inseparable from the colossal lies which decorate the throne of Jefferson Davis. How could it be otherwise? How could the political crabsterians of this country discover that the millions who have been working for *nothing* in the South, *are children of God* and the victims of wrong political circumstances, were it not for the moral, political, social, and civil degradations which those same circumstances have developed among the whites? White ninnies and black picaninnies walk side by side, and all parties are moving on the road leading to an equal success through desperate and blood-stained defeats.

Do you suppose that Abraham Lincoln would have felt the "military necessity" which prompted his first of January edict, if our armies had been successful six months before? The civilized world looks at the brave, strong, powerful North, and is amazed at its defeats. But the future will look upon those weeks and months of our national agony and despair with awe, gratitude, and thanksgiving. The "military necessity" of the 1st of January, 1863, will beget and become a "moral necessity."

Already the people of the North are opening their hearts to the conception that the black man is able and anxious to defend the rights of the white man. "This is a white man's war," said the proud, successful Northmen. "We will fight our own battles, win our own victories, and obtain much credit in the political heaven for achieving all this sublime success." Our private merchants and our public ministers, as with one voice, said: "We shall have the glorious honor of beholding a white man's laurel on the brow of the potential North." Well, we have learned, sadly enough, that all this boasting and presumption, this pedantry and heartless assumption of power, has been forced down with its knees in the dust. The whole people see that further humiliations are in store before real victory can crown the brow of the North; and so seeing, they are imperceptibly converted to a higher religion than the churches can impart. I know that a few churches begin to recognize this; but did they recognize it at the start? No! Ministers have been educated by this war as much as merchants, bankers, farmers, and mechanics. Brigadier-Generals know no more about the future than does the private warrior who went bravely forth from the mechanic's shop, the factory, or the field, bearing the musket snugly against his shoulder, and groaning (sometimes with homesick, despairing thoughts,) under the weight of his overloaded knapsack. But he knows as much, thinks as clearly, feels as much true patriotism as do the Brigadiers and Major-Generals who ride with plumes along the front, "the observed of all observers"—all being educated alike; all gone to school together.

Old theology teaches persons who go through these long avenues on to battle, that if they have not accepted Christ and the means of salvation, they will go down to endless night. But the divine truth of Nature (which is God's only gospel) speaking deep down in the soul of such persons, causes them to say, "I do not believe it." The minister says, "That

is Satan's voice." Intuition, however, takes the
responsibility, and so the soldier, without conversion,
marches on to battle. He vaguely, yet strongly feels,
in his deepest soul, that if he should die in the midst
of carnage, fighting for his flag and the country, the
duty which he is performing and the motive which
actuates him will be equal to the merits of Christ. So
he practically sees the goodness of God, and believes
in his own salvation. And what is more curious, his
mother at home believes it also. She says: "To be
sure, Charles never went to church; he seemed to be
irreligious on Sundays; but he was better than most
young men, and, though he was a little wild, yet he
died doing his duty, bravely and fearlessly at the cannon's mouth; and I know that our Savior is very mer-
ciful, and though he was not 'converted,' as was
supposed, no doubt God, who seeth the falling sparrow,
will take him home to glory."

THAT is the great gospel of Mother Nature! That
is the voice of the living God speaking higher than
theology, and above all the superstitions which crowd
the mother's mind. Let us pray that all mothers—
when the deep sorrow comes to the heart—may have
the great joy of believing truth direct from Deity.
Notwithstanding his waywardness, his evils, imperfections, cruelties at home, negligence even—still, over all
and through all, is the intuitive belief that the heavens
open and receive the soldier-son. *That*, I say, is the
word of God speaking in the woman's heart in the cool
of the day, when sorrow presses heavily, when the wine
of truth comes bleedingly out of her spirit.

But let a mother go on with social and worldly

success—let her feel the pressure of no great sorrow—
and her theology will be a pampered idol. She will
oppose the Reformer and sneer at the Spiritualist. She
docs not believe in the war; or, if she does, it is with
hate, like the politicians. But let a weighty sorrow
come to her heart, and forthwith she rises up into a
beautiful transformation of spirit; and then from ignorance she goes to knowledge, from theology to wisdom,
from despair to hope, from doubt to faith, from defeat
to victory.

For all these reasons I pity a village that has never
had a mob. Go into a Connecticut town that has never
had anything to disturb it worse than a few boys stealing melons in the summer time, or some dogs that kill
the sheep—suppose no great disturbance, no deep agi-
tation, had come to that town—behold the utter
imbecility there in regard to the great moving principles of the world! They read old newspapers that
were published half a century ago, edited by persons
who got their education one hundred years ago, and
who taught things that are two and a half centuries
old. They own the oldest books, which contain the
oldest sermons and inculcate the poorest thoughts.
They read the Bible with the oldest pair of spectacles
in the house, and they judge of modern things through
the Testaments, portions of which are at least three
thousand years behind the age.

Now look at the city or village that has been stir-
red. Some reformatory man went there, who aroused
the passions and prejudices of the people. They were
obliged to hunt up their unmarketable eggs to express
their profound disgust with the reformer's sentiments.

Perhaps he was an Anti-slavery man, or a Woman's Rights speaker, or some thorough-going temperance reformer, or—which is still more dreadful—some long-haired and large-brained Spiritualist. The community so visited has received a shock, a vibration, a movement from its center, which is the commencement of its success in development.

Now take this country. The·iron-clads and the Monitors that are to go forth to victory, have come out of defeats. In Hampton Roads, in sight of Fortress Monroe, the Merrimac had to come. She was the Confederate's victory. But we had to be defeated before a Monitor could come out of these machine-shops—freighted with prodigious strength, with almighty energy—blasting that invention of the Confederates in its very eyes, and giving such a demonstration of power as to alarm the North with its own success. Do you not also see that the Monitor had to *die*, to sink, before future Monitors would be made impervious to tempests and waves? Let her go; let her bravely sink. "It is but to another sea." The people rise up to a more perfect work. Our engineers, our machinists, our scientific men, our inventors--all spring like angels of light to the rescue! Give us defeat, not only in Hampton Roads, but also near Cape Hatteras!

Now, what has Disease done? It has brought the sciences of Anatomy, Physiology, Pathology, Therapeutics—these volumes of education upon which scientific and school men pride themselves. And what has been the result? The expansion of useful knowledge among the people, urging them to overcome the causes of discase and to learn the simple ways of Health. There is, consequently, only about one person in every twenty-three really sick at any one time. The twenty-two are not perfectly well—that is too much for the terrestrial sphere; but there is only one of the twenty-three who is prostrated, or silent, white, and waiting at the golden gate of the Summer-Land. So that, at this moment, while I am speaking to you, there are not more than 1,370,000 persons actually sick in America. According to the last census there were about 32,000,000 persons in the United States; and only about one in every twenty-three was prostrated by disease Why, the world is almost perfectly healthy—just sickness and suffering enough to keep us busy and on the high road to victorious Science.

The defeats of the Allopathic system—what have they led to? Why, they have led, through salivation, to salvation! Behold those crystal colleges, devoted to higher medical education, teaching the system of Hahnemann, or the system of Priesnitz, or both, and the system of Franklin—electricity, and the system of Mesmer—magnetism, and next the system of God—INDEPENDENCE OF ALL MEDICINE!

Let us thank all who populate heaven for our defeats, diseases, accidents, and disappointments. Why, Bull Run was but the commencement of that race which shall not stop until the golden summits of Liberty are fully attained! We have only "gone around Robin Hood's barn." There is vastly more courage and real success in backing out of fire than there is in going uselessly into it and dying foolishly. We had strength and wisdom enough to retreat when disaster was upon us. There was a Divinity shaping our ends—teaching us that Freedom is the *moral* as well as the military necessity of America's inhabitants.

Men in business do not arise to the true moral position. They cannot do it until they are bankrupt, and they may, therefore, soon become so. What makes slavery so popular at the South? Because of its great mercantile, and commercial, and local advantages, and not because of its moral, spiritual, and political advantages. It is popular because men and women, resting in the lap of luxury, can get money without earning it, can whip or hire it done, and out of the affliction of others realize two or three hundred per cent. on their hereditary investment. That is the reason why it is popular. Men are not constituted to continue long in that which brings bankruptcy. The slaves of the South have earned the wealth of the South. Many great folks who live in luxury in the North, are trembling lest these multiplied and triple-fold taxes will sweep away their fortunes and leave them at the altar of repentance. Many such persons tremble because they are living on the earnings of slaves. Men who have amassed large estates by the misfortunes and victimizations of the black people, have had the most miserable " success." Oh, what a desperate victory! It is dreadful, direful, devilful, hellful—damnation is the result! Every such estate will melt like a mountain of ice before the summer sun.

Before this war commenced many persons who were unfaithful to the ordinary obligations of truth became tangled up with and woven into this great national trouble. They ripened on the very sorrows and sicknesses and slaveries of the people. Let the moneyed institutions groan! It is an honest symptom of coming success for Truth and Justice—but remember, such success is coming through bankruptcy, through painful defeats! It is very gratifying to go into business and obtain money—mere animal excitement and happiness —have credit, so that no man questions you, with all your drafts instantly honored. Such a man does not care to attend Progressive Meetings. He goes to a popular church every Sunday, where it is only necessary to pay and keep still. But when the Sun of Righteousness comes over the horizon of disasters and melts away all his property, and when his great wealth floats down into the little rivulets of other individual possessions, then he goes in haste to his minister; he is spiritually sick, is alarmed for his soul, and begins to inquire the shortest way to the residence of the Holy Ghost. Do we not read in the New Testament that the young man was " very sorrowful, because he had great possessions"? He was materially successful—that was the hidden secret—so successful, indeed, that he was defeated every moment.

The man who is most unhappy, restless, defeated, is the man who *appears* to be in the midst of plenty and opulence. I wish mankind could see this immutable truth more clearly. They would then never become bankrupt. But not seeing it, they yield themselves to discord, to disappointment, and die with a thunder-stroke of Fate!

But a true Spiritualist cannot be cast down. He cannot be thrown into these vales of disappointment. No matter where he is, or in what he is laudably engaged, he finds that the eternal principles of the universe are filled with God's loving spirit, and in them he knows that he is safe, and beyond the possibility of defeat.

It is philosophical to believe in the benefits of defeats. The shipwrecked mariner contributes by his disaster just so much toward making all other ships safer. The Great Eastern had mishap after mishap in order that vessels hereafter should not be so ambitious in size, but more secure. Every accident on a railroad is but another step toward expedition and safety.

Seeing all this, I wonder how men can live or die worshiping the idol of theology, or believing in any creed in Christendom. I wonder not that they are mentally prostrated, with only what they call "faith" to give them a glimmering of rest just before the tomb-gate opens to receive them. They go *down* into the grave, and friends write on their tombstones that, when the angel comes and the trumpet sounds, then there will be a resurrection. But the true Spiritualist sees that there is no sepulcher, no tomb; that the world is regulated without accidents, and that death is nothing but a gentle "defeat," which excludes the cypress and includes the laurel. Flowers bloom o'er the death-bed of that mind which sees God's smiles behind frowning clouds and tempests. The Christian's "hope" and this knowledge among Spiritualists are the same in their effect upon the sentiments. When the Christian feels the "faith" which is peculiar to the Spiritualism of Christianity and identical with the knowledge of Spiritualism in these days, it is the light of a common Deity speaking through the intuitions and the moral faculties, saying to the prostrated one: " Thou shalt live beyond the tomb."

" The Summer-Land is not afar off. It is environing this world of ours, encasing it as the general air. It surrounds this world on all sides, so that, whether pointing up at noonday or at midnight, you point toward your home which is " eternal in the heavens." It is through the narrow, strait gate of defeat and of death, but it deepens into unutterable splendor and undying exhibitions of infinitude. That world hovers all around this world of winter, even as the golden era of peace is ready to pervade this terrible era of war.

War is the production of the cellar-kitchen of human nationality and progress. It never comes from the upper chambers in the temple of human growth. It is natural to have war in the basement of our life. There war is perfectly natural; not outside of God's providence, but as much in it as is the highest and most beautiful flower of peace.

The doctrine that you are fighting the devil when you are favoring the Deity, is worthy only of low and uneducated minds. Whichever way you work, you work for the ultimate glory of the universal system. God is in it. I mean by "God," the highest Truth, the highest Principle, the highest Virtue, the highest idea of whatsoever is Central and Perfect. The embodiment of these conceptions—the crystallization of all high thoughts and intuitions—is "God." God may be a monster to one in a monstrous state of mind. He is a heathen God to the heathen mind. He is a God of battle to the Major-general, but always a God of peace to " the pure in heart."

We have acquired a larger vision, and see principles in their grand, boundless operation, breaking out of the Infinite bosom with great success, which come from fine personal spasms and the awful experiences of rough public defeats. When men learn that war is to die, they will also learn that disease is to die; but while they believe that war is an inevitable part of human society and progress, and " will continue through all the cycles of human history," they then teach a desperate error, and are defeated through their lessons of faith in God and Humanity. Their misery, their despondency, their downcast hearts, and their deploring spirits, will constitute their best *teachers ;* but we believe that the time will come when they will attain to the summit of a better conviction, and say : " Sin abounded, that grace might much more abound;" discord, that harmony might come; ignorance, that knowledge might bloom and blossom as the rose; misfortune, that success could come; death, that immortality could crown the life of man; the sepulcher being necessary for the new truth, and the stone necessary to keep it entombed until the time should arrive for its out-bursting development. Behold! defeat is crowned at length with victory. The stone is rolled away, truth arises, and those who stand guard over it say, " Nay, this was buried, and it may now come forth."

Do you not feel thankful that the Romans came into England, and that when they found the old ancient Britons there they straightway put those Britons in bondage? What would England be to-day if it had not been for the defeat of those Britons and for the success of the Romans, and the Saxons, and the Nor-

2

mans. Their defeat was necessary for that great, powerful, commercial, arrogant nation, which to-day is giving America her finest lesson. It is the lesson of national consolidation—extending the front of education, of art, of commerce, and of liberty, though through a monarchial system. She became more liberal than Rome, though Rome was a republic. What kind of a republic? A republic for those who had arms to defend themselves against the Goths and the Vandals. It was not the Liberty, the high republic, which gives to every man and woman an expression. America, to-day, appears as a great success out of the defeats of these elder nations. England is not a perfect republic, because England came from ancestors who taught the monarchial system. She inherits the forces and features of the past.

But America threw off that hereditary disaster, and out of the defeats of the Past she is urging forward the victory of the Present. Suppose that persecution had never reached those old Dissenters in Nottingham, in England—suppose that persecution had never driven them to Holland—what would have become of Plymouth Rock? The Pilgrims laid the foundation for he Puritanic temple of perpendicular righteousness, nd of Yankee chicanery and machinery as well. therwise the temple could never have been erected. overnor Bradford were a myth, had it not been for ie great persecutions and the bitter defeats which ose early Dissenters experienced. Defeats drove them from Nottingham to Holland, and thence, in the midst of their physical embarrassments and great privations, they came all the way across the Atlantic to the

Western shore. Plymouth Rock is the victory of many defeats and misfortunes. But the descendants of that Rock are destined to develop the palladium of universal Freedom, and to make the immortal edict of Emancipation a *moral* as well as a military necessity.

THE WORLD'S TRUE REDEEMER.

" Wisdom's ways are ways of pleasantness, and all her paths are peace."

The beautiful and sublime truths imparted by the Harmonial Dispensation, will hereafter appear through lips more touched by the Promethean fire—more blessed by the enchanting powers of divine eloquence. My mission at present seems to be to utter, in plain style and understandable language, new lessons in spiritual progress, and to explain and enforce old lessons in a new and more practical, useful, soul-exalting, body-saving form.

I find a great many social and religious sewers in fashionable homes that need to be thoroughly cleansed; and one to enter upon such a labor must take off kid-gloves and put on corduroy over-alls. And hence, although it is hardly the form accepted in the so-styled best circles, (where dress passes par, and truth is quoted at fifty per cent. discount,) yet for the accomplishment of important ends in the day and hour and minute in which we breathe, such methods and dresses, and such unvarnished presentations of truth, are deemed expedient and appropriate. Therefore, as there are so many blessed witnesses to come after me, who will bring to you the clearly-defined pictures and express the highest melody of progressive truth, there seems to be for me the rougher labor of laying the granite foundation on which the temple of strong, vigorous Freedom, and of sturdy thought, can be planted and erected in safety as upon the everlasting hills.

I come before you at this time with the question, *" Who—What is the world's true Redeemer ?"*

A redeemer is one who takes up a circulation that has had a very wide diffusion on the credit system. The popular theory is that, from the first, mankind have been doing a credit business with the kingdom of heaven ; that the first thing we did as a race was to run into an everlasting, deadly, and diabolical debt with the Divine government, which is under the management and administration of that wifeless and melancholy trinity of co-equal gods—Father, Son, and Holy Ghost. Hence, according to this theory, the world needs some person, or thing, or principle, or transubstantiation, to liquidate this solid and solemn condition of things, and thus put mankind again on " interceding ground"—on the basis of a possible credit and acceptance at the bar of the Eternal in the heavens.

This, I repeat, is the general theory among so-called Christians. In searching human history, however, we find this popular theory to be nothing more than a hypothesis, based on Hebrew mythology and superstition. But this Hebrew mythology was originated in a genuine spiritual perception—crude, indistinct, and unphilosophical, but a perfect truth in germ—that, in the great *future*, mankind would come individually to realize that they were full of imperfections and weaknesses, and needed a saving power, a redemptive personage, an uplifting energy, a purifying principle. Thus originated the hypothesis of a personal Savior. What was first a mere speculation, at last became established as a positive fact.

The beauty and boundless catholicity of the Harmonial Dispensation are seen in the fact that, in freely and fearlessly sounding the deeps of all human history, its teachers come at last to accept the spiritual essence of all opinions in the world's religious creeds. They discover that in all things there is a sovereign, eternal truth, and their business seems to be, in part, to take off the coating and clear away the rubbish of the past—to divest history and mythology and experience of adhering superstitions, and thus aid to exhibit the majesty and harmonious perfections of the divine government, in its non-supernatural, inimitable, eternal beauty.

Hence we begin by rejecting the word " Redeemer," because it is a term developed by an hypothesis which is in itself erroneous. We discover that mankind do not stand in any such debit-and-credit relation to the kingdom of heaven. We are not doing a day-book and ledger business with God and Nature. Every instant of time the account in the " book of life" is balanced. The Bible is paper, and on the church theory it certainly is a paper basis of credit. Politicians and merchants, bankers and corporations, profess to dread and deplore this universal expansion of paper currency. Indeed! Then why do they not dread and equally deplore it in the religion of the world? It is nothing but paper currency in the popular churches, and much of it is exceedingly spurious at that. Multitudes of early Scriptures were counterfeits. This fact is inseparable from the history of all past negotiations on this paper basis in religion. In the Council of Nice the manuscripts which were rejected would make more than two such Bibles as are read in the churches of New York city. Those scriptures were repudiated as counterfeit representations of the real paper currency which it was supposed God had authorized to be diffused among mankind. On this theory the Divine government must have been exceedingly limited in suitable material for specie! The pavements of Heaven must have consumed all the gold and other metal they had on hand. The New Jerusalem, according to that old opinion, was so expensive in its metallic basis and ornamentations that the Trinity could not afford a *specie basis* for religion and morality. Of course they were obliged to issue several varieties of paper currency, and these are what men call the " Old and New Testaments"—legal tender notes, and notes promissory and on mortgages.

Now I ask, Why not be as reasonable in religion, theology, and spiritual necessities, as in this common affair of banking and of mercantile business? The answer is that men dare to use their reason, their common sense, and their educational sense as well, in all matters pertaining to the actualities of outward life, and the same men have resolved to be as nearly consummate block-heads and stumbling-blocks in matters of religion, as they can possibly be and still maintain a reputation for standing at the front of popular education, good manners, and good breeding. This universal acceptance of Reason on all practical questions, and this universal rejection of the same sovereign power on all questions in religion and spirituality, constitutes one of the most astonishing anomalies, one of the most consummate illustrations of imbecility, that ever started this side of the *upward* " Fall" of the first human pair.

This doctrine of doing all *worldly* business on what is termed " a paper basis" is, at the present time, quite unpopular. (It is not unpopular with me. I like it, and believe it will supersede the metals.) But in the world at large the plan is beginning to be rejected. Consequently, one of these days the same spirit of " repudiation" will strike into the organizations of religion. *Then* the kingdom of heaven will be appealed to—through vigorous prayers—for an exhibition of its supposed specie basis.

Is it not remarkable that people reject the idea of Progress in religion, in all the spiritual principles of human society, and at the same time *accept* it on almost every other subject in the domain of human life? It is everywhere held that man must not attempt to investigate the spiritual with his Reason. But, thank heaven ! Bishop Colenso has had the sublime audacity, in the midst of all his labors in heathendom, to make soundings down through the so-called infallible Pentateuch. He found and published to mankind, that the bottom had fallen out long before it was ever put in—that is, he broadly intimates that Moses is historically a myth. According to the history, the chronology, the mathematics of the Bible, good old Moses did not personally exist. But we find that in the *spiritual* history of the world the great Law-maker did live and does exist. This interior reality is all that is necessary for mankind. It is of little consequence, for example, whether

" Faith, Hope, and Charity," were three young women, excessively beautiful, in first-rate health, with fine digestion, good teeth, fine hair, and well acquainted with the wants of the human heart, or whether they were and are merely artistic personifications of interior sentiments and natural human necessities. It matters little; it matters not at all. The point is this: are they faithful representatives of *actual* principles and needs in the constitution of the human soul? All the world say " Yea," and therefore, " Hope, Faith, and Charity," are idolized images in our parlors—beautiful goddesses for the adoring soul to gaze upon—representatives of the internal, the eternal, and ever-present necessities of the human spirit—*hope, faith, charity !*

So Moses is related forever to the spiritual life and history of the human world. So is Jesus a *spiritual* fact—independent of history, mathematics, chronology, and the Bible. Whether they lived or did not live, is of little moment. It will be of little profit to persons who live so near the summit of the nineteenth century to make inquiries as to whether certain historical characters ever lived or not. Some minds seem to think that, because the old systems are so pervious to the waves of thought and investigation, therefore old theology holds no essential truth. Many ministers are thus troubled. The miserable gentlemen! They are affrighted at Bishop Colenso because they know nothing of essential Spiritualism. They know nothing whatever of the fundamental principles of the Harmonial Philosophy, by which the essentials of all things are saved; so that nothing worth saving is lost in history, theology, or mythology. If the world had more real

2*

intelligent, scientific spirituality in its religion—in its apprehensions of religion—it would never tremble if the bishops and priests of all countries came out *en masse* to-morrow and declared that the Bible itself, from end to end—in its literature, meanings, principles, and applications—was nothing but a worthless "paper currency" bequeathed to mankind through the Jewish Rabbi and early Christian Fathers, who firmly believed in their own honestly mistaken judgments and superstitions.

No; give men more knowledge of *real* spiritual truth, teach them of the philosophical depths of the immortal spirit, and they will have no more silly fears and hysterical tremblings lest the Bible should disappear and all Testaments be swept from the face of the earth. Suppose a great consuming fire should sweep across the prairies of the West and burn all the harvests that are garnered—with their fifteen to twenty-five miles of wheat and corn preserved in appropriate buildings—would the world despair of future cereal harvests? Would farmers and laborers never hope and believe that other corn-fields would again rustle in harmony with the music of the heavens? Would mothers and farming-maids never again look with *faith* for great thrift and burly health flowing up from the under-world, which brings in the new shocks of corn and fills the familiar scene with the affluence of new harvests? No, no! "Hope springs eternal in the human breast." The soul of the world would still feel assurance of future abundance. The summer comes, and with it come also those beautiful invigorating showers which awaken the slumbering principles of vegetation, and once more they bring oceans of food for the waiting millions, and all are fed.

So, also, if the present great spiritual and historical criticisms should sweep violently over the earth—rolling like the flood of Noah, sweeping Bibles and all books on other subjects wholly out of the world—nevertheless the men and women who feel the depths of these spiritual truths would not for one moment tremble or be cast down, except, perhaps, in a passing sorrow for the loss of so much property, representative of the industry and education of the past—for it would indeed be saddening to behold the destruction of the labors of those who have lived before us, and who have worked faithfully both night and day for years and centuries. The regret on this point would be deep, universal, and sorrowful; but there would be no spiritual trembling or vague fear; for very soon the divine harvests of Ideas would come again, more spiritual books than ever, and far better Testaments of truth, would unfold on the innumerable trees of human life. Singular, therefore, is it not, that men do not seek to comprehend and apply the law of Progress in their theologies and religion? It is because they *fear*, from the mere influence of their education, to use that sublimest power, the harmony of all the faculties—Reason.

If there was ever a flower from the soil of heaven planted in the garden of the human soul, blooming with an ever-increasing beauty and with an eternal fragrance, it is REASON. Men instinctively dread the absence of it in their children and in themselves; but nothing human ever dreads or deplores its presence.

The most *reasonable* person is the one you are inclined to love *most*. Reason always implies harmony of the faculties, for it receives happy contributions from all of the affections and sentiments. Reason, in this high sense, does not merely mean the power to think and talk logically from premises to conclusion, or legitimately to go in reflection from the outside to the center. It means the power to see not only outward facts, but the *essential principles*, also, by which alone the real significance of the facts can be comprehended. It is the German method. It begins at the heart of things, with fundamental Nature—is deductive, and goes thence outwardly, like God, through all the infinite spaces. God does not live and think on the surface of the universe as Bacon did. The Divine is not strictly an inductive philosopher. Every man of reason and every woman of intuition knows that God is in the deepest Heart—an inexhaustible fountain of Love, as well as of Wisdom—expanding through all that illimitable structure which we call " the physical universe."

Now God's method of living in the universe is the method of Reason in mankind. Rooting itself in Intuition, starting up with the lightning flash of thought, and with often an inexpressible conviction of what is and what is not true—such is Reason, blooming over the summits of the thinking and contemplative faculties—the first born, the last born—the perfect grouping of all the elements and attributes that go to make up the immortal human mind.

And yet men dare not trust Reason in religion! Behold how all the pulpitarians and crabsterians use Reason to prove that Reason is not to be trusted! Go to our logical clergymen—many of them are tolerably well-educated in logic—and hear how they habitually employ Reason, almost like thoroughly trained lawyers, to prove that Reason is most treacherous and *unreasonable*, and that it is unworthy of consultation in the presence of the Word of God!

Now I stand before you to announce the necessity of progress in the world's religion, and hence my subject is: "The World's True Redeemer."

I. In the first place I affirm that there is implanted in man a natural desire for knowledge. Men say that true human education did not begin until Christianity was perfectly established. It is astonishing that they dare so assert, when it is known that Egypt and Greece blossomed with institutions of learning, which have not been exceeded by anything educational in the present century—only we have *more* of it diffused among the people, and hence have made great progress in the adaptation of true education to human necessities. But in the fundamental germs of enlightenment and civilization the world was largely supplied centuries before Christianity was established.

I repeat, men desire Knowledge. They have an implanted desire to know more; they dread ignorance, and they repel with indignation that which is a recognized *discredit* to the Reason with which they are endowed. I know a perfectly honest, healthy, splendid-looking, wealthy proprietor of many whale-ships, who very frequently blushes because he is not educated. He began in the cabin, next went before the mast, and then became second mate, and so on and up until he went as sole master of his vessel. At last he became

the proprietor of many whaling-ships and store-houses.
He staid at home in his comfortable mansion by the
sea, and saw his many ships sail out and return to port,
bringing him wealth and luxury ; but he knew nothing
of French, nothing of Greek and Hebrew, and so he
fancied, as he was not educated in spiritual principles,
that he was shamefully destitute of education.   He had
never acquired the power of flourishing his pen, so that
he could not even write his own name very well.   But
that man was most trustworthy.   He was the trusted
friend of every man who needed his assistance and his
benefactions.   Still he would not accept the smallest
public office in his native town, nor assist in adjusting
public affairs, just because he was consciously deficient
in the rudiments of Education.   So he blushed and
remained at home, or rôde quietly out in his carriage,
looking equal to any man that walks in the halls of
Congress.   Thus the wealthy sailor lived, and at last
went completely out of sight in the midst of great accumulations of wealth—all because he knew that he was
not educated !   I relate this case to show that *people
naturally repel ignorance,* and that most persons blush
when they know that they are not well-informed and
accomplished.   It is a voice illustrating the natural
desire of the human heart for Knowledge.

Now who shall say that Knowledge shall not travel
into religious matters, as well as into navigation, into
matters of business, into the banking arrangements,
chemistry, the actual or the speculative sciences ?   The
desire for Knowledge with reference to spiritual things
is just as powerful as the desire to know anything with
reference to other departments of human interest.   I

think this question answers itself in every man's intuition.

II. In the second place I mention that man has a natural desire to make his knowledge Useful. He craves and seeks to acquire *natural and useful Knowledge.* When a boy sees a pair of skates, he wishes to know how he can use them. If he sees a ball, he wants to know how he can play with it; if a hook and line, to know how he can fish with them. So with the man. When he comes to recognize the facts of Science, or the development of these great discoveries in the world, he yearns to grasp them at once with the hand of Use. Why not carry that desire for Use into Religion? Why shall we not make our knowledge in spiritual things *useful?* The question answers itself. *We can and we must.* It is the inevitable tendency of the soul of every born human being to outgrow ignorance and to commence the investigation of spiritual truths. Mankind must make intelligent incursions through all these temples of ignorance, and error, and superstition—and over them, and through them, and in the midst of their demolition—he must acquire *useful* knowledge in spiritual and religious truths.

III. In the third place I will mention that man has a natural desire to be *consistent* in his Knowledge. He desires this jewel above all, in order to show the world that he knows the true *use* of his Knowledge, and to show that his use of it is exactly logical and everywhere intelligent and symmetrical. If a man knows a spiritual truth, he wants to make a *consistent* application of it. If he knows a scientific truth, he wishes also to be consistent with that.

This illustrates the intimacy with which one kind of knowledge is connected with another. If a man knows something of anatomy, he longs for a little physiology to make his anatomical science not only useful, but consistent; and if he has a knowledge of physiology he says: "Now, chemistry is really necessary to make my physiology at once useful and consistent." So he goes into chemical questions and investigates as far as his opportunities and prejudices will permit. If he gets interested deep enough in chemistry, he begins to look at the matter with a still broader view, and he says, "I must make these things useful in my daily life. I must show that I have *real* and positive knowledge. And, in order to make that exhibition indisputable, I must give it expression in my duties, in my daily avocations, and in my worldly career."

This illustrates the desire of the human to be consistent. In the Churches, both ministers and their followers plant themselves on certain principles or premises, and each one says: "I must reason correctly from my fundamental propositions." If a clergyman believes in the Trinity, his doxology at the end of the sermon and hymn will always be a logical conclusion from his creed. If the minister believes in eternal punishment, he will conduct himself like Henry Ward Beecher, who, although naturally anxious to discard the trammels of old theology, will, nevertheless, perhaps at the end of every third week's sermon bring out a logical hell-fire conclusion in harmony with an education received from his earthly father's orthodox premises.

This desire to be "consistent," too often allies

itself with the Satan of Pride. Some men having committed themselves openly and above board to certain fundamental opinions in politics or in religion, are actuated by the feelings of pride, so much so that they cannot be honorably open and simple-minded enough to know *where* or *what* a new truth is. They desire to stand by the old, and not to budge. They cling to the time-worn falsehood very strongly ; for they design to show, by their adhesion to it, that they have indubitable evidence that they are not mistaken. Thus Mr. H——, a flourishing merchant of this city, in conversation in Williamsburg several years ago, said to me that he was "a believer in total depravity." Then came the question: "What are your evidences, Mr. H—— ?" He answered by enumerating human evils, piling evidence upon evidence taken from history, quoted the crimes of society, the sins of individual men, &c., &c. Then we conversed concerning the hereditary and circumstantial causes of those evils and iniquities.

At length he yielded the point somewhat, and said : "Well, to be sure, special circumstances and lack of balance in phrenological organization, deficiency in the strength of will to resist evil, and various temptations, which flow in from the outside world upon the person, no doubt do explain away the intentional cause of many evils and vices ;" and so he measurably yielded the point that the human heart was not *totally* depraved, seeing that so many iniquities and evils came from the sphere of conditions and circumstances.

"Well," said I, "Mr. H——, where now is your evidence?" That unfortunate question at once reminded him of his position, and also aroused his *pride* of logical consistency, and said he: "I have, Mr. Davis, an unfailing evidence of total depravity." "Indeed?" "Yes." "Well, Mr. H——, where do you find that unfailing evidence?" "In my own heart, Mr. Davis."

I told him I admired the self-sacrificing spirit he manifested, but I detested the *pride* which caused him to do it; for he probably knew that he owned as good a heart as anybody, and it was not true that he went to his heart to find " total depravity." It was the ambitious desire to be " consistent"—the Devil of Pride— that held him to his first propositions. The imp of darkness thus shut down the vail over the good man's eyes, so that he dared not see the higher and more simple truth with all its rosy splendor. And so he became the zealous editor of the *Churchman*. His unfailing evidence of total depravity was simply the sacrifice of his own mind to his own avowed theory. He would rather stand before me a self-acknowledged spiritual criminal than to say that he really had no absolute evidence of total depravity.

Now the world is just in this condition of pride and fear with reference to the Trinity, or the doctrine of eternal punishments. The people and priests have not yet simple, spiritual, and interior childhood enough to acknowledge that facts, heretofore accepted, are perfectly invalidated by new scientific and historic evidence. They are not large enough to receive the new truth, and to welcome it, as happy mothers receive the new-born child.

Men love, in their pride, to be " consistent." But in such passion they make great life-long mistakes. If

I had labored to be logical and "consistent" in any of my discourses, no doubt I should have been, if possible, less useful to you than I have. It is a remarkable fact that I have sometimes attempted to teach you, but at the end of the Lecture I found, not unfrequently, that I knew much more than when I began, and was, perhaps, more benefited and more instructed than any other person. It was because a new phase of a great principle had been revealed to the interior, showing me that my internal life was still sensitively awake to the New, and that I was and am not wedded foolishly and indissolubly to the past, either personal or general.

Now I wish to call your attention to the points gained in this discourse: First. Internal desire for Knowledge; secondly, for Useful Knowledge; and thirdly, for Consistent Knowledge.

What is it in man that thirsts for knowledge? This inquiry answers itself in this way—that the harmony of all the faculties and attributes in the human soul constitutes what we call Wisdom. The Author of that harmony is also the Author of Wisdom. Persons who are yet not harmonized in spiritual principles, have only glimmering intuitions of Wisdom. It means the axis of the human mind coming to a parallel, so to say, in the plane of its orbit, with reference to the harmony of Deity. The unity of man's spirit with God's spirit is felt instantly when the fullness of wisdom is reached. It is the new birth. You then feel that your spirit is attuned to the harmony of eternal principles. The harmony of love shows you at once that you are part of an indestructible Brotherhood. Your partialities and jealousies die down, your little feelings and selfish traits depart, and the spirit of Fraternal Love, like the dove that went forth from the Ark, wings its way from your soul towards every son and daughter of the world. If you can rise to a feeling of that kind even once in a month, you have evidence that a new birth is taking place within you.

Furthermore, when you rise to see that the law of gravity is not merely physical, but spiritual also; that the laws that regulate mechanism and chemistry are spiritual as well as physical and mathematical, then you have attained to some perception of Wisdom.

Wisdom sounds through the physical and reaches to the profound depths where God sleeps and wakes every instant of time.

The penetration of the chemist is but a physical approach to the interior of things. He will take a substance into the laboratory and analyze it. He arrives at its constituents and names them; and they are thus marked and classified. And he finds that, by recombinations, they make this, that, and the other substance. But just where the chemist leaves off, the soundings of Wisdom commence. The chemist fails to touch the vital principle by which constituents are united to make the various compounds. He knows that he fails to reach the point where spirit moves the body, and so he goes once more to the threshold of inquiry. When he arrives at that place he stops short, but Wisdom hospitably opens the door into the vestibule of the immortal temple, just at this particular critical point; and thus, where the chemist, with his material methods of probing and analyzing, must, per force of his material methods, cease, there the penetrative spiritual philosopher commences his investigations. And thence he is led out through an infinitude of spirit culture.

Wisdom commences, I say, just where Science fails in its power to go. You know there are persons who all the time are in bondage to the sense. They behold gravitation, but to them the law itself is physical. Look at our material orthodox clergymen. They read the ponderous religious quarterlies—or the monthlies— which are lumbering and tediously elephantine in the treatment of things; what kind of knowledge have they? Talk with the most learned of these gentlemen, who day after day visit our best public libraries—men who dig through the great volumes that come across the Atlantic—and you will see how utterly destitute they are of *internal* perceptions of scientific and philosophic truths. Being without knowledge in these matters, many of them are skeptics; and although they attend church Sunday after Sunday, and go through all the forms, yet in their judgments they have no faith either in theology or religion.

THE WORLD'S TRUE REDEEMER IS WISDOM, because it passes through the dress to that which is essential, to the spirit through the body, to the life within the law, to the science within the substance; and not only so, but makes all of its discoveries at once *consistent, useful*, and *desirable*. But Wisdom seems, to most people, to be vague and abstract. Men do not see how they can put the teachings of Wisdom into operation. Well, then, let us see if we cannot make this truth useful, consistent, and practical.

Wisdom recognizes, as a central principle, the balance of things—the equilibrium of forces, the adaptation of one substance to another, of one force to another, of a fish to the water, of a bird to the air, of light to the eye, of sound to the ear, of flavors to the taste, of odors to the sense of smell, of substances to the touch, and so on throughout the whole system.

What is the image we see represented in poetry and in art on this subject? The image is JUSTICE. She holds the scales, which represent equality of proportion. Justice is the central law. It is recognized as the finest, most universal, and the highest expression of the Infinite Mind. The entire harmony of the planetary worlds, by which the stars move on in their sublime courses, never varying from the moment the pyramids were built to the present hour!—in all these splendid, vast, and incomprehensible systems, which make up the heavens—comets burning their way through space, crossing each other's paths beautifully, like well-trained dancers waltzing on lines most familiar to their minds; and the planets, too, moving on like respectable citizens in the high walks of the sidereal heavens—all in never-changing harmony with the original design. What causes that? It is what Wisdom recognizes as God's central law—JUSTICE.

Bring it to the person, and what does it do?

It gives us the two hands, two feet, two departments to the brain, two eyes, two ears—doubleness, duality throughout—all expressions of God's central law, JUSTICE. The foot cannot repel the head, nor the head the foot. The cerebrum cannot repel the cerebellum, the cerebellum cannot do without the cerebrum. Love warms Reason; Reason cannot exist and flourish without Love. How is it that a man can raise his arm? It is done by the laws of contraction and expansion—the two systems in harmony with each other. Justice breathes throughout all the system.

Again, we find in the world what is called *warmth*—red warmth—warmth which is mellow, which is penetrative, invigorating, and expanding. Wherever you find balance, you find warmth. What is it? It is God's central principle—LOVE. Not the physical universe, but that which gives us a physical universe, is naturally full of warmth, flowing from the center through all the minutest ramifications of the system—LOVE.

Now what is this all-pervading Love? Is it a Love which stops with a substance? Does it exist only in one heart? Does it take no interest in anything outside of itself? You know that the selfish love of the spirit brings no happiness to itself. Its happiness comes from its dependence upon the corresponding love of another, then the two depend upon a third, and the three upon a fourth, and the four upon the existence of the whole world without.

The system of human life and society is entirely dependent. One part is warmed by contact with another, and the heat is expanded and removed according to the principle of equilibrium. This is the divine LOVE. It is central with Nature, just as Justice is central with Deity.

Deity and Nature are counterparts, equals, and compeers; they are husband and wife, father and mother, wisdom and love, and are perpetually bearing children. The *warmth* and the *balance* go hand in hand, arm in arm, their arms about each other's necks, working without discord through the illimitable spaces.

Hence Love, which is not limited and selfish, and Justice, when married, constitute LOVING-JUSTICE—the best practical definition of *the world's true Redeemer.*

Justice without Love is the sun without heat—without its power to fertilize, and beautify, and adorn the world; and the world without its Justice would be the sun with only *heat*, that would burn, and parch, and consume, and destroy all things. The balance of the universe itself would be destroyed, so that where harmony dwelt, discord and conflagration would prevail. Thus it would be in a world full of Love, of warmth, but without Justice and light.

Try this principle in your homes. I know a young man in one of the avenues of this city who has been so petted and caressed by an over-loving mother—a maternal soul, who had Love in abundance, but not a corresponding sense of Justice—and that misdirected son is now the source of her daily anxieties and momentary miseries. She is every week put on the cross, and is sorely tried like one pulled joint by joint on the rack of torture. Why? Because when a little baby and a child he had all things given him that he wanted; never was practically instructed by Justice to recognize the rights of another child. Justice was left out of her Love. Thus the little one came up under the arms of maternal warmth; and this very day that son, now a young man in the city of New York, is carrying poiguards and stilettos in his disposition. He is to his mother a serpent that was nurtured in a house full of Love without corresponding Justice.

Try this principle with vegetations of any kind. Let them have the warmth which the sun might give, but without its regulating, adjusting, and balancing power, and soon you will find that the beautiful plants and harvests would disappear, crisped, parched, and destroyed, because the sun had not given down its cooling and harmonizing power, which would bring balance, and equilibrium, and proportion, and beauty, and symmetry, as well as the all-important results of warmth. I think you perceive that the world's true Savior is LOVING-JUSTICE, and that Wisdom is the apprehending and applying faculty.

How necessary it is that men should apply this principle throughout. I will not detain you at this time by describing its influence in the various departments of human interests. If, for example, these fashionable ladies could be made to see the *injustice* of their styles, with reference to other equally good ladies who are circumstantially unfortunate, they would not be guilty of another departure from wisdom. These fashion-ladies have been brought up under the warmth and wealth of the heart, without the cooling, regulating, and equalizing principle of social Justice. They have learned their arts from Mother Nature; but they have none of the wisdom of Father God.

So they are all fashionable ladies! They go to the churches. They would not attend a Progressive Meeting, lest it might impress an everlasting spot upon their reputations! And yet they do openly and unblushingly that which I believe not a lady in this cause would do. There is in nearly all they do a terrible wrong, which badly affects the domestic who gets the dinner, and the boy who serves at the table, and still worse, the children, who are readiest to imitate the

3

conduct of adults. I attended a party on one occasion where there were forty ladies exquisitely arrayed in the fashionable dresses of the day. By a careful computation I made out exactly 720 yards of silk and satin and costly brocade. Think of it, ye Christians! Seven hundred and twenty yards of most expensive cloth, on *forty* New York church-going women! I have also seen a party of forty faithful and industrious women, who had scarcely ten yards over the mere necessities of passable dress. They had scrimped themselves to just that pattern which was necessary for convenience—of course according to the style, so as not to be peculiar and conspicuous; but the calico they wore was way down in price, and they were ashamed to appear among the finely dressed. Yet these costly pagodas, these fashionable religious temples, are flashing and sparkling with Stewart's iniquities. Alas! they have not yet heard the central gospel of God—JUSTICE—down in the heart deep enough to regulate their habits and characters. Therefore, with all their religious professions, they are not friendly to the kingdom of righteousness.

Finally, I suggest to clergymen and to all teachers of public morals that they at once abandon the vicious doctrine of the vicarious atonement, as well as the preaching of all other mythological methods of getting rid of sin and evil, and come immediately on to the everlasting basis of LOVING-JUSTICE—the world's true Redeemer.

THE END OF THE WORLD.

—— " The original
Of all things is one thing. Creation is
One whole. The differences a mortal sees
Are diverse only to the finite mind."

The cheerful, yet solemn subject, announced for this morning, should have attracted the editorial staff of " *The World*," but it is more remarkable that there are not present editors of other and more loyal sheets who take an interest in the *end* of the " world."

My subject is the great question that frequently agitates thousands of honest religionists. In treating upon this subject I remark:

First, That the human mind begins to reason by taking a *literal* view of everything, whether spiritual or material. Its first apprehensions are confined strictly to the *apparent*—to what *appears*—to the *seeming*. Wisdom, mounting on the wings of untrammeled Ideality, penetrates to that which lives *within*. This state of mind judges "not from appearances, but with a righteous judgment"—that is, from the core outwardly, and *not* from the mere husk, burr, clothing, protection, appearance, or representation; thus wisdom renders an infallible verdict concerning that which is interior, spiritual, and eternal. To think or reason sensuously, is an error—a mistake—which is scarcely reprehensible, hardly blameworthy, because it is the inevitable step of the human mind when beginning its progress in experience, thought, wisdom, and intuition.

Hence there prevails a universal *externalism* among crude religionists with regard to the "End of the World." There are scores of persons, who, judging from the Bible sentences, fancy they read the fiery doom of the physical universe. All who live and move and have a being within the world, save "God and his holy angels," are marked down for a resurrected destruction. "His holy angels," according to the theory, will be manufactured out of certain earthly religionists, as their eternal reward for having believed the delectable creed in advance of their skeptical neighbors, even though the latter class may be respectable members of popular churches. The holy and sacred class are called "Second Adventists"—very pugnacious, warm-headed, discussionary characters, energetic and truth-loving, over-fond of debate—especially from a *literal* apprehension of the teachings of the Testaments. Taking the sensuous interpretation as the basis of all their reasoning, they have erected a system of theologic thought (based wholly upon literal apprehensions,) which they imagine logically leads—mathematically, prophetically, figuratively, and according to the biblical almanac—directly to a tragical and chemical termination of the physical world in which sinners now live. They fancy that they recognize the prophecy to be straight from God—of course through the mediation of the old prophets—and think that Christ announced the same awful fact whenever he spoke of the "end of the world." Beholding this unbroken chain of announcement, this concatenation of prophecies, this unmistakable literalization of the promises of God, the Adventists naturally work themselves up to believe that, in a very short time, the dissolution of the globe and the end of all physical things will surely come to pass. All this religious imagination is based on the fact that the mind first takes *a literal* view of ancient spiritual writings. It is the mind's first step in theology, in spirituality, as in everything else it encounters on the road of progressive thought, experience, and wisdom.

The next step the mind takes as it expands from intuition, is a *figurative* view of the Bible language. Minds in this state apprehend that the old prophets and the new apostles spoke in metaphors, wrote emblematically, with great opulence using figurative expressions. Bible-believers, thus thinking, throw off the *literal* letter and the materialistic conception, and swim out into the open sea of pictorial and figurative interpretation. They now seek for examples, correspondences, contrasts, and analogies. Swedenborg, for illustration, being both a scientific thinker and a philosophical religionist, started more systematically to give to all figurative, emblematic, metaphoric, and symbolic expressions, the basis and dignity of a Science—reducing, in his own opinion, all scriptural *externalisms* to an intelligible spiritual account. His principle of translation was something more than *analogy*, something more than mere *comparison*, something different from the purely *figurative*, something different from the *symbol*—it was what he called the "Science of Correspondence"— meaning that the *internal* of an object, person, thought, affection, subject, or thing, is always represented in its externals, and *vice versa ;* that while a sheep will represent nothing but a sheep to the *external* eye looking over the fence into the field, at the same time to the eye of the *spiritual* mind the sheep naturally represents and really seems to be nothing but the sentiment or principle of *innocence.* De Guay, in his " Letters [No. XII] to a Man of the World," gives the following familiar examples : " The *earth* in general corresponds to man ; its different productions, which serve for the nourishment of men, correspond to different kinds of goods and truths—the solid aliments to various kinds of goods, and the liquid to various kinds of truths. *A house* corresponds to the will and the understanding, which constitute the human mind; by house we here understand all that serves for lodging or retreat, the palace as well as the hut. *Garments* correspond to truths or falses, according to the substance, color, and form, which they present. *Animals* correspond to the affections ; those which are useful and gentle to good affections, those which are hurtful and bad to evil affections ; gentle and beautiful *birds* to intellectual truths, those which are ferocious and ugly to falses ; *fishes* to the scientifics which derive their origin from things sensual ; *reptiles* to corporeal and sensual pleasures ; and *noxious insects* to falsities which proceed from the senses. *Trees* and *shrubs* correspond to different kinds of knowledges; and *herbs* and *grass* correspond to various kinds of scientific truths. *Gold* corresponds to celestial good, *silver* to spiritual truth, *brass* to natural good, *iron* to natural truth, *stones* to sensual truths, *precious stones* to spiritual truths."

So Swedenborg goes through the mystic sphere of psycho-scientific research, and succeeds in reducing the whole Bible, or at least so much of it as, according to his superior illumination, was correspondentially written, to a consistent system of interior interpretation. It must strike every one as evident that the Swedish Seer ever and anon struck the core of Divine fruit on the biblical trees; almost every second step he planted his foot on the basis of everlasting truth. If he had struck solid ground every time, the world would find in him an infallible teacher. Unfortunately for him, perhaps, but unquestionably fortunate for the human millions, Swedenborg touched spiritual truth just unfrequently enough to convince many persons who read him that he was not infallible. Those who look at this question independently, see that, although it is very easy to think and say that a duck corresponds to a doctor of medicine and a goose to a doctor of divinity, still the so-called science is obviously arbitrary, and may not be true universally. For your spiritually-minded brother in Scotland, looking at the duck, may not think of seeing therein represented " a doctor of medicine," and not always in the *goose* a " doctor of divinity;" on the contrary, these twaddling birds or gawky fowls may represent very different affections, thoughts, persons, or professions, and may continue through all time to suggest something different from Swedenborg's meaning. And yet I hesitate not to say that the "Science of Correspondence" is the closest approach to a great discovery in the substantial sense of spiritual communications recorded in the Old and New Testaments.

But there have been, and are, persons who have conceived that, inasmuch as there was a *spirituul* sense tucked away in the literal Word, so it would be unfair if there could not be found a *celestial sense* still more concealed within the spiritual. These ambitious souls also think that it would be unfair for an hundred years to pass away without producing some "celestial seer" who could out-Swedenborgianize the Word. Among Spiritualists there is, or has been, a person who thinks and professes to believe that he has seen a *finer* sense in the Bible than Swedenborg saw, rippling all the way through from Genesis to Revelations. His first ambitious installment—"the Arcana of Christianity"—has been published.

On the same principle, and by parity of reasoning, you may apprehend that some other person will, by and by, arrogate the discovery of a "heavenly sense" as superior to the *celestial ;* and yet another who would say that there was a "deific sense" superior to the *heavenly*, and so the absurdity might flow on *ad infinitum*. The reasoning is deceptive and sophistical. They take for granted what remains to be established. Thus : Since the *literal* sense of your Bible is extinguished, since the *spiritual* sense is not sufficient, and since the *celestial* sense is already exhausted, is it not necessary now, in order to have the celestial sense perfectly comprehended, to cap it all with the climacteric discovery of God's own mind ? I believe that no such religious fanaticism will ever appear in a healthy human mind. Such an ambition could be nothing less than a parasitical development on the healthy faculties of human reason. Let us hope and pray that such religious monstrosities will never appear in the course of modern spiritual development and philosophic growth.

Let me now ask your attention to the universal fact that the internal and the external of all things are married, and do literally correspond to and represent each other; that what is true in the external, in anything, anywhere, is equally true of the *internal* in the same thing and place. Hence there cannot be such a thing as a religious truth which is incompatible or inconsistent with a scientific or a philosophic discovery in a corresponding department. There can be no incompatibility, no antagonism, between what religionists call a "revealed and natural religion." Paul has fully shown this; others have demonstrated it; and no man can escape the laws and logic of Reason. The changeless God who "built the palace of the sky," and talks to men through various mediators, could do no incohesive deed, could speak no inconsistent word ; but, when understood, both the Deed and the Word universally harmonize as do fellow-notes when speaking in the highest music.

This statement is the internal conviction of the world; the intuition of all peoples, both Heathen and Christian. If the people of Christendom would take those documents, which, bound together, are called the "Old and New Testaments," as simply and only a *portion* of the spiritually-written word of God, and hospitably accept the scriptures of all heathen nations with just as much reverence, and see that God spoke *through them all*, even as he speaks through the organization and habits of the meanest *worm* that ever crawled in mud, as through the beauty and perfections of the highest

seraph that ever sung under the finite sun, then indeed
would the earth rejoice in gladness; for all religionists
and Spiritualists would be enlarged and ennobled by
the presence and influence of perpetual and universal
inspirations.

~But, on the other hand, confine all authoritative
inspirations to a stereotyped volume—excluding all
God's words to the Chaldeans, Arabians, Chinese, and
the other nations who in past times have received truths
from the same inexhaustible Divine source—do this, as
Christians do, and you exclude golden sunlight, pure
air, blissful health, and impartial wisdom from you;
and, in consequence, you become miserable automatons
of a fashionable, popular, and outrageously expensive
religion, full of dried creeds and dead men's bones.

The application of the principle announced would
be this: Just what is true in the world of science, we
shall find equally true in the social world; what is true
in the social world, we shall find equally true in the
world of politics; what is true in the world of politics,
we shall find equally true in the world's laws and
governments; what is true in outward governments,
will be found equally true in the internal history of particular races; and what is true in all these, will be
found equally true in the geology of the globe and the
destiny of the human family; what is true in geology
and the destiny of the aggregation of persons, you will
find equally, intimately, delicately, eternally true in
every single component part of your mental existence!

Geology—a scientific knowledge of the earth—has
been practically born within the last quarter of the
present century. It has already arisen to the com-

manding position of the wisest commentary that was
ever written on book-religion. It is this day the pro-
foundest expounder and *pounder* of Genesis; for the
authority of the book and the source of the authority
have dropped out long ago to those who have had the
industry, independence, and talent to investigate. Perhaps, in this connection, it may be best to glance at the
outlines of the harmonial philosophy of creation in the
physical Universe.

The great original, ever-existing, omniscient, omnipotent, and omnipresent productive power—the Soul
of all existences—is throned in a central sphere, the
circumference of which is the boundless universe, and
around which solar, sidereal, and stellar systems,
revolve in silent, majestic sublimity and harmony! This
power is what mankind call Deity, whose attributes are
love and wisdom, corresponding with the principles of
male and female, positive and negative, creative and
sustaining.

The first goings forth or out-births from this great
celestial Center, are spiritual or vital suns. These,
after due elaboration or gestation, give birth to natural
suns—those that become cognizable to the outward or
natural senses of man. These again become centers,
or mothers, from which earths are born, with all the
elements of matter, and each minutest particle infused
with the vivifying, vitalizing spirit of the parent Forma-
tor. The Essences of heat or fire—electricity, galvan-
ism, magnetism—are all the natural or outward manifestations of the productive energy, the vitalizing Cause
of all existences. It pervades all substances and ani-
mates all forms.

THE PROGRESS OF FORMATION is from the lower to the higher, from the crude to the refined, from the simple to the complicated, from the imperfect to the perfect—but in distinct degrees or congeries. That is, the lower must first be developed, to elaborate the materials, and prepare the way for the higher. Thus, after the sun gave birth to the earth—and the same of all other planets—the action of the vitality within the particles of matter, and its constant emanation in the form of heat, light, electricity, &c.—first from the great Central sphere to the sun, and thence to the earth, acting upon the granite and other rocks, with the atmosphere, the water, and other compound and simple elements—then new compounds were formed, possessing this vital principle in sufficient quantities to give definite forms, as crystallization, organization, motion, life, sensation, intelligence—the last being the highest or ultimate attribute of production on our earth, and possessed or reached to perfection only by man.

A glance at the progress of creation, in the production of our earth and its inhabitants, will serve as an illustration of the same process and progress of worlds in the vast expanse of the universe, that are perpetually and continually being brought into existence, and ultimating the grand object of the whole—namely, to develop and perfect individualized, self-conscious, ever-existing, immortal spirits, that shall be in the "image and likeness" of the Central Cause, and dwell forever in the Summer Spheres.

I will now describe the process of the earth's origin. Within the circumference of the sun, elementary particles of matter gather around a nucleus, which continues to aggregate and increase in dimension and variety of parts, in its perpetual and endless revolutions and evolutions, gradually advancing towards the outer surface of this fiery orb, as it increases in complexity and density, until it approaches the extreme verge of the sun; when, by the impetus or centrifugal force it has attained, from its more compact structure and consequent increase of specific gravity, it breaks loose from its parent and flies off at a tangent into illimitable space. If a ball of lead and another of cotton, of the same size, be tied each to a string and whirled violently around until the strings break, the leaden ball will fly off in almost a straight line, for a long distance, before it makes a curve towards the earth; while the cotton ball will perform a graceful curve from the moment it breaks loose, and soon falls to the ground. The experiment will illustrate the movements of a planet, when first thrown off from the sun (being much more dense); or, in other words, it will account for the eccentric movement of comets, which, in fact, are newborn and baby earths or planets. The extreme tenuity, fluidity, and rarefaction of its particles, and its consequent feeble cohesive attraction, and its irregular orbituary and axillary movements, give the new earth elongated, attenuated, and many curious forms, as presented to the beholder on another planet. Sometimes it happens that the caudal extremity gets so " long drawn out," and so far from the center of gravity—the proper polarity or axis not being yet fully established—that a part or parts become detached or broken off. The detached parts become "satellites," or *moons*, which continue to revolve around and within the orbit

of the new earth. Our earth has one of these *parasites!*
Other planets several.

In the lapse of ages, the attractive and repulsive, or
the centripetal and centrifugal forces, become equalized,
the particles of matter have formed more intimate associations, the outer surfaces have locked up a large portion of the free caloric within the embrace of their own
substance, and have consequently condensed and hard-
ened—a globular form has succeeded the oblate sphere,
with its spinal extremity, and a *regular* orbit is defined
and maintained. Oxygen and nitrogen have united in
the proper proportions to form the atmosphere; oxygen
and hydrogen have combined to form water; oxygen
and silicon have entered into an adamantine embrace to
form quartz rock; oxygen and carbon have formed a
tripartite union with calcium, producing immense beds
of carboniferous lime-stone. Numerous other combinations of oxygen with gases, metals, and other elements
—and these again combining with other simple or compound substances—have brought out of this vast amor-
phous mass of elementary materials—as they existed in
an intensely heated and rarefied state, when first thrown
off from the sun—new, and more solid, and more permanent forms.

In all this beautiful, harmonious, and ever-progress-
ive flow of productive affinities, oxygen plays a very
conspicuous part, as a positive, energizing, vitalizing
principle. It appears to have grasped, and to have held
fast within its embrace, the very germs of vitality. Phosphorus is another form of its tangible development, not
yet understood by chemists or physiologists. No living
plant or animal can exist without it. It is always

found in the seeds and germinal principles, in the substance of the bone and brain and nerves, and in yet other parts of vegetables and animals.

In the course of time, when " the waters had subsided," the heat and light emanating continually from the sun—upon the waters of the seas, and in rain, and mist, and dew—acted upon the surfaces of the granite and other rocks, abrading, decomposing, and uniting with their elements to produce other new compounds of a more refined and perfect nature. Thus large beds of gelatinous matter were formed in shallow pools beneath the water-level, and a slimy coating upon the surfaces of the rocks above the water. (See second part *Great Harmonia*, vol. 5.) Thus soil was first formed—a preparation, elaboration, and combination of material, susceptible of developing vegetable life, marine and terrestrial. The first vegetable forms springing from these slimy rocks, were simple and not defined in their structure, being lichens, or cryptogamous plants, about seventy per cent. of whose substance is gelatin.

As one forcible evidence of the fact of vegetables first originating from the elements of the rock on which they germinate, and from the heat, light, atmosphere, and moisture, is, that each rock of different chemical composition, when exposed to these influences, will produce a moss peculiar to itself, and the same rock, in any latitude where it can grow, will always produce a plant of the same species, and each plant in its turn, of the thousands of classes, orders, genera, species, and varieties now in existence, will invariably produce an animalcule, or insect, peculiar to itself. These are facts that have been abundantly substantiated by the most scientific naturalists of the age.

The first forms of vegetation were brought into being, and perfected in their kind—elaborating from their own substance a germ .or nucleus of vitality with the impress of its own individuality, inclosed within a receptacle capable of preserving and sustaining it, till the favorable action of the elements (in heat, light, moisture, and the soil,) could bring forth from each germ or seed "an image and likeness" of its parent— the organized substance or body of the original plant, having performed the ultimate object of its existence, dies, and the elements of which it is composed mingle with the thin soil on the surface of the rocks, adding to its substance, increasing its complexity, and refining its particles; so that, with the return of the vernal equinox, and the genial rays of the sun, not only the seeds of the old lichen unfold and expand into the same species, but a new and more complicated plant, with distinct and marked differences (perhaps a fern,) makes its appearance, and rears its graceful stem and spreads its glossy foliage above the lowly moss.

Thus the ever-present and ever-active principle of vitality and creative Energy, acting and reacting upon the materials of our globe, started the kingdoms of Nature, which have and will ever continue to progress—from the simple to the more complicated vegetable forms: animalcule, infusoria, radiata, molusca, vertebrata, and Man as the Ultimate. The lowest and imperfect first, and the more complex and perfect after, in regular progression, but in distinct degrees. Each new type being dependent upon *all* that preceded it for its existence, but yet distinct and different from its pre-decessors.

Thus it requires certain conditions, proportions, and combinations of elementary inorganic substances to produce a vegetable—and vegetable growth is dependent entirely upon elementary regimen—while animals cannot be produced or sustained in their exist-ence by inorganic or elementary matter. The organic compounds of the blood, muscular fiber, gelatin, skin, hair, nails, or horns, &c., are all formed in exact con-stituents or proportions from the elementary particles that enter into their composition by the vegetable. The vegetable kingdom must, therefore, have existed *before* the animal—the vegetable realm being the stepping-stone, or connecting-link, between the elementary or mineral kingdom and the animal. Hence, if the vegetable kingdom should by any cause be blotted out from the face of the earth, the animal would soon be annihilated.

All types in the endless chain of inorganic and organized substances, are but links in the one system of cause and effect, and each type or species is so marked and distinct as easily to be distinguished, and each variety and unity of the human species is so indelibly stamped with its own perfected individuality, as to be recognized from the myriads of the species.

Thus, fixed, unvarying, and universal laws of the Father govern and regulate all his works. From the first fiat that was sent forth throughout all the ramifi-cations of the Universe, spiritual, physical, and celes-tial, eternal unity, order, and harmony reigns-—conception, development, progression, and perfection, mark all His work, and all point with the irresistible force of reason and demonstration to the immortality of the Soul.

In taking this philosophical view of the plan and progress of Nature and the works of God, how grand, how sublime, how comprehensive, how rational and satisfactory—to the independent-thinking and inquiring mind, who wishes to " have a reason for the faith that is within him"—how perfectly are the love and wisdom and justice of the Father and Mother conjugated and displayed! And how real, conclusive, and overwhelming the evidence—appealing directly to the senses, the intellect, and the affections—of the self-conscious, immortal existence and progressive happiness of the "spirit" that is within us! The human species being the last and highest Type upon our earth, and the only one possessing reason and intelligence that examines and investigates all that is beneath and around itself, and that has a consciousness of the future—endeavoring to raise or draw aside the thin, semi-transparent vail that hangs suspended between the physical and the spiritual existence—analogy, "reasoning from what we know," points directly not only to the probability, but to the absolute *certainty and necessity* of a future existence—in short and finally, to the Summer-Land!

All organic forms below man not only produce their like, but the substances of their material forms mingle with previously-formed compounds, to produce a new and *distinct type* superior to itself. *But the human type has no superior development*, and there is no retrogression in the works of Nature. Each new unfolding is superior to the preceding. Man, then, is destined for other and higher Spheres. In those Spheres, or new states of existence, man's spirit must present not only an "image and likeness" of Nature and God, but a consciousness of identity and individual selfhood. Feeling and knowing this, he should so live while in this rudimentary and preparatory state of existence, that all physical, intellectual, moral, and spiritual structure, formation, growth, and maturity, be fully developed, cultivated, and perfected; so that when the " mortal puts on immortality," and seeks " a home in the heavens," it can expand into a celestial being without spot or blemish to mar its beauty, or impede its progress in bliss and glory.

Thus Geology teaches, among her first lessons, the rise, perfection, blossoming, decay, and disappearance of various classes of vegetation. She teaches that the simplest forms—gelatinous fibers oozing out from the lonely margins of early seas—crept over the rocks, gave out their effluence, laid the foundation for something better, gathered the electricities of the air, absorbed carbon, became hard; then the rains washed them down into deep declivities and spacious valleys, and carefully packed them away for the people to dig out in the form of " coal" many hundred centuries afterwards! Those primeval mosses and early vegetations— the original plants and early trees, once the only glory of the physical world—are all gone into dense blackness, fit only for the stove, the grate, and the igneous stomachs of Monitors, iron-clads, ocean steamers, and locomotives. Then the earth brought forth higher orders—grand, large, immensely high trees, which packed away in their capacious trunks centuries upon centuries of growth and chemistry. Regally, supremely, these trees flourished. But at length, gathering their forces more closely within—deeper, with greater concentration—took fire and burned themselves to death! Soon out of sight, they became a portion ôf the floral history of that epoch.

Then, in the depths of the many warm seas, gelatinous compounds were slowly developed up into points of "life." The early minute fishes flourished in myriads throughout the seas, and also through infusorial organizations, propagating incomprehensible harvests of finer organizations, and then decomposing, becoming in hundreds of centuries petroleum for the machinery of the world—filling all the little crevices of rocks and valleys below the earth's surface, wherever they existed, and died in large abundance in the era of their greatest glory—now only oil, to-day being pumped up and burned in our most fashionable parlors. So the early *points* of life died, and though they were honored with no tombstones to mark their graves, they have arisen from the rocks and live in the world's best uses.

Let us go on through the animal kingdom, where yet more distinctly the same lesson is taught. The first animals were huge in physical organization—ponderous and immense—slow in their motions; they were filled with indolence—mere gastric receptacles or stomachs for the digestion of dense forms of vegetable matter—built for the reception and impartation of particles upon which they fed to form the basis of something better. Thus, primeval animals served for steps in a flight of stairs—for laws and materials to walk upward to the plane of finer organizations. You remember what Geology teaches with reference to the megatheriums, the mammoths, and the ponderous saurians that once roamed over the earth—the vast elephantine animals that were once so numerous and powerful that nothing short of an earthquake could extinguish them—now all gone, save those vestiges and remains of nobility which continue in the modern elephant, the camel, and in the various squirming vipers in the fields of civilization and far off on mountain-sides, each declaring itself to be nothing more than the relic of vast viprous and animal populations long extinct.

These great lessons come from Nature's and God's word. Say not, therefore, when you go from the reading of this Lecture, that you have been where infidelity was taught; but when asked: "What have you been reading?" you can in truth reply: "I have been learning lessons from the word of God." These truths are words of Deity, because they are written on the everlasting rocks and upon the beautiful hills, which show their secret instructions to those who will read and have "a heart to understand" God's infallible ideas written in the wondrous volume of Nature. Always the wisest mind is the best reader—the fastest learner, and the happiest.

It becomes now particularly important to observe that the higher grades of animals—those which exist on the earth to-day—are not the everlasting companions of the world. You know that it is even now difficult to keep certain animals in the world. Already science is concerning itself with the propagation of particular fishes. These animals and fishes are growing fewer, not simply because mankind feed upon them with such unbridled rapacity, but because, although they show the usual large preparations for future progeny, yet only a small percentage of their young are matured. Certain species of fish are, for this cause, almost utterly extinct. Certain birds, too, are growing "beautifully less" and less numerous, showing that their type is slowly becoming extinct.

On this island of Manhattan, on which we exist to-day, the time was when wild beasts—more wild than the worst people in their passions—roamed through thickets and dank swamps; the red man was lord of all; and fishes worked through the murky waters, and loathsome worms wriggled their happy lives away in the dirt and slime beneath. Behold, now it is a resurrected Isle! Like the new "Atlantis" prophesied in early Platonic history, bounded by the sea on all sides, opulent with science, and art, and happy homes, adorned by beautiful persons, filled with wisdom and affection, and bound together by united interests. These things for New York are prophesied on the basis of what now exists, because the departure of the wildness from the lower parts of Nature in the Island is a promise, in an internal sense, of the advent of that which is better, higher, grander, in whatsoever is human—in society and in government.

Many vipers that once lived and propagated in fearful abundance can now scarcely be found. Civilization marches onward and exterminates them. What is civilization? Is it the especial intention of the pioneer who goes to the far west, to destroy poisonous serpents or to kill wild animals? No. Civilization does not come of intention; it is the impulse of the

great law of Progress which gives to man's instinct
two expressions : one to kill for purposes of hunger,
and the other to kill to gratify the desire to overcome
—to give the pleasure of extermination. Nothing so
much as man is endowed with this double motive to
kill. The animals beneath man kill only to satisfy the
demands of hunger. But man kills by the force of a
higher propulsion—to destroy whatever is inimical to
his highest material interests, dangerous to the children
that play at the door, and baneful to the progeny that
will come after them. A man is not made to stop and
think, when he is first called upon to kill a bear or a
lion, whether it would be likely to destroy a human
being, or not, if left with life. It is the inevitable
voice of conquest that cries within him—the irresistible, sturdy impulse, to convince his own faculties—to
show by skillful marksmanship that he can destroy the
enemy or animal before him. I say all this is testimony
that the law of Progress—welling up through the human faculties and blundering through the stupid head
yet clear eye of the marksman—is exterminating all
serpents and animals which are incompatible with the
coming grand future of this planet.

Time is a fine-comb, and Progress is the strong iron
hand that grasps it—drawing it through all parts of
the head of humanity ; and it will comb it clean ! All
ferocious and venomous animals, all poisonous plants,
all meddlesome bugs, all summer flies, all wasps that
sting—everything that comes out of filth and opposes
refinement—everything that shocks civilization, that
comes as an insult and slight to the mind's higher sentiments—is destined, like these elder animals, and

fishes, and primordial trees, and early submarine vegetations, to go down and *die* out of existence !

You cannot escape the conclusion that the human
race is destined to pass through a similar experience.
The theologic, or intuitive dream of the " End of the
World," is based in *a fact* as well as upon a figure of
speech ; it is the upshot of a principle as well as a conception of its open manifestation.

When the early vegetation died out, to *them* it was
the *end* of the world. When the early saurians with-
drew, when the vast birds died, when the old dragons
and mammoth-bats which once roamed and flew through
the world became extinct, to *them* it was the *end* of the
world. When these various modern serpents, these
ferocious animals, these poisonous plants, become
extinct, to *them* it will be the *end* of the world.

Races and nations rise up ; they flourish, grow opulent ; they reach the maximum of material happiness ;
they slide down a rough declivity toward the sunset of
history ; and where another and a new nation is born,
there those once great nations are sepulchered. To the
dying nations it is the *end* of the world. The early
Aztecs thought that once the world was literally
destroyed by a mighty Whirlwind. The Chaldeans,
the Chinese, and others, have a myth that the world was
once destroyed by a general Flood. (I believe there
is a very similar myth recorded in the Old Testament.)
The earliest Greeks taught that the globe was once
destroyed by a Fire. Perhaps it will help the myth by
saying that many Greeks were Alchemists and believed
much in fire ! Famine was the means which hungry
races supposed the gods used to destroy the world. A

few tribes of Indians in North America believed in the destruction of the world by famine. There are, in fact, some twenty-five to thirty different doctrines in the world with regard to the means by which the physical world was once destroyed. Christians take one plan of destroying the world's population—that of *water*. By the amount of imperfection and corruption still remaining, one would be justified in saying that *the water* had been withdrawn several centuries too soon. It seems to have left the creed portion of the world *muddier* than it was before. World-makers and world-destroyers should not undertake to kill a population by water unless they can do the work universally and thoroughly. The world was not yet quite finished when that great Flood swept over the mountains and destroyed all; and yet the drowning was not sufficiently thorough; it did not destroy the evil conditions which caused the American rebellion! There was left in human nature a whole nest of evil eggs, which, when incubated by the law of Progress, will bring out, in the future of this country, the enactment of another Rebellion like this thing which is to-day startling and upturning all the nations of the world. And why? Because no literal Flood, however universal, however high over the peaks of the Andes it might have been, or may be, could not and cannot quite kill out all human imperfections. "Perfection out of imperfection comes," as flowers bloom out of the dark, dreary, and unresponsive earth. That is the reason why the end of the world does not come in haste. It is the infinite method of doing finite things—the perpetual going over dreary

4

wastes and imperfect conditions—up to that which is blooming, beautiful, and perfect.

Now the physical globe is to follow this progressive law. If a nation rises and matures, if it gathers around itself all the arts, and sciences, and splendors, and finally decays and dies; so mankind may surely expect that the globe itself, after its mission is all accomplished, will mature, decay, die, and disappear from space! Astronomy, geology, chemistry, and all the sciences, show that this earth *began ;* they demonstrate with equal certainty that it will also grow old and be dissolved. Its chemical affinities, in a few hundred thousand years, will become antipathies. Its atoms will rush to the embrace of thousands of other bodies.

The human race, properly so-called, is scarcely forty thousand years old. How old that is to a planet's population, you can judge by the aspect of the planet itself. What means it in this Temperate Zone, right between two great extremes, that we have these *changeable* seasons—these excessively curious exhibitions of climate and of temperature? Because, I reply, the earth itself is yet *new*—is not yet out of its teens! In its waters, in its mountains and valleys, in its chemistry, the globe is yet all undeveloped. Its treasures are yet locked up in trunks of trees and fastened in recesses far down beneath the soil. The atmosphere, even in the temperate belt, is yet rampant with a thousand-fold eccentricities; it is daily giving grotesque expressions of its innate, uncouth barbarisms; is not yet civilized enough to keep out of your doors even when you have locked them; not decent enough to cease "blowing you up" when you seek to comfortably and peaceably walk through the streets or open fields. Why, our uncivilized atmosphere is producing terrible havoc with navigation—is interfering every day with the commerce of the world—like a barbarian not yet wise enough to follow the ways of wisdom. The globe is like a wild boy. He tumbles down stairs when he should be walking, and falls through the ice while skating, when he ought to be self-poised and too wise for accidents. The atmosphere is like a powerful wild horse not perfectly trained. Ever and anon it gathers up its black powers, stands before a chasm with accumulated vigor and tremendous energy, and bounds to the opposite side with all the madness of unemployed power. A wild horse sweeping over the prairies: that is the earth's atmosphere. This all explains why the elements play mankind such pranks, unroofing houses, tumbling over chimneys, and paying no more respect to a church-steeple than to the pole of a hay-stack!

When Benjamin Franklin sent up his card, he simply obtained a slight indication that Mr. Lightning would, one of these days, be sociable and come to tea. He did get some of the fearful fluid bottled up; just enough to talk with it—nothing more. Now Mr. Lightning is social and chatty. He tells all the truth, and nearly all the lies, about the present war. "Electricity," *alias* "Lightning," cuts awful pranks with people in cholera times, and causes all kinds of unutterable mischief, according to recent discoveries, in the diseases of animals throughout the country. All because the fluid is not tame—it is wild, barbarous; it has not come into the best society; and it does not know how to behave among folks.

All this is equally true of the globe. The earth is eccentric; it is sidewise in its orbit; it does not yet know enough to get down and lie straight in its bed. Now it rolls in its path almost wrong end foremost. When the poles of the planet shall come into harmony with the plane of its orbit, then how beautifully the sun will cause all parts of it to bloom! The globe is not yet sufficiently good to be so blessed. It will not be so blessed while this orbital inequality continues to exist.

Mankind must not soon expect our oceans to be calm, nor our lightnings to save the churches, nor hurricanes to respect haystacks, or people, or cattle, nor that the atmosphere will soon be civilized enough to favor men in their Arctic explorations or coast-line navigations.

Men sneer at the fanatic who thinks he can ride in the air. Are you quite sure that the man is a fool who thinks that one of these days we will rise up in the air and be as safe, more certain, and far quicker, in our voyage, than when shipping for Europe on the best steamer? Men laugh at those who dare suggest its scientific practicability. Most people belong to the race who have the power and the pomposity to laugh at fanatics, until their children adopt the inventions of those fanatics, and until mankind enjoy all the luxuries which such improvements diffuse throughout the world. Now, I say, mankind are not yet old enough on this planet, nor is the atmosphere old enough, nor is electricity tame enough, and the mental world itself is not large and good enough, to realize aerial navigation. Therefore it will not come right away. But just

as sure as I am now speaking—as certain as birds fly—
so certain will safe, swift, and delightful air navigation
be man's achievement.

The earth is yet very young. . It is now only a few
millions of years old—in its early teens—has not been
in existence long enough to prepare the human race for
a higher degree of civilization. Only a few years ago,
across the Atlantic, in France, a man, although starving
to death,·gave to the world systematic intimations and
lofty demonstrations to the effect that a higher social
order would inevitably come. Of course it is popular
to slander him, and to blacken his character out of
sight; but the

"Truth, crushed to earth, will rise again."

Not all that Fourier or Swedenborg said is true; not
all that I say is true. True men make their words as
near truth as possible. Mankind must be catholic and
all-embracing; instead of excluding all the conflicting
creeds, better take them all in and pulverize them.

When you go upon the mountain hights, and with
your vision sweep the plain, and the whole horizon of
thought, can you not take the pictures home with you,
and tell your wife and children what you have seen and
enjoyed on the summit? Perhaps your wife and little
ones live in the valley of thought; they may look out
only through the open door, or through some panes of
broken glass, and see only a few pigs or the dirty fowls
that are squawking for something to eat, and crying
children that need bread to keep them still: this, perhaps, is what the valley-minded woman sees in her
lowly estate. Or, perhaps the wife is the progressive

member of the house. If the better-minded woman goes, I pray that she will try to attract upwards with her that ponderous being called " a husband." Go on together, if it be possible; sweep the horizon of Progression, take in the thoughtful scene; then, on returning, tell your listening neighbors, who have not yet gone up, of the rivers and mountains, plains, farmhouses, and beautiful trees—all the picturesque vision of higher forms of truth.

The mental world, I repeat, is young. The physical globe, too, is so young that it cannot be speedily called to order. The tempests of the physical world are only what we see mentally breaking out in the galleries of political conventions. Hurricanes are but parts of what occurs in the State Legislatures. Where political heathenism exists, *there* will be tornadoes and hurricanes! It is natural for people to be dirty until they are washed. People will be covered with political, social, and religious vermin, until they are perfectly cleansed and civilized, purely clothed, and thoroughly combed. All this is applicable to the physical world.

What of the races? The nations and peoples are not prepared for a higher order of society. They have not lived up to their present knowledge, and of course they are not ready for a grander social or political development. Best minds are ready only to say and believe that something better is possible, and that is all. But " humanity sweeps onward."

The great world is grand and sublime, because it rolls progressively away toward the coming centuries! The human race, about forty thousand years old, has but reached its thirteenth year in true civilization. In its politics, in its republicanism, in its democracy, in its poetry, in its music, and in its spirituality, the race is yet very young. Much will happen when 100,000 more of these rolling years shall have passed away! The notes of music which come through spiritual communications—from the lofty summits of heavenly inspiration—enable us to catch but imperfect glimpses of the " good time" when the earth shall ripen and blossom as the rose. All this shows what the world is fast coming to see.

When mankind shall have grown spiritually larger and finer in body, they will have fewer and fewer children. Down in the lower strata of society behold how populous! Take the early races: they propagated rapidly. Earth's mothers have been broken down by their exceedingly numerous progeny. Rise higher in the scale, and the married have fewer children and less frequently. Rise still higher and higher in the mental scale, and you can easily believe the time will come when reproduction will cease. There will then be fathers and mothers with their descendants; and the progeny will become as the angels—" neither marrying nor given in marriage"—having arisen above the mission of propagation—all ready for the wondrous apotheosis which will close the scene of the human race.

In the vast future (I wish I had another hour this morning, in which to speak of what will happen between this and the future,) when the race itself has grown to the highest point of maturity. Behold at last a family group ascends from the " perfect sleep" into the Upper life! They close the terrestrial drama, and the curtain falls. The great bell of chemistry is now struck, and instead of a conflagration, as the "Adventists" believe, slow *decomposition*—dying like a puff—decaying and dropping asunder like the stump of a tree without vitality—then spreading its atoms over millions of solar bodies that are ready to grasp these chemical opportunities—thus this planet will cease, and its population, all in the Summer-Land, looking down upon the closing of this sublime tragical drama!

The cerebellum, I again remark, will one of these days cease to have any function with reference to reproduction. The finest, most poetic and spiritual mind, gathers nearly all of its propagating powers and essences into the front-brain and top-faculties. Such persons have few children. Men who are yet full of the world's blood, and women who are full of similar vitalities, still believe that many children, better propagated, would be great blessings to the world. Only friends of Progress dare to speak the whole truth on this subject. Not a church-minister in the city, with the vast organization of moneyed men to support the pulpit, dares to speak the truth which lies at the basis of the happiness of mankind.

But friends of Progress are free to speak. We sing new songs. We have new wings of great principles just starting. We are ready to soar wherever the truth shall attract. We have free feet ready to scale the highest mountains. We are a glad and cheerful people, with unbounded hope. To our eyes the heavens are open, and our souls are filled with the attractive inspiration of the future. All this brings us joy and peace in the midst of carnage and confusion in the physical world. The true harmonial progressive Women and Men stand unruffled and unchanged. They know that, in the far-off future time, the better will dominate what is merely good; that the best will dominate the better; that fruits and flowers will yet blossom in the wilderness; and that, from out of the earth's dark places, the white lilies of peace shall bloom with an immortal beauty.

4*

THE NEW BIRTH;

OR,

THE SPIRIT'S PROGRESS IN TRUTH.

"To commune with God amidst the beauty of earth, in thanksgiving,
For life, health, our daily bread; and, by second birth,
A home in heaven."

The first view of this question that comes before the ignorant mind is the supernatural. It is incorporated with all religious education, and has been strengthened by the psychological influence of all ecclesiastical teachers. Hence there exists in almost every mind an undefinable conviction that the new birth—"a change of heart"—is a supernatural effect, produced by instrumentalities differing wholly from those laws of growth which bring mankind into existence, which cause the flowers to burst into blossom and the sun to shine; that in order to understand what is meant by a new heart, or to have the mysterious experience of such a "change," we must come into a state different from the whole system of laws, causes, and effects, which characterize and regulate the unchangeable universe.

Dr. Bushnell, a most classical expounder of the popular theory of the supernatural, holds the conviction that, above the will and reason of every person, there is a super-plane, an extra Divine sphere, differing from all the fixed natural laws and mathematical principles which move and systematically distribute the ponderable bodies of space. The supernatural, he would say, is the great voluntary system of God; the involuntary portion is the system of Nature, which is an organization endowed with laws, and with characteristics and attributes and forces, without inter-consciousness to operate throughout the interminable periods of the future, as it has through all past eternities, in unvarying accordance with the fixed plans of the Infinite Mind. If anything should occur in the departments of human nature contrary to the established laws and legitimate effects, it is a "miracle." It is furthermore held that God reserves to himself a realm of voluntary powers, with which, whenever in the depth of wisdom and love it seems best, he volitionally interposes, suspends, repeals, reverses, subverts any of the fixed laws of Nature—breaking them utterly—otherwise miracles would never occur, and the supernatural world would not be revealed and vindicated. Dr. Bushnell has probably given as complete an exposition of that side of the subject as can be found in the language, although necessarily very unsatisfactory and irrational, because the subject itself is involved in mazes of the greatest obscurity and superstition.

No miracle is possible without conflict with the established atomic laws of the physical universe. Whatever occurs in harmony with the requirements of any of these laws, is no miracle; though the occurrence might be a higher manifestation of the same general plan, not before fully understood. The definition of a miracle would be the development of something in contradiction, in antagonism, with the immutable atomic affinities of the physical universe.

The controversy between Progressive minds and the Church-people turns exactly on this one point,· viz., whether Deity ever contradicts the established laws of the physical and spiritual universe? Did he, or does he ever suspend the operation of natural principles, in order to accomplish anything for the especial benefit of any class of people, or for the sake of any particular person?

Desiring to ascertain the exact truth of the question, we have gone into investigations of what, in the past, have been accredited as "miracles," and which have ecclesiastically been and are yet considered marvels absolutely necessary to substantiate the peculiar claims and Messiahship of Jesus. The theory is, that he depended very much on these " signs and wonders" to arrest the attention of the people, and thus lead them, through their marvelousness, to a perception of higher truths. The different Churches say that the test of his Messiahship—the evidence that he was sent as the only begotten of God to humanity—is the supernatural power displayed in his miracles!

Now, we have investigated and analyzed this chapter of Bible-miracles, which these churchmen dare not do. They sometimes confess that they dare not take a miracle and probe it to its primal elements. Some clergymen cannot always afford to follow the plain truth; others are constitutionally cowardly; and others are intellectually incompetent; whilst many of the evangelical school eat too much, and are indolent. But Progressives have freely examined the question of

Bible-miracles, with a sincere desire to know "what is truth," and they find that there is nowhere recorded, either in the Old Testament or in the New, a transaction which, in any possible degree, violates the established order and fixed laws of Nature. If any one among you know of miracles, or fancy that you know of positive events, in direct contradiction to the unchangeable principles of human nature or of the physical universe, you should at once give a full exposition of what you think you know on the subject.

"A change of heart"—in the fact of which we firmly believe—is no supernatural manifestation of God's grace. We very earnestly believe in a "new birth;" yea, in a succession of new births. We believe that there are many individuals who need to be born again and patched up a good many times to be anybody worth mentioning. This is true because there are so many persons who seem to have been badly born from the first—"conceived in sin and brought forth in iniquity."

But there are other natures born in righteousness. We thank heaven for these beautiful bows of human promise, even though they come without especial intention or merit on the part of their progenitors. Halos of immortal effulgence now and then flash forth through the beautiful birth of approximate Saviors. In music, in art, in science, in philosophy, in every direction towards which human interests tend, or from which human needs are supplied, we behold well-born and highly-endowed sons and daughters of wisdom and liberty. A highly endowed person may be surprisingly "well-born" in one particular respect, and yet may

remain unconceived in almost every other department
of mind and soul.

No, we do not accept the doctrine of a supernatural
spiritual conception, nor a new, miraculous birth.   We
hold that man's mind is so constituted as to desire
sensuous Knowledge and also beautiful Wisdom, or
wise Knowledge, which is spiritual Understanding.   It
is natural for man to desire to expel ignorance from his
mind.   The soul throws a power from the center of its
being, saying to ignorance: " Get thee behind me !"
and then, turning to heaven, it says: " Give me understanding, I entreat Thee; and give me also wisdom ;
and oh, give me power, and true knowledge also, by
which that power can be made executive and practical."   The desire to *know*, is the first implanted ambition of the intellectual faculties.   Useful knowledge is
the next demand ; then knowledge that is *consistent*, as
well as useful ; then *beautiful* knowledge, as well as
consistent ; then *spiritual* knowledge, as well as beautiful ; then knowledge *celestial*, as well as spiritual—
these are the gradually awakening prayers and undefinable longings of the perpetually-borning human
spirit.

There are persons who pass on for years, feeling
only a feeble desire to know more—to have less ignorance in common, every-day concerns.   It is not
important to them whether they know " the whole
truth," so long as they have the common-place ex-
changes of a talkative society.   To this end they take
the established Quarterlies, read the political pamphlets
and the fashionable periodicals, and peruse such portions of the daily papers as inform them concerning the

common doings of the world. Such information seems to be a complete gratification to many minds. On Sundays they attend some established church, and during the brief moments spent there they hear music, and come under the influence of devotional prayers, or listen, it may be, to an eloquent, a beautiful, and perhaps a *spiritual* sermon, and, for the time being, such minds feel vague longings for something more "interior" which they do not consciously possess. But they hasten home to dinner. *That* settles all the fine emotions that were excited. Down they drop into their newspapers, and presently into a solid, snoring nap, and on waking, find themselves the persons they were after business hours on Saturday night. Others become excited. They feel enthusiastically warm all throughout their beating hearts. They feel that the physical dinner cannot come between them and the blessed truths of heaven. They go devotionally to their rooms to seek the Lord in prayer. Then they come under the influence of a new psychology; a finer feeling has commenced to flow from the mysterious fountains of spirit. They wish to know the will of their heavenly Father— beautiful, loving, saving justice, power, purity, and truth, which are God. Holy emotions rise from the depths of the spirit and set the moral faculties in action, and the whole religious group of organs bow themselves reverently before that newly-awakened desire to be at peace with God. With deep sincerity such minds go to their closets, shut the door, and prostrate themselves in prayer, or pray themselves into prostration. They attend the revival-meeting both day and night, until, like one of our celebrated pugilists, the overjoyed heart rises and boldly declares itself " saved by God," through the supernatural interposition of the sanguineous sweat of the Vicarious Redeemer. And the upshot of this excitement is called " a change of heart!"

Some are only spectators. Some have been through the mill. Others have been converted and " born again" a good many times. There are persons in all communities who have had the mysterious bewilderment of this experience, and have come safely and reasonably out of it; and they testify that, while in it, they were happier, but did not know as much; were not large in thought nor liberal; but they felt warmer, felt kindlier, felt a closer connection with something incomprehensible and mysteriously sublime. Young hearts, between the ninth and twentieth year, are especially susceptible to such Methodistical conversions; just as between the cradle and the twelfth year the physical system is susceptible to measles, mumps, whooping-cough, and kindred infirmities. I say there is an impressible period in each human life when a theological change of heart—a church-rousing among the young men and maidens—comes about and produces its devotional and probational effects as naturally as the little distempers of childhood afflict the tender physical organs.

A man just begins to be somebody when he is plumply forty-five years of age. Before that time he has an uncertain history and an unsolidified character. A woman truly begins to *be* when she is forty. There is then womanly beauty and practical strength. The orb of life is truly balanced at this age in its path around the sun of Duty. Hopes have been disappointed and buried, and they have been also resurrected and educated. Ambition and vanity have been checked and chided many times; and baseless expectations of worldly victories have been driven and punished out of the temple. The person begins to comprehend the solid facts of life, and to feel largely and sympathetically acquainted with the current wants, impulses, and experiences of human nature in general. After the fortieth year there occur few *sudden* conversions.

Almost every religious person in Christendom can remember to have experienced something like " a change of heart." Now and then, however, some one has dropped over-board in the voyage, or stranded upon some cliff by the way, and therefore she or he has never sensibly drifted into the ecclesiastical current. Some have stood upon the shore of religion and contemplated the mysterious voyage in which others were embarking. They stand to-day and remark: "I never was taken into any Church; I never was converted; I have tried to be, but never could be." This is the experience of a few religious souls in Christendom. Large numbers, on the other hand, testify that they have passed into the mysterious experience of feeling a oneness with Deity; and a certain conscientious reconciliation with the spirit of the historic Redeemer.

If you were intimately acquainted with the religious experience of the Mahommedans, Chinese, Chaldeans, or Persians, who have nothing essentially at war with the spirit of Christianity, you would recognize your own human nature with the same mysterious, subjectively spiritual experience, under the identical law

of psychological contact with Deity. They also obtain
and experience the " new birth," or " change of heart."
Many religious souls have had this experience who
never heard the name of Jesus—that " name" which
many Christians consider essential to the ultimate
safety of souls.

That celebrated religious phenomenon, which Unitarian missionaries obtained in the Eastern world—I mean
Mr. Philip Chunder Jogut Gangooly, who probably
cost about five thousand dollars to get him squarely
converted, educated, and shipped to this country—
testified that Christians, not excepting Unitarians, were
in need of true knowledge relative to the leading doctrines and ceremonies of Hindooism. He found the
American people religiously ignorant—found that we
knew but little, and what we did know was, like superficial drinking at the Pierian spring, calculated to
make all a little drunk with religious feeling and con-
ceit. His influence, however, had the effect of rendering
our missionaries more eloquent and our bumps of
benevolence more susceptible. Mr. Gangooly said
nothing remarkable about a " change of heart."

Bishop Colenso is a convert to God's preaching
through the unsophisticated, but highly religious nature,
of those far distant heathen children. They put questions to him which he would not answer dogmatically.
The noble bishop would " once more think of it." Once
more the teachable teacher felt that he must study his
own theories—go back again to the cardinal propositions of his Church—down to the primal principles of
his own long-cherished doctrines. And this accomplished and noble-souled gentleman was sent by an

evangelical institution to teach its religious dogmas to
the heathen, by which they were to be led to God! But
the entreaties of the heathen children led him prayerfully to a re-examination, to a new analysis and measurement of his creedal propositions, and lo! the result
is "conversion"—a new birth in the heart of the good
Bishop Colenso. And then Bishop Rochester attempts
to send the news to the kingdom of heaven, through his
formal prayers, and advises all the prelates and priests
of that region to send like word, that poor Bishop
Colenso has strayed from the fold of truth.* "Pray
for him! He is laboring under a soul-destroying
heresy!" What evangelical ignoramuses! what consummate twaddlers! what accomplished imbeciles!
Why, the priests and prelates are asked to pray against
the *very truths* which those simple children of the Most
High put to the susceptible and honest spirited Colenso!
The heathen converted the Bishop to a higher knowledge of God. Let all men and women see in the
teachable spirit of that excellent minister a beautiful
example, and let them not be behind him in simplicity
and integrity. "Are you quite sure"—they asked
him—"are you quite sure, Bishop, that all who never
heard the name of Jesus will eternally suffer?" He
could not reply, for he was *not quite sure!* Sent by a
great ecclesiastical power to teach the heathen, yet he

---

* The Bishop of Oxford has recently addressed a pastoral letter to
his clergy, in which he laments that Dr. Colenso has resolved to persevere in the course on which he has entered, and adds, that while it
is a matter of deep thankfulness that no leaven of this unbelief is to be
found in the Oxford Episcopate, it is not best to be contented with
mere immunity from error. "Rather," says the Bishop, "let the sight
of a brother so misled humble and warn us."

was "not quite sure"! Let us thank God—God does
not want us to thank him—well, let us be grateful to
the Heart of all principles, for the. teachable, the
beautiful, and child-like spirit of Bishop Colenso, which
caused him, with power, to say: " Dogmatism, depart!
These heathen children ask me if I am quite sure of
,eternal suffering for all who have not accepted Jesus.
No! *I am not sure !*" Then he goes to his New Testament; goes in deepest prayer; he prayed as good as
the best of you can pray, and with as sincere a heart;
and he finds therein what he never found before, viz.,
that the Divine never designs to cast off anything pertaining to the constitution of the human soul! He finds,
on the other hand, that the truths and real revelations
of the New Testament are worthy of the paternal Soul
of the universe. He says, therefore, to all the world:
"I am a *new* man." And we respond, Amen! He *has*
experienced a "new birth." And yet the dogmatic
Church, which holds that the new birth is essential for
a sight at the kingdom of heaven, is bowed down in
lamentations over his conversion! Presently another
class of religionists will undertake to wheel the Bishop
into line with their peculiar forms and notions.

If I were able, I would speak with an emphasis of
ten tons to the square inch, so that the whole world
should hear that the system of Christianity—I say
" the system," not the spirit, remember—as it is to-day
preached and presented to mankind, is, generally
speaking, just as monstrous a piece of quackery as any
practice we find in the discordant world of medicine.
Christendom is filled with ecclesiastical quacks and
charlatans on this very subject of " the new birth."

You cannot in American cities walk over five hundred
yards without noticing a new sign up, announcing a *new*
method of introducing you into the kingdom of heaven.
The Methodist differing from the Episcopalian, the
Presbyterian from the Baptist, the Quaker from the
Universalist, the Congregationalist from the Unitarian!

Every one who reads the Bible—as I am glad every
educated person can in the independence of consciousness and reason—sees in it precisely what his or her
state of mind makes apparent, and that is all. A man
will see its teachings literally or figuratively, symboli-
cally or spiritually, Swedenborgianally or quite otherwise, in accordance with the elections of his *state of
mind.* And he will furnish the "class-meeting" with
descriptions of his religious and spiritual development,
or new birth, in accordance with his intellectual cali-
ber, education, and worldly experience. If his priest
has impressed him to be a dogmatist, he will hold up
the stupid sign and say: "Lo! this is the *only* way to the
new birth, and the shortest route to the kingdom of
heaven."

Friends of Progress should help men over all this.
Let them understand that, by means of true spiritual
growth, they can become united, and thus destroy the
monstrous mistakes and expensive theological quacke-
ries which infest Christendom. No wonder so many
honest souls get so *badly-born* in the conflicting
Churches! No wonder so many come out sanctimoni-
ous and hypocritical, but not sanctified! True, many
tender-hearted converts in the Churches are inclined to
be spiritual, and some of them are permanently im-

proved and benefited for life by the mysterious shock, coupled with the institutional or societary check; but a far greater number, on the other hand, are rendered permanently small and limited in their understandings of the human world, of the great truths of Christianity; and the life-long moral consequences are—bigotry on most questions, narrow-mindedness, social bitterness, and a squeamish or malignant protest against the onward work of Reformers.

Now, all interior and common-sense men have practical and similar understandings of the origin, nature, and validity of the " new birth." Many of them, however, becoming utterly disgusted with supernatural theories, have gone to reading books of Medicine, or to reading Law, and have resolutely given up all speculative thoughts and the cultivation of all sentimental inclinations toward the popular Church, and toward spiritual things in general. Some of them still hold to progression and improvements in moral reforms, and such teach that the truest new birth consists in a true generation and a true exodus of both body and soul. "The true practical birth," say they—the only one which will save the trouble of all the pseudo-regenerative processes which the Churches have inaugurated, and do away with all the mysterious strugglings to get born again—" is to be perfectly born from the beginning." These results rest directly with the mother and the father—the true Joseph and the true Mary—who are to bring the gentle human Saviors into the world. The Christs are to be born from the spirit, without miracle, through the organs of human reproduction. There is to be a multiplication of Saviors, " both male

and female." Instead of one being born every ten centuries or two thousand years, there will eventually be
one born every ten years, and *ultimately*, every time a
child is born the angels will sing."glad tidings of
great joy," for each child will be a Christ-spirit and a
Savior. Let us, therefore, exalt woman's mission and
situation, and esteem man as the all-embracing, external, protective, and positive sphere in which woman
secretly performs her allotted duties. She is to be the
Savior in the sense of being a fountain from which a
stream, a river, a lake, a sea, an ocean of purer bodies
and souls will flow for the progress and purification of
the world.

Is not this a practical doctrine of being born again?
You know that few people are well-born. Their
spiritual genesis is defective; their deformities are
numerous—not only physiological defects, but also
mental and moral. Henry Ward Beecher is physically
hearty and morally stout enough—I am so glad that he
has made himself also *popular* and sufficiently acceptable—to convert a Congregationalist pulpit into a public
Sunday rostrum! The accomplishment of that "new-
birth" in the functions of a pulpit is a decided indication of his great inherent power, and of his great
mastery over the feelings and thoughts of his hearers.
And in the freedom of his Congregational platform, he
says, that *a man born right the first time* is very superior
to the man who has been "converted" under the influence of religion. (See PROGRESSIVE ANNUAL for 1862.)
The converted man—notwithstanding the restraints of
the Church and of Paul's gospel, and the additional
checks to bad morals constantly dropping from the

eaves of the sanctuary—is not *so good* a man as a man
who was born good and rightly trained from birth.
That is to say, a naturally good man is superior to a
converted bad man in the Church. I am so glad Henry
said it! I wish all gospel-ministers were sufficiently
stout in stomach and fearless in brain to make progressive platforms out of their pulpits, and then preach
the wisdom thereof to their astounded congregations!
Pity they are not more morally vigorous. They have
not the power of God with them. That is the cause of
their feebleness and bigotry. It would take twenty
Trinities to give Protestant clergymen moral courage
adequate to preach, investigate, and enforce new principles of human regeneration. But my Brother Beecher,
on the Sunday Rostrum, notwithstanding his substra-
tum of skepticism as to the existence of the Trinity
itself, is yet enabled to announce a most thrilling principle of redemptive Truth. He is not afraid to tell the
people that they had better propagate their children
right from the start—not in "sin and in iniquity," but
with the pure, beautiful, celestial principles of health
and harmony in the body, and with the balance of
righteousness in the spiritual organization. From
thence goodness in the subsequent individual flows as
from a fountain, while "conversions" do nothing more
than modify and patch up that which, after all, at heart,
is out of moral shape and due working proportion, and
the crookedness of which cannot be straightened for a
lengthened period in the Summer-Land. I wish my
Brother Henry had also said that the morally mis-
shapened and intellectually crooked do not quite
recover until the Summer-Land pours its fine discipline

and its healing magnetism through and over the affections and character.   But he has not got so far.

In the New Testament, in the third chapter of John,
we find a most practical view of this question of a new
birth, and yet it was given to mankind, as it were, accidentally, or as part of a common conversation.   It
makes one feel as though Nicodemus ought to receive
the thanks of Christendom for the spiritual answers
which his materialistic interrogatories elicited.   Nicodemus was a distinguished Pharisee.   The Pharisees,
you know, were almost all dogmatic men, just like these
American religionists and doctors of divinity.   They
held high positions, and filled all the important offices
in Israel.   Nicodemus was a Ruler.   He had heard
that the "young man" was teaching strange, mysterious
doctrines through the country; and, being a Ruler,
like the Governor of one of our States, he went to the
"young man," and very politely asked him to "explain
himself."   The Israelitish gentleman did not wish to be
conspicuous in such a matter.   Therefore, somewhat as
Mr. Lincoln left Baltimore for Washington, so the
Ruler put on an unusual coat, and a different hat, and
away he stealthily went to have a religious talk with
the son of Mary and Joseph.   Said he to the spiritual
man: "What is this doctrine of being born again?
What do you mean by it?"   So spake Mr. Nicodemus.
The "young man" held up the doctrine, plainly, substantially, that, "unless a man be born again, he cannot see the kingdom of heaven."   Nicodemus first paid
him a compliment; for, said he, You are a very influential, successful person; you must be "of God."   You
do these wonderful things—you accomplish these so-

called miracles among the people—consequently, you must be a Son of God, and I am willing to call you "Rabbi," or master. (Now-a-days we say "Mr.," instead of "Rabbi.")

The Ruler was investigating "for himself." Said he: "What is the meaning of all this?" Jesus gave him an obscure answer: "Except a man be born again, he cannot *see* the kingdom of heaven." Now, merely *seeing* the kingdom of heaven is not always satisfactory to one's spiritual cravings. You might see a very fine dinner in the next room, with a strong window between you and it, and you hungry and without money. Would *seeing* the dinner be calculated to satisfy the cravings of your appetite? Mr. Nicodemus did not seem to get much satisfaction out of the answer to his question. The theme itself was so extraordinary. "How can that be?" he thought. He took things *literally*. Said he: "How can an old man enter back through physical organs and be born again?"

Nicodemus naturally enough supposed he had the "best of the argument." His common experience and materialistic views, assured him. Says he: "That is absurd; I can bring medical books to show that the thing has never occurred." Jesus, on the contrary, did not need any medical books to convince him. He knew, by the light of Intuition, that the new birth in the Ruler's mind. was impossible. Miracles never occur. Jesus did not pretend that there was anything miraculous in his gospel of the new birth. He did not say that a man could possibly return and be born a second time through the physiological organs. He knew that such an event could not happen, any more than an elderly man could swim back to the baby year and begin life again—any more than any event which has happened can be annihilated from the history of the past.

Jesus did not admit that Nicodemus's thought was possible. But instead he said: " Unless a man be born of *water* and of the *spirit*, he cannot enter the kingdom." That is something more comprehensible. A man cannot come to dinner unless he pays the price. He cannot come to this feast of fat things—cannot drink the wine on the lea well-refined—unless he walks through water and in the Spirit.

Now of all this I believe that I never had any doubt. I believe it, and have long believed it, because it is utterly without miracle, and because the conception is so beautiful in itself. No spiritual person ever questions that beautiful reformatory principle divulged in the third chapter of John.

But Nicodemus was evidently astonished. He might have said: " I cannot make anything out of what you say; it is all incomprehensible stuff to me. I cannot comprehend your ideas about *water* and the *Spirit*." Then what did Mary's spiritual son do? Why, he cited a very interesting illustration of it—that is, interesting to commentators who make it their business to expound Scriptures, but very obscure to those who ask the question. Said he: " You do not understand the wind's mysteries, neither do you understand this. You cannot understand whence the wind cometh, nor whither it goeth. So of every person born of the Spirit." That limpid explanation must have been very unsatisfactory to Nicodemus. He very naturally said: " Well, I shall never succeed in being born again. If I cannot understand the process any more than I can understand the wind, then I am a gone case; for I certainly don't understand either how the wind comes or how it goes." And so he went away no wiser.

Missionaries who go out to teach the heathen, do not know any more about spiritual regeneration than did Nicodemus. When the affections of men are born again, the third chapter of John is of little moment. All truth is read with new eyes when the spirit is wise. If you be really "born again," the world's Bible, as well as Nature, will be new volumes to you. But you must be first born again, independently of the Bible, and become something within yourself, and then the Bible and Christianity will mean something more than a book and a system. The world also will become a new development to you from the day you become harmonious and new within yourself. The doctrine is plain and beautiful, that the new birth is not possible "except a man be born of water and of the Spirit." I am glad the account does not read "brandy and *water*," or "bread and wine;" for then, to follow authority, we would have to spread a table and proceed to celebrate the Eucharist. He did not say a man cannot be born again, except through the use of bread and wine, which is only a Hebrew act of commemoration. That will do as a Passover. (I always pass it over!) A human heart is not born again by means of brandy and water, nor alone by means of the "spirit." In some Churches they *dip* "converts" into a large tank, simply because the Bible-text reads "water"; and so *baptizo* becomes a very influential mystery in the regenerative vocabulary. I am so glad that Jesus was led into Jordan. It seems to promise that, one of these days, people will adopt the rational means of securing physiological perfection. There will be sweeter people on earth when *bathing* becomes universal. Swedenborg and all spiritually-minded people say that water is a beautiful emblem of purity, renovation, or regeneration. What a sparkling element it is, going through the world, with immortal music on its bosom, flowing down mountain-slopes and forming cascades, and forever hymning gratitude and praise to Deity! No man can enter into the kingdom of harmony unless he be born, first, through physiological harmony, or " water," and, second, through the balance of his affections and faculties, or through the " spirit" of wisdom and justice.

Many of us will know something more substantial about being "born again" one of these coming days. Mary's son put " water" *before* " spirit," and so do we. It is true physiological reform. There is no miracle or mystery in it. He said: " A man (that is, anybody,) born 'of water'—of physical cleanliness, physical neatness, physical harmony, and away from disease—and 'of the spirit'—that is, of the balance of the powers of the heart and faculties of the brain—such an one can enter into the kingdom of heaven." (Have you tried it? If you have not, suppose you begin to test the truth of it to-day.) He says the Son of Man shall be " lifted up"—the only begotten of God. What is the only begotten? It is the spirit of Truth issuing from this beautiful marriage between " water" and " spirit"—the nuptial union between " body" and " soul." The power and the spirit of Truth rise out—

the only begotten—and thus the individual is "lifted up." Then what? No man can be *lifted out* unless he be first immersed *in* something. What is he lifted out of? Out from his personal Satans—out of sympathy with his unclean spirits—out of the pit of his demons. What are they? Passions, appetites, and inversions. "The only begotten" is the principle of Truth—rising out from the secret recesses of the superior faculties, and "lifting" man out of his passions and appetites, which are demons and unclean spirits.

It matters not how great a man's reputation may be, if he is, to any extent, in bondage to his stomach, to his passions, to any bad habit or acquired appetite—such a man is not "saved." He realizes nothing of the new birth. A selfish man, a deceiver, a hypocrite—a man who lives in his family like a beast and before folks like a gentleman—has not experienced a change of heart. A swinish character always gets "lengthwise in the trough." He stretches himself at full length in the advantages of his home, and closes out the choicest friends of his wife and children. Or the fashionable religious woman, member of whatever Church, who will require the coachman to go out in the storm to drive her to Church, is not born again. And these women who work and slave, who are deprived of their just rewards, who labor in the kitchens, and who garnish the rooms where maidenly attentions are most required —these are cheated of an extra twenty-five cents a month by persons who go to some graceless church. And are such born again? "Can't you work in my kitchen early and late for six dollars and a quarter a month?" Bridget thinks she deserves seven dollars.

Who would labor for less? (I would charge twenty, if I were Bridget.) It is the hardest thing in the world for an intelligent person to be Bridget, and to do Bridget's work. She ought to have ten or twelve, instead of six and a quarter dollars per month. But the favorite orthodox minister gets all the extra money which Bridget ought to have for her tedious labors. All because the religious lady of the house is not just— is not " born again"—but is under the dominion of popularity, style, fashion, churchianity, and orthodoxy.

Look up these opulent Avenues, so full of dressings and great mansions. Do they not administer to the destruction of the principles of human liberty, justice, happiness, and fraternity? Persons who live in them lose much of their simplicity of character, and they are not teachable. They are unhappy and in " outer darkness." There are " weepings" in the basements, " wailings" in the bed-chambers, and " gnashings of teeth" whenever the large bills come in for payment. I do not wonder that they live in outer darkness, nor that they go to church to see whether there is anything " cheerful" in the prospect after a death by gout. The man who needs a Church, or the woman who needs a Minister, or the bishop who needs a Bible, or the religionist whose feeble faith needs the bolster of a Miracle, is not born again. Such may have the form—the signs and symbols—but not the spirit of Truth.

A new birth lifts the mind above dependence upon externals, for the " only begotten" in the spirit begins life by drawing upon the Infinite Father for truths and principles. A new birth, therefore, consists in a marriage between the affections and faculties of the social, intellectual, and moral nature. The spirit will produce its kind. Jesus also said that. Did he not say truly: "That which is born of the flesh, is flesh; that which is born of the spirit, is spirit"? Don't you believe it? If·the Nazarene were in New York to-day, he would undoubtedly be thankful for an opportunity to re-announce that beautiful principle. Spiritualists would all enjoy it, and each would say: "Well, I have heard that before—a thing produces its kind." The physical body, however healthy and perfect, will produce only *physical* happiness. Aromal emanations from the pure body are always precious, life-giving, and beautiful; but the harmonious human mind gives off far sweeter aromal fragrances which elevate and chasten all who come within their celestial influence.

Now the body—"water"—and the soul—"spirit" —become balanced and married. That is the true relation. When there is marriage between body and spirit, what is the result? Progeny. Next comes a "new birth." Unless that true, private, interior mar-riage takes place, you will experience only an illegiti-mate birth. Many obtain such births in revival meetings. They deem themselves "converted." But think the subject all over, and see if you do not decide that all such "conversions" are illegitimate births from the spirit. Let there be a true marriage between the body and the soul—be blended by "water and the spirit"—and then observe how purely the offspring is legitimate Truth. Then, truly, you begin to compre-hend high motives and ideas. First, whatsoever is *good ;* second, whatsoever is *useful ;* third, whatsoever is *consistent ;* fourth, whatsoever is *beautiful ;* fifth, whatsoever is *spiritual ;* sixth, whatsoever is *celestial ;* seventh, whatsoever is *heavenly* and *eternal.* The truer your marriage, the higher and more beautiful your spiritual children. Just in proportion as you grow independent of externals—just in proportion as you rise out of passions, appetites, unclean spirits, and demons—in that same proportion you enter into the kingdom of harmony. No matter where you reside, or with whom you live, that glorious emancipation and consummation will be the result of your interior growth.

Now, therefore, let us all go to work with "water" —I mean, let us cleanse out our affections. Water means purification. Regulate your bodily appetites, discipline your hidden passions, harmonize the action of your thinking faculties. Erect for yourself a high standard! Set out for personal harmony! You have a watch in the spirit. Just wind up that spirit-watch, and see that every second of time is kept right. Wind up your habits, and set your house in order. When you attain to "inward peace," you are born again. Then you can each live a spontaneous, easy, free, orderly, happy life. What will be the result! TRUTHS! Beautiful children are they! and ever and anon another "new birth." There is recorded on the blank leaves of the old Family Bible, by our parents, a memorandum, thus: "Born on the —— day, in the year of our Lord," &c. But there are theological births which occur under the psychology of the orthodox minister and pulpit. These theological births are seldom recorded in any book under the sun—most rarely in the "book of life." As before admitted, sometimes such a birth is a true one, and the person

5*

does begin to live a well-ordered and more beautiful life. Such cases are extremely rare. The rule is, as my Brother Henry truly said, that a man who was good before, is essentially no better after his "conversion."

There are many "changes of heart" in one's lifetime, and very many "new births." The marriage of the body to the spirit—this is a delightful birth. It is delicious harmony, producing what Epicurus termed "bodily ease and mental tranquillity." He never could have uttered and enforced the principle unless he had experienced its birth in his mind. Out of that marriage spring attractive and powerful *truths;* the progeny are exceedingly pure and beautiful! You can begin to count your new births from that time—the birth of *good truths;* the birth of *useful truths;* the birth of *consistent truths;* the birth of *beautiful truths;* the birth of *spiritual truths;* the birth of *celestial truths;* the birth of *heavenly truths;* the birth of *infinite truths;* the birth of God in the heart; and in all directions, eternal Progression.

THE SHORTEST ROAD TO THE KINGDOM
OF HEAVEN.

"Oh, restless spirit! Wherefore strain
　　Beyond thy sphere?—
Heaven and hell, with their joy and pain,
　　Are now and here."

We start with the question, What does the religious
world mean by the "kingdom of heaven"? Almost
every one's educational memory will answer that by
the expression is meant, a place far off—the residence
of the Father, Son, and the Holy Ghost; a solemn
celestial abode where mirthfulness is not permitted;
where persons appear as monks and nuns, beautifully
arrayed in white, but always with a thoughtful, medi-
tative, abstract, poetic appearance, and on their faces
an indescribable expression of unsmiling, cadaverous
piety. The whole population of the Paradisaical realm,
according to the world's estimation, wear an unsport-
ful, reverential, pious aspect; all engaged in the same
rapt devotions to the august family of Gods. It must
be a cold and dreary place for human nature as it is
now constituted; a place of unbroken circumspection
and habitual interiority. It makes us feel as though
we were on the verge of an everlasting graveyard to
think of it; the churchyard, with its white mementos,
with its many reminders of that ghostly purity which

is to characterize the few who are saved by the blood of the Lamb.

The religious world, you know, not only looks upon the "kingdom of heaven" as a place afar off, but also as a situation attainable alone by means of the supernatural miracle of the atonement. Thus both the "kingdom" and the "road" are absurd to human reason and comprehension, and very properly the preachers repudiate the independent use of Reason on such pulpit questions. The miracle of the Atonement constitutes a sort of Air-line railroad to the kingdom of eternal monotony! No one pretends to know how his reddened iniquities can be whitened. No one pretends to know why the angels will adore the blackest sinner the moment he arrives, *via* Atonement Railroad, and knocks at the great magical gate of St. Peter. It is all a stupendous miracle to the thick-headed sinner; but the Church tells him, "Believe; it is all the more gracious for its mystery, and all the more like God because of its incomprehensibility." And thus the stupid sinner, not having thought ten minutes consecutively on the subject since his birth, drops out of skepticism and rolls into the lap of that mysterious conviction, and next permits himself to fall into a slumber of dogmatic faith most deceptive, which the Church pronounces the "sleep of the blessed"—all, if only in his soul he adopts the Gospel of Miracle by which the consequences of all sins shall be purged away.

In the course of my lectures on the "Summer-Land" it will be shown that no atonement-treated sinner realizes beyond the tomb, what these pulpit accoucheurs say he may in unbounded confidence expect to receive at the hands of the Savior. Memory is an undying thinking power, gathering its education from all the faculties, and from every thing or influence that ever *touched* them—a power which weaves and winds every impression up snugger, and snugger, and snugger—reeling all thoughts firmer and more close together than threads on the roll of the silk-spinner—all which is to be unrolled through all the post-historic labyrinths of the great future, standing at every moment in the temple of personal consciousness as an accusing angel. And then, what men call "Conscience"—the sense of rectitude which every faculty bestows upon its possessor—locks arms with Memory, and thus the two dwell always with the individual, however ideally dressed he may be; however angelic in personal appearance; however accomplished in the scholastic arts and fashionable attainments.

But we will not dwell upon that subject this morning. I have but simply alluded to the world's theological conception of the miracle of "Atonement." How many believe it to be the directest road to the kingdom of heaven! My object in speaking on the point was to declare against that foolish and pernicious doctrine of miraculously saving sinners from the legitimate consequences of sin. As a theory it is immeasurably worse than the system of the allopathic medical schools, which hold that men are better for swallowing a dose of calomel on every disturbance of the liver. This error is not a whit more pernicious to the body than is the doctrine of the ecclesiastical schools, that "faith" in the vicarious atonement is permanently good to save mankind from the consequences of sin in the soul.

To enter directly upon the subject, I will call your attention—

First: To the fact that every person has an Ideal, which to realize would, in that person's opinion, constitute " perfect happiness," and perfect happiness is the usual understanding of the " kingdom of heaven." Every one will remember his or her Ideal. An ideal comes, first, out of the particular organic structure of the mind. Second, out of the *condition* of the spirit which lives within that structure. So that a person's ideal is material or spiritual, little or large, just in proportion to the construction of mind ; and besides, the ideal will always represent the *status* of the spirit, which resides beneath those organs and behind those structural conditions.

Second: Every person's Ideal is modified by the force and flow and shape of Circumstances. And hence the mind's Ideal will partake invariably of the image and likeness to the circumstances with which it is surrounded.

Third: These influential and shaping circumstances of your organization, and then the *conditions* of your spirit, are what originate and modify your Ideal. All persons receive some form of education—all experience some kind of development of the internal powers. Much valuable education to the faculties comes by friction, contact, imitation, and the force of discipline in the society of those about you. They constitute your severest teachers, and the effect of their painful teaching is education. Perhaps it will be a mis-education ; perhaps an un-education ; perhaps a complete- education ; perhaps it will be nothing but consciousness of unhappy ignorance and discord.   But whatever the mental effect, which may be comprehended under the general term "education," *that* is sure to greatly modify the Ideal which your circumstances, your organization, and your spiritual *status* first developed within the sanctuary of the mind.   And this "Ideal" is the first thing for us to analyze, because its complete attainment, its actualization, the embodiment of the internal image, is the individual's conception of the "kingdom of heaven"— or, perfect personal happiness.

In order to ascertain what is meant by the spiritual *status*, also what is meant by the *structure* of the mind, I will reaffirm the fact that man's spirit is constituted of several fundamental principles. These principles are internal and inseparable. Phrenologists have enumerated them up from 30 to 39; some have subdivided and counted mental organs to the number of 40. I am not impressed that this enumeration is the practical one for an internal and final. analysis. It has always seemed to me, nevertheless, that the classification of phrenology was valuable to the mind, inasmuch as thereby it came into a sort of external acquaintance with itself. These cerebral convolutions, formed and forming from within, are real indications of exercises in specific nerves and substances of the brain. Thus Phrenology demonstrates that these nerves are inhabited by mind, or spirit; and where the spirit is most exercised, there will take place and be visible the largest protuberance. Phrenological classifications have been based almost entirely upon this understanding, that wherever there is a projection or depression, there the brain is either exceedingly much used, or greatly too idle. This organ-plan of the

brain was primitively necessary; and the Phrenological classification will continue to be necessary for many
ages.   It is a kind of gate-of-invitation through which
people can go easily in and out—thus, to some extent,
forming an acquaintance with themselves, and particularly in a pre-eminently practical way.

Now, if it be true that there are thirty-eight or
forty brain-gates to your spirit, as the best phrenologists say, then you will be obliged intellectually to go
through each one in order to attain to a knowledge of
yourself; not only so, but you would also be obliged to
flow out through the brain-channels in order to express
yourself truly to a wife, to a brother, to a sister, to the
world in general.

Now I think it is every one's conception that happiness consists in an equal development of the spiritual
parts and physical organs, and the equal gratification
of their natural desires. I suppose this to be the shortest and completest statement of what would constitute
the "happiness" of a person—the supply of every want
without friction, and the gratification of every desire
without exorbitant expense or excessive industry.   In
fact, the ability to bring ends to means, and to adapt
physical conditions without friction to the requisitions
of the spirit, would constitute the first, clearest, quick-
est, directest fulfillment of the "ideal" of personal rest,
peace and satisfaction with life—in a word, Happiness.

I wish now to show you that the realization of such
an "ideal" is at present impossible on the face of the
earth.   But let me here mention that the *fundamental
principles* of the human soul, according to the cassifica-

tion of the Harmonial Philosophy, are only twelve in number. There are six fundamental principles of Love, and six of Wisdom. [See 3d vol. HARMONIA.] The six radical affections are the ingredients, constituents, or the fountain sources from which flow life, motion, sensation, and also the mysterious consciousness of consciousness—the wondrous psychological fact that a human mind is conscious of its own consciousness—aware of itself—the ever present " I," which is the central reality. Hence the power of the human mind to go into deep solitude, and yet be in the midst of things. Hence the power of the human soul to retire on the far-off isle of the sea, and call poetry and music and thought and affection and friendship and philosophy and angels and Deity, all into its service and consciousness. These twelve faculties in the spirit, these twelve principles, are like all other principles, everlasting ; and not only so, but it is true that each separate principle *makes a perpetual demand upon the everlasting universe in which it finds itself ever-recurringly conscious !*

Hence the doctrines in the intuitions of the soul that man *essentially* pre-existed, and also that he is destined to live after the destruction of all these physical appearances. It is this Intuition that gives the sense of weight about the spirit. The soul longs to leave this realm of dust and discord, and to sweep on through interminable spheres—endeavoring thus to realize her 'treasured " ideal" by striving to attain to the *ultima thule* of the present aspiration.

Each of these twelve radical and eternal principles in the constitution of the human mind makes, as I before

said, requisitions more or less vivid, positive, and energetic, upon their individual possessor, and that, too, even
in this state of existence. Out of their wondrous depths
spring the onward-drawing "ideal," which, attained,
is termed "happiness," but which, not attained, is productive of unrest and dissatisfaction, and a feeling of
incompleteness which ever and anon flashes painfully
through and through the self-conscious mind.

It is indisputable, I think, that "happiness" would
result from the harmonious action and melodious blending of all the faculties. Discordant minds cannot be
happy. Only those who travel without friction along
the "shortest and directest road to the kingdom of
heaven," can realize what it is to tread the high royal
road that leads to happiness unutterable. But there is
many a person who has the constitutional misfortune to
be a sort of *grindstone*, revolving in the center of outward circumstances and weight. Such people not only
make other people and things with which they come in
contact awful *sharp* and *severe* in feeling and disposition, but exceedingly like a cross-cut saw—working
against each other with irresistible strength and with
painful, destructive friction. Such minds reciprocate each
other's favors by spinning and rasping off the surface-
steel. They work and chafe and wear away the nap on
the spirit of those about them, until they get down to the
bleeding sensations of life itself, and then come the
depressions of despair, with the feeling that the wound
which is bleeding day by day in the family, under the
very roof of apparent and reputed happiness, and in the
society which is recognized as fashionable, can never be
healed of the feud or forgiven the offense.

Unrest is the testimony which the Eternal of the universe has implanted in the constitution of the spirit, saying, " *You cannot spiritually die so long as there is an unsatisfied desire.* Your life will continue so long as there exists within you a want that has never been met, a condition that has not been fulfilled, or great prophecies that have never met their entire satisfaction in the unfoldments of Science, Art, or History." This intuition is one of the strongest arguments in favor of the immortality of the soul.

Men undertake by prayer to bring " the kingdom of heaven on earth." It is the old error in masonry of building an impossible temple, which the children of Babel first attempted in their ignorance, and which, as the story most beautifully illustrates, was a stupendously practical failure in materialistic religion. The ambition to make a mammoth broad-church balloon, to construct some theological Great Eastern, or to erect some skyward pointing temple upon which mankind can, without losing their present physical relations, reach the kingdom of Peace, is nothing but a foolish dream of error and ignorance.

Perfect happiness, be it remembered, is the received definition of the kingdom of heaven. This is what all the world is after, and it will have nothing less. But let me ask, Why do many apparently practical persons go " through hell" in order to arrive at the heavenly kingdom? Is it because they fancy that " the underground-railroad" in experience and religion, is the shortest and the safest way ? or is it because such persons *err* in their fancy and judgments as to *the means* by which happiness is attainable and procurable? These questions are important.

It is instructive to note the mistakes and errors of men respecting the means of happiness. I saw a man who supposed that his present happiness and success would be promoted by *stealing a horse* and riding swiftly across the State of Illinois to meet a companion who was expecting him. Not having the money to purchase a conveyance, and not being able to go in the regular way of travel, he attempted to secure his happiness by the adoption of spurious and vicious means. He supposed that he would secure present comfort by securing his ends; which, instead, secured him a great deal of physical confinement in jail; for nothing like spiritual rest could issue from his mistake. At first he was intellectually infatuated by the conviction that if he could only but steal a horse he would be, for that time, at least, comparatively happy. Did he not sadly err as to the *means* of personal happiness? Yet somehow I never supposed that *that* man designed to be evil—in fact, I believe he did not premeditate a crime, but adopted the readiest means of immediate success? but, like hundreds of others, he found that the path of error and injustice is the most "hellish road" he ever traveled to reach the heaven of development.

Once I met a young lady whose "ideal" was a mansion—one just out of Boston. She was beautiful, unmarried, the darling of rich and accomplished parents; the father a distinguished, influential banker, and the mother once a belle at Newport and often a central figure at Saratoga. In noticing this case it is well to recall our propositions. Her mind had inherited a peculiar *structure*, and the structure gave birth to her *ideal*, and the ideal, borrowing itself from the spiritual *status*, declared that "perfect happiness" consisted in the splendid equipments and proprietorship of a beautiful mansion near Roxbury. I saw her and heard her ideal expressed several years ago. In three years from that time she was a wife, and in two years afterward (as I have been informed) she formally and proudly entered upon her ideal life in a great, rich, domestic establishment. I have heard of her twice since that year. Is she happy? Just think of a "material house" for a spirit endowed with *twelve radical, eternal principles!* That young wife's mind was harnessed to her home, which rises up with mystic grandeur, and which is dressed from base to attic in the most fashionable style, with all the appliances of compound comfort and distressing luxury—indeed, so beautiful are the chairs, and sofas, and *tete-a-tetes*, that they had to be immediately clad in very common looking stuff, and so concealed were they that an observer hardly knew, without being told, whether the gorgeous furniture was made of anything superior to pine boards. Chestnut or red-oak saplings, whitewashed and dressed up in coarse brown linen, would have looked quite as well. Beautiful things! So costly, so exquisite and so fragible, that not a child dared to move round among them; and as for grown persons, it was to them almost like treading upon the honey-combed edge of Vesuvius. The young wife was nervous all over the house. Her nerves were just as numerous and as much present in the bedroom as in the kitchen. I know a gentleman who said he had tried to find a place in that

great splendid house where her nerves were not. Nervous ladies are all so *very happy* in great city houses!
City doctors know that many patients have had their
"ideals" beautifully embodied in the possession of domestic splendors! Servants and waiting-maids know
the ubiquitous nature of the nervous system. Dust! it
is the special horror of the soul with twelve radical
principles. Well, there is, perhaps, a *spiritual* meaning
in such abhorrence. If my friend Emerson were here,
perhaps he would say it means the testimony of the
spirit against the crude earth. That interpretation is
poetical, philosophical, and constitutional. But the
habit of being *more* conscious of dirt than of refinement,
is the chronic difficulty with a great many people who
pretend to be "perfectly happy" in great town or city
dwellings. The cook in the aforesaid lady's house was a
portion of her happiness, and the girl who kept the cook
at work was another happiness, and so was the girl whose
special duty was to see that the girl who attended
to the cook did her work, and then the other girl, whose
labor was to visit daily all the extra rooms, and to
see that all parts of the house were exquisitely arranged
and put "to rights" just ten minutes before two o'clock,
P. M.—all parts of the lady's ideal! It was all deemed
necessary—all beautiful! And when the time came for
parties! You know what exquisite *joy* there is in the
flutter of a fashionable party! And physicians know
what a healthy pulse is, and they also know when it
beats way up ten or fifteen beyond fever-heat, which is
always the case when there is "perfect happiness" in
the ideal possession of a great mansion, and especially
when a Party is about to be inaugurated on a grand

scale, "regardless of expense." Joy everywhere! but *not* in the "ideal" of that mistaken, miseducated, but wealthy wife in old Massachusetts. She would not attend a lecture like this; would not go to hear James Freeman Clark in Boston; would never hear Theodore Parker; thinks that the Devil, William Lloyd Garrison, and Wendell Phillips, constitute the infernal trinity! Oh, *so* "happy!"

Once I met a gentleman whose ideal of "perfect happiness" consisted in roving o'er land and sea. He longed to get away from the perpetual embarrassments of home; to throw off the entanglements of a wife who had borne him many children. At length he was at liberty, as he thought, to pursue his idea of happiness. So he started on a journey, which terminated in China; then it lapped over and terminated in New York; but he was *scarcely* perfectly happy yet! Though he had all the buffetings of journeying and all the mishaps and losses of unfortunate enterprises, yet he found, on his arrival in New York, that "perfect happiness" consisted in doing almost the same thing right over again, only he had concluded that he would embark for a different port and on the other side of the rolling globe. I do not know how *perfect* his present happiness is, but I know that when he had made the tour of twenty-four thousand miles he reported himself, and said that journeying was a good deal of "a tax," and he would give it up if he had not acquired "the habit," which, like tobacco, must be chewed over and again in order to be perfectly *enjoyed!* Poor fellow! He has cherished that "ideal," working on through the dreary wastes of ice and snow in the Arctic regions, seeking in desola-

tion for the experience of perfect happiness. It comes
not out of his mistaken ideal. I asked him one day
concerning his mother, and found that she had never
been away from home long enough to gratify her desire
for an excursion, and this desire was strongest in her
just before *his* birth. Thus the great law of reproduction is reaffirmed : her desire to take a journey not
being gratified, became the source of misery every hour.
She was relieved from it only by exhaustion and disease, but never by a natural gratification of the imperious desire. Inheriting this consequential construction,
and also imbibing the spiritual *status* which that desire
necessarily imparted, on the law of reflex action, to the
depths of her nature, her child was unreasonably cen-
trifugated from his wife, and from all the endearments
of the family and home. The blind impulse actuated
his thoughts and led him into the open field of loose,
aimless, objectless journeying. Of course he is not
happy. How can a man be happy who holds in his
constitution *twelve* radical principles, when nothing is
done to feed and gratify them save journeying over the
outward world ?

I know a person who supposed that marriage would
be the climacteric point in the happiness of the soul.
Many there are who look upon that as *the* relation.
All such are, I think, truly inspired with a sovereign
and eternally important conviction. But those who
expect that even the highest gratification of Conjugal
Love will satisfy the *eleven other* mental principles, will
find themselves mistaken in eleven parts of their existence. I have known persons who sought the marriage
relation and found it, and who considered that, at the

time, it was the coronation of the heart; but at length they found that the crown of happiness had not settled upon their heads, and that yet *other* and equally imperative demands were made from within. Ere long the unsatisfied pair quarreled with each other, *because* they had not wisdom to see that *eleven* parts of their existence could not be at rest and satisfied with the gratification of the one. There was restlessness in the eleven parts of their existence and complete gratification in only one; so they *complained* to each other *of* each other; and from their discord came diabolism, and out of that a brood of Satans instead of angels; and thus the conjugal home was rent asunder like the temple, because their idea of happiness was built upon a foundation of sand; and although they were beautifully and truly married, and were, as a consequence, capable of building up the "harmonial union," yet they sadly and madly separated, and will probably remain so until some divine attraction either brings them together, or else sets upon their hearts the seal of eternal divorce.

How many beautiful love-temples you and I have seen, in the once happy home, all in ruins! Temples of domestic conjugal happiness rent in twain by these great, burly ignoramuses, who have much money, but deficiency of judgment. Such men are strong in the arm, but "weak in ye head." And ladies, too, perfectly accomplished in the externals—knowing by intuition what it is to love, and as well what it would be to be loved, but who have not met their mates on the philosophic basis; and so both men and women, in all parts of the world, do not often travel on the

6

directest, shortest, safest road to the kingdom of heaven.   Standing socially against each other like sworn enemies, the quarrel begins through the use of affectionate terms in excess, beautiful little epithets. Even before persons they begin with a little curl of satire around the mouth, to name each other "My dove!" "my darling!" "my precious!"   Alas! it is to be feared that they have each purchased a ticket on the under-ground railroad.   All because the married do not know that conjugal love is but one-twelfth part of the individual's life and being.

You know probably that I have been, for the last fifteen years, so related to the public as to receive applications from persons in every imaginable situation. Some have lost faith in prayer; they do not believe in the confessional, nor in the dismal doctrines of the Protestant clergy.   Many such minds do not know what is best for them to do.   Some of them frequently visit "mediums;" others go to "clairvoyants," who have some secret knowledge of things, persons, &c., and may be able to vouchsafe true counsel.   I have received almost innumerable letters from every class of persons. (My correspondence during the past ten years is a remarkable chapter in the history of human spiritual necessity.)   I have sometimes almost commiserated the orthodox God, if his ears had to hear those selfish prayers that are uttered during the weakest and most contracted and foolish days, hours, and moments of men's lives.   Awful is the internal history of human shallowness which the world's prayers betray—so full of practical imbecilities, of insanities, of special self-interest, of inexpressible follies among people who really have reputations for being sensible—men praying for God to do for them what they would not of themselves deem reasonable for any brother to ask of them. I remember the case of a lady whose " perfect happiness" she thought would consist in becoming a mother. Some two years afterward she became a mother, and I distinctly recall the experiences which she related. After the second year, she found that perfect happiness would consist, not so much in being a mother, but in *knowing* for a certainty that her darling little Eddie would grow up to be " a good man." She was exceedingly anxious to get away out of the city into a beautiful little retired place, where no bad children could molest him or teach him bad habits, but her finances forbade it. Hence the lady's "perfect happiness" on becoming a mother was nothing but the beginning of solicitude, anxiety, and unrest.

Now, what was that good lady's error? I need not mention it. You know that she had eleven *other* elements in her spiritual organization which a child could never more than partially gratify. Parental love is *one*, and only one of the radical principles of the human spirit; and even when that is perfectly gratified there are yet remaining *eleven others* which have equally imperative demands that " will not down at your bidding." And the lady's error was her irrational belief that her "happiness" would be complete with the gratification of one-twelfth part of her nature. There was her mistake, and it is the error of thousands. Indeed, this illustrates the entire secret of nearly all human mistakes. The error consists in mistaking the *means* of happiness. By the attainment of *one* point you thence proceed on the false notion that all the *other* parts of your nature will receive corresponding gratification and be at rest.

How many are there who are made "perfectly happy" in the actualization of the "ideal" that fortune or wealth is in itself the only important ultimate! You know how few there are who are made truly happy in *that* way. Many there are who wish to-day to try the experiment of acquiring property. John Jacob Astor attained *his* "ideal." I suppose that many of you remember what his past testimony was—he merely received "his victuals and clothes;" and yet he was the man of fortune. The more fortune, the more the slave. When the cares of property multiply and replenish themselves in your path, the greater becomes your servitude and the further you recede from the kingdom of true peace and happiness. I am glad that Mary's and Joseph's son saw and uttered this spiritual truth. No merely rich man, with his money-bags "strapped upon his back," could enter heaven any more than could a camel go through the eye of a needle. When the young man of fortune came to him and declared that he had done all the unutterable things, had performed all the virtues and made all the trips to obtain happiness, then the Spiritual man said, "Sell what thou hast"—that is, put it beneath you, make it subservient to true human interests, let *it* not be your master. That is what is meant by selling your "possessions." It is not necessary to throw away your property upon Thomas, and Richard, and Henry; but the true way is to use your wealth for good purposes, and not be used by it. The Harmonial Philosophy teaches that self-possession—

true self-ownership—is one of the paths leading to the *shortest* road to the kingdom of heaven.

I know many citizens who are made corporeally happy by the wealth of others. At least a hundred and fifty persons are made daily more comfortable, their existence is made to them vastly more tolerable, and their paths of labor are strewn with perfumed flowers,- all because certain good property-men *are not servants to their riches*, but they have "sold all they have"—that is, they have become spiritual philosophers, and are using their means with discretion and with gratitude, for the augmentation and expansion of human happiness. That is for them the "shortest road;" they walk therein; and such men are, therefore, always philanthropic, cheerful, and happy.

I know a man of this stamp who has a beautiful social and moral presence; his very breath is imbued with purity and benevolence, like the fragrance of roses. Such a human spirit has in itself the beautiful realization of sitting down in the kingdom of heaven with Abraham and Isaac and Jacob—a sweet, harmonious, largely magnanimous character, beaming and graceful out of his goodness. I also know ladies of this noble, regal, heavenly pattern. They generously give of their abundance, but are not the less wealthy. They do not squander on personal ornamentation; neither do they throw away riches without thought into the treasuries of old Missionary Societies, when it requires $4.99 to pay the expense of one cent to the heathen. Nay, nay. They give their money to the worthy objects that are within their gates, or to cases of want just within the radius of the eye, and to humble, industrious poor who come within the reach of the spirit.

I wish, therefore, to bring to your mind clearly and distinctly, without one exception, that the secret of happiness consists in removing *unnecessary friction* in one's own pathway, and in assisting to remove it from the pathway of others. Whoso doeth such deeds is a possessor of tickets on the shortest, safest, directest road to the kingdom of heaven.

First, however, it is philosophical to take it for granted that this world cannot bring you the perfect and complete realization of any one of your interior "ideals;" and, secondly, that an ideal which is but partially fulfilled can never fully satisfy the twelve radical elements of the human spirit. Hence your nature demands a Sphere of life *after* death for the purpose of growth. Mankind are made upon imperishable principles, each one of which is the harmonial voice of God, which speaks through all parts of the tree of life, moving its leaves in the winds of circumstances, and vibrating them in the currents of terrestrial affairs. Each one of these principles, I repeat, is *a word from heaven*—from God's own central spirit—saying, "Your best *ideals* are not attainable in three score and ten years; no, nor in a century, neither in a hundred centuries, nor in myriads of millions of ages, through all which time you will yet be young in the Summer-Land.

The Spiritualist is a philosophic believer in eternal life. He cannot help it. Every voice from heaven proclaims *eternal ideality*, and, at the same time, gives promise to reason for an *eternal opportunity for actuali-*

zation ! It is this fundamental, natural, spontaneous, intuitive *logic*—dominating all the schools of Material- ism—that will not down to any man's argument, which is the upwelling revelation of truth from within, that no ideal, however perfectly realized, can *satisfy* the whole spirit! And this dissatisfaction, this unrest, this yearning, is a *premonitory symptom,* so to say, of the future which is in store for man's mind, and which must open, like a flower in the garden of truth, to receive and welcome man to the inextinguishable light of the future. By planting yourself upon these twelve radical principles, the destructive *friction* of the present will be measurably removed, and at once you will find yourself a pilgrim on the shortest road.

No man can be perfectly cosmopolitan and wholly catholic. No man can do all things with equal skill, pleasure, or profit. A natural merchant cannot be as good a mechanic; it is neither easy nor pleasurable for him to be. It is not easy for a natural musician to be a successful merchant, nor for a mechanic to be a suc- cessful musician. It would not be easy and pleasurable for Blondin to enter the pulpit, nor for the devotional minister to be a pugnacious and logical lawyer, nor for the natural lawyer to enter upon the practice of medi- cine. It is not easy for man to take the position of woman, neither is it easy for woman to merge out into externalisms and do battle with the entanglements which give pleasure to the physical man ; but, at present, each one is hampered and bound to a special sphere, neither realizing the implanted "ideal." For the present stage of human progress this incompleteness is necessary and unavoidable. But by removing *friction,* the life which we are all involuntarily leading will be more freighted with solid happiness. The road of life would be less dusty and more attractive. And then, most of the present iniquities and miseries which clog and throng our way—the stumbling-blocks of ignorance in each one's path on earth—would be utterly destroyed. If, for example, you have any habit which causes your daily physical and domestic life to be a source of annoyance, *down with it !* Because, by inherent strength, you are "master of the situation."

There is no primogeniture in this harmonial doctrine. No man inherits special wealth and extra power because he is the *oldest* son in the family of God. No ! Every man and woman inherits equal wealth and power from the *innermost*. Every one is born with an equal fortune. Alas ! some there are among us on earth who yet live in the slumberous quietude of idiocy, leading only an imbecile life; others there are, among all races of civilized man, who have not yet escaped beyond the animal plane of feeling and conduct. But it is your prerogative to look from a high standpoint, and with great tenderness, upon the less fortunate in the world. Remember that each human brain is a nest of *eggs* destined to hatch out twelve immortal doves, which are twelve radical, impersonal Principles. Your mission is to remove " stumbling-blocks," not only out of the way of your individual paths, but the paths of others—-not merely not to " lay a straw in the path" of your neighbor, but to take away straws that some *other* less spiritual person has laid there to work a brother's or sister's misfortune. Take them all away ! Down with your Satans ! (I mean your Appetites and your Pas-

sious.) Of course I do not advise any one to attempt
to live without appetites and without passions ; but this
is the point: let no man or woman be mastered and
overcome by them. Put all "unclean spirits" beneath
your feet ; bruise the serpent's head, crush and kill
him.

If you belonged to these popular pagodas—if you
worshiped in these temples of the gods that are without
these walls—I could not "preach" to you such things.
You would be unfriendly to the ideal of progress, and
would have a *different* conception of the object of life ;
and as for your sins, why, you would expect happiness
only by and through the "atonement." But I will ask
you, friends of Freedom! whether, standing as you do,
firmly and independently on your own feet—feeling all
the way up your back the ascending vertebræ of harmonial and independent life, each vertebra representing
a round in a Jacob's ladder on which influences descend
and ascend—the brain being a *nest* of the faculties to
be hatched into immortality—the whole a conscious
oneness—standing thus, are you to consent to be *mastered* by "demons" and "satans" that are nothing but
personal *passions*, and by "unclean spirits" that are
nothing but your own over-indulged *appetites ?* Never!
You know as well as I that the "shortest road to the
kingdom of heaven" is to *become master of your own
proper person !* Whatever your situation in life, whether
you reside in the city of New York, or away in some
rural home— whether your business is to cook or pro-
vide dinner for the family who employ you, or whether
you are partaker of a dinner which others have prepared—in either case, as under every temptation, your

6*

spiritual mission should render you "a peace-maker," and thus remove friction. By so doing, or even by so desiring to do in secret, you *shorten* the road to the kingdom of heaven, not only to yourself, but for every other human pilgrim on the globe.

And yet, let no one suppose that he or she is to be "perfectly" happy in this world. It is a shallow, idiotic, and illogical dream; it is the very opposite, the antagonist of the doctrine of universal progress. What is a perfectly contented person? What sort of a mind is that which feels no onward-drawing needs or wants? It is an idiot, with no ambition to move from its place—a nobody! What brought you out from your warm homes on this cold, wintry morning? Because you thought you would be *happier* by coming · to this Hall. What is that which will soon take you away from this Hall? Because, when this discourse is finished and the choir have sung, you will then think you will feel *happier* to go away. Whatever motive immediately moves you, it is all traceable to that impulse within which dominates logic—the spirit of " change," of " progress," of " development," which rises higher than the highest steeple in this city, saying, " Onward! father, mother, brother, sister." And onward you go into the open air—and away toward other attractions, Central Park, Brooklyn, to the meeting of friends, to your home—anywhere, to get *happiness*. Never *perfect* after all!

Well, that is what you should always expect, and not be disappointed. For myself I am glad that I find just what I philosophically know that I shall find, not " perfect happiness," but the present partial gratification of honest, healthful desires—just this, and nothing more, nothing less, unless I should greatly err in the *use* of means and opportunities.

Can you not, therefore, be rational? To be *rational* in everything is a ticket on the "shortest road to the kingdom of heaven." Try the opposite course. Make the *worst* of your life, as millions on the earth do, for want of true knowledge of means, uses, and opportunities. Some shallow heads think it is very fine to be full of *taste* and full of *petulancy;* they fancy it is smart to be able to scowl at every annoyance, and to wrinkle up the thoughtful brow, and to make decided speeches with inflated language on very small occasions; very smart to use the word "infinite" about the limited varieties of pocket-handkerchiefs; and lastly, it is the hight of sense and of fashion to join the vast army of ladies who go shopping at Stewart's great Broadway agony. All this looks to many people like being as high in wit and happiness as anybody can be outside of pandemonium.

I tell you now the day will come—and each of you will remember it after it passes as well as the fact of being here this morning—when mankind will look down upon all this externalism with unutterable *contempt,* and not less with self-sorrow and unpardonable shame. Why should this be? Because such a life is unworthy! That is the reason, and it is sufficient. Every intelligent person knows that the "shortest way to the kingdom of heaven" is, not to expect in this world the perfect fulfillment of any one "ideal," but, instead, to remove *friction* from the track of progress, to be industrious and comfortably happy in the midst of what you may have—this is the surest and safest side-road leading toward what is better and superior in the straight and harmonious way.

I stand before you as an illustration of the truth of what I am now affirming. I will not refer to my history—every step of which is a living demonstration that a man can come from the *darkest* place in the social Egypt and find the promised Land. In the superior condition of mind a man can stand on his own feet, the proprietor of those great truths which no man's material wealth can purchase. A person with such a history may stand as a representative merely—a kind of philosophical promise—of what is possible in the ultimate of every human life! Let all welcome whatsoever gives hope to the millions.

And now, Sisters and Brothers, it is just as easy to commence from this hour as any future time. Commence to make the best, and not the worst, of what is yours or what may come. Shorten the road to human happiness, and you will greatly lengthen the duration of human life. Do not wait for the future. Begin to-day! Now, from this moment, say, "I will not be a grindstone; I will rather be a fountain and a day-spring on high. I will not be a moon to anybody; I will be either a sun or a fixed star."

Can you not say so, and indorse it by practice? It will sweeten and strengthen your feelings as soon as you commence. You will look in the mirror with vastly more satisfaction. How few wrinkles there will soon be on your face! How much cleaner and purer your skin is! The eye looks beaming and cheerful, and there is a clear, heavenly light in it, which testifies that you have adopted a new life! And when you awake in the morning, it will seem to you as though everybody's existence had commenced anew, and that there is no dreary past in your own history! All *this* goes on the fact that you have ordered *down* your vehement passions, and said to your unclean spirits and demons: " *Away to the dark and dreary past—away! I turn my back forever upon you! You shall not again come before me! If you do, you shall be at once consigned to an everlasting death!"*

These sayings are not fictions. I know that a true Harmonial Philosopher—a real, spiritual, living soul— can rise up and live *a higher life* in the midst of his circumstances. Neither his bodily diseases, nor his habitual passions, nor his great wealth, nor his extreme poverty, nor his ignorance, can utterly deprive him of heaven and angels. Whatever his situation, he may become a candidate for an eternal voyage; for his spiritual ship is freighted with every means of happiness and progression.

THE REIGN OF ANTI-CHRIST.

"Be thou like the old apostles,
   Be thou like heroic Paul :
If a free thought seeks expression,
   Speak it boldly ! speak it all !
Face thine enemies—accusers,
   Scorn the prison, rack, or rod !
And if thou hast TRUTH to utter,
   SPEAK ! and leave the rest to God."

I shall not be able to say more than half that I feel ought to be said on this subject to the hundreds and thousands who live and think within sectarian walls; but, according to the law of progress, the time will arrive when *all* ears will hear and *all* hearts understand the gospel of God in contradistinction to the prevalent gospel of Diabolism.

Past peoples followed the course of human prejudice concerning the faults, evils, and iniquities of their neighbors. Nothing was easier to understand than the supposed or real imperfections of souls outside of themselves. And yet *self*-knowledge was esteemed to be the highest attainment of wisdom. Every true Philosopher, Spiritualist, or Progressive Bibliarian—every person, in short, who taught or teaches from a high point of spirit-culture, advocates and urges that true *self*-knowledge is the highest and most valuable education. But those conceited minds who are not truly self-informed, who do not yet begin to *know* themselves, who still need the hints and revealments of phrenologists and psychometrists, who most ardently wish to have themselves analyzed—are the very minds who judge, with great assurance of perception, the character and conduct of their nearest neighbors; they assume to fully *know* their neighbors' motives and the most secret thoughts that led to individual manifestations, as much in social life as in the public arena.

Nothing is more illustrative of the truth of these remarks than the history of theology. When Buddhism appeared, the Brahmins, who were the aristocratic religionists of ancient Asia, rose up and said, "That is Anti-Brahma, and should be overthrown." When Buddhism became perfectly established, and when its doctrines were sufficiently respectable to exert a wide influence in China and in many portions of the East, then Brahminism, suspending its opposition, cordially shook hands with it; then the Old and the New exchanged compliments, and sent letters of fellowship to each other; but, notwithstanding all this, one never got invited to the other's temple or pagoda. They became somewhat tolerant and respectful, but never reconciled to each other. And they are perfect illustrations of the Mosaic and the Christian dispensations.

When the Mosaic dispensation became very respectable, and great synagogues and costly temples and vast cities were consecrated to it—to the laws of Moses, which were, in a religious point of view, as complete and inexorable as were the laws of the Medes and Persians—then a pious Eastern lady had the unparalleled audacity to believe and to declare that her first babe was conceived and "sent of God." And then the star, according to the story, went over and stood—where? Not over a palace, but over a stable! Wise men went thither to learn, and some of them to worship. Thus began a new chapter in theological history.

But when the babe grew to a young man, and became sufficiently "meddlesome" to interfere with the Rabbinical wisdom and religious authorities of the times, then the learned doctors and profound Israelites, concentrating the opposition of both sects—of the Pharisees on the one side and the Sadducees on the other—made common cause and set themselves as one man against the young Reformer. And when the meddlesome carpenter attained his thirtieth year, and as soon as he bravely began his three years' work for the common humanity, then they rose up as one party and said : "He hath a devil!" "This is Anti-Christ!" "Crucify him, crucify him!" And when he was outwardly successful—for it is human nature to.admire and almost worship "Success"—when the young Spiritual Reformer was successful, then very gladly large multitudes "followed him." They gathered in vast congregations to hear the amber words of wisdom as they dropped from his inspired lips, and in their enthusiasm the disciples cried, "Hosanna!" ("three cheers"—that was what they meant.) "He is successful in his signs and wonders; he is our man." But when what the sightless world terms "defeat" overtook him ; when his sweetest truths evoked a public hissing ; when his associates were openly scorned ; when the Sermon on the Mount was derided on all sides by the learned in the temples; and when there was a great startling convulsion of the world's political relations, which struck terror to the highest officers in Judea—then human nature, undeveloped and full of pride, declared itself, and many of the enthusiastic persons who followed him—some of them the most conspicuous among his friends—betrayed and forsook him, and sided with the opposition and largest party, and cried: "Crucify him!" "He is Anti-Moses!" "He is a pretender to the throne of Judea!" "He assumes to be what he is not!" "He is an impostor!" And then a Jewish magnate held his court of inquiry. The young Spiritual Reformer was there arraigned and accused. His crime was said to be sedition and conspiracy against the Roman government. He had aroused the prejudices of the Israelites. They heard him not in self-defense. That was a packed jury! And I believe that every juryman there had in his ear a private whisper, not from the angels of heaven, but from those prejudiced Israelites who prowled round about, saying,: "He is not fit to live!" "Crucify him!" "Let us defend, obey, and save good old Moses, and let us cling firmly to the Laws and the Prophets!"

But why dwell upon this event? You all know the history. It is a clear, simple narrative, and is in almost every one's external memory. Jesus was Anti-Moses. That crime was sufficient. Consequently, down he went perforce into the earth beneath. But at that moment he was greater, vaster, more almighty than all the world above ground! When the hour arrived for the eternal truth to manifest itself, the birth of it only astounded those who saw with their physical eyes. But the civilized world, to-day, looks upon that august apotheosis—the going up of a Spiritual Reformer to live among the Gods—as one of the grandest victories over materialism, and as one of the sublimest spectacles that was ever painted on the canvas of the past; and nearly all the accredited eloquence of this age is thrown about it; all the resources of rhetoric; all the devices of grammar; all the symbolic reasonings and pictorial conceptions of Christian scholars. Music, fashion, wealth, and all the civil and political institutions of this country, more or less, harmonize with the conviction that when Jesus died the world lost its central figure in the tragedy of salvation.

Now what is this that is called "Christianity"? What is the history of Christendom? I tell you, in plain truth, that its history, from first to last, is an exact reproduction of its tragical origin. As soon as it attained to adequate power, it became the *persecutor* of every Scientific and Spiritual Reformer. In its turn, it has echoed the word "Anti-Christ" all the way down human history. The record is before you. Henry VIII declared, in the midst of his regal selfishness and personal lustfulness, that he would not be bridled in his seekings after various companions in marriage. The prelates and bishops at Rome assembled and sat in judgment against him. They shouted "Anti-Christ," and denounced him, declaring that his relation to Catharine of Arragon was holy and valid, and that any other conjugal relation would be false as hell and opposed to the gospel of Jesus. You know the sequel of the story. He immediately broke with the whole Roman Catholic world, and from that day to this the Catholics have been denounced by Protestants as

" Anti-Christ;" and as "one good turn deserves another," the Protestants are denounced as " Anti-Christ"
by Roman Catholics the wide world over.

Martin Luther and. his companion, Melancthon, who
stood on the threshold of that vast religious reform
which brought the blessings of freedom of conscience
and free speech, were deemed "Anti-Christ" by the whole
religious world then called Christendom. These were
early and bitterly denounced as disbelievers in the
Bible. And then, as soon as Protestantism became perfectly established, (I will not go into details of its
history, which arc familiar to all,) it began the anti-
Christian work of persecuting and crucifying every
Reformer that has arisen. And in nearly every instance
the *new* man or the *new* movement was stigmatized as
" Anti-Christ" and opposed as " Anti-Christian."

Now the real anti-Christian—whether man or movement—can be easily known and recognized. The
genuine Christian is one who goes about doing good, or
does good whilst staying at home—not evil anywhere.
A theologian—a mere theorist in religion—is a very
different person. " Christ signifies Savior"—the opposite of evil and destruction. Anything, therefore, which
saves, or partakes of and imparts the saving principle,
illustrates the true Christ. Such a person, or such a
principle, is truly " Christian." On the contrary, anything which militates powerfully and intensely *against*
the advancement of a Truth, which sets itself against
the growth of a Science, or opposes the light of Reason
and Intuition, is necessarily an antagonist of the good
principle, " anti-Christian," and practically an enemy of mankind. The Word of God is composed

of Love, Justice, Truth, Wisdom, and Liberty. PRINCIPLES, wherever you find them, whether in religion or out of it, are infallible and imperishable *words of God.* A Christian is one who wishes to live in relation to his fellows as he would have others live with reference to him. It is the adoption of the principle of perfect justice and reciprocation—of doing to others as you would have others do to you—having unbounded sympathy, saving charity, practical benevolence, crowned by a warm love of truth, and a reverence for what is truly Supreme. Therefore to cherish a worshipful love of Father God and Mother Nature is to be Christian and religious also, in the largest spiritual sense.

The opposite is easily comprehended. To be the opposite of all this is to be " anti-Christian." To live unjustly and combatively, so as to produce discord and enmities among your fellow-men ; to give misinterpretations to the plainest truths that you may hear; to act falsely, with duplicity and hypocrisy ; to deal with mankind maliciously and selfishly ; to hold passions, to harbor prejudices, to foster intemperate appetites ; in short, to do, or feel, or think, whatsoever breeds discord and destruction in human family or society, is to be necessarily and diametrically opposite to the redeeming principles, and is, strictly speaking, " antiChrist."

But sectarianism does not judge by this standard. Each Church holds that everything is anti-Christian which does not fully accept its adopted creed. Thus the Methodists are Anti-Christ to the Presbyterians. Calvinists could not endure John Wesley's anti-

Christianism; not that Methodists were not just as good pietists and citizens as the Presbyterians, but because Wesley's followers did not receive the gospel which Calvin taught as biblical and infallibly true. In like manner when Unitarianism appeared, it was everywhere denounced as "Anti-Christ." The same denunciatory spirit is written in the history of the Dissenters in England and Scotland. They fled to the mountain-glens and sought safety among the distant valleys. The Waldenses and the Huguenots—how cruelly they were persecuted in consequence of not adopting the religious *creed* which passed current as God's Word among those in power at the time! Not because the Huguenots were not just as good as others; not because the Waldenses were not upright and honorable persons, industrious and frugal, exemplary in their families; but simply because they did not believe in the various cardinal principles which were authoritatively called "God's Word" in the creed of the dominant Church.

The same persecuting spirit appeared and was applied to the early leaders and teachers of the Universalist denomination. They were all "Anti-Christs." Universalism was so terribly Anti-Christian because it was not in harmony with the doctrines of eternal sufferings for a few years of sin. John Murray did not take a large amount of stock in a personal Devil nor in a literal hell! and so he was opposed to and denounced by the Churches that flourished in grandeur around him. And therefore these Churches said, with one voice: "He is Anti-Christian—crucify him! crucify him!" You know the history of George Fox and of

Elias Hicks; it is all the same story, a repetition of the same outrageous conduct among the evangelical sects.

Now look at the evil spirit of sectarianism in connection with the world of Science. The Churches say: "Any Science that conflicts with the doctrines of our creeds, is no science, and it must not be taught in our schools." That was the early trouble of the so-called Christian world. It was seen that the doctrines held by scientific men, with reference to Nature, were calculated to destroy utterly the creeds of the Churches not only, but threatened to destroy as well the foundations of Christianity. Science and common sense—both powerful agents from God—early began to destroy the fiction-basis of miracles, and to reduce all mental and physical transactions to the systematic operations of immutable law. The Churches said that this scientific and rationalistic opposition to their creed was "Anti-Christian," not because these scientific men and rationalists were bad men; not because their families were less respectable than the families of believers in the Bible; but because they taught the impossibility of the Trinity; because they found nowhere in the boundless geography of God's universe a place for the eternal explosion of soul-burning sulphur; and, more especially, because Science and Reason said this world was not the center of the physical Universe, but a very insignificant part of the material system—on account of all this, the Churches rose up and said: "Anti-Christ!—down with such Science! Crucify its first apostle and advocates!" You know that the first scientific astronomers were obliged to seal their lips, to carry the beautiful truth upon the heart, and to worship the divine secret in the silence of a prison. When Science said, " God is more illustrated, and magnified, and vindicated, in these distant planets than on this small globe," and when it said that " this globe revolves around the sun, and not the sun around it"—then the sects cried out in great bitterness: " This is surely Anti-Christ!" and they rose in monumental resistance to the development and diffusion of such information. They opposed Science because *it* was opposed to the accepted " Word of God," as written out in their sectarian creeds.

Universalists, Unitarians, the Quakers, the Nothingarians—the evangelical and respectable sects, all the way down to the bottomless pit of old Hebrew mythology—have arisen, as one man and one power, and said: " Spiritualism is ' Anti-Christ.' " The respectable sects say : " There is no question or doubt about it; at last we have found out the evil one who is among us. He comes in ' the garments of light'—which the Devil sometimes either borrows or steals—and calls himself *Spiritualism*." Therefore the leaders and teachers of this new truth must be opposed and vanquished. Not that Spiritualists in the community are any worse persons than their Christian neighbors; not that they act offensively; not that they keep their children from the public schools, or fail to pay their taxes, or decline to make Presidents or unmake them; nor that they fail to fulfill their responsible relations as citizens, as husbands, fathers, brothers, or sisters, wives, and mothers—no, the opposition comes from the fact that modern Spiritualism is to popular theology what Christianity was to the Spiritualism of the Egyptio-Israelites. The modern

movement began about fifteen years ago. It has
gathered strength and momentum every hour since.
Impelled by its original moving-power of principles,
it rapidly rolls past the Churches of Christendom,
although they shout "Anti-Christ!" No imaginable
opposition could now arrest its progress. In addition
to its inherent motive force of principles, it adds the
strength of "facts," which have been accumulating in
all past Spiritual history. But there is a vaster and
more influential attraction—viz., the discovery that the
Future is larger, grander, and more permanent than the
present; and that when we go forward, it is towards
the light out of darkness, toward purity out of imperfection, toward harmony out of discord. This is the
powerful attraction that draws onward the Spiritual
movement. Its inherent momentum, and the vitality of
its central principles, lift it far beyond all the growling,
barking institutions that pride themselves on not being
Anti-Christ. I will now ask your attention to eight
points of Sectarianism—each being a form of "Anti-
Christ."

1. What does sectarianism do? It breaks up human sympathies, divides families, breeds animosities,
leads to misrepresentations, brings confusion, and ends
in war. It goes out into politics, separates the country, divides limb from limb. This is what it does in
the civil, social, and political departments of the world.
Has Spiritualism brought sectarianism into the world?
What is its spirit? Love of mankind—brotherly love
and sisterly love—comprehending the Father and
Mother principles. That is Christian, and it is also
Spiritual. It is the opposite of sectarianism. Sects

have arisen out of theology and priestcraft. Each decides the question for the other. But Spiritualism stands to-day as the boundless Protestant, as the Luther of Luthers in the midst of this jargon, saying, "Away with creeds and party walls! Break down the partitions, and build up liberty, sympathy, and unity, among these discordant, chaotic, and estranged elements." And this is what is called "Anti-Christ!" We say that evils, even if they be stubborn as goats, may become white and gentle sheep one of these days. Some believe that a portion of the human race will be consigned to the great goat-gridiron, to be fried forever. Goat-steak for breakfast—broiled goats for dinner—stewed goats for supper. But to teach that all goats are on the way to the sheep-fold; that all may become brothers and sisters; that all are on the way toward the infinite, approaching from a countless variety of paths which lead toward one Positive Mind, and toward one encircling sphere of immortal glory and happiness, preparatory to a larger and a grander experience in individual progress—because Spiritualism asserts and advocates these principles and ultimates, it is denounced as "Anti-Christ."

Orthodox ministers could do nothing without "a personal devil" or something equivalent to him—could do nothing for the salvation of souls without these cells in the lower portions of God's universe, where lost souls are burning and seething with unutterable suffering. Anything opposed to those beautiful cardinal principles is Anti-Christ!!! Spiritualism, Quakerism, Unitarianism, Universalism, Atheism, and Deism, are oppo-

7

nents of such teachings in old theology. Therefore they are denounced.

II. Next we will. consider Vindictive Punishments. Did Spiritualism bring into the world such punishments? The teaching of the pulpit is, that God punishes arbitrarily; not as the natural result of violated principles. The principles themselves (we say) contain the whips of justice by which both the criminal and the victim are brought to repentance and compensation.

The Churches teach that "man is to be arbitrarily punished, and that God may justly punish to all eternity for a few years, a few hours, a few days of sin. But reason rebels; for the relation of punishment to the crimes committed, is out of all human sense of proportion. Orthodoxy regards it all as God's great wisdom, and it teaches that men ought to keep still and not criticise. But human nature insists that punishment and crime should sustain some relation to each other; that if a man sins a certain number of weeks or years, he should experience punishments which extend over something like a corresponding period of time; or that his punishment, if shortened in duration, should be at least equivalent in quantity and quality to the nature and extent of his crimes.

Perhaps the best thing that can be said of Spiritual reform is, that it brings in this Gospel—that punishment and crime are always in harmony with each other; that one is balanced by the other, and that there is no vicarious atonement, and no virtue in what is called death-bed repentance. Theology says, "Our faith will sweep you all clean, you miserable sinners; it will get you into the kingdom all beautiful at last, even though you may have destroyed the lives of hundreds of your fellow-beings!" Spiritualism holds a very different doctrine with regard to the future of all such persons. Although there is no despair, there are opportunities and privileges, labors and schools, influences of example, and the magnetic attraction of love, all tending slowly, winningly, lovingly, to develop better faculties in such sinners, and to conquer their imperfect habits and badly developed powers. That is what Spiritualism teaches. Is it Anti-Christian?

III. In the world there is the doctrine that God sends War as an arbitrary punishment. Spiritualism teaches that War comes as a concomitant of human misdirection, of miseducation, and undevelopment. War is in harmony with man's lower mental and moral conditions. When he unfolds a more beautiful character, then Society will be sweeter, then nations will be harmonized, and then bloody Wars will cease! The Church says " War comes out of heaven; God sends it as a punishment." Spiritualism teaches, on the other hand, that War comes out of man's lowest estates, and that it is *natural* to those inferior conditions. But this is what the churches call " Anti-Christian Philosophy."

IV. Next look at the universal passion for Selfish Aggrandizement. Spiritualism comes as the opponent of such selfishness. But the churches do not oppose it. Did you ever hear a revival-minister stand in the pulpit and teach the doctrines of social reforms, by which alone mankind can be developed out of their selfishness? Nothing of this at a revival. But the people are told that Christ died for sinners, not to cure you of your selfishness, but to make it possible that, although you are as *red* as fire with iniquities, you can be made as white as snow—not saved from the commission of sin, but from its "consequences." Spiritualism teaches that the doctrine of vicarious atonement for the consequences of sin comes out of undevelopment, out of a lack of justice in man, out of a low, selfish condition of mentality. When men learn the principles of community; when they discover that large cities may become corporate bodies, as really and practically as these Insurance and Banking corporations; and that the whole city may become a monopoly in human happiness, instead of a mill for social, commercial, and mercantile conflicts, then will come among men the delights and beauties and equilibriums of the kingdom of heaven. Spiritualism teaches the absence of selfishness and inculcates doctrines of justice and truth to cause men to unite their interests. It will be easier to live *for* each other's interests than to live *against* each other's interests.

V. Next, I think it will be admitted that the doctrine that Woman should occupy a position equal with man is not "Anti-Christ," though the Church affects to look upon it as such. The Church says: "The woman should not teach, or if she does, she should do it in private, and with her head covered." Paul, a great authority in the Churches, held that woman had a place more brilliant, more attractive, more grand, away from the public arena. There are many intelligent persons who agree with Paul; but it will come to be seen one of these days that Paul and all who think with him are Anti-Christians. And those who hold to the doctrine that woman is spiritually, socially, intellectually, and physically man's equal, but in a different way—that woman will have a career parallel with man's through all the eternal spheres—such doctrines one of these days will be called good orthodox Christian truth. Now, however, it is " Anti-Christian " and is denounced as the Woman's Rights movement. Not a church in New York City is open for a speaker upon this question. Dodworth's Hall, or Peter Cooper's Institute, or some lesser place, must be hired, to advocate the doctrine that the mother is equal to the father, the sister to the brother, and that in the future of society and of government they are to stand side by side as compeers and mutual supporters.

VI. Next, take the question of Slavery. Slavery must be several years older than Spiritualism. It started some time previous to the development of the heathen mythologies. You find it before Calvin taught, before Luther declared himself independent, or before Henry the Eighth broke with the Romish Church. You can trace it in all the lower, brutish, and selfish conditions of human society. Spiritualism declares itself the fixed and unalterable opponent of all human chattelism, servitude, tyranny, and despotism. It emancipates the individual, and proclaims freedom alike to man and woman, Jew and Christian, child and adult, black and white. Such is the philosophy of this new dispensation, which the Church calls " Anti-Christian." I know it is anti-creed and anti-church, but it is not Anti-Christian.

VII. Again, Spiritualism teaches that all Excesses are vicious; that persons who indulge in anything excessively are guilty of vice, which is certain to be punished; and that no vicarious atonement can save them from such legitimate suffering. But the Churches hold up the doctrine that man can be cleansed by a miracle, and so pass off into the other world pure as a child born from the bosom of God. Spiritualism teaches that intemperance is as much applicable to eating as to alcohol, as much to activity as to idleness, as much to spiritual as to any other human manifestation. Intemperance in any of these departments is vice, is wrong; and balance, equilibrium, harmony in all things, is right.

VIII. Lastly, look at the doctrine in the religious world that men are spiritually fallen in animalism, and that if they live hereafter it will be by some miraculous arrangement. Ask the Church people what they think of the future; they will give you the most vague and unsatisfactory answer. The Future, in their creeds, is an incomprehensible Supernaturalism. They seem to think that the other world is as different from this as truth is from error.

Spiritualism, on the other hand, proves the other world to be as much a part of this existence as the human brain is a part of the spinal marrow. The spinal-marrow has been gathered up, and folded over, and in and out, and over again, and convoluted into the mental organism. The spines of all the lower world—working up through fishes, reptiles, birds, quadrupeds, and bimanals into the human, growing finer and finer until they become human cerebrum, or front brain—flowering out from the animal world through the cerebellum, or back brain, and hanging itself over on the front, the receptacle of the immortal mind! Thus we trace the first particles of this human brain back through the history of all the organic kingdoms of the world below.

The Churches do not seek such knowledge, and they openly repudiate it as " Anti-Christian." But we look upon Science and Philosophy as the hand-maids of this new Religion. Spiritualism opens the human brain as the sun opens the petals of the flower, when it trembles and bursts into fragrance and beauty ; and as Minerva sprung from the brain of Jupiter, so the human spirit comes forth and rises into that existence which is a con-tinuation of this. When these soldiers, facing and fighting the enemies of Freedom, are struck down, they are not *down* except to the external physical eyes, but are in reality immediately shot *up* and *out* into a larger, sublimer existence. With this knowledge they can march on without trembling. They need not be one moment in bondage to the fear of death ; there is no grave for the immortal spirit, only a natural and imme-diate resurrection.

But all this the Church calls " Anti-Christian." Christian clergymen have ventured to call it the rhap-sody of a fanatical brain ! Spiritualism brings a great knowledge of the future. The old materialistic school of Infidelity has no chance with Spiritualism. Men who had no knowledge of the future and no faith in man, have now a scientific assurance and a beautiful hope. These truths come as an illuminating religion, expand-ing the human heart, refreshing the senses, and opening the reasoning powers, enabling the mind to see that there is no break in the laws of individual progress. If such a doctrine is " Anti-Christian," then human intuition has no power by which it can distinguish the truth from error. Anti-Christianism is teaching that which is opposed to the future and to God, to purity and to progress. Reformers are obliged to marshal their forces against the Anti-Christianity of Christendom. Anything which militates against the doctrine of Spiritual freedom and progress, and the development and expansion of fraternal love, is Anti-Christ, and it is undeniable that the Churches are the worst opponents of Freedom and Progress. Hence you perceive that THE WORST ANTI-CHRISTIANISM IS THE CHURCHIANITY OF CHRISTENDOM.

In conclusion, I have but to remind you that the era of Spiritual harmony is approaching; it is coming to be part of the common inheritance. Not by any miracle, not by any supernatural arrangement, not by the death of Christ or any other reformer; but the New Age is coming by the principles of an eternal Divinity, which are imperishably implanted in human nature. When the new truth comes, it is natural for persecution to come also. The opposition is necessary to bring out a grander and more perfect development; so that, while we deplore and denounce this sectarian opposition, we see that it is natural and proper in the course of human progress.

I would not have any man or woman believe these principles any sooner than Nature and Reason will aid them to believe. Be just and natural in your spiritual growth; then you will be as firm as the everlasting hills. God is the central magnet of the universe; the spiritual world is the continuation of the natural world; and man's spirit comes out of his brain at death just as the flower comes out of the bud in the garden; it is all beautifully natural, and there is no miracle; and, therefore, when you ascend to the higher life, it will not even surprise you; but will seem like a welcoming stream of water to the thirsty, and like a feast of wholesome food to the hungry.

This spiritual truth gives help to all and extracts help from all. Instead of finding an antagonist in popular science or philosophy, or an enemy in any of the reforms, Spiritualism finds in each and all of them true friends, dear relatives, and old acquaintances. Therefore, when a man is a Spiritualist, he will very likely be something else beside—a Woman's Rights man, an Anti-Slavery man, a Temperance man; and he believes in the development of higher governmental organizations. He is loyal to the government while it must exist, but is ever working and longing for something better. He is in favor of punishment, if it be reformatory and not vindictive. He is therefore in favor of Justice, and is the opponent of all forms and degrees of oppression. A Spiritualist is very likely to be cosmopolitan. He will have a tender and saving regard for his fallen brother everywhere, and feels solicitude for the man who occupies a place higher than himself. He extends the fraternal grasp to those who are above and those who stand beneath. The modern Spiritualist stands erect between these positions—between social and religious extremes—and becomes a central influence, a medium for the expression of the principles of progress, and a friend to all who would grow in wisdom and harmony.

7*

THE SPIRIT AND ITS CIRCUMSTANCES.

"The weapons which your hands have found
Are those which Heaven itself has wrought :
Light, Truth, and Love ;—your battle-ground
The free, broad field of Thought."

A startling proposition was offered and then urged some time since, to this effect : That, although all human minds are constituted upon and with the same fundamental principles, yet each differs from the other both in quantity of mentality and also in the quality of the ingredients. By quality and by quantity men are less or more in contact with the divine principles that regulate the spiritual universe.

It can be shown that an " adjective" is all-important. People pay for an adjective when it is properly applied to fruit, to grains, or to goods of any kind in the physical world. For example: If a peach, without an adjective, is worth one penny, then a *good* peach is worth three cents, a *better* peach is worth four, and the *best* peach is worth six cents. The value is enhanced by the adjective, the superlative degrees always commanding the highest price.

This reasoning is applicable to man's spiritual nature. As fruit is improved by cultivation, so the development of spiritual *quality* and excellence is dependent upon true mental education. All persons do not inherit the same amount of spiritual property; some minds are born comparatively millionaires in their endowments and attributes, and some correspond to musical instruments in the arrangements of their attributes; while others are born in the lowest physiological dell, and are compelled to enter society through the lowest doors, and must plod their way through the coarsest circumstances.

In meeting certain persons, do you not perceive that there is either an excess or else a deficiency in their mentalities? Other natures are large and opulent from no 'definable or apparent reason. Their personal presence seems to fill the whole' space. They may not utter a word; and yet their very silence—which is the twin of mystery and the chief indication of power—pours itself with eloquence into your consciousness. Do you not sometimes feel the immensity of particular persons who are, through their whole life, habitually silent and thoughtful?

Other persons, however demonstrative and garrulous, impress you as being empty and void of soul. They may utter, and write, and do things that are precious and agreeable to your convictions—may hold to ideas that are sympathetic with your long-cherished sentiments—may tell political or religious truths to the people that you have long been waiting to hear uttered—and yet these same persons will impress you with a hollowness of character, with a sense of sounding brass and tinkling cymbals, which repels you from them, and all this without any well-defined reasons or cause that you can understand or express.

Others, again, are "passable." They impress you

indifferently, or not at all. Such seem to be about fairly equipped for the voyage of life. They neither impress nor depress the social sphere about them. They are comfortable passengers, sleeping in the middle cars, between the two extremes.

My work this morning is to trace out the causes that lead to so many battles between the Spirit and its Circumstances, and, if possible, to give suggestions by which those conflicts may be avoided or shortened, and the conquest of the individual all the more perfect and permanent.

When a great and important battle is contemplated, it is one part of good generalship to ascertain all the directions whence your enemies can approach; and not only so, but to examine and estimate their resources, study their tactics, find out their nationality and temperaments, learn what they design to do, ferret out their motives, and pierce them to the heart by the most searching investigations. Then take an inventory and make an honest estimate of your own powers and resources—neither under-estimate nor over-estimate them—be wholly calm and steady, without heat or trepidation, but with great self-preservation and conscientiousness, having perfect reliance upon the virtue and integrity of your motives and the divinity of the ends to be accomplished. Find out, first of all, *what* you have to battle with and what weapons you will be called to use. This forethought and preparation will give you a true estimate of your own powers and resources, and you will know the various obstacles with which you will be forced to contend.

In investigating the constitution, and resources, and

responsibilities of the human mind, I find that few persons think—few persons give themselves time enough to stop to think—what it is to live in this world. Few realize that life to a human being is infinitely more important and more significant than is life to an animal. Take the most perfectly trained and learned animals of the age, and you will find that their progeny return to the first animals of like species in all their characteristics. Their progeny never improve in any habit; they never acquire new thoughts or instincts; never adopt new methods of living in this world. They are entirely harmonious—soul with sense, inward life with external parts. They have no war with their circumstances. They are embodiments of but few principles. Motion, life, and sensation—these constitute the whole of an animal. The soul fills the physical parts to overflowing, and that completes an animal's existence and happiness. Its senses are balanced and in perfect harmony with that combination of powers and instincts. There is therefore no controversy in the single-consciousness of an animal. Its mind hesitates only when two things, like two bundles of hay of unequal size, happen to be presented to it; then there is a momentary exercise of inclination in reference to a purely selfish gratification. The animal mind is swayed and governed invariably, *not* by a moral conviction, but by that simple sense of attraction which moves its feelings the strongest. The same is true of all human beings who are yet on the animal plane. Yes, there are plenty of human beings who walk through society in just that sensuous way. You will see, on analysis, that all such, while so permitting themselves to live, are nothing but quadrupeds in many of their sensations and tastes. They have not arisen to experience the noble feelings and large spiritual proportions of true human souls. Of course I know that, under some conditions and peculiar circumstances, all persons have such sensuous experiences—occasionally that all mankind so "live, and move, and have their being"—and thus all are, by the instincts of their constitutions, made conscious of one truth in our philosophy, that the animal world *preceded* the human; that our ancestral roots are deeply driven into the great physical under-world of organic life; that we have inherited all of their instincts, inclinations, and attributes; and, therefore, being legitimate offsprings from the Divine source, through these pre-human instrumentalities, mankind have inherited all anatomy, physiology, phrenology, and social propensities of their remotest pre-human ancestors.

Man is alone capable of knowing the difference between *himself* and his *circumstances*. When a " circumstance" is realized to be a circumstance, and when man's spirit feels itself to be a "centerstance," a suncenter, around which all circumstances and satellites are destined to revolve in orbital obedience, then is born within him the first assurance of his implanted prerogatives and kingship. This sense of supremacy may come in such memorable moments as when a man is driven to his highest mental point through excitement—sometimes through sublime indignation—at the climax of which comes the terrific fire and the thunder-shock from the soul's Sinai; then descends a flash of celestial lightning from the spirit's heaven, and in an instant is born a strong divinity within the soul, which

brings mountains to the valley and raises that which
was low instantly to the level of its will.   It is rarely
that an appeal so sublime as this comes to human nature.   But something of it is known in nearly all private lives.   There comes to every one of you a moment
of decision which will demand and compel the culmina-
tion and climacteric determination of all your powers.
The strength is declared from the inward fountain, and
in that moment you realize, perhaps for the first time in
your life, that there is an infinite difference between
yourself and all that is moving about you— that *you* are
spiritually a master, and that every " circumstance"
which proposes to conquer and govern you is designed
to be subservient.   I say that such a conviction may be
born in you for the first time in your life, in the midst
of some ordinary transaction.   When it comes, you
should hail it as a prophet ; it is a John the Baptist.
It is going before experience, announcing that a better,
grander, sublimer era will dawn in your autobiogra-
phy, when "circumstances" will be comparatively your
servants,. and you their immortal king within the
temple!

The world is filled with substances with which
spirit is constantly in contact.   Why ?   Because Spirit
is substance itself.   Spirit is something and substantial.
It is connected, through the finest substances, with all
the coarser substances in the visible world.   It is all a
system of perpetual centrifugation.   Man's spirit is like
a sun.   It is revolving on its own axis, in its private
orbit, and, as it revolves, throws off, by its centrifugal
power, first, its most delicate substance—that is, the
" body of the spirit ;" and then a yet *coarser* substance—

that is, the "physical organization;" and, lastly, still coarser substances, which are the "circumstances" round about it in the world.

Every one is either a king in that central kingdom, or else a subject. It depends entirely on your constitution, education, and state of mind, whether you be master or servant—whether you be "a thing" or "a power." Your position and your progress will be determined by your power, not by your force. There is, as you perceive, a great difference between force and power. Force is animal; it is filled with impetuous vital electricity; and after manifestation, it suffers from a corresponding degree of exhaustion. When it retires, you are fatigued. Power, on the contrary, never subsides. Power is linked with the eternal Spirit; always feels its identity, and has no other ally. Do you suppose that God ever gets tired, as the old theology teaches? that he needs to rest from Saturday night till Monday morning? Such seasons of rest will do for force. Force requires it; power never. Power is the deep ocean of omnipotent life. It flows through all physical and mechanical laws, and through all the organic phenomena of the visible world.

This perpetual evolution of the infinite power is silent. It is only when forces meet that there occurs an earthquake, a revolution, a war, or a battle. Where power is, there is only an overcoming, attended by no war, by no discord. The crooked is straightened without conflict. That which was rough is smoothed as by the omnipotent spirit of Deity. When filled with "force," you feel impatient and largely capable of accomplishing rudimental ends. When filled with

" power," you are overflowing with riches, feel no haste. Impulse subsides under true " power," and a quiet, earnest, indefatigable sensation sweeps all through the vine-clad groves of the spirit. This feeling of divine strength refreshes every faculty, gives you a new volume of confidence in the omnipotent God, and opens the truth that he liveth and reigneth in all things.

Old Testament writers seemed to be filled with the spirit as well as the power of Jehovah. That is, they realized the difference between force and power. When they dropped out of it, they acted just like our modern warriors and politicians. They said and did coarse and crude things. But in Jeremiah, Ezekiel, Daniel, and in the Proverbs, you get words from the " superior condition." When they felt the Divine " power," when their impatient *force* was subdued and tranquilized, you know how beautifully and reverentially they wrote and sung of the Infinite Spirit. How sublimely they reposed on the unfathomable bosom of unknown Deity. " God," " Lord," and " Jehovah," were expressions they frequently used. What they called the " promises of God," we, in modern days, call the fulfillments of the unchangeable laws of Destiny. These promises or fulfillments of fixed laws are mapped out from the heart of the universe. We behold them in all the physical phenomena, and feel their operations infallibly in the life of spirit.

Now, in arranging ourselves for the work of individual progress, we must ascertain the sources of our private enemies, and comprehend the magnitude and variety of our inevitable struggles. First, to begin inductively to examine the field of battle, we must commence with the outermost surfaces and go toward the center—go toward the internal man or spirit. You will observe, therefore, that physical circumstances first attract and demand your constant attention. They are the soil, water, air, heat—the physical elements and the social conditions of the outside world, in which you happen to be born and reared. You will always notice the difference between persons born on opposite sides of the Atlantic; also a difference between persons born on different portions of the American Continent, and still closer, the difference between individual members of the same family. Plants, in like manner, indicate, first, the soil from which they spring, and then the kind and amount of attention they receive. Moisture or dryness, the amount of sun-heat and amount of sun-light, will be clearly visible in the growth of the plants. Their history is within. If you had deep-seeing eyes, each one of earth's flowers, trees, and vines, would give you a careful account of the " circumstances" which superintended its development. Of course, in flower-gardens and orchards, there are intermediates—such as human eyes, and human skill, and human magnetism, and the gentle encouragements to growth.

Trees, plants, vines, and flowers, are all affected more or less by the human beings who superintend their development. Thus their external history is like that of persons in the world. Cross to the opposite side of the Pacific—go onward in the west until you arrive in the east again—and you will see that the mystery and philosophy of the Egyptian race—all they did in science and art—are characterized by and inseparable from the sands, plains, plants, valleys, and the almost monotonous world in which they lived. People and country correspond; the country first, next the people. On this principle, every tree, every plant, all vines, will form among themselves very small organic beings—animalculæ—if you will but give them opportunities and suitable conditions, so that the omnipresent organizing principle can operate through their parts. The bugs and worms on plum-trees always differ from those upon vines and plants in the garden. The apple-tree, the cherry, the pear, and each flower, bring out living creatures peculiarly adapted to their own productive sources and circumstances.

It is even so with the physical and human world. The constitution, propensities, and characteristics of human beings, are in keeping with the constitution, propensities, and characteristics of the soil. The amount and kind of sun-light and heat, the kind of lunar influences, the amount of star-shine, the kind of water, the nature of the vegetation, and the character of the animals—all go into the formation of a people or a race. Since the Egyptians left their soil, the soil itself seems almost to have died. Let a spectator examine it, and it would appear as though the valley of the Nile, with all its primeval abundance, had gone into slumber.

Those great mountains and exceeding floral splendors, which are so wonderfully beautiful and grand and startling in the southern hemisphere of the globe, are far from where the Egyptians once lived. In southern regions you at once see that the *physical* "circumstances" are fully reported in the temperaments and tendencies of the people. Volcanic peoples in volcanic countries. Silent, stealthy impulses in human nature just where Nature is impulsive. Volcanoes take a long time to mature. When they get ready to break open the crust of the earth, they do so, and immediately swallow whole cities with one terrific elemental convulsion. In such countries you find yourself among people who have in their characters corresponding impulses and designs. Give them time, and they, too, will silently incubate the largest revolution and produce the most ponderous monarchy; they will remorselessly overthrow and utterly destroy any government or constitution which shuts them from the indulgence of the largest interests and propensities. Thus the volcanic "circumstances" of the world are repeated and reproduced in the temperaments, tendencies, and morals of the people; and thus, too, are visible in folks the water and the soil, and the sun-light and heat, the lunar influences, the star-shine, and also the millions upon millions less noticeable circumstances of the age and clime.

In this connection I adduce the reflections and facts of a mother concerning the influence of parental circumstances on offspring. She says: "The precise character of the father, or the mother, is, probably, never reproduced in a child; the characters of children are a variously proportioned compound of father and mother, modified, often in a great degree, by the circumstances and condition of the mother during her periods of gestation. The circumstances, or the condition, of both, differ in most of, probably in all, her gestations, sometimes greatly. The influence of the father on the personal and mental characters of his children, which is evident, makes it probable that that influence varies with every child; according to the varying circumstances, the varying surroundings, pursuits, cares, pleasures, occupations, and states of mental and bodily health of the father. But the varied influence of the father is not easy to be traced out; though we may make some probable guesses, that some of the most lamentable variations in the children of the same family do proceed from variations in the father. But the varying influence of the mother is evident to all observers; and the observer by questioning even very unphilosophical mothers can make them, by the facts they can recollect, readily admit that certain of their experiences during a period of gestation do coincide with the peculiarity of the child of that period.

" The mother during one gestation may be sick— during another, she may be in health; she may be lethargic and indolent during one, and active in mind during another; be delighted in reciprocal conjugal love, respect, and confidence, at one period, and be desponding, under blighted hopes and blighted affection, at another; or be experiencing suspicion, jealousy, and hatred, under real or imagined injuries; at one period her intellect is beneficially active under the influence of the highest feelings; at another those feelings are dormant, causing the feelings that we call the worst (because when not under the control of the higher feelings they operate injuriously) to have undisputed sway; and her intellect becomes devoted to melancholy, or to bitter and revengeful ideas; at one period she may have pecuniary prosperity, at another, poverty, or the dread of it; she is excited or depressed by the varying conditions of her family and her friends; by varying elementary conditions; and by varying conditions in her locality, or in her country. The variety of combinations from all these circumstances is without end ; and, as they are ever varying, it is very unlikely that the condition of a mother can be alike during any two periods of gestation ; while it is certain that they cause it frequently to vary very greatly.

"Can we expect the children formed under very different conditions of the mother to be exactly alike ? We see that they are not alike in form, size, and health ; and as most of the mother's variable circumstances act diversely on her brain, and all her other variable circumstances act indirectly upon it, it is only reasonable to suppose that though we cannot weigh or measure the different portions of the brains of children, their brains must differ more than their bodies do. And as even those physiologists who say that mind is a spiritual existence added to matter, admit that the manifestations of mind, or mental character, will be according to the size, organization, and condition of the brain, modified by the condition of the body, both Materialists and Spiritualists agree that differences in brain and body caused differences in character at the time of birth.

"That children are affected by transitory impressions on their mother's mind, is proved by the cases of physical markings, and deformities, familiar to every one as consequences of some short-lived desire, or fright, in mothers during gestation. I know a case of a child whose right hand is without fingers, as if the four fingers had been cut off; the mother had experienced a momentary fear that her fingers would be cut off, as she placed her hand under the descending knife of the butcher, directing him where to cut the meat ;

she received so slight a scratch that, as she says, she 'thought no more about it' until her child was born. If such transient emotion can cause such a variation, we must suppose that the more permanent mental conditions of the mother, often lasting through the whole period of gestation, must have a marked effect on the mental character of her child. Intelligent observers have collected a mass of facts upon the subject which amount to proof (as nearly as proof can be obtained on a subject that must be inferential) that differences in the mother's circumstances-caused condition do produce mental differences in children. I will narrate a few of the facts known to myself:

" A wife with good intellect, and still better moral feelings, during her last gestation, forbearingly, from past love and respect, sustained a melancholy secret, a suppression of any expression of disgust and fear of a husband, who, by natural intellect and by education, once seemed her superior, but who, at this time, debased by drunkenness, had brought her to poverty, and to dread of debt and want; and who, in the frenzy of delirium tremens, was seeking to take the life of the wife he still respected and loved. The child of this gestation (now in the prime of manhood) possesses the intellect of his parents and the moral worth of his mother; but, unlike his parents in their happier days, unlike their earlier child, but like his mother when she bore him, he has ever had a manner of sadness, and has ever been eminently secretive, so uncommunicative of his ideas, feelings, and plans, that he can be estimated only by his actions.

" Another wife, of different character, during her

last gestation, was deserted by her husband, was left to poverty, and to experience the pang of jealousy in a high degree; her feelings were not controlled by any remembrance of former respectful love, for her husband was not so constituted as to excite that for himself, or to feel it for her, and in the time of her great trial she had but little moral restraint on her feelings—she indulged in hatred and in bitter, vindictive feelings; her child, now fifteen years of age, is, as he has always been, the personification of sourness of temper and of that ill-nature that likes to give pain by word and deed—and such is his character. His features wear the same expression that his unfortunate mother's wore while she bore him.

"The mothers, in most cases, recognize the connection between their feelings and the character of their child.

"Mothers of several children, having one especially passionate child, have admitted that they were unusually passionate while bearing that child, from the circumstance that the husband or somebody else had been more provoking at that time than any other.

"A mother, rejoicing in the serene and happy temper of her fourth child, told me that the circumstances of a hope of a better state of society, which she was experiencing during her gestation of that child, and her having then learned that her temper would affect that of the child she bore, had given her happier feelings, and caused her to guard against ill temper and to cultivate kind feelings.

"A married couple, with a medium amount of brain between them, were happy in mind and in pecuniary condition—the wife was without care, and without pursuits, when their first child was born; that child had a smaller proportion of brain than either of her parents, and when she was twelve years of age, her mother said of her: 'She is just as thoughtless as I was when I bore her;' but during the wife's second gestation, there was a variation in the circumstances of the couple; the pecuniary failure of a trusted friend reduced them to poverty, and to the necessity of finding some new means of supporting themselves and children; this aroused every faculty of their minds that before was sluggish—the change being greater in the wife, who then, and ever after, participated in earning their living, and who became active in contriving to obtain for her family the utmost comfort that small means could afford; the second child was weak in body, but active and vigorous in mind; the third child had a quiet, thoughtful force of character, and they and all the succeeding children had larger brains than the first child had, and they promised (under ordinary mental culture,) to have larger brains than their parents have.

" These cases will suffice to illustrate the principle; such cases come within every one's notice. The existing national circumstances will have marked effect on many children now in the womb; hope in some minds, terror in others; timidity in some, courage in others; and all the various states of mind that the war engenders will make many children, born during its continuance, differ in character from their brothers and sisters."

America is a new continent. We have here the

8

richest and most expansive prairies. Do you see anything corresponding to them in the American people? Yes! Broad, rich, expansive, enterprising minds! In the far-spreading West, where great prairies sweep away like shoreless oceans, there the most impressible people are largely liberal and prairie-like in their ambitions. I do not mean that those who have recently gone from eastern States are in character like the external prairie; but especially do I mean those who were born and reared there, who have received their first impressions of Nature from the windows and doors of a prairie-home. Such minds are like the physical "circumstances" which surround them. They show muscular tendencies and mental powers which have been imparted by their physical environments. They are like the soil—very independent of embarrassment —not always deep, but very broad and sweeping in their opinions of men, customs, and fashions. The spirit of Freedom, like the fire that unrestrainedly rolls over the ocean land, gathers strength every hour in the West. It is to be the most remarkable seat of social and national experience in this country. The most remarkable battles will be fought in the West. Freedom there is not the New England idea of Freedom. It is the spirit of do-what-you-have-a-mind-to-do-ativeness—a sort of individual license not yet attuned to either justice or freedom. It is the prairie-form of national independence, however, which is beginning to rapidly educate and expand the powers of the Western mind. I do not mean to say that these "circumstances" will mature and culminate in a revolution in the West. But this I am impressed to say, that the Western world is affecting the minds of the people in such a manner as to cause them, in one of these coming years, to lose all national and political relationship to the people of the great mountains of the East; and the people of the mountains in the Eastern States, who will aid in determining these historic events, will be ready to yield to the West the most wholesale independence. The people are being educated out of old-time opinions and institutions. They are emancipated from their primal soils and climates, and they begin to forget the sunshine and starshine of previous generations; so that they easily glide into new "circumstances," by which they are imperceptibly molded and developed to a different plan.

The American mind, I think, is gradually assuming the form and tendencies of the mind of the Aborigines. The American mind is every day becoming less governable by old-time codes. It will no longer import its ideas of government; it no longer can import its religion; music for the people can scarcely be copied from trans-Atlantic sources. Fifty years more, and the American mind will be setting up for itself in religion, in government, in music, in art. New schools upon the new soils will spring up. Americans have hitherto imitated and profited by the old examples and masters. Possible artists yet go over to Italy to study the old pictures. But the true American would rather study the artist, when he gets home, than to study what he has studied. When the art-lover returns and receives again the " circumstances " of his own native country into his mind, then he rises out of slumberous Italy and above all those Medieval schools of inspiration, and becomes once more loyal to the providential spirit of Progress which pervades the Continent of America.

The aboriginal spirit is bold, defiant, incorrigible, and independent. It can be broken and dispersed; it cannot be conquered. Some minds pride themselves upon their Anglo-Saxon origin. They think that that race is unconquerable. That is not history. If we are really the descendants of Anglo-Saxons, we shall be conquered; because they were conquered in the very first stages of their development in England. And they have in them the spirit of "obedience" to "law" to such an extent that a potentate would be welcomed by them. There is a welcoming prayer put up, especially through commerce and politics, for the safe and speedy arrival of some Dictator. Many descendants of Anglo-Saxons would vote for the inauguration of a Monarch in this country! But the spirit of the true people of the country has not yet been declared. That is supremely aboriginal. It is the spirit of personal independence, of national largeness, of great commercial expansiveness, and of unbounded research and enterprise. These conditions in the minds of true Americans come from physical "circumstances," from climate and the soils, including water, the action of the sun through its heat and light, the influences of the moon and stars, and from yet more powerful effects bestowed by the Summer-Land.

Next come the nearer and more potent "circumstances" known as societary influences. Fortunately, they are transitory. But they come very near. They almost touch your nervous system. They control your

actions more than any or all the other influences mentioned. Not more positively, perhaps, but more sensibly and immediately. When a human mind is touched
by its immediate discordant surroundings, the soul feels
them as quickly and as disagreeably as you feel a dress
that does not fit your form, or a new shoe that pinches
your tenderest toes. Societary influences act directly
upon your character. If I should let fall but ten drops
of ink into a tumblerful of water, those ten drops would
be instantly dissolved and diffused through all parts of
the fluid, and there is no chemistry that can restore that
water to its original condition. The new element
becomes incorporated inseparably with the receptive
water.

So the circumstantial and potent drops that have
been added to your soul's fluids from the streams of
society have not been thrown off, but have been absorbed. They have become parts of your sensations and
exterior character. Your outward faculties are impressed to assume the shape and properties of the nearest and strongest powers. Societary influences are
positive and imperative, and they mold mankind in
proportion to their nearness. They are inevitably connected with family relations, with particular duties,
with business obligations, and always with selfish pursuits and interests.

The next set of "circumstances" which are always
around a man, and which are still more inward, and
influential, and potential, are phrenological. It is not
customary to say that the brain organs in a man's
cranium are "circumstances." But if you examine
yourself closely, you will find that you have a *phrenology*

which *you* are not, but belonging to you as tools belong
to a mechanic.   You naturally say to the Phrenologist:
"I wish an examination of my phrenology—of my organs"—thus making a philosophical and perfectly
accurate distinction between *yourself* and your *phrenological* "circumstances." You say to him: "Sir, I wish to
know what powers (organs) I have, according to your
science and measurement." You thus get mapped out,
for future reference, your phrenological circumstances.
You take the book containing your Chart, and examine
the names, and figures, and sizes, and functions, as one
would look at a box of carpenter's tools.   There is
"tune," and here is "ideality," "sublimity," "conscience," and close under the brain is "combativeness,"
and so on—all the time separating *yourself*, and reserv-
ing your individual judgment and consciousness, from
the details of the map which locates and describes your
phrenological circumstances.   A thoughtful man never
naturally says: "I wish the phrenologist to examine
me." He who so addresses himself to a phrenologist,
says something he does not comprehend. The comprehending power in the spirit never so speaks with reference to itself.   It speaks only of something which is
"circumstantial" to its most interior consciousness.
However analytical you may be, you never undertake
to analyze the consciousness of the consciousness which
first sought and suggested the investigation.   At one
time I supposed that I could ultimately comprehend my
own inmost.   The consciousness of consciousness in me,
which longed for and dictated the investigations, would
not submit to self-comprehension.   I found, what every
one of you will find, sooner or later, that your inmost

consciousness is an eternal reservation. It touches infinitude on every side. It demands and permits no final self-comprehending analysis. It allies itself eternally with infinite Principles, and takes little interest in evanescent "thoughts." Spirit indulges the sportive play of "thoughts" in a supplementary way; merely tolerates them, but always with graceful concessions to their fleeting juvenescence.

Now it is to be remembered that these *phrenological* "circumstances" affect us more potentially than do our most intimate *social* "circumstances," because the former are so much more closely identified with the brain's workings. We are incarcerated within these cranial walls, and we reflect truthfully that we did not erect them. Many find entire justification, as they suppose, for any eccentricity, or for the habitual gratification of any impulse, or for any misconduct or mismanagement of which they are culpable, on the ground that they have rceived, by transmission, a bad phrenological organization for which they are not responsible. They justify themselves and say to mother and father : "Look at my phrenology ! How could I help it?" Do you not see that there is *reserved power* in spite of which you seek justification in your " circumstances "? But while you will not always find justification, you may find plenty of pity and sympathy from kindly-natured persons, who estimate carefully your circumstances, and who try in charity to comprehend what measure of influence they exerted upon your motives and actions. Phrenology proves that "organs" about the soul exert upon personal disposition and character a distinct and positive influence.

Next, we are to examine our *physiological* "cir-cumstances." We did not primarily make our physiological organs, but we do make the "conditions" under which those organs are required to perform their functions. Our physiological conditions come out of our foods, and drinks, and methods of living, and out of our habits—out of too little sleep, or too much of it; out of our industries, or out of our continued idleness—in short, whatever we may do, or not do, contributes to the formation of our physiological "conditions." But our physiological circumstances (by which I mean *organization*,) were bestowed without premeditation from our parents. We inherit the bodily forms and functions with our phrenology, as the latter came with our social and physiological surroundings. Thus it stands: A man is born into his *physiology*, born into his *phrenology*, born into his *society*, born into his *geography*, into his *climate ;* so that each individual is deposited (so to say,) amid many and various concentric circles of shaping and molding influences. Mark you, the man is born *into* them ; they do not make the man. The human spirit is born into the center of these concentric dynamic circles of circumstances; and the circle nearest to the spirit will first exert its constructive influence upon disposition and character.

Your physiological circumstances are first predominant. The contents of your phrenology—the brain organs—do not first influence you. The child first responds to the demands of its physiological circumstances. The young mind is affected first by the shape of the spine, by the action of the several joints, by the tendons and ligaments, by the size and proportions of the organs within the body, and, lastly, by the performance of their functions. The little child is in sympathy with its bodily organs and forces—with the ponderable parts and imponderable powers that make up the physiological circumstances of its inmost life. Its mind and feelings will be in bondage to them. Its life-manifestations will be in accordance with them until the phrenological circumstances begin to exert themselves upon the feelings and character. Then the little child changes from a physiological to a phrenological being.   ·

This dependence upon phrenology may continue for years. Then come the constructive powers of social and physical circumstances. The child-mind then begins to exhibit the action of social and physical circumstances upon both its physiology and phrenology. The · young constitution very soon responds to the most outward "circumstances"—the physical globe, its climatology, its topography, and the soil ; the action of the sun, its heat and its light; moisture, dryness, &c., &c. ; whatever, in short, is considered appropriate or existing in the world of physical circumstances, is concerned more or less conspicuously in framing and making up the human character.

Spirit is in the center. Begin thus, at the pivot, and count the concentric circles. First, its physiological circumstances ; second, its phrenological ; third, its societary ; fourth, its physical or geographical—the most external of all. Now do you not know that some persons remain through life under one or two of these concentric "circumstances"? Certain minds allow themselves to be molded and fashioned by whatever is

8*

nearest and most allied to their interests. They die at the end of fifty, sixty, or perhaps one hundred years, having been molded and shaped by one set of circumstances, and only transiently affected by the others.

Spirit, the inmost and eternal, is no such victim. It is the source of power. Force is animal. The soul is composed of motion, life, sensation, and intelligence. In the animal but little; in the man, much. That power which is at the center of life, which is destined to gain the mastery, which takes hold upon infinitude, which is allied with whatsoever is divine and omnipotent, which is twin-born with justice, and truth, and virtue, and with all that is pure, and noble, and sublime—that power resides at the heart-seat of your life, the coming Lord of all circumstances. I am now speaking to that power in you. Some will hear; others will not. In the millions the Inmost has not yet asserted its supremacy. Of course such do not feel themselves even partial masters of their influential circumstances.

The spirit's battles are to be fought through power, not through force. But "force" is necessary. It is part of man's intelligence—is natural to motion, life, and sensation. But there is invariably as large an amount of *defeat* as there is of *victory* in battles of mere force. "Action and reaction are equal;" so say all who study the laws of mechanics. They must calculate for loss of power by reaction in all mechanism which moves by means of motive power. Now what is man? Does he not start out as a mechanism—the most perfect and the most fearful and wonderful piece of machinery in the world? The necessities and circumstances of his physiological organs cause him to call for drink, for clothing, for protection, for home, for love, and the ineffable attentions and blessedness of that love. Then his phrenology brings in its influence. All his brain-organs have motives, impulses, and powers, hidden in their centers.

But the time comes when, over and above all, a divine power—according to the definition first given—is born and revealed from within. This power comes through the soul. The soul is the battle-ground. Forces, instead of powers, first prevail. People are weary with battling with intellectual error, and, most of all, weary from battling with their " circumstances"—fatigued, annoyed, exhausted, despairing. Certain minds grow disloyal to principles by means of too long indulged indifference. They cease to take an interest in themselves, and they retire from the battle-field vanquished and " demoralized." Others go through all of life's battle, then they lie down at the end of the many struggles, and finally die from sheer mental exhaustion. But it is only " force" that fails. *Power* never feels exhaustion, never desponds, never " gives up the ship." Force, through the organs of your intelligence, plans the way. Power, however, will often conduct you to a very different plan and different result. You begin life with the impulsive ambitions of " force" —with many inclinations for worldly distinctions—and you fix all your intellectual plans to consummate the ends of such ambitions. But presently you find that there is a " power" *behind* and *within* and *above*, shaping your destiny! And every step you take in your plans is a disheartening *defeat*. The very end which you supposed " impossible" is the *only* thing " possible" for you to do. And those things that seemed to you most desirable and *possible*—most in the direction of your selfish preferences and energies, and most gratifying and attractive to your ambitions—were just the things which could not be done by you, because you had not power to control your concentric circles of "circumstances," which included the affections, thoughts, plans, and wills of many people. Society would not permit itself to be marshaled into the files of your aims. Therefore you could not conquer by " force"—something deeper, something higher, which may be termed " power," was needed.

What else have you with which you could conquer? Use mere " force" and you are utterly vanquished. Church people talk very beautifully and approvingly about those submissive, pious souls, who say, " Father, thy will, not mine de done." Well, there is in that moral condition an interior truth. Do you suppose that those who were lovingly engaged in laying the foundations of the Christian system, were all mistaken in their spiritual experience? Certainly not. They uttered and wrote memorable words from an inward conviction and experience. What does it mean to be submissive to God's will? It means that " spiritual power"—not mere vital force—must be permitted to have its own way in mapping out and regulating your destiny, and thus always to have the predominance of authority in the shaping of private experience. Power is long and patient in suffering, can unmurmuringly bear great outward persecution and contumely, and can bear up under all the trials and defeats which afflict you in the pilgrimage of life. Power, which is always from spirit, is never conquered. Force, which is always from vitality, or soul, is vanquished at every step. Sometimes, indeed, it commits suicide. It loses breath and drops below from the very climax of its victory, because force is only an animal energy arising from the physiological and phrenological organs, and its efforts must necessarily be violent, exhausting and suicidal.

Whoso feels this " power" feels also what we term a Principle. Whoso feels what we term a Principle, also feels good and truth, or God, invariably in that same proportion and to that same measure of interior consciousness. And whoso feels God living in the form of Justice and Truth in his soul, is never conquered.

Suppose the soul that feels Truth, or Justice, or God, be put on a cross and crucified—what does that outward persecution amount to? I never could understand the " Much Ado about Nothing" in the Churches. What soul-harrowing accounts of the heart-crushing persecution which attended and destroyed " the Man of God"—that is, the Man of Power! One of two things is certain—either that when " the Man of God" was being crucified he failed to realize the presence and power of his own immortal Spirit, or else the whole Calvary scene was spectacular and dramatical, and permitted for " effect." It was either a performance, or else there was a failure on the part of the persecuted to realize the presence and power of Truth. If it was no failure in this particular, then we must conclude his physical sufferings were not different, nor more severe or agonizing, than were those of numbers of human beings who have innocently died on gibbets, in flames, or upon scaffolds. Physiological suffering is the same with all organized humanity. Very sensitive persons experience inconceivable intensity of suffering for a few moments. But who believes that any human being has ever sweat " drops of blood" in consequence of his physical suffering? If, at the moment of the crucifixion, either by cross or by other means of destroying human life, the spirit should lose its conscious contact with the source of " power," then, indeed, the sufferer might almost sweat blood in the throes of his mortal and spiritual agony. Blood might flow out from a bursted vein. But there is too much said about " the sufferings of Jesus." The exaggeration of his agony, in simply dying as part of his mission, is unjustifiable; the tears of sympathy that have been shed over the mortal agonies of a man who died a no more terrible death than thousands of others have, ought to have been shed for more genuine sufferings. Jesus first carried his cross to the place of execution, and was then physiologically put to death. There is no logical proportion between the physical sufferings of the individual and the dramatic effect with which pulpits " harrow up one's feelings." One view or the other must be taken—either Jesus died in great agony to emphatically impress the world with the importance of his mission, or else it was really true that he felt that God had departed from his soul, and that, perhaps, he was suffering without any just and sufficient reason. An overwhelming feeling of agonizing doubt might have caused blood to rush from his veins; but if he had a full sense of his perfect spiritual unity with the Divine Source, what would it have been to be

" shot," or forced to drink " poison" like Socrates, or " gibbeted," or " burned at the stake," like the early martyrs and patriots? What would such bodily agony amount to in a righteous cause? Nothing at all. Look at the brave-souled martyrs, in the consuming fires, all going heavenward with songs of praise on their lips! How many of them were moved with prayer and to expressions of gratitude while standing in the midst of flames! Vastly more sublime, many of them, than was the scene of the Cross-death on the mount. Why be absurd in weeping over this matter of a teacher of Justice and Truth dying in vindication of his testimony?

Let us now return to our theme. The shortest method to conquer " circumstances," is to ally yourself with Principles. Suppose you say: " I can comprehend only one thing, viz., the idea of Progress." Keep in mind, now, that the idea is a Principle. Now, suppose you say: " To *that* Principle I will be loyal, though the heavens fall." Can you not take that positive position? Whatever seems to me to be true, *that* I will adhere to, though I lose the whole world. And I will adhere to it with power, not with " force." Force is animal; it is not " power." Secure your spirit by an indomitable adherence to some divine Principle. Fix your nature in its true orbit, and forthwith you are above anger, above enmity, above petty vices, above low motives, above vindictiveness, and, therefore, you are master and governor of all those demons of discord that beset your path. In proportion as you are loyal to a Principle, you will receive inspiration, and thus " power" is added to that life which is integral and eternal. The divine, in ultimates, always gains a victory over what is earthly

and unworthy. In theology, however, the devil always
has the upper hand. But, in fact and in truth, the devil
is always under—in outer and in *utter* darkness. Discord—force—the war element—is finally put down.
The animal world is beneath man; the angel world is
above man; higher worlds roll over the angel-world;
the divinest Sphere through and within them all; and
the Supreme eventually conquers. In this rudimental
world of ours, the man of war is not a conqueror, nor is
the earth itself a conqueror; but the *sun*, with its
inconceivable opulence and abundance, is grandly
triumphant. And yet how silently the sun does all its
omnipotent work! It does not send out a flaming
letter to say: "I shall give you a very fine day
to-morrow; I shall show you a worldful of warmth;
a great flood of light will I pour over your habitations."
But it rolls right on, and shines beneficently, and
warms the fields, and brings mankind a wondrous wealth
of golden harvests. The sun is the "power" of wise
affection personified.

Whenever the consciousness of a Principle is born
in the human spirit, from that moment it ceases to be a
"thing," and becomes a "power." In *force* you see
what is rudimental; in "power" that which is sublime.
No defeat in power; always defeat in force.

Take any divine Principle; such as Liberty or
Brotherhood. Learn the beautiful lesson of strict loyalty to your deepest conviction. Become harmonious
with a principle, and you become, to the same extent,
"a power." Instead of feeling weary in battling with
circumstances, you receive accessions of celestial strength
from invisible sources. A friend may ask: "Do you

not grow weary with labor?" "No," you reply. "I never think of it." Why? Because God and Nature, or immutable Justice and Truth, breathe into your nostrils "the breath of life"—that is, if you are absolutely *loyal to a Principle.* Loyalty is power, as knowledge is power; and in true power there is victory, without exhaustion. You stand as "a power" in the center of substances—a centerstance—in the center of your physiology, in your phrenology, in your society, and amid still more external atmospheres and soils.

In the Bible you read that if a man does not single-heartedly and absolutely follow Truth, if he does not leave his father and mother "for my sake, he is not worthy of me." That is what Truth said to the world. long, long ago. The writer, unfortunately, wrote down the name of an individual instead of "Truth." To some minds, "the man" personifies a Principle. It is reported that he said, "I am the *way*, the *truth*, and the *life*." Matthew, Mark, and Luke, have reported the Nazarene as identifying himself with the principle of Truth, or with God. "If a man does not forsake father and mother, son and daughter, he is not worthy of Truth."

Let each identify himself with divine Principles, and if wife, or husband, or son, or daughter, or Mrs. Grundy, or any other relation does not choose to harmonize with that Principle, but is determined that you shall be an apostate and a rebel to it, then you should say, "Clear the way. My path is chosen. I shall walk according to my deepest, highest, most sacred convictions, though the heavens fall." Feel and follow the principle of Truth, and you will find that no earth-relation is important. Take any Principle your soul may choose, and be *faithful* to it, " come what may." Suppose you be driven out of your business to-morrow; suppose your children starve; suppose they should perish and die. Some of you look upon the death of a martyr as " sublime." Or you go back in your imagination to Calvary, and there you behold another " sublime spectacle." There you behold the death of a man who went into society at the lowest door, who was persecuted and despised in the midst of his philanthropic labors. Did he set a very good example of obedience to his mother or his father when the doctors in the temple needed his instructions? His mother, you recollect, was very apprehensive about him. Did he stop for that? It was more important that he should be engaged in the impartation of what was welling up in his soul than to obey the requisitions of his mother, who had no distinct idea of what her son's mission was. The Catholics, however, have made a Saint of her. Beautiful picture! I love the painted Madonna: there is an idea in the conception. Anything truly beautiful is eternal. But the son did not seem to know anything very important about his mother. He had to be *loyal to Truth,* even if seemingly disloyal to heart-requisitions.

Now we are all children. We have parents, and grandmothers, and grandfathers. These relations make positive social requisitions upon us. A kindly religious mother says: " Don't! I beg of you—don't go to Progressive Hall; if you do, I shall get heart-sick and die." Well, if it be necessary, let her die. Be strong and firm. There is much folly in " compromise." If you have a Truth, *stand by it !*   Let people see that you, like a miner in a dark world, carry a lamp in the front part of your mind—" the light that lighteth every man who cometh into the world"—shedding its effulgent rays over all your terrestrial path.   If you be faithful to your best experience and highest convictions, it will shake the citadel of old theology to its foundations, and your expanding influence will revolutionize the cities and the kingdoms of the world.   If you try it, there will be a great struggle among your relatives to rule your course.   In these days, however, you will find plenty of spiritual company to aid you in your struggles.   But the time was when a person had to make spiritual struggling all alone.   Happily, that time is passed.   Let your spirit fully identify itself with Principles.   Then you can surely and noiselessly "overcome evil with good."   You will go on, quietly conquering and to conquer—victorious every step of the way—and thus reach the inmost heart of the Eternal Mind.

ETERNAL VALUE OF PURE PURPOSES.

"A good man is God's best legacy to this straying world."

The human mind irresistibly seeks for uses, ends, results. It is impossible to repress this tendency of our intellectual and imaginative powers. They naturally trace out ultimates. This is true, because the mind is constituted with a specific ultimate—because it is itself the development of a central design. The mental organization carries out its tendencies as naturally as the dancing streamlets flow from mountain-sides to the welcoming plains. It is the involuntary flow of the interior—through the reasoning powers—toward ultimates! If the reasoning powers are well-balanced, vigorous, and pure, the rule then is, that the understanding, by moving steadily along the line of logic, will arrive at the most reasonable solution of whatever problem is presented. This uniform reasonableness is what men call "common sense." Persons having this *sixth* sense—this admirable arrangement of these beautiful and immortal endowments—can take in a large field of observation, and arrive rapidly at healthy and certain conclusions. It is, so to say, a clairvoyance of the reasoning powers. Some minds, by the exercise of such common sense—that is to say, by obtaining the verdict of a well-balanced class of intellectual thinking powers—seem to see as accurately through the incoming future, and to prophesy events and results, as though Clairvoyance itself sat enthroned in the spirit.   Clairvoyance is the far-soaring eagle's flight—the lightning's flash—along the line of cause and effect.   It arrives at remote results without the exercise of the reasoning powers.   Hence the clairvoyant may not, in the ordinary state, possess what is called " common sense."   Clairvoyance, in many minds, gets the start by years, and, in some instances, it may be centuries in advance of the moral growth and out-rounding of the soul.

The forecasting abilities of the intellectual faculties—the grasping healthily all parts and details of the field of perception and consciousness—is the normal exercise of man's normal and beautiful endowments. Their exercise promotes and advances the individual to the superior state; to attain which, many minds are obliged first to be magnetized or mediumized.   Very great mediums are sometimes no better or wiser in matters within the sphere of common sense, even while under the influence of the afflatus, than are some persons who have no such experience, but who, by the natural and just exercise of their energetic and well-balanced powers, philosophically see principles, causes, effects, and their results.

This irresistible tendency, streaming through all the thinking powers, demonstrates the central fact that the spirit is constructed on a plan of pure reason and harmony.   This harmonial design lies in the very foundation of the human mind.   The spiritual universe is filled with Designs.   You naturally ask, " *Cui bono ?*"

—what use, or what good? This question was asked of every new thing that ever started. The irrepressible tendency of the spirit to put this question, is owing to the fundamental fact that the mind itself is constructed upon a living divine Design—upon Use. Nothing grows, nothing walks, nothing wings its way through the free air—whether great or insignificant, beautiful or otherwise—but gives rise to questions of Use, in the little child as well as in the mind of the fullgrown man or woman. The first conception that a man or woman must attain to, before the spirit-mind is rounded out and fashioned into the beautiful and harmonious proportions of a pure Purpose, is this conception of inborn Use. You remember the Platonic, spiritual verse in the third chapter of John, where the materialist, Nicodemus, came and held a conversation with the illuminated son of Joseph and Mary. How beautifully and truthfully it was said that " That which is born of the flesh, *is flesh,* and that which is born of the spirit, *is spirit.*" We know by the universal testimony of the world—yet more certainly by experience and observation—that that which is flesh dies, goes down, sickens, and despairs; while that which is spirit goes up and on—because retrogression to it is impossible—because, like truth, it is immortal and cannot die! A Purpose that is conceived in the spirit, which is brought forth in the beauty of its powers—a Purpose which goes before the soul like a pillar of guiding light, drawing it magnetically onward —is certain to consecrate, to lift, to renew, to baptize, to round out, to make perfect, angelic, heavenly, even as the Infinite is perfect.

A high, pure Purpose, be it remembered, is possible only to *spirit*. Ambition is earthly; aspiration is spiritual. They are analogous, resemble each other, just as common sense, in its healthful exercise, bears a likeness to the superior condition, with its pure and independent clairvoyance. A human mind may be actuated by "ambition," and the individual may successfully go on in the road which the ambition indicates, but its success will be parallel with the earth, with society, with what is for the hour called "success," "victory," "conquest;" while the mind that dreamily and confidingly floats in the celestial rivers of "aspiration," may not be successful according to popular standards of judgment. Such a person may seem to fail, or really fail, when measured by the world's rules of success; but, believe me, that soul surely succeeds in whatsoever is permanent and glorious, because its pure Purpose brings the inmost spirit into harmony with pure Truth, which is eternal! There is no failure, no defeat, no killing disappointment, in the mind that is exclusively moved by a high Purpose in its external relations to mankind. Success always attends the steps of such an one. But when a person is moved by an "ambition" to accomplish an ordinary end—which would be considered by society a high and victorious result—he is sure to be defeated. This wretched experience dates from the time he starts, and is continued until he sits down in his uneasy chair to review the ill-spent past.

The Jews killed the spiritually-unfolded son of Joseph and Mary. They were pre-eminently "victorious" in the judgment of the whole Roman Empire. His arrest, trial, condemnation, and execution—each step was pronounced a "success" as far as the circumstances were known. (The fact is, however, that little or nothing was known of the transaction, except locally.) The crucifixion was considered a great "triumph" of law and order over anarchy and heresy. And many thanked those who nailed his body to the wooden cross. But there was *one* in the midst of all that row and riot, bloodshed and diabolism, who was momentarily and perfectly "successful," viz., the man who had a PURE PURPOSE enthroned in his spirit, magnetically and perpetually calling him onward and upward in the divine line of his work.

It has been shown that Nature, through all her forces, works for the development of individualized human beings; that all the lower kingdoms and systems of life, combined, are but the scaffolding of the building; and that all parts subserve the elaboration and perfection of human bodies and souls. From the lowest monad to the animal that comes nearest man, in association and usefulness, there is visible this continued beautiful flow of "Design," mounting up to the well-proportioned, harmonious human organization.

Nature, then, has a high Purpose, and she works to no other End. It is not merely to organize a physiological being, to make a perfect anatomy and a fine physiology. Our great Mother's purpose is far, far higher. It is, to so construct an anatomy and physiology that the soul, like a garment, may be accumulated and folded about the more interior being, the Spirit, which is golden and immortal; which will be so beautifully and so harmoniously arrayed, that, when we each pass from this existence, the revolutions of eternal spheres and the destruction of innumerable stars can never impair our youthfulness, or in any degree disturb the deep flow of the heart's exalted happiness. Yea, Nature has a high and pure Purpose. If her work was simply to make a fish, she would fail. If she had not a mission far above and beyond all fishes, reptiles, birds, marsupials, and mammalials—a Purpose to which those organized forms of life unitedly labor, of which they are but parts and fragments—she would " fail" utterly in all her movements and ministrations. *To individualize the immortal human spirit,* and to make for it a garment—an enveloping soul—after the fashion of the physical body, which shall withstand the revolutions of eternity, and always be young and beautiful to look upon—this is the high *Purpose,* the pure *Design,* which consecrates the unalterable labors of Nature, and lifts the whole system into a divine and glorious significance.

Nature, therefore, has given the lesson. Can you not follow it? How can you fail to respond to the vibration of that electric current of " Design" which the Divine has communicated to all parts of the spiritual universe, and which goes quivering and shimmering through systems of suns as it throbs through the faculties of your immortal mind? I know you cannot resist it. You begin life by asking, *" Cui bono ?"* This is the beginning of Use. In the most inferior and ridiculous expression of that interrogatory you may see the alphabet of that harmonial poetry of pure " Purpose," which will be epical and lyrical as it sweeps through eternal years.

Suppose a young man enters college. He is induced
9

to study for some particular profession—a lawyer, a physician, or, if he be not in mental and physical health, a clergyman. But if he be bodily robust and intellectually sturdy and strong, and is good with his jack-knife, why, then, perhaps, his best friends will want him to study for a boss-mechanic. If he has inherited large scheming powers, with the outlines of a lawyer, but deficient in the intellectual substance required for a high post in that profession, then he may direct his education toward Congress or for the Presidency. The young man is solemnly admonished to "aim" his studies at something. But this is true, that, if his aim be for nothing more than what is called "success" in the chosen profession, he is extremely likely to turn out a mistake and an ordinary character. If his Purpose in life is embodied in the thought of being ordinarily "successful" in any one of its departments, then he will be "defeated" and crippled from the very moment of his graduation with such an ambition. What percentage of the students, who come out of colleges, amount to anything, as men among men? About twenty in every hundred of those who graduate from our best colleges amount to something in the world's esteem—all the rest "fail." Merchants fail in a very much larger proportion. Politicians fail at the rate of 140 per cent. Men fail in all situations just in proportion to the immorality of their motives.

When a man desires to be of service to the Universe, when he yearns to live not for his own sake, not for his own personal benefit alone, but for the benefit, advancement, civilization, and spiritualization of the millions, then he has in him that Savior which will preserve him from harm and from defeat through all disasters and earthly besetments. He can not experience what is called demoralization or discouragement. He may overwork, he may lie down, as did the great-minded Theodore Parker, in the midst of his gigantic industry, and die up into the Summer-Land; but as surely as that transformation takes place on earth, so surely, if you will but look with your intellectual telescope, you may behold a new, bright, beautiful orb, shining in the spiritual heavens. The politician dies at the same time—the man who lived for himself, for little earthly, sickly, temporary purposes—and goes also to the Summer-Life at the same time. You would be obliged to look with a powerful microscope to see who or where he was. One man's spirit shines out goldenly and immortally in the firmament that spans the heavenly sphere. The other man's spirit, on the other hand, hovers and shivers in the midst of all that diversified beauty and ineffable glory of the Infinite—is small and mean and cold beneath the heat and light of myriad suns—and would fain become a part of even one of the heavenly rays.

What are we Americans doing? What has the administration been trying to do? We have been trying to " conquer a rebellion," but not to improve anything, either institutional or constitutional. The immoral purpose at the start was, not to improve a man, woman, or child on the continent, in respect to their civil, political, or religious circumstances, but to " crush the rebellion" and to restore things as they were—a philosophical absurdity, a political sham, a religious impossibility. Thus our people started with an impure purpose, filled with immoral designings, only to accomplish the traditional ends of conservative power. Such is political power when not consecrated to divine uses! The result has been "failure" on all sides, or at best, but indifferent temporary success.

You have read about a Father who so loved the world that he gave "his only begotten son" to rectify its errors and to save it—in short, gave his son for the pure purpose of doing all the good he could. On the same principle a great many fathers and mothers have also given "their only begotten sons" to march and die for Freedom. Why all this sentimental weeping and this sickly lamentation over that glorious sacrifice of the infinite heart that had as much power to endure as to propose the work? (We are now supposing the theological notion to be a truth; not that we accept it literally.) Here are mothers and fathers, I repeat, who have given their "only begotten" to save American Freedom from destruction ; not only so, but those sons have been sent to expand our Liberty, to multiply it, and to cause it to abound from the Atlantic to the Pacific, from the remote North to the far South. How many of those dearly beloved "sons" have been crucified! How many of them have been in our hospitals, drinking gall and the bitterness of wormwood, and swallowing as medicines all sorts of contemptible trash! How many of them have had bayonets thrust into their bleeding sides? How many have freely poured out their whole lives that Liberty might "believe, be baptized, and be saved"! Would it not be wisest to search outside of the realm of creeds to find objects sufficiently touching and sacred for the shedding of tears and the building of monuments? Let us have real objects and

genuine causes for sadness and lamentation, for holy
sorrow and devotional gratitude; but no more of this
dramatically-manufactured "holy sorrow," taught by
men, who, perhaps, sincerely believe it, but who have
not the courage to investigate it to its silly mythological
foundation.   Here, in this war, we have the real sacrifice of truly begotten sons. The purposes of these fathers
and mothers have been high and beautiful. They have
in them a source of consolation that no Bible or church
can either impart or remove.   Their patriotic sons are
slain—crucified on the cross of battle.   Look at their
downcast and weeping friends.   No minister can
assuage their sufferings.   Their heart-pains cannot be
mitigated by prayers.   Nothing will do it but time
with its upliftings, and the onward march of the
soul of each.

There were many in need of useful and profitable
employment.   Some of these enlisted for the war as
they would go into any hazardous labor.   I saw and
conversed with a Massachusetts soldier—a fine enough
looking man—going as a private down to New Orleans
with General Banks.   I said to him, "Why did you
enlist?"   "Well," he said, "wagon-making was poor
business in our town, and I have a beautiful wife and
two darling little ones, and they must be supported,
and I got a bounty—more money than I could possibly
get if I had worked at home for a long time—and I
gave it to them and made other provision, so that, if I
should not get through the war, my beloved family
will be as much benefited as though I were to remain
with them."

There was dwelling in that soldier's soul a "pure
purpose." He took his life in his hands and went to

work for his beautiful wife and his darling two children. But if he had felt the urgent demands of Liberty also, how much more noble!

Thus, if a man enters as a merchant into business, or, as a mechanic, accepts of labors, however low and undignified or however high and commanding, *with a desire to benefit others by his labor*, he is in the same proportion made spiritually buoyant, and the ordinary friction of life that would otherwise wear upon him is chiefly removed. He goes lovingly on to his business, not " dragging one foot before the other ;" because he feels lifted and is blest—baptized and strengthened by the purity of his intentions.

Live selfishly for yourself, and you will sit down at the end of life dissatisfied with human existence. You will be misanthropic, no matter whether you are surrounded by wealth or by poverty, by enemies or by friends.

Therefore take to your heart the motive which is beautiful and heavenly in itself, live to make *others* better, and you will make yourself rounder, sweeter, more effective in all you do, gladsome, cheerful, buoyant, never cast down, always ready for good deeds; and a beautiful warmth will pervade your home, will follow you into the street and into society, and noble beings will associate with you wherever you mingle wisely and lovingly with your fellow-men.

Great men are always *good* men. " A good man is God's best legacy to this straying world." Such never " fail." The truly good cannot be unsuccessful. The son of Joseph and Mary was not defeated when crucified. Verily, there is eternal value in PURE PURPOSES.

WARS OF THE BLOOD, BRAIN, AND SPIRIT.

" If more would act the play of life,
    And fewer spoil it in rehearsal ;
If bigotry would sheathe its knife
    Till good became more universal ;
If men, when wrong beats down the right,
    Would strike together and restore it ;
If right made might in every fight,
    The world would be the better for it."

The impression comes to speak this morning on the subject of war—first, of the Blood ; second, of the Brain ; third, of the Spirit ; or, in other language, (1.) the war of *Gehenna*, which means the underworld of passion and selfish lusts that burn perpetually ; (2.) the war of the middle world, or *Hades*, which means the transition and wintery sphere in which we now live ; (3.) the war of the overworld, or *Heaven*, which means the moral and spiritual sphere of the immortal mind.

Let your minds contemplate the universality of war. You will discover, after investigation, that war is universal. War is not excluded from heaven—*i. e.*, from the presence of the inmost Spirit, although it originates only in the blood and in the force-departments of the brain. I speak now of the universality of the struggles, the encroachments, the infringements, and of the aggressional tendencies of all forces locked up and embodied in the organization of matter—beneath, within, and round about us in the great universe that fills immeasurable space.

All investigators discover penetralia within penetralia, truths within truths; or, as it is commonly expressed, wheels within wheels, designs within designs, and uses within uses in endless succession. Such inquiring minds come at last to the wise conclusion that, in the inmost of things, is written the unchangeable commandments (the laws of Nature) by which all things are regulated and governed in perpetual order, goodness, and perfection.

A handwriting in milk held to the fire, becomes plain, though invisible before it was so subjected. So the infinite designs and immutable laws written in human nature, as upon the whole universe, do not become plain to your understanding until you are fully subjected to the fires of infringements and transgressions, and tried by the irrepressible tendency of your investigating powers to pass through, and over, and between all things. Something important to the whole universe takes place every instant of time. No tide is perfectly inert. Water presupposes motion, forward and backward, or rising and falling. The action of rising and falling tides upon substances pulverizes and converts them into itself—dissolves solid rocks and makes them flow with its movement. Physiologists discover that the liver is composed of an infinite number of lesser organs; or, more strictly speaking, they find that the liver is composed of very minute lobes, which in appearance exactly resemble the whole structure. The liver is a cellar, because it is composed of cells. How many persons experience the truth of this! The liver is Hades. It is the dark repository or grave-yard of whatsoever is broken-down in the constitution of the arterial blood. It is always gaining and always losing. Disease is produced just as quickly by an excess as by a deficiency.

Now what is the world's system of politics? Is it not the *liver* or kitchen department of human government and enterprise—a desire for system and regulation and order—composed of an infinite number of lesser policies, as the liver is composed of a countless number of infinitesimal livers?

It was said that a writing in milk when exposed to fire, becomes plain to the eye. So the Infinite laws and ultimate designs, exposed to the progressive abrasions and fiery frictions and irrepressible conflicts of human mind and moving matter, are brought into open revealment; and only those faithful seers, who have wise eyes, can read the handwriting clearly, and truly interpret the Idea at the heart of the infinite designs. How do scientific men stand before the great universe of design? They say, "Matter is regulated by unvarying methods. These methods are laws." Here the spiritual philosopher approaches. He discovers within laws principles, within principles ideas, within ideas the infinitely and eternally thinking Father-God, and the impersonal love-fountain of the universe, or Mother-Nature. The spiritual philosopher finds something deeper and better and more interiorly satisfying than that which is brought to the world through external science. He discovers that the impersonal love-fountain, from which all things flow, is NATURE, and that this productive heart of infinite love is "Mother." He

9*

discovers that Nature is *not* matter. Nature is a general
term for the Mother-fountain of Love which moves and
forms and molds all things, in conjunction with the
masculine laws of Wisdom. The impersonal mind-
fountain—of formative laws and organizing energies—
is the Father-Nature. "God is a spirit." The New
Testament adds: "And he seeketh such to worship
him."

Why use the masculine adjective with reference to
Deity? Because the mind instinctively thinks of God
as the source of *thought* and energy—executive, formative, and legislative.

If I were a clergyman (which, fortunately, I am
not,) I should state this theological proposition in very
different phraseology. Undoubtedly, I would employ
New Testament language, or such words as would correspond to lessons that I had learned from authoritative
books on theology. And yet, although I do not so
employ language, I believe that I am not in conflict
with the essential truths at the center of enlightened
minds. I know not a civilized clergyman in the land
with whom I might not shake hands on some of these
theological principles. For example: They believe, or
profess to believe, in a Supreme Source. So do we.
They give it the theological, religious, and oriental
name—"God." We give it the spiritual, philosophical,
and scientific name—"Father-Nature." The sectarian war rises and continues from a vastly different use
of human language with regard to identical meanings.
Not interpreting the meaning which we intend to convey—by the use of different words, we kindle up
antagonism in our neighbor's mind; and on the other

hand, when he announces his thought, the meaning whereof not being fully conveyed to our mind, a corresponding fire is kindled up, and forthwith an explosion takes place—and an everlasting enmity and opposition drive out the angels of peace. There can be no reconciliation so long as men will not stop, in their haste, to give each other the central meanings which they designed should flow through their educational use of language. Let all men be cautious and just. Within all this mountainous mass of educational verbiage and controversy you may find, if you look patiently, the beautiful flowings of *identical* immortal truths. The brotherhood of truth makes this "fraternity of ideas" absolutely certain in all true human hearts.

Mother-Nature and Father-Nature—who might with propriety be named the Love-life and the Wisdom-power of the universe—live in eternal conjugal relation each with the other. Matter is the indestructible chariot in which they together ride through the illimitable star-strewn spaces of infinitude. We must learn to think deeply on this subject. We must deepen out of words into meanings, and penetrate through meanings to the source of inspiration.

Water is the expression of inherent contention—the to and fro movement of the material and spiritual universe. By means of this movement—this perpetual overthrow of equilibriums—all things are organized, inspired, and brought forth. Not only so, but they are also made to continually advance along the onward way; yea, all improvement is accomplished and guaranteed by the reciprocal action, or warlike contention, of opposite forces and immutable powers.

Let me illustrate. Justice is recognized by a perfect balance—a state of exact equilibrium. Place a stick across your finger. There is a point in that stick from which both ends will be precisely alike—each will weigh the same—and, as a consequence, the stick will rest exactly in balance, without the least motion. If the universe were constructed upon that principle, all throbbing hearts and the infinite powers would cease to move; not a heart would beat; not a brain would think, not a tide flow, not a bird sing, not a tree would grow, but inertia and death would be universal. And yet the universe is constructed on JUSTICE. But one end of the stick must weigh more than the other in order to produce motion. Then comes in a governing power to restore the lost balance; by the act of balancing it, the power loads the opposite end, and thus is established the principle of reciprocation. The weight, (by changing from point to point,) produces every description of motion. So the planets revolve about the sun. So also your blood flows from heart to brain, from brain to feet and hands, and back again to its central sources. All this illustrates the spirit of contention. This is what I mean by "the universality of war."

Right is the source of true might. An organ is not the cause of motion. The heart does not make the blood flow; it is rather a regulating and modifying organ—chairman of the movement. Neither do the organs of the brain cause the blood to flow. The brain is not the primal source of its energies. The cerebral organization cannot keep itself in motion. It continually inhales and exhales; always giving off an equivalent to what it may have taken in; always expelling the body of that which has been duly appropriated ; the magnetic and material weights are thus constantly changing from one pole of the cerebral battery to the other. The perpetual change is perpetual motion. This ceaseless motion produces refinement; this refinement insures advancement; and all true advancement is progress. Whatever is refined is expanded ; whatever is expanded occupies a larger sphere than it did a few minutes before; and whatever is refined and expanded is more powerful, because it covers a larger radius in space, and permeates and inspires a larger mass of gross matter.

Now do you suppose that God is a person, confined like a fountain of energy, at the very center of things? Theology taught an astronomer to say that God sent all these orbs that sparkle through the infinitude ; that they were projected, as balls from the cannon's mouth, out of his formative powers. No man or woman, who thinks truly, would ever attribute such works to an Infinite Spirit. An Infinite Spirit must be diffused through infinite space; and is therefore omnipresent in matter, and infinitely and universally powerful. Confinement, to the limits of personality, would limit its presence and power. In the infinite depths of the visible universal whole you will find the beautiful Love-Fountain, and the Fountain of Wisdom, which are to our spirits both "Mother" and "Father"—both Nature and God—sweet, pure, perfect, beautiful—living with celestial and unchangeable harmony through all the life of things.

What most satisfies your best affections? It is that holy experience by which you touch and feel the warm love of Deity. Where can you find that love, if not in the divine life of living things? Can you find it in dead books, or in lifeless sentences? Is it possible for bookmakers, down at the Bible House, to turn out that which will communicate God's love to your mind by actual impartation. Reason tells you that it is not possible. True, a spiritually-inspired sentence may arouse your slumbering thoughts to high action; but if there be an impartation of life to your soul, it is from the life of things—from some hovering angel, or from some beautiful principle of truth that is both within and without. I admit the conviction that beautiful sentences, contained in the Bibles of the world, do, now and then, rouse dormant natures to thought and meditation, and to progress; but I deny that anything within these printed words is the cause of that progress, meditation, and growth; for all life proceeds from the living, breathing, palpitating Father and Mother, who are within all immutable laws and within all impersonal principles. It is the ideal and heavenly presence of their love and wisdom, which awakens and rouses, to a blooming grandeur and holy meditation, the inmost of your deepest intuitions; for, under such influence, you feel as though you had just heard the "voice of God" in the "cool of the day," while you were silently walking to and fro in the garden of thought.

War is the outward method by which laws, principles, and ideas work. (1.) Blood is animal; (2.) brain is thoughtful; (3.) spirit is heavenly. Heavenly wars? Yes. Every man's spirit is a soldier. Brain wars too? Yes. Plenty of illustrations in the world's intellectual and political history. And also blood wars? Certainly, all beneath brain wars on that principle. I said the brain does not circulate the blood; neither does the heart; but that the heart is a regulator, a sort of chairman, and that the brain is conductor or superintendent of the movement. What, then, is the blood? And how is it moved? It is circulated by the laws and perpetually-broken equilibriums of reciprocal powers. The venous blood is negative; the arterial blood positive. Each overbalances the other by turns. How so? By the respirational processes, and also by the magnetic and electric actions, through the breathings of the lungs and skin. All parts of a living body are inhaling and exhaling, every instant of time, like summer flowers that receive golden life and give off the spirit of fragrance. The blood contains the power of its own motion. Human life ceases when the blood is poured out and lost, or when the vitality has been pumped out of the blood by the magnetic powers of the brain, which keeps drawing and pumping in order that its own forces may be renewed and existence guaranteed. A physiologically well-balanced man or woman is one whose blood flows independently of either brain or heart; that is to say, the circulation is from the intrinsic motive-energy of the blood itself.

Blood wars, consequently, are inherent. Who taught the lion and the bear to go out and slay for their food and subsistence? Not a teacher of war have they ever had, save the inherent voice of blood. It is constitutional. "What do you mean by that?" I mean that the animal is acting in accordance with a Divine "idea" (design) expressing itself irrepressibly and unconsciously through the throbbing blood.

Blood wars are *Gehenna*—full of fire and destruction. Hades is the middle world, and the liver is the
dark repository or grave-yard of the debris of the
victims of war in the chemistry of life. In like manner
the whole organic world is a burying-ground or repository, a hepatical-hades, for the victims of progressive
laws, which, in the animal world, as in man, operate
through the life of the blood.

All mankind inherit animal blood. We received it
from our predecessors in the order of organization. No
theology, no science, no philosophy can refute the doctrine of the rudimental origin of human beings. I
speak not of man's spirit, but of his material organization. Love and wisdom, in man and woman, came not
from the lower world. But this organic machinery,
which we name the physical body, and this blood which
flows through its parts, and these elemental forces which
constitute the body and final covering of the spirit, all
these came out of the reservoir of matter and principles
which preceded mankind in the growth of the universe.
Blood wars are described by the burning words of Dante,
who saw, in "The Inferno" of his thought, the wars of
demons, and now and then an "angel of light" flitting
through the darkened sky. Pollock and Milton, and
indeed many other poets, who were gifted with powers
adapted to conceiving and giving embodiment to ideas,
have described wars in the lower world. Poets, unhappily, have located these conflicts to suit the Christians,
in their fabled hell which God is supposed to have
made from the foundations of the world. Poetry and
theology will, in their details and geography, have no
value in the grand analysis which is to come. We

accept only the inward flow of meaning. It is this: Poets have set to words and to music the actual "war" which originates from the combative forces that are accumulated and treasured up in the blood.

Next, we come to consider the conflicts of Brain. These wars are based on differences of organization. There is no spirituality, no moral 'restraint, in brain wars. Intellect does not conciliate. The thinking powers are animated mostly by policies, convictions, ways and means, and expedients. They resolve upon the execution of their purposes. In this respect each man's brain is alike. Hence the origin of brain wars. It is thinking-force against thinking-force. Men cipher out problems through their intellectual organs, and each sets all his forces to work to accomplish results most congenial to his own interests. How many governments have gone to war upon the principle of brain—thinking that it would be best.

All the kings and emperors, all tyrants and potentates, go to war from the dictates of the brain. These are the wars of aggrandizement, wars for more power, wars for the possession of larger territories, wars for the acquisition of greater resources of wealth, wars for the establishment of kingdoms already possessed, wars for the accumulation of wider privileges on sea and land. These brain-wars are planned and premeditated with as much indifference to the claims of humanity as one would cipher out a sum on a slate.

Spirit is not heard from in the jargon of such wars. It is very still—in the depths of the mind; locked up, imbedded, as life sometimes is in the germs of trees. The wars of the spirit—how different! Such

wars never occur except where RIGHT is in jeopardy.
Men of blood and men of brain avail themselves of all
enginery, powers, and forces, that are known to be most
destructive.   But the Spirit, on the other hand, goes to
war from its highest standard; to penetrate the darkness of ignorance and error, and to shine lovingly into
and through the darkness that rejects it; to persevere
in warring its way through, until it reaches the "point
of light" in the world, or in the kindred spirit of a
brother man.   The moment the heart of love is touched
by the penetration of spirit, like the rod that smote the
rock, the waters of truth and affection flow, reconciliation takes place, and the lion and the lamb lie down
together.

A war in the spirit is "a war in heaven"—per-
vading and penetrating, impressing and uplifting, chastening and purifying, harmonizing and rendering
universally happy the discordant forces and conflicting
elements which come up to dwell with Spirit from the
kingdoms of the under world.

The man who fights "the good fight" from his
Spirit, is infinitely more of a power than he who proceeds to battle from the forces of his brain and blood.
Neither man nor animal fights from blood except when
its fires arrive at the point of a Gehennal-conflagration.
The blow is struck somewhat as the ball leaps from the
cannon's mouth—from an inherent, propulsive, explo-
sive energy that cannot be repressed. Blood goes for
the instantaneous destruction of its antagonist. It takes
no thought; therefore it is frequently forgiven in our
courts of Justice. Unpremeditated murder, the destruction of life in the heat (hell) of passion, (*Gehenna*,) is
not as punishable as is murder of the calculating brain.

This form of Justice is intuition coming up through drunken judges ; it is the spirit of truth in man reaching out clumsily, yet really, after justice, love and right.

The effect of the war of the Spirit upon the lower world is marked and lasting. The mythological statement is that Diana, by her long, eternal kiss of love, woke the dead Endymion " to life." Thus these spirit-wars in man's highest powers lift out of the " lowest darkness" the impulses of blood and other imps of self-ishness. As lilies of purest celestial whiteness grow in ponds, and bloom in their loveliness from the depths of corrupt marshes, so from *Hadean* and *Gehennal* regions in mankind—from the regions of the liver, the blood, and the brain, which are fed and filled from the darkness and corruptions of the physical world—out of all these come results which will ultimately bring happiness, and ornament, and beauty, and progress, and that sublime courage which is the hope of the world. The war of the Spirit may be represented and characterized by the picture of Raphael. He has beautifully and powerfully painted St. Margaret standing with her foot on " the great dragon." St. Margaret may be called " the Spirit" conquering the impulses and abolishing the wars of Blood and Brain. The human world is constituted of races somewhat as ethnologists have classified them. Commence at the top and count down, thus: Caucasian, Mongolian, African, Indian and Malayan. These five races may be subdivided, or they may be made more homogeneous and brought much nearer together. They would then literally represent Blood, Brain, Spirit. The Caucasian race (which, according to mythology, came from that beautiful mount from which the name is derived,) may be called the race of Spirit. Their greatest wars will be wars of spirit—the wars of Thought, of Ideas, of Principles—against the darkness of ignorance and error, against the brain and its calculating selfishness, against the blood and its passion-fed fires and gehennal impulses. The true, forthcoming Caucasians will be conquerors; they will be masters of the races of the human world. The Mongolians are not conquerors; the Africans are not; the Indians are not, but are, in fact, passing away.

Now the blood-races are beneath, in *Gehenna;* the brain-races are transitional, in *Hades;* the spirit-race, the Heavenly-family, is to come. Promises of the spirit-race have always dwelt among men. The race of brain will flower out and become spiritual inspiration, seeking after principles and ideas, seeking after God, liberty, fraternity, harmony. Members of the Spirit-race believe that all lower wars will be abolished; that all men will be converted at last to the beautiful ways of good and truth; that the might of the lower world will be directed by the whole world's Right!

The Spirit-republic, unhappily, is not yet born. Its faintest foregleams are just now visible in the transitional republicanism of the land. Present signs presage the erection of that glorious future temple of truth and Brotherhood which will be carpeted with the beautiful designs of the Infinite mind—designs that will be revealed plainly to man's understanding by a full exposure of the world's life to the fires of blood-wars and brain-wars, which will cease only when the harmonial era is fully unfolded.

TRUTHS, MALE AND FEMALE.

"The Truth only needs to be for once spoke out,
And there's such music in her, such strange rhythm,
As makes men's memories her joyous slaves,
And cling around the soul, as the sky clings
Round the mute earth, forever beautiful."

Nature, left to herself, expresses outwardly what is inmost. Her truest and largest expression is two-fold —male and female—a divine revelation from the central golden fountains of the universe. It is a common intuition that the universe is sexual. All human tongues, in one form of speech or another, name and address the different objects in Nature as though they were sexual. Full-grown men, like little boys, when speaking of a steamboat, say—"There *she* comes," or "How beautifully *she* sails!" Of the sun, " *He* shines." Of an iron-bodied and fire-heated locomotive the friendly engineer will very tenderly say, " *She* is the best machine on the road." Throughout the world you will observe the same instinctive, unconscious acknowledgment of this universal truth. Not an intelligent man on the farm or in the garden but what is obliged to recognize these dual principles—male and female—in the swaying vine as in the animal stock, in the fruiting tree as in the blooming flower. Everything that grows, mani-

fests the internal and immutable principles of husband
and wife, or father and mother. Enshrined in the
golden fountains of the spiritual universe, is the central
law which expands throughout infinitude, and expresses
itself through an infinite variety of apparently opposite,
but really united, principles of action, organization, and
distribution.

This subject comes challenging your reverent attention this bright morning. Mankind do not naturally
or intuitively associate and combine " God" and " Nature" as though they were *one* under different forms of
expression. I know that it is possible to reason oneself
into a proposition admitting the total identity and
unity of the two ; so much so, indeed, that the absolute
individuality of each may cease for a time to occupy any
place in one's thoughts. But the moment you cease to
think on the question of the difference between " God"
and "Nature," or when you settle down into your
normal consciousness, then Intuition from its deep
sources declares fully of an eternal difference. Unconsciously, or rather without intellectual consciousness, you will allude to God, or to that mental something
which represents the Divine source, as a *masculine*
Energy, and then, as unconsciously and unthinkingly,
you will speak of "Nature" as a *feminine* Fountain of
love, beauty, and tenderness. It is natural, therefore,
to feel and speak of NATURE as " Mother" and of GOD
as " Father." The human spirit left to itself, unrestrained and unwarped by educational impediments,
instinctively adopts this form of expression.

Here it becomes again necessary to say that I mean
by the word NATURE, something *different* from the phy-

sical constitution of things. The term is often used to
signify merely the phenomenal universe—the objective
world or system of worlds. I have often used the word
in that commonly received sense. When so used, it
should always be written without the capital N—
simply, *nature*, meaning the objective sphere or the
nature of things. When used in an interior spiritual
sense, it should invariably be written with the capital
N not only, but the whole word might appear in capitals, because it assumes a new and far loftier situation
in the spiritual order of thought. Vastly more interior
sentiments and infinitely higher reflections are awakened
and symbolized and expressed by this use of the term.
"Nature," in the interior sense, is the love-center of
all Existences—the mother-heart of which "God" is ·
the father-head or positive principle. NATURE is the
center of which GOD is the surrounding sphere of order
and organization.

NATURE means, therefore, the internal love-source
of all being. The common dictionary signification
makes the word mean the fixed order of things. But,
in the interior, the word will be found to signify and
express the fountain-heart of the life of things. The
physical universe—the objective sphere of matter—is
not NATURE. The following proposition is more truthful and philosophical: The phenomenal universe is a
physical organization, and the spiritual universe is a
spiritual organization ; and the two are expressions of
the male and female principles, which are interior and
invisible, and are not easily perceived nor comprehended
by the external mind of sensuous thinkers. Nature, the
infinite heart, and God, the positive sphere, like soul

and brain married indissolubly, propagate both the physical and spiritual universe, which is interrelated to summer-spheres beyond all comprehension. Objects in the physical worlds, and human beings, including the higher grades of intelligences, are children born from that beautiful, infinite, central marriage of the "Father" and "Mother," the union of the Eternal heart with the Eternal head—the conjunction of Love and Wisdom—the positive and the negative in unchangeable conjugial harmony, giving rise to all that *is*, and to all that will *ever* be. As you behold in your children your propensities and your tendencies, your attributes and habits, your complexions, your hair and face, and the tone of your voice, so in the external workings of the physical universe, you may behold the attributes, the elements, and the primal principles of the Infinite Father and Mother.

When you come to truly investigate the composition of mind, you will find in thoughts that are evolved two varieties of sentiment, or two classes of truths, that are strictly in harmony with the desires of the intellect, which the intellect alone recognizes and harmonizes with as its own legitimate offspring. These purely intellectual truths gain your respect, and sometimes your admiration. And yet they are not warm and loving; they are cold and calm, the keen-eyed children of the reflective and perceptive faculties. They may be mathematically accurate, and geometrically perfect in all their forms and expressions; yet they eliminate only that clear, calm, electric life which the moon gives off to artists, and to the photographers, who too soon discover the absence of another principle by which alone chemical action can occur.

Investigate further into the mind, and you will discover another class of truths which are nearer your affections, which cling like loving children around your heart and sympathies. Do they not belong to more interior parts of the mind? They are sequestered and deeply vailed. They are inexpressible and indefinite. They float and sail like beautiful birds through the mind. They come together, they perch and sing for a moment, then depart for months. Other truths rest within; they dwell in the heart, and are a part of it. We call these always-present truths the tendencies of the mind, or the instincts of the heart, which will express themselves in the various sentiments, actions, and relations of individual life.

There is yet another class of truths which seem to have been born since we were born, that are not necessarily a part of us, that come in and go out in consequence of contact with other minds. These correlative or transmitted truths well up in us during the course of our ordinary development; while those truths which were born with us, which are parts of the spirit itself, cause us to love flowers and music, poetry and beauty, affection and wisdom, Nature and God. They are the principles which should systematize the external action of men—should regulate and govern mankind during all their lives.

Nature gets the start of the judgment, forestalls all discipline, and anticipates the highest experience. Education may greatly modify the inherited impulse and action of temperaments, yet the cure is not radical; for

10

when the temperaments have an opportunity to declare themselves, they will utterly centrifugate all educational restrictions, and will express themselves freely, and that too from their own resources of instincts and tendencies. Such natures are called "incorrigible" by teachers in the different schools. They do not long submit to be ruled and disciplined by the methods of the schoolmen. There are multitudes of both men and women, of girls and boys, who are thus untrainable and unsusceptible; they are not necessarily "wild," but have, from the start of life, adopted their own determined instincts and tendencies, and are unhappy, even miserable, unless they are left undisturbed to live the life of congenial proclivities.

Other natures, perhaps born of the same parents, are plastic and easily molded. Such minds are more conscious of two different classes of truths than are either of the others. They can realize that there are truths which come into the mind from without; and yet other truths which come up from within, as water springs from the earth. Before these truths came you were like sealed fountains, waiting in fullness to flow. Every soul waits for some magic power to break down the embankments between the spirit and its external expression. That awakening power is remembered pleasurably through all your life as the captain of your exodus, when the whole current of life's inner being was turned into the celestial channel of a new experience. How many there are who seem, even to themselves, to be treasurers of great innate powers—waiting for some person, influence, or event, to give them the golden key with which to unlock their never-fully-expressed existence.

These natures are waiting for the approach of those male and female principles. They are waiting for the approach of the masculine truth, or for the coming of this feminine truth, and they are alone until the right truth arrives. The spirit is in its bachelorhood, or in its maidenhood; it is waiting for the bridegroom, or for the bride.

It is the presence of male and female truths in the soul, their nuptial relation, the joining and interrelationship of what before had not met, and which, when joined, will never be sundered. In Solomon's Songs, (so many of them seem unfit for human reading,) if your eyes be deep-sighted enough, you may go beneath the verbiage, and find that by the "maiden" is represented the female-principle in religion—the mother-soul, the wife-nature, the unmarried, a beautiful virgin going forth and seeking her mate. What is Judaism but a marriage of Egyptian philosophy with the religion of the Israelites? The children of Israel were spiritualists in bondage in Egypt. The Egyptians were a people learned in science, in the objective facts and realities of the world—master Masons; were vast and strong and ponderous in their thoughts and in many of their deeds, and thus they displayed the principle of masculinity. The Israelites furnished the female principle, and the marriage of those two made Judaism. There is no other way of accounting for the coming of that offspring. It was born legitimately. Judaism, however, was a masculine element. It was not a fine order of cultured and reverent affection for truth. It was objective,

ceremonial, full of law. It had not its mate. Judaism
was therefore a great, strong, religious giant, holding
fast to Egyptian laws. It was obliged to meet its mate
—the feminine element—before progeny could come ; a
true marriage was necessary before something better,
more adapted to future generations, could be born.
Hence the feminine part of the Grecian element, represented by the Platonic philosophy, had to be blended
with Judaism before the world could receive what is
called Christianity. .

It is the sheerest folly to say that Christianity began
with Jesus. You might as well say that music began
with Mozart, or that the principle of independent conscience began with Luther, as to say that Christianity
began .with a person. Christianity is the legitimate
child of the marriage of the female Greek principle
with the masculine Judaic principle. Coming from such
parents, it inherits traits and truths from both of them,
does it not? You who are acquainted with Christianity
find the characteristics and features of both parents represented in the child, do you not? Do you not see
Platonic philosophy and religion and theology in
Christianity? What is the Gospel of John but a
Platonic epistle? Is it not original Platonism from
first to last? The most beautiful writing in the New
Testament is the beautiful Gospel of John, and that
Gospel is almost a perfect embodiment of the spiritual
teachings of Plato. You read thus: " In the beginning
was the Word, and the Word was with God, and the
Word *was* God." (John I, Verse 13.) And again :
"The Word was made *flesh* and dwelt among us, full
of grace and truth." Platonism, you recollect, teaches

the same doctrine; that *things* are the *forms* of pre-existent *spiritual* patterns or *ideas*. In other language, *things* are the incarnations of archetypal thoughts that were God, or were with God in the spiritual universe. Saint John and Saint Plato both taught that spiritual types or ideals were prepared before creation, waiting for embodiment; and that when the time arrived for expression, or " creation," (as some writers term it,) then expression came. Wherefore we read in the Testament this Platonism: " The Word became flesh and dwelt among men." To this conclusion you arrive: What you find that is superior in theology and ethics in the New Testament, is but an offspring of the marriage of the Grecian female philosophy with the masculine element of Judaism. In the theology and ethics of Christendom, we find representative traits and impressive propensities of its father and mother. In examining Christianity you will discover the distinguishing characteristics of the father and mother, both parents and grandparents; the feminine Greek philosophy and the Judaic masculine element—the latter an offspring of the spiritualism of the Israelites in marriage relation with the masculine science of the Egyptians.

In Christianity, however, we recognize also a masculine element which required new companionship, and went abroad seeking its true bride. It found no companionship in Greece. Plato was not the founder of a masculine philosophy—Socrates was not. But Aristotle, and those of his school, were founders and champions of the masculine in Greek philosophy. Many of them taught and represented perfectly, long before the element went out to seek its companion, the full development of the male principle in the spiritual life of the world.

It was this masculine element, which, going into Rome, formed a marriage relation with the Roman feminine principle; which was exhibited as an internal fondness for whatsoever was at once decidedly beautiful and strictly useful. A union of the Roman principle with the Greek principle, in this intimate relation of marriage, introduced Christianity to all Europe. Without such marriage, Christianity could not have lived through the medieval age and obtained an expression in the Western world. The feminine in Platoism and in Christism, blended with the masculine in Judaism and in Greek philosophy, brought out the latent attributes of the Roman mind. The Roman mind was strictly and perfectly pledged to the development of Use and Power. Utilism, strong political and legal institutions, and energetic devotion to what was deemed the most beautiful and lasting. The Roman did not possess a philosophic mind. His was not an artistic, poetic, or musical mind. Greece alone furnished the feminine principles of which Art, Poetry, and Music are expressions to mankind's five senses. In the Roman mind you find the Greek expressions cropping out, because in the offspring you always behold more or less of the characteristics and ruling propensities of the progenitors. Therefore in Rome you find the Art and Science, some of the Philosophy, a good deal of the Music, a little of the Poetry, and a very large proportion of the Drama, Tragedy and Comedy of ancient Greece, and also of the Arabian and Persian world. Children always receive from their parents, by physiological and psychological inheritance, and the same is true of nations, races, ages, and institutions.

Now when Rome arrived at the climax of her power she was substantially a rich giantess and the supreme head of the earth's law-makers. In the latter respect Rome was masculine. It eventually became necessary for this element to seek a new relation. That new relation was easily found in more Western Europe. The marriage resulted in the large and beautiful family of Literature and Art and Science and Music and Poetry, and resulted also in all the various forms of the State and Church, of Law and Democracy, of Philosophy and Progress, and in the public spirited movements of the present age. The masculine and feminine principles—the whole family of them—seemed to have culminated and gathered for their first and most grand expression in England and in France. The conjugal blending of those opposite principles was the gathering of long-estranged elements into a happy group to dwell for a time together in peace. It was like the gathering of the scattered and discordant tribes of Judea. When they should be gathered together, there was to be great rejoicing, for the foundation of the New Jerusalem would soon be laid. (So says the pleasant dream.) But the New Jerusalem was really nothing but the meeting of those long-wandering male and female principles— the children and grandchildren and the great-grand- children—the aunts and uncles, nieces and nephews, and cousins near and distant—the various feminine and masculine principles past and present which assembled like a Congress in the age of Charlemagne. Then they found their finest and sweetest expression; but how very crude, how very barbarian, how exceedingly far beneath what is to-day seen and known of them!

Grave and slow old England, when many of these principles were gathered in her heart, openly exhibited a masculine development. The blending of the masculine Roman principles with the feminine principles of the age of Charlemagne, gave the purest and clearest development of Science through the mind of Bacon. The German inductive philosophy came also; and this, unlike the English Science, was truly and healthfully feminine.

Anything which engerms and inspires a love of truth in the soul, is feminine. Science, which insists upon facts and accuracy in things, is invariably masculine. The spiritual effect of Bacon's philosophy is masculine, or inductive; but the truly German philosophy is feminine, or deductive. *Phileo* means to *love*, and *sophia* means *wisdom*. Hence the term "Philosophy," literally signifying *the love of wisdom*. Love signifies the seat or heart of the affections; the life-principles and impersonal ideas of the inmost spirit. When the heart, therefore, goes out toward a truth, it is a bride going out to meet the bridegroom. The offspring of the Baconian philosophy are all great healthy boys—that is, strong, vigorous, progressive, irrepressible *Sciences* —the positive methods which that school of philosophy has developed throughout civilization.

What comes next? When a perfect marriage takes place between these outer sciences and a love of truth, the world is soon blest with young saviors. Such is the origin of the Daguerrean and Photographic arts, and of every new invention for human good, each being duly baptized and placed upon record, just as a new babe is added to the family and a new hand is made for industry.

A truth goes out from one mind and obtains a hospitable recognition in another mind: only an intellectual apprehension and entertainment. But there is also such a fact as a *spiritual love of truth.* No mind can develop anything good and beautiful unless he first feels in his deep soul a love for whatsoever is good and beautiful. First, he must have the *feminine* inspiration and aspiration for and toward truth ; and next, the *masculine* intellectual apprehension of the scientific details by which that truth can alone receive its finest and highest expression. Thus, Daguerre went to work with the love of heart, which is the bride of truth, and also with the Baconian philosophy, which is the bridegroom, or form of truth, and the result was the development of a new art. When he received into his mind the masculine apprehension of those exact facts in chemistry concerning the action of light, and when he united with that apprehension the *love* of the good, the true and the beautiful, the next event was a marriage in his being, which in due course of time unfolded that wonderful art·by which the sun is made everybody's artist.

Wherever mankind are, there you will observe this blending of the bridegroom and the bride. In the smallest, least, and most unimportant, as in the grandest, most essential, and magnificent, it is clearly and truly like the marriage of the beautiful maiden with her own beloved mate. It is indorsed by NATURE, our spirit Mother, and by her eternal companion, our spirit Father ; and no union can be more sacred and pro-

10*

ductive of human progress and happiness. The issues of such marriages are legitimate—beautiful offspring called "society," "education," "art," "poetry," "music," science," "philosophy," "religion," and "civilization," and giving "hope" and "courage" and embellishment to the great temple of human "liberty" and "progress"—these are the darling offspring, the legitimate progeny, of the perfect marriages of principles of male and female truths in the human mind.

You know, by your own experience, that you have intellectual conceptions of truths which bear no fruit—truths that are sterile and barren of children. Do you not also think of friends and acquaintances, who apprehend high truths and principles as clearly as you, and yet whose lives and characters have never been improved and beautified by those truths? Their lives and homes have never been modified or softened or sweetened by that which in you has been a perpetual source of great strength and spiritual fertility. The secret is: The unchanged character has only had in his mind the masculine element of the truth—merely an intellectual apprehension of the truth, and of course it does not bear fruitful results in him. Perhaps in your own nature you have a beautiful and holy truth that has not improved and strengthened you. Perhaps you do not feel invigorated by your truth for any great work, either in private or public life. You may have a clear, sweet, reverent, religious devotion to some particular beautiful truth, which has been alternately nestling and slumbering in your bosom for years, but it has never imparted to you a ray of strength—never given life and light enough to enable you to carry out a millionth part of its dictation and positive requirements. What can be the cause and the reason? Because, perhaps, instead of a male, you may have a feminine truth, which may never have met with its masculine counterpart or principle. If there be no marriage there can be no parentage or results. Suppose now that you should hear some preacher, politician, orator, or some man or woman, who said "just the *right* thing"—just what you had been "longing" to have said, but knew not before exactly what it was you so longingly wanted, and which you were never able to give a tangible expression. It may be but a single word in the whole discourse, but that "word" struck your pent up and barren soul as Moses' rod struck the rock, and forthwith the deep fountains of your interior life are unsealed, and they send forth their golden spray into the great world about you. You are spiritually, morally strong. You go out into the world and you return to your family with a new life and a new comprehension. The explanation is, that the opposite element has entered your spirit. The bridegroom has sought and found his bride, or the reverse has transpired, and marriage was perfect and immediate. You rise strengthened, built up anew, and are, as it were, "born again;" the light of new skies is showered upon you, and your awakened mind is all starry and begemmed with new and beautiful conceptions of the Divine. Persons susceptible to high religious influences, know the reality of these experiences. You may read the best books, you may attend the highest order of literary lectures, you may go to the most living churches for years; but unless the "right thing is said," and said in "the right way" to your inmost, you will still be waiting and longing. The bride will be waiting for her mate, or the masculine for his feminine companion, within the temple of life.

I used to think, uncharitably and unphilosophically, that men were very blameworthy for all deviations from what is deemed just and right. I have not wholly arrived at that conscienceless and comfortable point where " whatever is, is right;" but I do most clearly see that men are not as culpable as they are supposed to be by the religious creeds of the world. Men and women wait for the advent of the master—the masculine and the feminine principles—the interior union of love and wisdom in the spirit.

See, for example, how in these days America waits for champions to lead her armies to battle. Men had military principles and tactics taught to them at West Point; the masculine science of planning and fighting great battles. They knew, in theory, how to march and countermarch, to plot and counterplot; they understood commanding, and the management of the sword and musket. They understood also, by theory and illustration, all the pharaphernalia of an army in its march to the field of battle. But all this learning was the masculine element; it amounted to nothing for the world's progress. The West Point Cadets, when in the city of New York, appeared like the other people, except in the matter of their uniform. But the day and the hour arrived for some of these men to receive the feminine principle. What was it? It was the *love* of an unchangeable principle; the love of Liberty for all the inhabitants of this continent. When this *love* entered into the soul of these men a marriage was celebrated through all their faculties, and instead of being mere uniformed officers, they rose to manhood, and the faithful among them equaled the might of a thousand men. Some of the military leaders wait for opportunities. They will yet show you grand and valorous generalship; they hesitate, waiting for the expression of the interior marriage that has not yet occurred. Others again go into the field mechanically; are nothing but military men, with no love for any ennobling principle, having never felt the marriage of the principles of Liberty and Justice with the principles of military science.

Now take spiritual truths. In our motto you read, "Fair truth! for thee alone we seek," &c. Does that sound as though you were addressing a masculine principle? A great many men may think they ought to be so addressed, but you know that it would be an inappropriate use of language. "Fair truth!" Did the poet not see truth to be a female—the woman principle? William Cullen Bryant, in his well-known lines, says:

"Truth crushed to earth will rise again ;
The eternal years of God are *hers*."

After recognizing thus the *feminine* of truth, he adds:

"While Error, wounded, writhes in pain,
And dies amid *his* worshipers."

What man is there that will not shrink from the poet's testimony that error is masculine? We men, however, can read Genesis for consolation. We find there that *woman* was the *cause* of the world's universal damnation. *She* began the quarrel! But, on the other hand, we are compelled to acknowledge that the Prince of Darkness was *masculine*. We have not heard that the Christian's devil was a woman. The great sphere of action, energy, force, is masculine; and force, in its desperation and ambition to gain its point, falls, as did the Prince of Darkness, from these mountain-hights of joys delectable down to the dreary depths of hopeless perdition. Such operations and overthrows occur throughout the world, in all history, and in much of private experience.

The woman element, on the contrary, visits all these various recesses of darkness. Lovingly she goes to every part of the inhabitable globe as a missionary. Woman-life is a divine power; it is not force, which is masculine. Woman, in essence, is love; she is not intellect. Rarely does the principle of ambition gain highest expression in the woman mind. Force and ambition are masculine. If a woman's ambition is great, and if her love of admiration is also great, her conduct will correspond with such temporarily predominating masculine elements. But when the feminine principle in her spirit rouses, then she is affection, full of gentle dependence and of healing sympathy; she is the interblending and transforming power of love, endowed richly with the missionary spirit. All women, when in their freedom, are missionaries in their homes and in all hearts. No mother can live without the inspiration of unselfish love for children. She goes as a missionary every time she visits her babe in the cradle; thus, too, she visits the sick one in the chamber of sorrow and suffering. Man goes to lift up the body of the little one; to change its position in the bed; to *do* something for the suffering. A woman goes, not only to *do*, but also to *rescue* and *save* and *heal.* The mother-nature comes to teach, to bind up the broken-hearted, and to pour over us all the streams of unselfish affection. The father-nature, the masculine element, holds up the physical relations, keeps the positive principles in action, and does the outward work of life. But the action of the mother-principle in the human mind is identical with the action of the masculine principle. For if a soul loves a spiritual truth, it will give that soul, whether man or woman, warmth and zeal and enthusiastic fertility. If love does not exist in the spirit by the side of an intellectual apprehension of the truth, there is no growth, no improvement. But let the love of truth be blended with the intellect's admiration for and apprehension of it, and there very soon occurs "a new birth." The person henceforth not only *is,* but begins to *be,* and to *do* and to live from that divinely fertile center. Deeds, righteous and wholesome, are the darling progeny. Instead of bringing over-action and fatigue, such offspring bathe the spirit with rest and happiness.

A recent writer on the "Poetry, History, and Wisdom of Words," unintentionally gives the substance of our philosophy in his solution of the origin of languages :

"The causes of that marvelous identity we call the English language, lie deep in the manifold influences [the conjugal relationships of the previously existing male and female principles] that have made the English Nation. The history of a language is measurable only in the terms of all the factors that have shaped a people's life. A nation's history is the result of the double action [*i. e.,* the sexual meeting and marrying] of internal impulses and external events ; and language expresses the infusions from all these—subtilely absorbing the ethnology of a nation, its geography, government, traditions, culture, faith.

"The heart of our language is Anglo-Saxon. This is the spine on which the structure of our speech is hung. And yet had the Saxon been left to itself, it never could have grown into the English tongue. It needed a new element. This it found in the Norman French introduced with that great political and social revolution, the Norman conquest, which was, no doubt, precisely the best thing that could have happened. And here we have to mention the deep debt we owe to that illustrious nation, Italy—which for so many centuries led the van of European civilization—in operating the renaissance of Greek and Latin language and thought. The breath of antique genius passed over the English mind like the air of spring, bursting and blossoming in luxuriant growths of thought and speech. Of those three grand factors --Saxon, French, and Classical—is our language made up. It is the mutual influence and action of these that form the warp and woof of our English speech. Not but that other elements are, in greater or smaller proportions, present, and weave their threads into the divine web; but these are the main sources whence our language has enriched itself.

"Of course the English language must take on new powers in America. And here we are favored by the genius of this grand and noble language, which, more than all others, lends itself, plastic and willing, to the molding power of new *formative* influences. [What new "formative" influences can there be but such as are rendered fertile and *reproductive* through the *meeting* and marriage of male and female principles?] The future expansions of the English Language in America are already marked in the great lines of development this idiom shows. It is for us freely to follow the divine indications. The immense diversity of race, temperament, character—the copious streams of humanity constantly flowing hither—must reappear in free, rich growths of speech. Over the transformations of a language the genius of a nation unconsciously presides— the issues of words represent issues in the national thought. And in the vernal seasons of a nation's life the formative energy puts forth verbal growths, opulent as flowers in spring."

Science, I repeat, is masculine; philosophy is feminine. Poetry, when genuine, is instinctive—feminine. It is the blending of outward and inward truths at the heart of the spirit. Poetry is spiritual; Music is spiritual; therefore both Poetry and Music are feminine. But the science of music, as of poetical composition, is mechanical, or masculine; the great, strong, beautiful Apollo is a representative character in old mythology. Pandora's box was the source of innumerable evils. That is also mythology. But for woman's cause it should be remembered that it was not Pandora's heart, but her *box*, in which she was supposed to have accumulated evils and pestilences and disorders from masculine sources.

Perhaps there is more truth than mythology in the story. Look at the feminine principles in your mind. Unless they be married with something which is *masculine*—full of energy and full of action—they will often be sources of annoyance, pain, distress, and disaster to those about you. The most beautiful and affectionate principles in the human spirit, when not properly balanced with their mates and counterparts, will assault and break down the most beautiful relations subsisting in the social sphere between men and women, between women and women, and between men and men. We all need more balance. We are frequently imperfect. All men should have the power to modify and contain as well as the power to impart and express.

Now the deductive principles, the method of the German, come fom the heart of thought. This method is always feminine; reasoning from the center, outwardly. Intuition is thus revealed; it is the spirit of Nature; the life of our Mother, going from her central fountains toward the surface. Intuition always starts from the germinal fountains of the immortal spirit; it throws its showers of golden spray worldward—sometimes in music, sometimes in poetry, sometimes in affectionate speech, sometimes in terse affirmations of great truths. Whatever way it expresses itself, it is still truly feminine. Truth is incessantly busy gathering to itself the means and objects of gratification. Science furnishes the parliamentary forms by which men may deal with each other in their relations to the truth.

Women are not great inventors; neither are the womanly elements in any mind. The uncompanionated *love* of principles in a man's mind never invented anything. The love of truth is a source of inspiration. It is the intellectual sight and comprehension of truth, calm and cool, without enthusiasm, full of steady-eyed science, with an abiding sense that something like philosophy is at the bottom—from such a mind, whether male or female, inventions will come. The sources and causes of inventions are the same in individual minds of either sex. Men are quicker in the sphere of physical results. No womanly element, however, in either man or woman, can invent. Hence many men, like women, " die without issue." The woman element will inspire, give life, love, affection, unchangeable devotion; but the masculine element gives form, proportion, manifestation, embodiment. The woman-nature imparts inspiration to the intellectual faculties. The man-principles of mind think; they plan; they move; they bring in the details of heartless science; they open the way through swamps and mountains; they dig the channels and prepare for the inflowing of the golden rivers of Paradise. The conjugal blending of male and female truths in the mind, is happiness; the healthy, beloved, beautiful off-spring of these married truths are deeds of use and beauty, of philanthropy, fraternity, and progression.

How can you put the doctrine of this lecture into daily practice? I answer, easily. First find out which is the predominating sex in the state of your mind—whether there be more *love* of principles than an intellectual comprehension of them; or, on the other hand, analyze yourself to find whether you have not more *comprehension* of principles than *love* in your deep affections for them. Whichever way you find yourself unbalanced, proceed at once to adjust your life to the married law. For example, in America we find the sentiment of liberty—*i. e.*, the *love* of the principle—fifty years in advance of the *comprehension* of the requirements of the principle. Few persons, therefore, are competent to define what Liberty *is*. In this respect the great mass of the world is dumb. But as to the sentiment—the feminine love of liberty—they are over-glad to sing it and have it sung, and are willing to contribute their property, their lives and sacred honor to defend and establish it. And yet the intellectual conception of the requirements of the Idea has scarcely entered the heart of any American. Because the masculine side of the principle is not yet married to the soul's love of it.

How can you be large, unsectarian, broad and philanthropic until you have the conception of justice, as well as a profound love of it, so that you will *give* as much freedom as you will take? You will not be large-souled enough to open the doors of freedom to all human beings, until you see, and *love* to see, that the divine idea of Liberty positively calls upon you to be just and true to its requirements, " at whatever cost."

And thus, also, with all the other truths. Take, for instance, the principle of marriage between the sexes. Love, unless regulated by wisdom, leads to discordant expressions. The masculine element, the intellect, recognizes adaptations--the science of physiological and temperamental relations between men and women—and yet no relation known as marriage could exist without love. The protecting sphere of wisdom should be thrown around the conjugal love. That is what is meant by having truth dwelling *with* and *in* you, and your dwelling *with* and *in* the truth. How can you be " at home" unless you have a true conception of what it is to be a man—a woman—bound together in true marriage? Unless these conceptions and these loves dwell with you every day, giving you largeness of thought and warmth of soul, you will be restless and discordant with all about you. People who have none of these loves and conceptions in their homes, live like animals—full of strife, sensuality, profanity, evil-speaking, and destructiveness.

The inmates of these fashionable city homes repel the doctrines of "woman's rights," no matter how plausibly or reasonably presented, saying that they do not want more rights than they now enjoy. They detest such controversies. Why? Because they have not yet so much as the *love* of human rights born in them, much less the far-reaching idea, the intellectual conception and comprehension. A masculine truth in the mind is simply admired. It does not warm your affections; it is not necessary to your present happiness. You may admire your own truth; you may think it is superlatively good; the best thing; and yet you know it is only a part of your intellect. If it be a truth which you *love* also, it will always cause you to glow with gladness and work with joy.

The conclusion of all is, that all truths in the mind need to be truly married. There can be no balance of character on any other basis. Any guardian angel, any passage of poetry, any strain of music, any scene in Nature, that will blend any two truths together and make them *one* in your spirit, is the high-priest of life to you. From that hour you will go happily forward in your proper sphere of labor, doing good, and exhibiting the pleasant ways of wisdom and righteousness to your fellow-men. The marriage of all principles in the mind will be known as a revelation to that mind of " the unity of truth."

FALSE AND TRUE EDUCATION.

"A voice within us speaks the startling word,
'Man, thou shalt never die!'"

Education means eduction—drawing out from within—extracting that which is deposited. It is the work of quickening and bringing into active life dormant genius. True education is a process of incubation—the internal is roused and evoked to a natural revelation.

Long ago Dr. Channing asserted that culture was the guardian angel of civilization, and the Unitarian organization has ever since been largely pervaded by the beautiful spirit of his teachings, through which a refining influence has gone out upon the whole world. Universalists have proved useful educators in doing battle against the dismal error of eternal punishment. Orthodoxy has never recovered from the effects of their blows.

We now stand upon the threshold of a new dispensation—the most golden that ever rolled in from the sea of the centuries. We recognize the truth that the human mind is a soil, and that Education is a cultivation of that soil. Education brings out that which is hidden, straightens the crooked, embellishes the unsightly, and equalizes the vigor and action of the faculties.

Mark how educational processes inaugurate a new dispensation in the garden, on the prairie, in the Central Park! See how the uninviting waste has been converted into beautifully-carpeted lawns and walks, the dirty frog-ponds and cess-pools cleansed and dimpled all over with Heaven's smiles—because they have been educated. Accidents have been built up into beautiful caves, and craggy cliffs subdued and embellished. How we admire the beauty, purity, and attractiveness of what before was filthy and repulsive! Such is education in the physical world. And see how the inhabitants of this planet are growing out of their sectarian bonds by cultivating a higher knowledge of rocks, and shrubs, and trees. All days are sacred in the universal temple. It is open, like the atmosphere, every day of the week. How beautiful and chastening to dwell with Nature.

Education is the same when applied to the human mind. Look at the boy not truly educated, and you see what the Central Park was before it felt the magic hand of artists. Imagine what the Central Park will be one hundred years hence, and you will obtain a hint of what true education is destined to accomplish for the human mind.

By education is not meant a knowledge of Latin and Greek, nor familiarity with the routine of popular fashionable accomplishments. The truly educated are those who have come out from Within, who have grown up from the mental quadruped state to the full-blown development of the immortal faculties and attributes.

Imitation is not the basis of true Education. Many are but learned pigs! Some talented men are but trained animals. They walk and talk after the manner of their masters. Medical colleges and theological seminaries inculcate simply the lesson of consulting and following rigidly in the footsteps of certain authorities. Their students are taught to diagnosticate and minister to diseases, and to pound and expound the Scriptures, in strict accordance with an established rule. Their ministrations are simply a routine, a trained performance. Depart from the prescribed methods, and a withdrawal of the good opinion of teachers and patrons is sure to follow. And the excellence and importance of these established codes are profoundly felt by fathers, who give their money, and by mothers, who offer evening prayers that their sons may become ministers. Take, for example, a family of boys. The strongest and most vigorous goes out upon the soil, or he wields the energy of his existence in the machine-shop. Another, with sympathetic nature, chooses the practice of medicine; another the law; while the last, who is fond of graveyards and poetry, and is likely to have the dyspepsia, and is not over-fond of manual labor, studies for the ministry. Like a young ghost he goes to the theological school, and in due course of study comes out a fashionable goblin of old orthodoxy. But no such person is truly educated.

True education, instead of cramping and incarcerating, liberates the mind. It has no programme beyond the discipline whose object is freedom—emancipation from the Teacher, and perhaps also, from the doctrines taught. Spiritualists, like all who labor for the diffusion of this true type of education, are incubators and social agitators. How powerfully have the recent efforts of such educators moved the thinking world!

Teachers often become consolidated, established, and finally infidel to the progressive principles which underlie true education. Time was when one Quaker could shake the country for ten miles in every direction. Now it takes a section of country twenty miles every way to shake one Quaker! Whitefield and Wesley each brought a new magnetic light and a higher spiritual enthusiasm. They spread democratic religious convictions, and broke down the church barriers as a locomotive would demolish a temple of glass. Methodism was a great Protestant movement. It was a religious democratic innovation. We welcome the general liberating influence of the lessons they taught. Now, however, the Methodist Episcopal Church has become fashionable, proud, respectable, consolidated, immovable, and a stumbling-block.

True education visits man somewhat as the true horticulturist goes to plants, the pomologist to trees, the agriculturist to the field, the astronomer to the heavens, the musician to harmony, and as all true minds labor in the departments of science and art. Such influences are exerted not to embarrass and imprison, but to open, to extract, to call out, to unfold and perfect from properties and essences that exist within.

Pythagoras listened, as he passed a blacksmith's shop, and heard different musical sounds from the blows of different sized hammers upon the anvil. By those sounds he was educated. He went to his room, suspended four hammers of different weight and form, and striking them, elicited different notes, and so began his education in the science of music. Aristotle worked differently. To him the different sounds were different

11

facts, to be used to put his pupils in bondage. His lessons were heavily freighted with the despotic and absolute. All who differed from his propositions were
pronounced to be in error. Those who went out from
his school were simply his disciples. They lived and
died as such. The students of Pythagoras, on the other
hand, went out feeling that philosophic truths, and not
the teacher of them, were of eternal importance. But
they were not strong to withstand the influences and
temptations of the times, and they fell from power. So
will fall all Spiritualists who commit themselves too
largely to popular influences and aristocratical institutions. Let all reformers learn by the example of the
disciples of Pythagoras, to avoid every attempt to
accomplish great social and political changes by means
of popular institutions. The lesson is, that new social,
religious, governmental, and educational developments require new means and new men. Old forms
and institutions subserve the ends for which they were
established. Such organizations usually die when their
purposes are fulfilled and their objects attained.

Nutrition, not education, is the first natural want
of the little child. The first things that interest the
babe are its fingers, its toes, and its stomach. These
define the conscious needs and furnish the amusements
of the opening mind. In these it finds delight, wonder,
and satisfaction. It soon, however, discovers that fingers, toes, and stomach, have limits. New sources of
diversion are sought. New toys must be brought in.
The desire for nutrition being quickly gratified, other
and higher wants are unfolded; and so on and on,
and in and in, until you begin to hear from the spirit.

The body's dispensation slowly passes, and almost imperceptibly the spirit begins to unfold its nature and needs. The young spirit takes the shape of its physical home. Impressions are thus made upon the young mind that cannot easily be eradicated. Still more important is it to know that the child will, ever and anon, manifest traits and characteristics in accordance with what acted upon it before birth.

Young Safford, the remarkable mathematical genius, received his powers from his mother, who, before his birth, became almost infatuated by her love of figures. Another mother was so circumstanced with a penurious, niggardly, and oppressive husband, that she was compelled to steal her pin-money from her legal master, habitually resorting to evasions and deceits to conceal her practices. Petty lying and theft became a settled habit with her, and as a result, her next-born child was as great a prodigy in lying and stealing as young Safford was in mathematics. The ante-natal law in both cases is precisely the same.

According to this ante-natal psychologic law, some persons are born prodigies in music and others in murder. This is the law of ante-natal true education or mis-education. Spiritualists do not fear to speak in public on this subject—to mothers and to youth in each other's presence. Thus Reformers are out-growing the restraints of vulgar gentility or genteel vulgarity, and do not hesitate to proclaim and redeem truths that shall make mankind truly glorious, beautiful, and righteous in all things. Spiritualists, more than any other class, have dared to investigate education back of birth, back of the marriage relation.

Science and Philosophy truly educate and liberate. They open up a broad field, and lead the mind far out into the spheres of infinitude. They bring facts, principles, and laws, to the understanding. Music and Art also tend to liberate. Not always are artists and musicians truly liberated, because of the false constraints and circumstances of social life which hamper them; but the influences they involuntarily exert, through the instrumentality of their works, are emancipatory and exalting to all human kind.

But for one moment look at American theology! That assumes to *settle* all doubtful questions. Ecclesiasticism is the great Apollyon under the shadow of whose wings are all the educational institutions of the country. Children and young men usually come out of them very sickly—if possible, more sickly in mind than in body. The established system of Education under the wings of the Church is a system of *monotony.* All must appear, think, and act alike. Members and supporters must not differ. No vital controversy is permitted. By this system Science is regarded as dangerous, and Philosophy as the handmaid of the devil. Art and Music are good, and the Church approves and appropriates them. Poetry, too, it needs and uses. But touch upon philosophic truths that tend to liberate, to break up authority, and knock the bottom out of perdition— destroy the devil, extinguish the fires of hell—and at once the Church says: "You go too far;" and forthwith the occupants of thirty thousand pulpits unitedly oppose and strenuously resist your efforts, and they zealously pray for the Almighty to restrain such infidel tendencies.

Education, as well as the State, should be divorced from the Church.

The human mind contains within itself all the elements for the development of a perfect character. The child is an ovarium. The inmost mental germs ask to be quickened, brought out; for then harmony and balance of the faculties will result. It is well to teach Science, but we should be cautious and not overload one side of the mind. The world longs for balanced and industrious minds.

Parents should not be obeyed because they are parents, but rather, because they are worthy of obedience. No wonder that some children set up for themselves; it is because they have no real parents. Parentage means more than physiology. The temple of Childhood is built without the sound of a hammer, and obedience (in the true family relation,) is as natural as the revolution of the planets. The sun does not compel obedience, but is simply in harmony with the immutable laws by which obedience among lesser bodies is natural and inevitable.

The Church teaches benevolence and charity for the reason that Christ was charitable and benevolent, which is no reason at all. Yet I accept the record, and I there read that Jesus, when a child, went with his parents to Jerusalem, and after the feast of the Passover he remained in conversation with the doctors. His parents returned for him, and his reply to their questions and invitation to accompany them home, was: "I am about my Father's business." Here is an example of disobedience to physiological parents. He felt that he had a spiritual Father, and hesitated not, under the

pressure of the higher obligations, to transcend the prerogatives of his physiological parents.

The record informs us that Mary " laid the words
to her heart." Let all mothers do likewise. If your
child disobeys, lay the lesson to your heart, and learn
which was in fault. Who knows but a child is " about
his Father's business" when he seeks the fresh wholesome air, in defiance of the parental command to stay
pent up in the house? His spiritual Father tells him
that he needs air, exercise, and sunshine; if denied an
opportunity by the physiological parent, he steals away
out of the house, and thus learns burglary and deceit.
Apply the lesson and introduce a new law—the
God-code—in your families. Woe be to the fashionable
code, conflicting with the divine, for thus come discord
and evil!

In the same record we read that spirits were
preached to in prison; shut out from the light of
heaven. Those who were free, as the truth alone makes
free, went to them who were in darkness and proclaimed
glad tidings of great joy. This morning it seems necessary to preach to minds in like condition.

The constant reproduction of human experience—
which is owing to the spiral progress of the race, causes
many to disbelieve in human improvement. It is true
that there are a few lost arts; a few fragments of
human discovery have been jostled out. Still, when we
examine the national tumults of the past, the wonder is
not that we have lost a few arts, but that we have saved
so many discoveries from oblivion. Some arts have
been lost because of the excess of business consequent
upon the immense accumulations of higher arts and

sciences. The universal currental drift—the unbroken tide of material and spiritual progress of the centuries—has gathered up and floated onward the fruits of all nations and the inventions of all peoples. In our physical garments, in our furniture and adornments, in our arts, sciences, mechanics, &c., are seen the wealth, experience, discoveries and industries of Egypt, Europe, and Asia.

Holding complete and perpetual communion with the supernal world, is regarded as one of the " lost arts." Yet justly regarded, the experiences of peculiarly qualified persons, here and there in the past, give golden promise to the individuals of all nations, that, in the full-orbed future, every truly unfolded man, woman, and child, shall have a distinct consciousness of an environing spiritual sphere. This fine art of holding communion with the Superior Life is not "lost," but is demonstrably reaffirmed in modern experiences. Time never was when man, as to his internal nature and career, appeared in such regal splendor. Mankind are just learning of man.

Men's minds are imprisoned by whatsoever is false, evil, erroneous, authoritative, and respectable. We are here on earth expressly to grow. The gospel we announce is not essentially different from the spiritual past, which commenced in Egyptian darkness. We do not ignore this past, though we are Protestants on a boundless scale. We would speak to all who live in mental prisons, for so the teachers of another world frequently speak to us.

The prejudiced people of the churches are " in prison." Their very beautiful compartments are numbered as are the cells of criminals. The prison-keepers (the clergy) would fear to have me speak to their people, lest our spiritual truths might make their prisoners too free! Not a-pulpit minister in this city would exchange with me, through *fear* that the lessons of mental freedom we teach might overthrow authority and liberate imprisoned congregations.

Now, think of the wealth and beauty of the immortal human spirit! Artists and poets almost exhaust their powers in portraying the beauty and glory of outward creation. But this great natural universe, in all its sublimity, is nothing when compared with the essential properties and immortal capacities of man's spirit. A man who can conceive of an eternal Truth, gives evidence that he, like the truth, is eternal. His career is coextensive with his truth.

A man who conceives of Beauty demonstrates that he possesses it within himself, and that he is destined to become that which he conceives. The power to conceive of an immortal spirit, stript of perishable flesh, deprived of its material avoirdupois, guarantees to the conceiving spirit a future and immortal existence. All Truth, all Beauty, all Philosophy, and all Science, that crop out from man's mental tree, are prophecies that mankind are to *be* what they thus have the power to apprehend or conceive. In the depths of the past, spiritual men dreamed of a great political and social Republic. Americans have come exceedingly near realizing that dream. Plato's *Atlantis* is more than realized in America. The wonders of Arabian Nights' Entertainments, however surprising, do not begin to portray the real scientific developments of the nineteenth century. Man's mind is superior to Art, Science, Philosophy, and Theology. All these have come *through* him in the course of the centuries.

We have, I repeat, no hostility to whatever in the past is good, true, beautiful, or great. The good of the olden time is living still. But those who are shut up in prisons by the foolish education of the past do not dare to open themselves to the education of the present. To bring such out of religious darkness we are first to teach that all men are yet in slavish bondage to their various habits, passions, and popular opinions.

We live in the midst of a great city. People are thrown into "prison" by the police of custom. Our children are educated to resemble each other in dress, in public movements and private deportment. Children must not differ from the neighbors' children; ladies' bonnets are all of one absurd pattern. " Better be out of the world than out of fashion."

Any principle of Truth that will emancipate you is a Moses or Jesus to you ; no matter whether it comes to you in the form of a book, a tract, a piece of music, or a fragment of a poem. Any thing—person, influence, or principle—that lifts you out of your mental prison and emancipates you, is worthy of your truest devotion until another and a newer teacher comes in answer to your newer necessities.

It was remarked by an intelligent lady in my hearing that she had taken into serious consideration which should take the precedence, Reason or Rags. After due deliberation, with prayer superadded, she concluded that Rags had it, and Reason, with its protests, was forced to allow the trial to go by default; she wears

11*

dresses as long and as graceful as others, and yields her judgment and experience to the tyrannical bondage of a contemptible Fashion. Not only do women need emancipation, but men also—for they are in prison to Custom. The leaders of Fashion cannot take a step forward without the approval of fathers, husbands, and brothers. It is almost in vain for women to seek to emancipate themselves from this despotic rule without the aid and support of their associates and masculine acquaintances. Thus men imprison women, and women turn the keys of Custom on the young members of the household. Prison is built upon prison, but the Spiritual Reformer should work to give freedom to the captives.

Many intelligent persons are in prison to "the fear of death." Modern light comes as a savior to the dungeon-door to all in this gloomy prison. It comes, also, to teach the lesson of charity for those who entertain conflicting opinions. The Christian and Jew are to be regarded as equally honest. If you have not equal charity for both, you are in the prison of prejudice. Accept the idea of human progress, and you rise out of the " slough of despond," and forthwith begin to enjoy the glorious liberty of the Sons of God.

Some Spiritualists have been inclined to move off from the world, like Shakers, and combine themselves for the establishment of industrial and economical communities. They will not be successful, because they do not entertain sectional opinions, but believe in the private efficacy of universal principles, and repudiate individual authority. For this reason practical Spiritualists will remain in the world. They will wield a wide influence directly on the institutions of society. They have the true idea that the way to reform society is not to remove from it, but to make it what it should be from its centers. The theory and practice of isolation are to be overthrown by individual growth from within.

The spiritual principle recognizes germs of immortal excellence in the lowest, meanest, and most depraved. Every man on earth is your compeer. The recognition of this fraternal truth not only gives dignity to your character, but leads your Brother to lay aside all narrow prejudices and passions toward you and others. No man or woman, educated to realize all the noble capacities of the human spirit, can consent to pass a life unworthy of innate powers and endowments. When every man comes before you as a compeer, in his innermost, you will not be unfaithful to the spirit of universal love. Popular religion does not fraternally recognize any who differ from a prescribed standard. How different the influence of the doctrine that all human beings are to meet in the Summer-Land!

Strive by will-power and inward growth to live less in bondage to circumstances. No matter what or who may be your prison-keeper, put him or it under your feet. Accept the higher convictions, and you will experience a beautiful interior resurrection. Then you will also become a minister of love and wisdom to those about you! Internal growth is the only real growth. Start from the *center*, grow from *within*, and expand fraternally and lovingly day by day.

Truths cannot be engrafted. You cannot argue a belief in immortality into the skeptic's mind. Some change may gradually or suddenly come over him—an accident, an impulse might awaken and quicken his interior consciousness—and he may rise into fellowship with principles and " feel his immortality," without an argument. A man who can be educated to a belief in immortality, can be also educated out of it. The understanding takes its bias from outward circumstances and education.

Soon as you see that malformations of character come from internal and external conditions, you rise up into a new and more charitable estimate of mankind. You enter the temple of Brotherhood. As you grow from within, so are you liberated. You may not be able to escape physically from the prison of your circumstances, but you can with these truths rise from within, and thus grow as naturally as a tree blossoms. One such emancipated individual is a Redeemer to the world. When all are thus emancipated, all will be redeemed. When all are redemed from ignorance, the whole world will live in accord with Deity.

THE EQUALITIES AND INEQUALITIES OF HUMAN NATURE.

> "Why, when all is bright and happy, should a gloom
> Be spread around us ? Oh, blind and thoughtless soul!
> 'Tis *the same* POWER that reigns, and *the same* LOVE
> Is traced alike, in sunshine and in shade."

This morning I feel impressed with this subject: The application of the law of Love—*i. e.*, the God-code—to the equalities and the inequalities of human nature.

Since the advent of the harmonial dispensation, thousands of minds have become familiar with the idea that God is essentially present in the compounds of the physical world, as well as in the finest and most sublimated substances in the spiritual realm. This idea does not affirm that there is as much of Infinite love-essence in the organism of a bird as there is in the constitution of a globe ; but so far as the *life* of the bird is concerned, it is just as truly and essentially God as is the life of the globe. Drops contain the properties and principles of their fountain. The heart is the companion of the brain ; the lungs co-operate fraternally with the heart ; the stomach receives, digests, works, and imparts for the whole body. It should be remembered, however, that the brain receives from the heart just what the lungs are empowered to communicate to it; that the lungs receive just what the stomach is permitted to afford; and that the stomach does its best (I suppose you think that is bad enough) with the unsuitable material which you thoughtlessly cram into it, often when the body does not call for anything. The clock says "Dinner is ready," and the bell rings, and you eat, whether hungry or not. Many of you know that you eat "to the damnation of your body;" meaning the destruction of your physiological harmony, which is about as much damnation as most people can bear. And yet a man may continue to damn himself all the way across this terrestrial life, but must stop when he sees the Summer-Land. Public opinion there, and the divine codes of government as exemplified there, array and combine themselves against him. And yet man's power to think and to act remains. He may double and treble and quadruple the intensity of his troubles. He may become infatuated with the idea that, through voluntary discords and consequent sufferings, he is working out God's secret design. He is, however, altogether and unhappily mistaken; and yet there is another side to this conviction, as I shall partly show in this morning's discourse.

The stomach, you will recollect, does its best with the materials furnished and consigned to it. Give rose leaves, however beautiful, to the silk-worm, and do you suppose it would spin you any silk? Not a fiber could it centrifugate. It must have its own food—the multicaulis; although it may feed on other leaves besides those of the mulberry. Give the noiseless worm its appropriate aliment, and beautifully it will wind off for human use the fibers of its silken vitality. Such is the God-code outside of man.

Now let us apply this law to ourselves. Suppose we feed the human body with inappropriate aliment. Under such management can the lungs receive from the stomach what the heart most needs? Do you suppose that the heart, which depends on the lungs for its blood, can bestow upon the brain those blessings which are its just rewards and requirements? The brain is the source of which the heart is but the regulating center—the point of government and administration through which all the blood flows—the viaduct, the governing organ; and the lungs are the channel of the river which flows into and feeds the heart; and the stomach is the originator of the stream that flows into and feeds the lungs; and the substances you eat and the fluids you drink are the sources out of which the streams, the rivers, the lakes, the seas, and the oceans of motion, life, sensation, and intelligence, are made.

By too well-remembered experience you know that " the troubled sea casts up mire and dirt." That is the reason why so many people get angry and swear; anger is the " mire" and the profanity is the " dirt," which is thrown up from incompatible foods and drinks, or from your discordant relation to the outer world and its inhabitants.

God is just as truly exhibited in the operation of the stomach as in the operation of the brain. Discord is opposed to the Spirit of God; Harmony is an expo-nent of the Divine code, and is infinitely expressive of the Divine heart. The revelation of spiritual principles, in the present age, has brought to human comprehension this wondrous gradation of the degrees of deific power and love and wisdom, showing that the social subordinates, or what are called low-natures in the human scale, are indispensable to the existence and reciprocations of the highest. The principle of music runs, ripples, vibrates, throbs, and sings through all degrees of life; the principle of God everywhere present, over All and *in* All.

What is God? Let us not stop to answer, because every mind in the universe is organized to furnish for itself the answer, which will be appropriate to the necessities of its state and phase of moral development. You may behold God as a person, or as a trinity, or as filling a whole pantheon, if you be so educated; or, if your education has emancipated you from personalities, trinities, pagodas and pantheons, then you may be at liberty to assume that "God is a Principle." Said the Platonists, "God is love." But love is a principle; therefore must you not say that God is a principle? But you thus dispossess him of personality, which is "atheism" in the opinion of all Christians who cling to creeds. Love is a fountain! It comes not as a person; not as a man or woman. For love is a principle by which all things are filled with vitality, animated, expanded, and made beautiful for the temples of eternity. This fountain of love *is God*, if the Bible definition be accepted. If love is God, and if God is love, then God is a principle; so that, according to the rules of reason, the Divine personality is dissolved in the immensity—of the conception.

"Fair truth! for thee alone we seek," is saying, "God, for thee alone we seek." This statement is true, whether you say it with your will or not. Why are you drawn *onward* from day to day and from year to year? Why is the insensate particle that floats in the sun-beam drawn toward its proper place in the physical world? The particle moves onward not because it knows its proper sphere and destiny, but because there is a subtile principle of mysterious attraction [love] which fills the particle, to which it resistlessly responds, and on the bosom of which it harmoniously floats to its place in the universe.

So onward are you moving, in the will of the God-code. In the golden beams of an eternal Sun, floating in the baptismal fount of infinite love, [attraction,] mankind are moving onward to what is beyond; leaving the past to take care of itself, to bury its dead—pressing strenuously toward the great surrounding immensity—ever expanding and ever reaching into the beautiful future. Not because we will it, but because we cannot but obey the attraction of God. The essence of the divine love is within all—just as truly in the warrior as in " the man of peace ;" just as truly in the cannon that projects its message of iron as in the beautiful plants that load the air with fragrance. The laws of mechanics are supremely beautiful. Angles prophesy ovals ; octagons indicate the coming of circles ; spirals foreshadow onward moving principles. Rocks in the globe presuppose the ultimate pulverization of them into tillable earth. From crude rocks come the beautiful soils on which flowers and harvest grains grow, feeding the lower animals first, then the higher, and finally the highest; thus preparing the fine atoms of earth for the formation of a Summer-Land, in a higher and more glorious realm.

. And the equalities and inequalities of human nature are all comprehended by and reconciled with the grand scheme. To those who do not see the comprehending plan and principle, the inequalities and iniquities of humanity are regarded as the manifestations of the devil and of original sin. But to those who do see the plan and the principle, mankind's involuntary missteps are deemed the incidental manifestations of the progressive development of the Divine Spirit through the human family. Men will act toward their fellows in accordance with their estimates of human nature in general. If, for example, you consider that the asteroids, which occupy the space between the planets, were once one globe, but thrown asunder in consequence of the exceeding moral depravity of the people who once inhabited that globe, as one Rev. Dr. Cummings holds and proclaims, then you will very likely also believe the same with respect to the discords of men's homes and habits, and you will be inclined to act in accordance with such conviction, rendering you a very morose neighbor and a bad citizen. But, on the other hand, suppose you conceive and receive the glorious gospel, that " God is present in all things," that, as David said, if you should descend to " the belly of hell," or to the uttermost parts of the earth, yet you would find the spirit and laws of Jehovah there ; do you not think that your belief in intrinsic evil would depart, and that a flood of love and worshipful gratitude would pour from your soul toward the whole humanity ?

The equalities and inequalities of human nature are

from the infinite fountain of progress, just as drops of water contain the properties and principles of the ocean whence they came. Individual qualities contain the properties of the Father and Mother. You remember Pope's couplet:

" All are but parts of one stupendous whole,
Whose spirit Nature is, and God the soul."

If Pope will permit this emendation, his lines will meet the discoveries of later times. The qualities of human nature partake of the properties and principles of the Infinite Spirit. Equalities and Inequalities are incidental to these qualities. These manifest themselves first, in affection. The little child clings lovingly to its mother; the little bird that is born does the same. The progeny of the different animals do not learn to love their mothers. The lesson of love is born with the heart. Every living soul returns to the fountain for sustenance of affection—for the loving magnetic embrace, and finally for all the fertilizing influences which eventually emancipate the little one from its immediate dependence upon the fountain. Such love is deeper than the intellect; it comes from the essences of God and Nature.

The inequalities of human nature, when particularly traced and analyzed, arise *not* from the Fountain of Love, but from the sphere of relations, adjustments, and manifestations. The Fountain is always the same, and the streams are like their source, but in the sphere of matter and of its organs, inequalities are manifested. Spiritually unfolded minds regard inequalities as imperfections incident to the ascending flight of progressive principles. Think how differently mankind are put up in their physiological and phrenological organs! One person is sensitive and impressible; another is clad, as it were, with impenetrable iron. One is alive to the impulses and requirements of love; another treats affection as though it were a piece of merchandise. One mind has the faculty of analyzing propositions; another has not the slightest conception of such a faculty. These special inequalities are *equalities* in the grand system. One person is incased in powerful organic armor, adapted to the most Roman and heroic work among the world's solid unresponsive substances; another is so constitutionally built as to tremble and shiver, like an aspen leaf, in the slightest breath from society, or from an antagonistic emotion in other natures; there are yet others, who, positive to earth, are easily moved by the fine celestial currents that flow through the encompassing atmosphere from higher spheres. How differently organized, how unequal, are those persons! Suppose society should accidentally jostle them into the marriage relation! The iron-clad character legally bound to the sensitive. Progeny come, but they are discordant. One child is born with little brain and much body; the next, perhaps, all brain and no body. One dies from an excess of physical vigor, producing fevers in early childhood— croup, obstructions, and inflammations; another dies from an excess of cerebral nervousness, not because the brain is too large, but because the body is too small. In these cases it is possibly well that they do not live. The great GOD, both Father and Mother, careth for all —" taketh knowledge of the falling sparrow, and lights a world with glory;" just as attentive to the lilies of the valley as to "the highest seraph that adores" in the infinite temple of truth.

I am sorry for every mind that cannot, from a lofty eminence of interior growth, contemplate the empire of inequalities as a part of the plan. When one has tasted of the Pierian spring of immortal truths, and drank deeply thereof, and descended to the terrestrial valleys of discordant experience, then regret and sorrow for others blossom in the troubled and sympathizing heart. Those who have never been on the Alpine summits of ideas, know nothing of the high countries and magnificent scenes above their heads.

The gentle Nazarene was filled with concern for people who had no concern for themselves. He understood their conditions, and appreciated wants and needs which they had not arisen either to express or comprehend. What mean these pulpit sayings that some people ought to be condemned for not taking as much interest in themselves as a high-minded, benevolent, spiritual person may feel for them? Is not such preaching illogical, and philosophically absurd? A child takes as much interest in itself as it is qualified and educated to take. The Nazarene wept in deep sorrow, and would have philanthropically gathered the chosen people together "as a hen gathers her chickens." But do you think that the "chickens" deserve to be consigned to hell because they did not feel in their own behalf what "the hen" felt for them?

Inequalities in human nature are equalities when viewed from the center of the system. They are not necessarily imperfections. Some men are by nature inclined to work in iron and stone, to delve and dig, to

scrub and cook, to eat and to sleep; other men are
qualified to do many exactly opposite things, and to
turn the labors of the other party into channels which
widen as they approach the world's wants. These inequalities are imperfections tending to correct themselves through humanity's growth. There must be
different notes and ascending scales in music—octaves
one above the other—and whole notes must be divided
and fractionalized. Feet and hands, stomach and bowels,
liver and pancreas, and kidneys, are as necessary to
society as individual man. What would society do
without governing organs—without lungs, and heart,
and brain? And there are individuals who, by organization, seem qualified to perform these various functions
in the social body.

I come now to make the application. The God-code
develops the inequalities as well as the equalities of
human nature. Men who hold that benevolence is an
intellectual abstraction, consider themselves, on account
of their large mental capacities, authorized to use people
who are weak enough to allow themselves to be used.
But persons who have a high feeling, which, like amber,
pours over the intellectual faculties and gives a divine
color to all their decisions with reference to those
beneath them, are certain to make the laborers feel that
they are not useless, or menial, or subordinate, but as
essential in the great plan of the Infinite as are those
whom they may be serving. And this is the practical
lesson of this discourse. No mind under the influence
of the Divine principle, will ever intentionally cause an
inferior to feel his inferiority. In the true order of
humanity no souls will ever realize that they *are* hands

and feet, or inferior parts and indifferent organs, in the social economy of the rudimental sphere.

Such is the divine government in the Land of perpetual Summer beyond the stars. Can the head say to the hand, "I have no use of you?" No wise head ever thinks such language. The feet and the hands are delicately cared for and preserved by wise brains, even with love's refinement; for the hands and the feet are regarded as both spiritual and beautiful. "All are but parts of one harmonious whole." Look at the feet and hands of society in the South, whose skins are dark, who are down at the very basis of human concern and interest. The Divine principles of love and justice teach you to consider them as essential to the great workings and ends of the infinite plan as you are.

There are two kinds of ambition : one causes you to desire the elevation of the world ; the other to seek to elevate yourself. If you would be truly elevated, aspire to lift those about you ; you will rise with the tide of the divine power which you freely pour out upon others. The ocean which ceaselessly throbs, and is so remorseless to thousands, is not possessed with the silly ambition to be raised in the estimation of the world. The ocean contents itself with being truly and faithfully an ocean. It is unselfish, and is therefore Godlike. It buoys up innumerable vessels, freighted with countless human beings, each the center of diversified interests. They float confidingly on its bosom, flying the flag of the government that authorized their sailing.

Thus you have embarked for the voyage of immortality. The ocean is the God-code of the universe, the love-ocean of principles, filled with countless personal loves and individualized minds. This ocean floats us all upon its bosom, together with inconceivable myriads who have gone before us in the voyage of eternity. Now if this divine love-ocean was concerned with and for itself—was exceedingly anxious that somebody should get on the shore, and prayerfully tell the universe of its " greatness" and " wisdom" and " love," it would be a very selfish and treacherous ocean for you to trust your barks upon. But unlike the Atlantic, the divine ocean sympathizes and throbs harmoniously with the vessels which it lovingly floats; and in this way, (for no other way is possible,) it is lifted and made unutterably happy by the accumulated happinesses which it has bestowed unselfishly upon others.

Inequalities are as natural as equalities. All efforts to fix human beings upon a social level of life and government, are illogical and impracticable. We are qualified to breathe air alike, to see alike, to hear alike; for the principles of life are the same; but some can hear no music in the songs of birds; and take no high happiness in the joys of others beneath them. Men and women cannot become alike in any of these great spheres of action; and yet the divine principle of Love gives to each an equality of existence to the extent of his or her capacity. It is always " more blessed to give than to receive." Self-elevation is based in selfishness; it is the wrong road to happiness and self-improvement. Forget how you personally look when working in a good cause; keep away from the looking-glass of public opinion; be natural, thoroughly honest, and full of integrity; then virtue's influence will always flow out from you, healing the spirits of those who are crushed by misfortune and sorrow.

We read that miracles were performed in the olden time. What were they? Christ raised " the dead." Can you not go and do likewise? How often you might be a Christ to people about you! How many minds and hearts are dead and in their graves—the graves of unemployed faculties. Spirits who have come to you may have raised the dead in you. Can you not also do something for the dead in others? Intellectual and Spiritual faculties, in many minds about you, are yet in their dark tombs. They await the heavenly summons! Can you not be the one to sound the trumpet of resurrection? Can you not knock at the door of the sepulcher? Can you not speak the magic word that will awaken the sleeper and bring forth life from the silent tomb? Many faculties in those about you are perishing for lack of air and exercise. Do you not feel sad for such? Do you not often feel more sad for many people than they do for themselves?

If you would perform miracles, if you would raise the dead, if you would bring the kingdom of heaven on earth, apply the God-code, which is impartial love and progressive wisdom, to all who come within the circle of your consciousness.

12

SOCIAL CENTERS IN THE SUMMER-LAND.

"If I have told you earthly things, and ye believe not, how shall ye believe if I tell you of heavenly things?"

It appears to me that the foregoing words are peculiarly applicable to the subject-matter of this discourse.

The third chapter of John opens one of the richest mines of Platonic Philosophy. You remember that the doctrine of the "new birth," or what is theologically called "regeneration," is there introduced in behalf of persons who were imperfectly generated and badly born to start with—minds only half or two-thirds made up, "sent into this breathing world" full of physiological mistakes and psychological errors; which must be either voluntarily outgrown, or else involuntarily agonized through to a successful issue—"regeneration" being theologically prescribed as the true medicine, the only Divine plan, projecting over immense sins, shortening the road to Abraham's bosom, economizing or transcending the methods of justice, and saving the sinner from the pit of eternal and well-merited punishments. But I believe that all who voluntarily leave the world, the flesh, alcohol, tobacco, and the other devils, practically set their spirits and their bodies sailing toward the immortal Future. Such pay the genuine coin at the ticket-office of repentance ; they comply with the conditions, and are guaranteed a safe and happy voyage to the heavenly kingdom.

But look at the Church plan.   From the many probations that are granted and accepted, and judging from the many false steps and moral mistakes made by the converts, it is probable that multitudes run off the track.   Notwithstanding the fact that they voluntarily enlisted in the spiritual army, purchased tickets in the pew-department, and started with all the best sympathies of the brothers and sisters in Jesus, with the combined prayers of a mighty congregation to keep their souls steady toward the goal ; still great numbers switch off and run for years in the world's popular tracks.

Nicodemus could not properly understand the mysterious simplicity of a spiritual birth.   I never saw a Nicodemus that could.   A materialist, a man who believes only in the obvious, in weights and measures, who acquires his knowledge through the external, is a man whose thoughts extend only to the question which was put by Nicodemus.   One of the most beautiful Sons of the Infinite Father replied to him in astonishment: " Art thou a master in Israel"—that is, art thou a learned lawyer, a doctor of divinity, a responsible public man, a governor over many people—" and knowest *not* these things ?"   Think of a leader of the people, standing up in authority·before multitudes, influencing their feelings and conduct, and yet knowing not that " that which is flesh, *is flesh*, and that which is spirit, *is spirit*."

To be born of " water" as well as of " the spirit," is

too much like the hydropathic system of cure to be congenial to most persons. It is supposed to be more pleasant and less laborious to be " born of the spirit"— of sentiment, of good endeavor, and of the conscious possession of high motives. But it is quite too practical to be also born of *a clean body*, which means " water." I am rejoiced and grateful that some such man as John the Baptist—the " forerunner"—perceived the beautiful emblematic induction, and made the demonstration that the *physical* temple is the basis on which the intellectual and spiritual superstructure must be erected—that a true " new birth" begins in the body department.

" If I have told you earthly things, and ye believe not, how shall ye believe if I tell you of heavenly things ?" That is to say, if a person, when testifying of common earthly things, is known to be *as truthful* and unimpeachable as others who believe a very different creed—known to be as reliable in his speech and in character as his orthodox neighbors—why can you not as readily believe the same person when he soberly speaks of elevated things, which exist out of and beyond the sensuous sphere ? The question is very simple. Nicodemus, not being acquainted with the science of electricity and meteorology, could not understand what caused the wind to rush from one place and blow into another. Inasmuch as he could not comprehend the law of the blowing tempests, nor the wafting of the gentle evening zephyrs, how could he understand the simple mystery of the " birth of the spirit" ? The progressive growth of the spirit in truth and right is more mysterious than the coming and going of terrestrial

winds. Inasmuch, therefore, as most men are yet ignorant of the common phenomena of the physical world,
is it not presumptuous in them to stand up in the midst
of this temple of God and proclaim their superficial
skepticisms concerning profounder, deeper, vaster,
more elevated things? Hundreds pompously denounce
spiritual things while they know little or nothing of the
underlying laws and refined conditions by which these
marvelous visions and rich experiences are obtained.
Such minds arrogantly presume to sit in final judgment
upon the spiritual experience of others. The Nazarene when answering Nicodemus, was compelled to raise
the question of personal veracity. "If," he said substantially, "I am worthy of being believed when telling
you of ordinary things—if I am entitled to be trusted
in earthly things—why should not my testimony be
accepted when I speak of things elevated, supersensu-
ous, celestial, and heavenly?"

Every mind intuitively recognizes the eternal value
of pure purposes. The converse of the proposition is as
self-evident—*i. e.*, the eternal disadvantage of immoral .
purposes, nesting and breeding in the centers of individual life. We should urge this statement of the
question, were it not true that the divine constitution
of the material and spiritual universe so works, that out
of darkness light is born—out of evil, good—out of
lowest imperfections the flowers of purity bloom on the
high summits of all things, principalities, and principles. Were this progressive redemptiveness not true,
it would then be true to say—as do the orthodox, who
see only absolute and irreconcilable *opposites* in the
structure and method of the Divine government—that,

inasmuch as eternal value is stamped upon the soul with pure motives, so is there " eternal condemnation" written upon the soul that is moved with immoral motives. In all statements, you perceive, there are *some* items of truth.

The material point of the present discourse is now reached—viz., the influence which immoral motives and impure purposes exert upon man's interior—upon the centers of his life, character, endowments, and faculties of his inmost, deathless spirit. High purposes invariably expand and exalt the best powers of the immortal mind—giving harmonial roundness, symmetrical beauty, and celestial completeness of inward growth. Pure motives go before the individual like a divine magnet—drawing the impressible spirit pleasurably onward, over all surrounding evils and prevailing embarrassments. There can be no defeat in that spirit which is actuated every day and in all moments by the largest, highest, purest purposes of which it can conceive. It has been clearly shown that the rich and powerful Jews, who persecuted and finally killed the body of the poor divine friend of humanity, supposing themselves successful the while, were really and totally *defeated*—bankrupt and overthrown in every exalted sense ; but the Man, who passed so completely through the terrific ordeal, was *victorious* every instant of time—outriding the temptations of passion, quelling the storms of the ages, and stilling the tempest of cupidity and selfishness. The Jews, successful in worldly matters, were in all other respects utterly defeated. Behold the effect of that martyrdom upon the world. It is teeming with beautiful sentiments of love and charity—with glorious civil aud educational institutions, that have cropped out and blossomed from the fertile influence of that one example of a good Man dying that his truths might live.

High purposes alone presided. If the Infinite Father was so moved from the interior—this is the orthodox proposition—as to prepare and send to earth his only begotten, then the Father was actuated by the highest, deepest, and most heavenly purpose. He intended good to all and harm to none. Orthodoxy makes a sad theory of it.   But the spiritual thought, within the crude doctrine, is not destitute of truth. The theory of the flowering out and incarnation of the Divine Spirit in a human being, exhibits love infinitely higher than force, and broader than intellect, and more influential—subduing enmities, overcoming evils, and banishing from the earth, passion and strife and war. This is the spiritual picture within the theoretical incarnation. In this light the incarnation has been a success. Practically and philosophically, he alone is truly successful who is capable of embosoming and exemplifying those high motives which Mary's Son felt, inculcated, and manifested in the far distant past.

The infallible history of each person is written in the Summer-Land. A man who lives for himself, *loses* himself. If he wishes to gain the world, he as certainly loses it. The death-dealing immoralities of his purposes demoralize all parts of him, curtail his beautiful powers, paralyze his natural energies, and defeat him every step of the way, from the cradle to the coffin.

But a consolation is at hand. Death is a chemical screen—a strainer, a finely-woven sieve—through which, by the perpetual flow of the laws of Mother

Nature, individuals are passed on to their *true* stations in the Summer-Land. The squares in the death-sieve are so exceedingly fine, that only finest particles and certain powers and principles can go through; while on the earth-side is peeled off and cast down a lifeless mass of bones and fleshly corruption.

A process of refinement is this wondrous chemico-sieve death-experience. The spirit with the encasing soul, hidden centers of life, all the characteristics that have distinguished, and all the motives that have influenced the person—all these easily pass through the death-strainer, the screen or sieve; while the physical body and its particles, which cannot pass through, are dropped; and what is more gratifying, with the physical body are left behind many of those hereditary predispositions and abnormal conditions which gave rise to discordant passions and false appetites, called demons and unclean spirits. The *causes* of these demons and unclean spirits remain on the earth-side of the death-strainer, while the *effects*, which those causes exerted on the soul, being so fine and so mixed with the soul-substance, pass through, and remain with the individual long after he has attained to his social center in the Summer-Land.

Persons, or, rather, individualities, are not therefore destroyed by death. Nothing is changed save the dense physical form and the low material world in which they live. This chemical screenage, this extraordinary refining process and preparation, is one which all have to submit to at the end of the present life. The effect there is like the birth of each into the present world. Much is elevated to the world into which we come at birth;

while, at the same moment, and by the same process, much is left behind in the reproductive sphere.

In the temperaments and characteristics of the individual are laid the foundations of the different "Social Centers" that exist in the different mansions of the Father's house that was not built with hands. Those mansions, or, to continue the figure, the different rooms, are inhabited by classes of persons who have taken with them, through the death-strainer, different intellectual, spiritual, and social characteristics—integral attributes and temperamental individualities of character—ruling affections, and the effects of propensities that have been generated and strengthened by long-continued practices in this world before death.

Regeneration is a spiritualizing process, the same after death as it sometimes is before. If the person starts from earth interiorly cleansed, he will arrive at the next sphere in a corresponding condition. If the persons start from their death-screener with the earth, the flesh, and the demoniac influences impressed upon their souls, they will arrive at and sojourn in appropriate "Social Centers," with the accumulated effects still influencing the inner life and the manifestations of the affections. Thus radical differences in men and women cause different societies in the next sphere. Are there not many persons about you, perhaps dwelling every day in your homes, who have "no part or lot" in *your* cherished sentiments and happiest experiences? You sit at the dining-table, you look into the eyes of a person on the opposite side, and lo; you are strangers by leagues, perhaps you are whole ages asunder. Different sentiments, different attractions, and different social

12*

habits, give rise to different societies. Perhaps husband and wife, or brother and sister, though living in this world in the same house, eating at the same table, will become members of spiritual societies as far apart as the poles asunder. Society would be everywhere monotonous, both on earth and in the succeeding sphere, if individuals were all alike, all cast with the same combination of temperaments.

You begin plainly to comprehend, I think, that if these things are true on earth—about you and *in* you—death not destroying you, there must be great "diversities" among the inhabitants in the Summer-Land. These various super-mundane societies are predicated upon the continuation of the radical distinguishing characteristics of men and women. There are, consequently, societies embodying many of the effects of the immoral motives and degrading purposes by which women and men have been actuated and made miserable in this world.

This is an important and momentous truth. The Summer-Land is a *natural* state of human existence—growing out of the universal system of causes and effects, laws and ultimates, just as logically and scientifically as to-day grew out of yesterday. Are you not to-day, in all parts of your being, the legitimate result of what the laws, conditions, and experiences of yesterday made you? You are dead to yesterday. Your life is here and now. All you know of yesterday is remembrance. No man or woman can live in any *past* hour, except in the chambers of intangible memory. You live NOW, and thus it will be innumerable ages hence. The universal verdict of reason will be this ever-*present* con-

sciousness of existence—the Past a ghost of the memory;
the Future an unfinished picture, illuminated by the
inextinguishable lights of eternal hope.   Throughout
innumerable ages, the Past will appear like a dream;
while the Future will be a subject of curiosity, of surprise and attractiveness, in the succeeding ages of eternal life.   To-morrow is new and attractive to those who
live truly in the Present.   None can tell with absolute
certainty what will happen to-morrow.   There is, nevertheless, an universal confidence in its coming, because
of the immutable and perpetual flow of Nature's laws,
causing the revolution of the planets and the rising and
setting of suns—thus all men believe that to-morrow
will surely come.

Now I will put a question : If your common reason
tells you so clearly of earthly things, why can you not
believe your wiser intuitions and their superior logic
when they tell you of heavenly things ?   If ye believe
that the progression of months and years will surely
bring you up to the chemical *screen* called Death, why
can ye not also believe that the shining river which
flows skyward, in harmony with the noiseless rotation
of this planet, will float you through that screen to a
Social Center in the Summer-Land ?   All men go forward with their thoughts and anticipations—believing,
with the simplicity of very young children, that to-morrow
will come.   This, I say, is the uprising voice and irrepressible logic of Intuition, aided and confirmed by
experience, and made practical by the constant, habitual
exercise of the reasoning faculties.   All men naturally
expect to live over the present, into To-morrow.   Thus
mankind buy lands, and hire carpenters, and build

beautiful houses, and nicely furnish their new-made homes, as though everything, including personal existence, was vouchsafed to last forever on earth. But this is the usual experience: After all is completed and fully prepared—the house garnished and swept, and everything put in order for a long, luxurious physical life on earth—then the death-screen drops, the interior person passes through "in the twinkling of an eye," and the rich, lawful heirs are left to weep, to put away in the ground what the screen refused, and to live as long and comfortably as they can upon "the property of the deceased."

It is easy for the human mind to fix its imagination upon a long life in this world. So common was this inverted testimony of the fancy, that the ancient Jews supposed "the kingdom of heaven" was certainly coming "on the earth." Mankind, they thought, were not to ascend a progressive Jacob's ladder. The heavenly kingdom was to be drawn down out of the supernatural realm and made literally manifest here—a fancy in religion to which Adventists are strongly attached—so that great wildernesses would blossom, animals internally opposed to each other would become harmonious, and lions and lambs would, in peace and friendship, lie down together. Christians, with more Ideality, put a *spiritual* interpretation upon the literalness of the Hebrew Scriptures, and thus made tolerable common sense of what thousands of Jews believed to be true from a very different standpoint. In the Lord's Prayer, which contains many Jewish thoughts and expressions, we find this double-meaning allusion to the kingdom of heaven. Now what, think you, was intended by that prayer?

This answer seems correct: It was designed to float the mind out of materialism into spiritual thought and holy aspiration. " The kingdom of heaven," to the soul that uttered the prayer, was a condition of intellectual, social, and spiritual harmony; in which mental condition pure truth would reign triumphant, even as it prevails in every beautiful and harmonious family in the Summer-Land, with whom dwell harmony, peace, and eternal happiness. The Lord's Prayer is a conception which, interiorly viewed, does fully harmonize with the deductions of philosophy; but it was as legitimate a development from the Jewish basis of literalism as flowers are natural growths from the germs which precede. them. The prayer was constructed with a literal " kingdom of heaven" in it, so that the Jewish mind could grasp it, and adopt it in its rituals, and thus pray for the down-coming and universal expansion of the spirit's beautiful truths.

Now this is my testimony : The Summer-Land, as to the origin of the social centers, is made of persons from all parts of this inhabitable globe not only, but populations also from far-distant planets that are constituted like this earth—each globe producing an infinite variety of radical personal characteristics and temperamental differences. All these individuals carry upon the life within their faces, as well as in the secret chambers of their affections, the *effects* of life on the globe that produced them. If the person has been moved and governed by high and beautiful motives, he naturally and instinctively seeks association with those who have been similarly actuated and developed. If, on the other hand, the person has been led by low and demoralizing motives, he as naturally seeks those, who, before death, had been correspondingly influenced. There a man can elect his friends and gravitate to his own congenial Social Center—in fact, he can tell before he goes, by looking through the death-screen, or strainer, with what manner of minds he will probably live; at least until the redemptive evangel of "regeneration" through repentance and progression reaches his affections, until perfectly pure purposes are born in him; the same in effect whether he starts from a Methodist prayer-meeting in New York City, or from the center of some spiritual society in the fragrant groves of the Summer-Land. Progression out of imperfection is a purely spiritual transaction, growing out of the same general causes and resulting in the same internal effects upon character. Societies, in general terms, are natural exponents of the interior realities of the societies of men and women on different planets. .

There is there a society or province called "Altolissa." Persons have returned from it and testified that they were, while dwellers of earth, almost wholly influenced by the idea of gaining money, position, power among men. And it would seem that these invisible characters are influential still among those who are similarly organized and influenced in this world. When persons are actuated by the selfish motives to accumulate wealth, power, position, and influence, they become mediums to some extent. As the violet absorbs all but the *blue* ray, or as a red flower absorbs all but the *red* color, so is the mind of man in its impressibilities and mediumship. He will take on all that for which he has affinity. He will absorb from each society in the Sum-

mer-land precisely such influences as are in accordance
with his magnetic powers, and he will exclude all other
influences, from whatever source.

Now if the death-strainer, or screen, was not perfect—if, when passing through the chemical change, we
do not leave the *causes* of appetites and passions behind
us—then, in truth, men in this world would really be
injured and degraded by contact with the unseen populations.   But men are benefited, and not injured, by
such contact.   Now and then men are stimulated somewhat in their course; but they are not degraded, are
not made worse by the contact; only patted on the
back, flattered by unwise spirits, and sometimes approved,
as a too fond mother approbates her pet child even in
its errors. So men, moving in very low and demoralizing
circles in this world, will sometimes experience a sort
of self-satisfaction and contentment.   They do not have
those "fine compunctions" of conscience, which so many
pious people imagine they must necessarily have ; these
feelings are for a time laid aside, not by the use of
tobacco, alcohol, and opium, but by sympathetic contact with those spirits who are not wise and grown in
purity.

Such characters on earth absorb the rays of spirit-
life that are congenial to them, and exclude all the
others.   Thus you see men moving as earnestly *against*
the truth as for it.   It is a matter of astonishment to
many Northmen how the Southerners can have their
religious meetings and political gatherings, appoint "a
day" for sincere "prayers" to be sent to the kingdom of
heaven, and do all things just like the "loyal" and
"religious" people of the North.   Do you suppose that

men who have gone from the ranks of Rebeldom, and who have passed through the screen of death, suddenly lost all religious and political notions on the death-bed? No. The rule works both ways. They have a political scheme and a religious experience, and both were to them genuine. These return to their brethren in the South. When earnestly engaged in devotion and prayer, the Southerner feels as heaven-approved as the Northerner. You know that the discordant man, who walks Broadway with murder in his heart, can *see the sun* as clearly as can the man of peace. A morally bad character can physiologically eat and drink and sleep just as good as can the best. The laws that operate in your physical being operate the same in his. He goes round with the planet, experiences the flow and recession of emotions; but he can only absorb those influences from society with which he has affinity, and he knows nothing of what others experience. Suppose, for example, that I should " exchange pulpits" with the evangelical Brother who lectures every Sunday in Grace Church. The ladies and gentlemen there would absorb from me only those thoughts and sentiments for which they have an educational sympathy. They would reject everything else. There would be between us no sympathy, no fellowship; yet they are constituted just like ourselves, and in ten years from this they may come to feel as we do; but it is not at all likely that we shall ever feel as they do, because souls cannot go back.

Hence those who go to the Summer-Land cannot return just as bad as they were before they started. Going through death cleansed them largely of *causes*, conditions, and temptations, leaving with them the *results* treasured up in their affections, in their sympathies, in their antipathies, inclinations, disinclinations, loves, hates, attractions, and repulsions. Of course they have sympathy only for congenial associations in that better life; but such associations are, necessarily, on a higher plane than though they were of earth. The " higher plane," however, is so little removed, so slightly shaded off from that in which they lived while here, that it requires but little change to feel themselves " at home."

True, contradictory characters often go to the Summer-Land. Sometimes imagination gets the start of conscience. The youth feels, thinks, hopes beyond his powers to grasp or attain; but as the years roll through the spirit, he grows gradually solid, and strong, and practical. Conscience is not fully born in some souls until after death; that is, the idea of right and wrong is to them " a theory." I have seen persons, who, having a very large sense of right and wrong, wondered how their most intimate acquaintances could *do* things diametrically antagonistic to such sense without being surprised or astonished, and still live among folks just as though nothing had happened. It is because the conscientious part of the spirit had not yet been fully born. The person might have been born on three or five sides of his character, and yet there remain other parts not born from error and wrong, and hence the defectiveness; hence, also, the monstrosity which the character · and conduct of such a person presents—deceiving, murdering, robbing—yet thinking nothing more of the self-condemnation of his crimes than most men do of transacting their ordinary business. It is because these men have not as much light in principles as you; they do not yet perceive the white ray of pure justice; they cannot take it in, any more than a red plant could take in the red ray. So a man who cannot absorb the principle of justice is a man who cannot comprehend its requirements.

Society is constructed so as to require regeneration and progression. The Christian system prays for the better time. Nicodemus asked how a man could be taken out of his .defects—brought out of the flesh and made as pure as spirit. Jesus did not answer him in common words, but told him that as he could not understand the ordinary phenomena of Nature—the blowing of the wind, for example—he certainly could not understand that which was interior and far more extraordinary, like the birth of the spirit.

It has been ascertained by multitudes of witnesses, by experiments, and by conversations with those who have returned from the Summer-Land, that those who have demoralizing motives in this life have the greatest density on their arrival. In Altolissa, the section where many persons go, who, in this world, lived wholly under the influence of selfishness, the population seems about as comfortable as general society on earth. Jews still believe in the doctrine of their fathers—Abraham, Isaac, and Jacob: the Roman Catholics hold the same views they did before death; and there are other sects in Altolissa who think and believe in the same things and forms of faith they learned on earth. The sects will long continue in their various sympathies and educational associations. Of course, progressively and quite imperceptibly, this world will grow better and more harmonious. Men will intuitively differ less and less upon fundamental principles. But in the "details"— in the ramifications of thought—this endless variety of convictions and affinities will prevail. The foundations for countless and various societies in the Summer-Land are thus laid and established. Death is largely a cleansing process, and is the hope of the world, not its point of darkness. So beautiful are its siftings, strainings, and other processes, that the active *causes* of passions and appetites are dropped and left on earth with the gross materiality. So beautiful is the law of Progress, that even the *active effects* that accompany the individual cannot be perpetuated (as evils and discords) throughout eternity. Why? Because in the center of the universe a positive power reigns, breathing its spirit throughout the illimitable spaces; and, and by the slow workings of its progressive laws, it cleanses all personalities of their transient imperfections. Only eternal GOOD can eternally exist. There is a universal gathering of all spirits and angels—not in one place, under the blaze of one heavenly central sun, but under the influence of musical distributions, of harmonious varieties, each adding completeness and happiness to the other. Many persons are harmonized in this world when they are "born again," and thus lifted out of their low motives and consequent imperfections. Hundreds and thousands of "things" that annoy, vex, and wear the spirit, before it is thus born, cease to exert any bad effect. Such minds grow sweet, and gentle, and loving, under the new life; before, the same persons were hateful, discordant, and full of consuming passions. The evil woman, who had "seven devils" cast out of her, is an instance of what good can be accomplished by exchanging bad motives for good ones. How many hateful propensities, how many demonic habits, and how many unladylike characteristics were cast out of her by the psychological power, is left to every one's imagination.

The Catholics believe that each purified soul has " died" to the influences of this world. The Shakers hold a similar white banner over the redeemed— " Come in and dwell with us, put on the plain garb, renounce the world's evil habits and cruel customs, among other things the evils of marriage and marriage itself, and you will be saved; for thus you die to the world." Nuns enter convents under the psychological impression that before death they can leave the world and its sins, become spiritually sweet and beautiful, and acceptable brides for the only Son. There is a poetic sublimity in the thought.

Now there are persons yet in the world who know that they can put their crushing heel on the serpent's head. They have learned that *they can resist* striking a brother, in passion ; and, what is far better, they can resist *the passion* which would suggest the blow. Strong, vigorous, full-blooded men, have conquered the demon of passion. Such conquering heroes would not go among the Heenans who live in sections of the Summer-Land, except as Moral Policemen, as philanthropists, but never in the capacity of associates. And yet you know that there are men, and women, too, who " hugely enjoy" the Heenan style of life; they like the very thought of it, the exciting manifestations of it, and the large, beautiful, abandoned animality which it displays

and indorses.   If they enjoy it, *how* do they enjoy it?
Do they by means of their physiological or phrenological organs?   They enjoy it by means of those talents
and faculties which live *within* physical organs, and
which the screenage of death does not refine away and
crush out of the person.

Therefore there is a great individual work here to
be done.   The ounce of prevention is wanted which
will make the tons of cure unnecessary.   Each person
can start on the right track before death; this is the
best place to get under full sail for a happier harbor.
To-day is better than to-morrow.   The sooner you
begin, the farther you will find yourself in the path of
harmonious life.

This is the doctrine which we are impressed to
teach.   I think all should commence at once to see
what can be done toward preparing for a better,
sweeter screenage at death, and to insure a beautiful
entrance into superior societies.   No one can hurt the
Infinite Father nor the Infinite Mother—you can permanently injure only yourself.   This being the truth,
we have but to proclaim, " Repent ye, for the kingdom
of heaven is"—next door, just beyond, on the other
side of the death-screen, through which each must
sooner or later pass.   How many persons will feel,
after attaining the elevation of self-control, that they
have begun anew!   But how many cross, sour counte-
nances, there will be while going through the trial of
trying to be good.   If Nicodemus could have understood that to be " born of water" was a natural and
indispensable forerunner of being " born of the spirit,"
he would have first given attention to the correction

of his personal habits and physical appetites. Thus he would have had more harmonious, more sweet, and more beautiful bodily sensations. He would have become a better neighbor and a truer Governor in Israel, a more agreeable companion; and there would have been a cheerful, buoyant, juvenile flow of light, joy, and peace, within his lifted spirit; in short, he would have soon experienced the difference between a son of God and a son of Belial.

I know it is a hard doctrine to preach, that *now* is " the accepted time." But this death-screen, which hangs before us, is as certain to fix upon each the *effects* of habits and mental conditions as that to-morrow will be the natural result of the causes and conditions of to-day. Each person can in this world select his associations after death. It is, therefore, important to get a passport to harmonious central societies in the Summer-Land. You should feel no enmity toward any human being, however much you have been injured. The lion and the lamb lie down together only within the *purified* human spirit. The hidden, cave-like cerebellum, the back-brain, is a den full of untamed animals. Spiritual TRUTH is the only conqueror that can enter and still the passions, tame them to peace, and hold them in abeyance until the outward disturbance is gone. Motives, when high, lift up the soul, which is thus prepared to be a better neighbor and more successful in all the genuine enterprises of present life.

All true progress brings an immediate and glorious satisfaction. We discourse upon " life and immortality," not because it is a spiritual fact, but because it is the foundation and inspiration of immediate personal improvements. It stimulates us to beautiful effort, and causes us to teach practical reforms. We can bring innumerable tests and mathematical evidences that these things, which we relate with respect to the other sphere, are true; but time will supply you with all necessary testimonies; many of them you have already heard, many of them you know by heart, and ask for nothing more. Now, therefore, the time has come for each to step upon the solid rock of Truth—of eternal principles—which will surely stand, while the spirit makes substantial progress toward higher and more beautiful societies which blossom beyond the stars.

POVERTY AND RICHES.

"All is the gift of industry; whate'er
Exalts, embellishes, and renders life
Delightful." "More precious
Than gold are the treasures
And rewards of wisdom."

The outward body exerts an imperious mastery over the will, affections, and inclinations. In consequence of this imperious dictation, growing out of the physiological and phrenological organization, the mind finds itself electing motives in the place of ideals, and pursuing the object of such motives with all the instruments at its command. Persons therefore, as a result of their organization, adopt and foster habits which they would not, if the congress of all the faculties were consulted. When there is lobbying behind the ears, caucus meetings on the sides of the head, political legerdemain, wire-pulling, log-rolling around the basilar faculties of the mind, then the person is carried with the wild impulsive energy of youth, to consummate an object not worthy the whole character. It was an election of only a portion of the congress of the faculties; a minority report. The majority report is not heeded, scarcely received, until the person has arrived at a point far beyond the meridian of human life. The traveler sits down and thinks over the misfortunes and successes of this journey. Then, possibly, some religious question is broached by the spirit to itself. Or, he takes up a newspaper and reads that the celebrated revivalist from England will preach to sinners at —— Hall this evening. The traveler goes there, having no object but pastime and curiosity, and he listens. He finds that the preacher is addressing a class of faculties which have for years regularly whispered "religion" to him through the interstices and crevices, meditations and intuitions of his experience. The speaker's descriptive appeal is so entirely suitable to his own private and never-before expressed convictions and emotions and impulses, that he takes all the rest for granted. It matters not what the preacher's creed may be; the listener does not stop to consider. He feels for the first time in his life that "religion is the chief concern of mortals here below," and instantly yields. Down he goes into the valley of humiliation, on knees unaccustomed to bending before any religious idol, and bows his head in veneration to his God. After the conversion is perfected, he rises in class-meeting and reports a long series of sins; tells what the good Lord has done for him; that he has at last taken a position through the grace of the Lamb of God; that all his past life has been a mistake and a sham, and that henceforth all his life shall become new. He thinks nothing about the theology of his religion. A convert seldom knows anything about the creed of his church. No convert has had any real conception of the goblin doctrines taught by the preacher who just converted him. The experience of conversion is a serious internal experience, a

13

report from the superior faculties that the *inferior* faculties have been log-rolling and wire-pulling and having their own evil way for years. A variety of unworthy objects have been pursued, and the person has employed unworthy instruments for the accomplishment of those objects. The conversion was brought on by the psychology of the pulpit, which impressed the sincere conviction upon the listening mind that its life was an insult to the firmament of the superior faculties. Such a mind gains his soul, perhaps, while he loses the whole world.

The ambitious person does not want money, but rather power, though money subserves his object. The vain person does not want either money or power, but admiration, and money and power only so far as they contribute to securing the largest amount of admiration. Only the passionate acquisitive mind seeks money for money's sake. The mind possesses its object by the automatic elections of the lower faculties. They clamor and shout through the galleries of the interior legislature. They drown the voices of the respected, venerable powers; the most wise are the deepest, and the last to speak the words of protest. Those most cultured in spirit wait until the noise and tumult of inferior powers are allayed; then they rise in their seats in the sanctuary of the soul and announce the claims of justice and liberty and truth and virtue. St. Augustine, Fenelon, Jesus and others, who have spoken and written from their higher faculties, echo just what has been uttered from the inner chambers of the temple of every true mind.

The conviction in the religious world is, that great riches are identical with great wickedness. Such is the accepted theory, and yet the religious world is walking in the footsteps of Mammon. You know that Mammon sits in the gates of the temples of commerce and dictates the maxims of trade, saying "Get all thou canst, and give as little as possible; so that thy neighbor may fail and thou be successful upon his ruin." Talk about "practical Christianity" in this state of society! Talk about bringing the kingdom of heaven on earth by prayer, or precept, or example! Men are moved not by their higher inclinations and inspirations, but by the imperious automatic election of their most sensitive faculties. They are full of the force and fierceness of wild animals; to them the locomotive is a savage gratification, and the terrible earthquake a thrilling delight. No wonder that Dante, Milton, and Pollock, find readers throughout the world. Their most thrilling descriptions of infernal spheres are gratifying to the basilar faculties. The back of the head swells and the neck throbs. Power meets and welcomes power with luxurious embrace. It is like the nuptial meeting of mighty forces in the physical world. Thus electricity and magnetism meet in their own appointed way—each rushing into the other's embrace, with terrible earnestness and increasing frequency, bringing forth new elements, new powers and new principles, developing new centers of energy for new forms and manifestations of matter. So man's faculties draw into themselves their own proper foods and drinks. In the lower states of civilization their appetite is rapacious and fierce—blood, the fires of passion, and savage sports are its bread and wine.

Agar in his prayer, said, "Give me neither poverty nor riches." What is the golden mean of virtue? If

I have riches and great abundance, I shall be over-fed
and too well clothed.   I shall feel indolent, proud, and
luxurious.   I shall lean back in my easy chair and say,
" Who can tell me what truth is?   The Lord—who is
he?" I shall be too comfortable and superficially independent.   O let me not travel so far into the forest of
evil and despair.   He says, " Give me not riches."
Well, then, why not give him poverty?   Because he
may thereby lose his self-respect, steal from his neighbor, and take in vain the name of all holy and beautiful
things.   Agar's prayer suggests the glorious independence that is found midway between extreme poverty and
exceeding riches.   There is no evil in having riches, but
in fostering a love for it in blinding excess.   Neither is
there evil in having poverty, in being decently and
honorably poor ; but evil consists in the excesses of
squalor in which many spend their lives.   Balance is
the basis of harmony. It is like the golden belt between
the equator and the polar regions, where the greatest
fertility and industry are possible and practicable—a
band of land and water between the two extremes—so
is the pleasant, independent, comfortable place between
excessive poverty and extravagant riches.

This is the gospel of all beautiful relations.   Disease, one extreme, is not attractive.   No one's veneration is excited by bodily discord.   Sympathy and pity
(which hold always a little of the element of contempt)
are excited by disease.   You may have rich pity and
beautiful sympathy for the afflicted.   If your sympathies
for the suffering flow from a large love-fountain, and if
at the same moment your magnetic powers are fully
awakened and active, then you are to the afflicted one a

perfect magnetic savior. To such an one you can say, " I WILL, *be thou healed!*" And the condition of cure is established. Because your WILL is not merely an intention in such a case; it is the uprising of the healing virtue from the life-fountain, the springing of divine energy from the heart of the spirit; which, showering down and refreshing the soul-aura of the sick one, fills the exhausted nerves, refreshes the impoverished blood, and balances forces long since spent or over-worn; and so a sweet rejuvenation and the conditions of pure health come to you from the one whom you should name a " Savior."

But suppose a person treats your case by the exercise of mere will, and by magnetism coming from the psychological power of ordinary intention, then all you will receive is metallic or animal heat. It is nothing but the breathings of Satan. (Of course, I use this hateful word in a symbolic sense.) Whatever is simply galvanic or willful, coming from the decomposition of metals or from the clash and clank of the animal brain, is degrading to the spiritual sensibilities. Everything which intends forcibly to assail the private rights and intentions of another person, is freighted with a subtile poison. It defrauds you of personality, and to that extent it is your enemy. The best friend is he who gives you to yourself. A true friend does not throw any power over you, to circumscribe or limit the natural expression and perfect expansion of the elements and attributes of your being, although , he may caution, counsel, and develop the beauty and the might of Truth before you.

Disease, I repeat, is not attractive. Neither is

poverty. It is said that the poor shall always be with us. I do not wonder that the ancients thought so. Anything which flows far down in the channels of experience, which is in the earth beneath your feet, which compels you to live down where crude forces move, is an attack upon the selfish dictates of your self-esteem and pride. The position itself is poverty. The lesson is, that machinery, not human hands, must go down and do the dirty work of the world. In this manner all true needs will be supplied, and all true desires provided with their fullest gratification.

Riches, on the other hand, are attractive to all men. There is no disputing this obvious fact. The human mind goes toward riches as inevitably and gladly as the birds spring from earth into the blue space in which they are at home. It is the power and privileges of wealth which the mind craves. It is similar to what Hannibal longed for when he was crossing the mountains; something that would soften and melt the solid substances which opposed his march and his purposes. Every man is a Hannibal on the question of riches. Man has by inheritance the aggressive elements of the great Napoleon. He wants to be pecuniarily independent, and he *will be* monarch over the domain of poverty; he must be emperor in the field of ownership, or he makes war upon his neighbors. This super-power—this magnificent feeling of personal monarchy—is what each soul wants. Autocracy is the perfect and entire emancipation of the individual. The autocrat is a self-centered governor. Every person wants to be a self-regulated and rich autocrat. America, in political organization, is not yet up to this conception; and the church is even a greater stumbling-block than the political combinations. It says, "Thus far and no farther. You shall not become independent of restrictions; you shall obey the laws of these religious organizations." Order implies organization, and organization necessitates discipline, and the authority of discipline must not be questioned. How can you induce bigots of this stripe to investigate a new truth? You even shrink from asking them to look at your positive facts.

Autocracy is the rich and comfortable democracy of the human mind. This view of riches is creeping into and through all parts of the human imagination. Money brings anxiety, pride, and power; and these bring admiration for a time. Mammon is more worshiped to-day than are the Father and Mother of the everlasting universe. Mammon is not worshiped with genuine spiritual veneration; yet he is followed and obeyed as is no other leader in the round world. He dictates all measures to the ministers of both Church and State. He is in the path of every nation. Golden hammers have arisen over the firmament of the American people; and it seems as though great authorities are to be subverted and large capitalists crushed in the twinkling of an eye. It is a great trial that the world is passing through. During the years of these national travails and trials, new ideas of Progress will take root deeply, will grow up vast and mighty, and will spread out their thickly-woven branches through and over all the institutions of both Church and State. Legislators in the capitals and ministers in the pulpits, and men who are masters of the press, and those who stand upon the rostrum, will rise up as so many redeemed angels of light, and there will be a unity of thought and a unity of purpose more complete and spontaneous than was ever before seen.   Like a spiritual Aurora Borealis, it will give to mankind a world of light and joy, and a roseate and a golden opulence to the whole horizon and firmament of human history.

As men do not love disease, so they do not love poverty.   Health is richly attractive; even so are riches.   No man can say that he hates just and whole-some wealth. He may hate the misapplication of riches. He hates acquisitiveness, penuriousness and miserly covetousness.   He hates the evils of wealth; he does not hate the riches.

It is the destiny of all men to become rich.   Man-kind have no business to be everlastingly sick and ever-lastingly poor.   All men will become ashamed of it, for every one has the power to help himself out of both disease and poverty.   This shame will come with a larger inward growth.   The time is coming when men will see that their interests are co-ordinate and co-operative.   Men who have only muscle are brothers to those who have only brain.   Skill, however, is in the ascendant.   One true Idea in one master mind sets a thousand men at work, because there are thousands of men who have millions of muscles, but scarcely one clear idea.

Why is it that our Yankee girls, as they are called, cannot be found at work in basements? They labor in our factories only just long enough to get a couple of beautiful rooms filled with more beautiful furniture, a wardrobe abundantly supplied, and two hundred dollars laid away in the Savings Bank.   They very soon get married,

leave the factories, and settle down in happy homes.
Then only the Yankee husbands go to the factories;
the young women, their wives, remain in the homes
their own industry has purchased. The American female
mind will not long dwell in the presence of wheels and
pulleys and spindles. It will not stoop many times to
scrub your floors; it will not garnish up and put your
house in order; for it is independent, artistic, and in-
ventive, and cannot be repressed nor subjected.

Anglo Saxon blood is nearly buried; but the
"American blood" is fast coming into active life. The
old branches of the Saxon family will, one of these days,
come in embattled conflict with the new-born flood of
America. When that time comes, the empires of Europe
will crumble and tumble forever, and political freedom
will prevail. The American blood is the best channel
for the introduction and widest distribution of advantages, opportunities, and national wealth. Where does
the world get its gold in the greatest abundance? From
the valley of the Nile? From the Libyan mountains
west of the valley, or the Arabians to the east, or from
the Orkney hills of Scotland? Does it come from the
great mountains of the far South? No. The Eldora-
dos, and Colorados, the shining placers and auriferous
leads, the sparkling channels and gorges, full of magnetic particles, which draw muscle and not skill, are
found in the bosom of America. Skill remains in the
cities; it works through the machinery of commerce;
it sinks the deep shafts, sends down great buckets into
golden wells, and draws up millions of the precious
metal. Vast territories on the Pacific side of the continent are destined to furnish the world with the metal

13*

which, like all other kinds of material riches, will take
unto itself wings and fly out of sight and out of mind.
In after years it will fly back and come down heavier
than lead, and become worthless except for useful tools
and personal ornaments.   Gold exists in great abundance.   Every little child can have a gold watch and a
gold breast-pin and a gold finger-ring.   The metal will
become popular and correspondingly cheap.   Let commerce and the mercantile power bow to the god, Mammon, who grimly sits in the gates of trade and holds
the scepter, and is the exactor of this tribute of adoration—a sacrifice for which all men will in the future be
unutterably ashamed.   I have taken great precautions
not to invest largely in metals.   I have made investments in health—a form of riches far above the metals,
and one unsearchable and unattainable to those who
have not obeyed the laws of their existence.   Miners
and merchants and ministers are bowing and searching
down in the bowels of the earth.   They look downwards for the means of attaining their miserable terrestrial objects.   What is it all for?   Do you not
suppose the time will come when the silver and golden
metals will take a very inferior position in your mind?
Suppose between this and next Sunday one of you should
depart for the Summer-Land.   Of what value would be
all this fret and foam about the metals of the mineral
world?   Metals are not riches.   They do not even
represent riches; they only represent the materiality
and dross-mindedness of the world of commerce.

Labor and skill alone bring riches.   Skill is in the
ascendant, and first exhibits itself through science.
What is science?   It is a true knowledge of facts and

forces, of ponderable substances and the visible organs. The next manifestation of skill, is art—a true knowledge of *how* to control forces, organs, and substances. Art is the control of those powers of which science gives you a true knowledge. Skill, therefore, is the master. The man of mere muscle cannot contend with the man of mind. The ignorant giant might as well give up before he begins the battle. The conflict in the world to-day between the poor and the rich, is, when ana- lyzed, a battle between skill and muscle, or bones and brains. The poor man's salvation is alone possible through his mind.

The American blood is already making these demands and these manifestations. The poor man is kept down because of two things: first, he has not the money by which he can " take advantage" of conditions and cir- cumstances about him ; second, and first of all, he has not, as a general rule, the skill by which, if he had suf- ficient money, he might make himself " master of the situation." Mechanics and other working men, not American, are generally of this stamp. In the old countries poor men and women seldom get property. American poor men and women, on the other hand, fre- quently become rich and masters of their position. I begin to see glimmerings of an industrial pathway by which all the poor of the country are to become pos- sessed of homes and acres of their own, so that they shall grow neither rich nor poor, but even more inde- pendent. But this prospect does not open for those whose blood is not legitimately progressive. Muscle and breast and digestion and brains and the automatic ener- gies will obey the skill and ideas of those who have the inspiration and positive intelligence. Myriads in the old countries are to be benefited by the exaltation of minds that are skilled and rich in divine ideas. The churches do not see any such prospect. A man standing in his pulpit, seeing in one of the front pews a person whose business is that of wine-selling, or who gets all his money by " taking advantage" of the rise of the markets in flour and in necessary staples, upon which " the poor" must pay the combined profits and the largest percentage, does not dare say to that man that *he is not as righteous* as the hypocritical righteousness of the Scribes and Pharisees. Because that rich wine-dealer and stock-jobber and popular swindler holds communion with the one god which the minister is compelled to acknowledge and worship, Mammon ! Tinseled rhetoric is subject to the command of metal. If the minister, in a moment of moral bravery, should denounce the sins of the pew-holders, he is very soon visited by a committee, who inform him that he is " void of ideality; that he is not poetical enough ; that the congregation wants a preacher who is more refined and impersonal in his conversation, more ecstatic in his style of sermonizing, and not so direct and vulgar in his references to supporters of God's holy word," &c. And the committee very soon hear that there is a minister for sale. Such a preacher is sent for. He puts his ear to the mouth of Mammon, and the metallic god whispers " a high calling ;" and he listens all over ; he accepts the congregation in obedience to the " call," and you know that hymns, and prayers, and sermons always go just where the minister goes ; and the minister goes just where the implacable metal-and-greenback gods bid

him, even in spite of himself. Then do you suppose that
the speculator and the stock-gambler, who lives and
fattens upon others' misfortunes, will be talked to from
the pulpit? Will he be told that his apparent righteousness is *nothing*? Dare the minister tell him that
without sacrifices, and without integral virtues, he cannot enter into the kingdom of harmony? Never! And
the speculators' wives will be delighted. They will
say, " What a delightful change! Why, the minister
we had last year was such a coarse and vulgar person!
He would talk his notions ' right out,' and preach all
sorts of reforms. He spoke his mind on every-day
' religion,' and talked ' politics' right out in meeting.
Now, how delightful! We have a *gentleman* in the
pulpit who is cultivated and poetical; he has ideas,
and never interferes with every-day matters."

It is the misdirection of the love of wealth which
we are called upon to denounce. All men should and
shall desire to have homes and property and position.
It is sad to behold a person so far down in the deep
valley of disappointment, that he does not put forth
adequate exertions to make for himself a home, if it be
but twenty feet square and one story high, with only a
place overhead for boxes and trunks. Uncultivated
land all over this country is calling for men and women.
The unworked fields of America put forth thickly-
matted vegetation, saying, " See what I could do, if you
would only bring to me your hoes, your plows, your
implements of industry. I will bring you great harvests.
Open me deeply, let me breathe, then give me the germs.
You have but to sit in the door afterward, and under
your own vine and fig-tree, and behold the blossoming

of the material abundance with which I will bless you."
Behold the prairies of the West! Gardens are they
that could support the entire population of the globe,
if we but give to them our skill and our working-
muscles.

Riches are inevitable. Mankind will not remain
poor. If they do, they are sinners. America is remarkable for her tendency and her power to equalize wealth
and distribute knowledge. Here fierce blasts topple
down steeples that are too lofty. A farmer may stack
and store large quantities of grain for the market.
Some great tornado may destroy his property in a single
afternoon. That is what the country prophesies as possible and certain in all great accumulations of wealth.
John Jacob Astor's property will very soon melt out of
his possession. Let the owning and watching mind
depart, and forthwith the decomposing process commences. Here is no primogeniture. The property of
the family does not descend to the eldest son. Sometimes, instead, the greatest financial misfortunes descend
to the first child. Here is disintegration and diffusion.
Why, the climate itself is full of democracy. Property
concentration in America is possible only for three-
quarters of a century. Some few New England families are opulent, and have been ever since the country
started. But the young men and the war are now
making those properties fly to the four winds. The
sons of once rich parents are looking about for business,
to prevent their entire impoverishment. They descend
from families once aristocratic in wealth, but in mind and
spirit they were very poor and valueless to the world.

Now, *mind* is taking a lofty position that money can

never reach. Skill, in the ascendant, indicates mind. The superior faculties are declaring their aristocracy. This declaration will show itself in the growing *independence* of our working men and women. They will accumulate property. They cannot help it. Spiritual riches, however, will soonest save all from poverty both in matter and in mind. Such riches develop the superior powers, by which man puts down diseases and all forms of poverty in his spirit. Ideas, at last, will be the Saviors of the world. But "ideas" are considered vague. *Are* they? Look at their incarnations. What is a locomotive, a factory, the invention of the sewing machine, or a watch, but the incarnation of ideas? Ideas antedate all literature, art and science. Ideas will change and revolutionize the world. Poverty, in the physical body and in the world's circumstances, will be overcome and destroyed. Spiritual riches are impersonal ideas. Present physical life is a struggle for bread—a battle of selfishness from which very few persons come off with clean hands and a pure heart. Society is full of worn and weary workers for the daily wants of their bodies and families.

It is not always to be so. The moment a man gets a true education with an Idea, in itself clear and capable of being transmitted to a fellow, that moment he takes precedence in the field, work-shop, or factory. He is foreman, an assistant on the side of government; his wages are increased, and he is thereby put on the way to something better. For it is the American's ambition to acquire, not money, but mind; ideas, instead of gold medals and personal luxury. I would rather have my invisible brain with its boney-casket than the wealth of the wealthiest man. Who would not? If a man has a true education, and a brain-power adequate to the wheeling of circumstances into line with his intentions, the wealth of the rich and idle man, who possibly has no brain-power, will melt into his hands. Truly educated men will become rich through the country; and thus every poor man, through his ideas and his ceaseless industry, will have a home and a garden. The world is on its way to vast accumulations of spiritual riches, not from any special individual intention, but from the direct election and development of its innate constitutional powers.

Let no one, however, expect that people will catch an idea to-day and act upon it to-morrow. To-morrow people will manifest their characteristics and dispositions according to their circumstances. They will act from their long-accustomed habits and ruling inclinations. Mankind do not rapidly change. They will not be quickly impressed and swayed by great ideas. The most powerful principles will give but a momentary inspiration and direction to the general mind. The dominating characteristics of the people will be those which spring from their organic conformation, modified by passing inclinations and swayed by fleeting circumstances, and all more or less independent of the individual wish or will.

Suppose your superior faculties should come down out of their heavens and touch your internal being, awaken your divinest and sweetest sensations, and bid your spiritual nature to yield to holier emotions. What would then occur? "A voice from heaven" means a voice from the interior of spirit. It is a divine feeling, also, which the inhabitants of the Summer-Land will in your heart increase with aerial music and songs of joy and anthems of deathless gratitude. The upper and higher faculties speak in silvery tones to that which is ordinary, earthly, and external in you, saying, " Rise! Live worthier! Be thou whole, healthy, rich, happy!"

Mankind are on the straight road to ultimate success. The harmonial era is coming through this beautiful nuptial relation, which will, at the right hour in history, be formed between the upper faculties in men's minds and their ordinary powers and propensities of externalism and selfishness, which to-day are highest in authoritative power, dictating the movements and constructing the mechanism of Church and State. The superior nature in man, the kingdom of heaven, is gaining the ascendency. Its methods and its resources will be mankind's true Saviors.

There is always greater "joy in heaven" over one person so lifted and converted than over a thousand who have walked along sweetly and noiselessly through. life. Moderate saints are moderate sinners. They are neither rich nor poor, neither benevolent nor penurious, but live unobtrusively and indifferently in an even way—letting their "moderation be known unto all men"—exciting neither joy nor sympathy among the philanthropic in the Summer-Land. But one of those hard-headed, hard-hearted, thick-skinned sinners, who has been induced to listen to and obey the voice of the higher powers, who has substantially resolved to live henceforth in the sanctuary of his immortal spirit, who has given evidence that he will be a better, a wiser, a larger, and a more truly rich man—such an one, when freed from his bad habits and earthliness, kindles grand joy in the heavens.

The era of harmony, which is to come, will consist in the coming together of the powers between the lower and the highest in man's nature. Such a race will come out of America's blood. They will conquer the soil, will subdue the climate, will destroy disease, will rise above the metals, will overthrow all known standards of wealth, and will arrange themselves in harmonial brotherhoods, and will live as they live who inhabit the higher mansions in the Father's house.

The soil of the globe is in a very undeveloped and low state. Its inexhaustible resources have not yet declared themselves to the eyes and skill of the wisest men. Science has not yet probed the recesses of visible matter. Religion has done nothing more than to say, "The coming of the kingdom of heaven is a subject of prayer." We affirm that it will become a fact when mankind pray hard enough in *deeds*. Religion has soothed you in your struggles. It has essayed to make you feel satisfied with bereavements. It attends your death-beds. It goes with you to your grave-yards. And it has made light with faith the dark and dreary walks of the world. Religion, stripped of its theology, has had in it much for mankind in all these things. But it has not lifted you to the heart of Mother Nature. It has not turned you out into the fields of progressive truth. It has not shown you " the unsearchable riches" of the physical world, which came out from the unsearchable opulence of the spiritual. But true religion will be the El Dorado of the new world. It will be a Colorado far more spacious and grand than the golden mountains of the world. Those who love most and wisest, will have the largest and richest investments. Such riches never fly away.

"Ideas" will preside over this conjugal blending of the superior with the inferior in the mind. Wealth is natural and accessible to all. Economies and simplicities in dress and in foods will be consequences of the new birth. Simplicity of habits at the table will increase your health income. You will be astonished, when you attain to the life-hights of the new birth, how independent you are by nature of these external things which give you such anxiety and such selfish distress, and for the possession of which you must think and sweat and labor from Monday morning till Saturday night. Misled and miseducated, by the false habits and customs of the world, ladies will search through New York to find a certain ribbon, for which they will freely spend the entire day; but the same ladies would not be induced to do one hour's needle-work for the amelioration of some suffering person in poverty. Miseducated ladies are not the intentional defrauders of other people's right and riches, but are the victims and exponents of a false social start in the world.

. The only substantial riches are spiritual; all outward wealth is convenient and transient. It is not necessary to bedeck the walls of an artist who lives in ideas. Who thinks, when in the presence of angels, that his floor is not carpeted? I used to think that a studio for high contemplations must be beautifully decorated and visibly attractive; that my elegant writing-desk must have a beautiful blue silk velvet cover on which I might write these spiritual thoughts; and that the pictures on the wall must be high-toned and very suggestive. I then thought that many beautiful things in my room were indispensably necessary to induce a state of mind appropriate to these inward truths and more beautiful revealments. But one day I suddenly awoke to the conception that these externals were parts of my enthralled feelings. When I entered into the interior for association with higher things, when in communion with principles and ideas, or with the beauties and glories and blissfulness of the Summer-Land, when contemplating the beatitudes of the state future to man, I never thought of or felt these outward things. My room at such times was never seen; nor was my body necessary to me; neither did I realize my circumstances. I was in communication with the spheres of real life, and they with me; we had formed a true nuptial relation. When out of that condition, the mastery of place and objects was perfect over my external; indeed I could scarcely write my investigations unless I was snugly seated in my beautiful furnished room. At length I said, "This slavery will not do! A man with ideas must be free as are the sons of God." I resolved upon a completer and higher education. I lived at the time in Hartford. I went through a silent street to the store of a periodical dealer. In the back room of this establishment I found barrels and casks and bundles of dirty paper, and repulsive piles of yellow-covered novels, and all sorts of things in dire confusion, dirt and disorder being in extravagant abundance. I seated myself and deliberately made up my mind that *I would* go into " the presence of divine

ideas" *then* and THERE; for I had awakened to the fact
that I was dependent upon pictures and furniture and
carpets for my harmony and tranquillity. I worked
every day for three full weeks, and in that dirty place
every day I entered into the presence of riches that
are unsearchable and permanent. I did it in the rear
of a store frequently filled with people, hearing the
voices of purchasers, talking and bartering. Customers
every day receded until they ceased out of my thoughts,
and the store also vanished, and with it all the world's
externals. Then carpets of imperishable texture and
pictures of immortal beauty were mine—in a word, I
passed from poverty into the possession of eternal
riches.

THE OBJECT OF LIFE.

"Let each man think himself an act of God,
His mind a thought, his life a breath of God ;
And let each try, by great thoughts and good deeds,
To show the most of heaven he hath in him."

The other day a friend who has listened to this course
of lectures, remarked to me, " It seems to me that you
always leave off in the *middle* of your subject.   There
is a great deal of introduction, but no completion of the
subject at the end of your lecture."   Yes, I proceed as
a tree grows—step by step, from its first beginnings
deliberately onward to fruitage ; and I leave off just
when you first get a glimpse of the fruit, and begin to
be hungry for some of it.

The gentleman who made that remark will discover
that he will resign his physical organization, at the end
of this section of his external life, in a manner somewhat as I cease in my discourse—just at the place where
thoughts and ideas begin to be interesting and valuable.
Men usually die when life begins to be full of sweet-
ness, magnitude, and significance.   When, through many
accidents and sorrows, you have learned the beginnings
of a rational way to live, then there sounds a signal
bell telling you that "your work on earth is over."
Thus I speak on the subject before me—begin and

end, not with the end of a subject, but rather with the first sentence in an introduction. Every theme is susceptible of being amplified and lived through ages yet to come. You cannot sound to the lowest deep of any principle that is infinite, nor reach to its highest pinnacle, though you think and speak upon it every hour between the cradle and the coffin.

The object of life? The careless skeptic thinks and says, " This existence is the result of a fortuitous concourse of accidents." Aristotle said, " the fortuitous concourse of atoms." The accidental meeting and confluence of atoms, congregated, making a whole, the universe, and having inherent vital powers and consequential galvanic energies that work everlastingly or until they wear out, is the sum of the skeptic's careless creed. What does such a skeptic think and say of humanity? He says, men are here by accident. We have stumbled out of matter into a temporary organization, into breathing, conscious life, and we shall in like manner stumble back again and drop into the chemistry of utter extinction. What then? What is the sad conclusion? Why, that the "object of life" is to eat, drink, propagate, be merry, and die.

I am acquainted with refined ladies and talented gentlemen who are, or have recently been, in this state of mind; they particularly think and say, " Let us eat, drink, and be merry, for to-morrow we die." They reject the fine Gospel of Epicurus, and, instead, adopt the purely sensual interpretation of his grand sentence, that " True happiness consists in bodily ease and mental tranquillity." Epicurus was not one who debauched his appetites and defiled the organs of his body. Pure

and simple was his style of life. Music in flavors, music
in odors, harmony in compounds prepared for the
stomach, purity in the fluids for drinking, and perfect
health in all parts of the body, which is the basis of
tranquillity of mind and repose in the spirit.

There is another interpretation of the object of life.
The Assembly's Shorter *Cate*chism gives the *dog*matic
answer to this grand question. I suppose it is natural
and right that the catechisms and dogmatisms of the
world should be kept securely in the same cage of creeds.
They always give the same hideous howl to the soul's
freest questionings, "What is the chief end of man?"
You remember the answer—"To glorify God." The
chief end of untold millions already gone, and of innumerable millions yet to go into the higher spheres, is
simply to serve and glorify God, a supposed personality,
and enjoy his presence forever. What does the dictionary say about "glory"? The word "glory" has
two or thee definitions; one is anything that is bright.
A bright day is a glorious day. Anything that is
resplendent and beautiful, is glorious. Thus the object
or "end" of all these countless myriads of human
hearts and heads will be one—what? "To glorify
God;" that is to bedazzle his existence, to brighten him
up, to make him shine—that is the first work, the middle work, and the work eternal! What next? "To
enjoy his presence forever." This is the chief object of our
creation and immortality according to the catechism.
Who will stand or sit in the front ranks? Will everybody
have an equal amount of enjoyment? If the Christians
are countless, how can they be all stationed for this
"glorious" work in one place? Will there not be some

vanguards and some rearguards, some safeguards and
unsafe guards in the midst of the pent-up kingdom?
Those who are nearest the throne, would naturally have
a better chance " to enjoy his presence" than those who
are from the necessity of space farther back. Or, do
they take turns in coming to the front to see and
" glorify" and enjoy the Trinity? Is such a life to be
the basis of your employment throughout eternity?
Made, as each human soul is, with twelve loving, energetic, intelligent, immortal attributes—fitted for ceaseless and variable industry, for art and for science, and
demanding for their full gratification not less than the
circle of the whole universe—and yet through the endless ages to *live* and *think* and *work* and *sing* only to
brighten up God, and " to enjoy" the radiant smiles
and gratified approbation of the Trinity! Outrageous,
imbecile theology! An insult to the mind of every
reasonable man! Our children, thank heaven! are not
taught these heathenish doctrines. To rational minds
the Catechism is like a controversy on the Trinity;
nothing but " an oblong blur," a spot on the sun of
progress in the development of religious ideas.

Again, suppose we take the definition that to " glorify God," means to worship and to praise him. Does
that help it any? Think of a deity whose bump of
approbation and other selfish organs must be constantly
stimulated by the speeches and songs of his children, so
that he may be comfortable and in a happy " frame of
mind." Glorify God! Why, a noble human being is superior to requiring that service from either his children
or peers. A true man is above acclamation or adula-
tion. He stands upon the sublime inherent indorsement

14

of eternal right and truth! What other definition can sectarians give to the words, "To glorify God"? Any theological definition will be an insult to your common sense, and an outrage upon a true idea of the eternal Father-Spirit, who, like the sun, warms and lights all with love and wisdom to the ends of the universe.

There are spiritually-minded men and women, truly religious people, ardent lovers of justice and humanity, who feel that there is nothing better for the sustenance and elevation of the soul than the truth of Deity. These minds are many times tempted to ask each other, "What is the object of life?" They would "do good," but the "way" does not open with the "will," and they flounder in uncertainties. I know a person who persists in thinking that woman's highest and only mission consists in keeping house, multiplying the race, and obeying her husband in all things; and that man's strongest and most enduring interest in woman, under the laws of nature, is wholly of "the earth, earthy," and so he scouts the modern notions of woman's equality and independence. And this man, both a husband and father, began life with high hopes and sublime anticipations, believing that something heavenly and grand would grow out of the reformer's *ideal* of the holy mission and beautiful progress of woman. Of course, such a man was too weak to withstand a few of life's disappointments. Others suppose that the best way to answer the designs of life is to accumulate riches and to enjoy the power and commanding position which wealth gives. The Rothchilds and the Astors can give no other reply out of their practices and experiences. But the upshot of all is disappointment and oppressive cares, with nothing but a place to sleep, something to eat, comfortable clothing, and only such assistance and attentions as you receive from those to whom you pay the wages due to labor. A few fine souls think Art is the object of life. Some say that whatever they feel themselves intellectually, morally, or passionally drawn toward, is the true indication of the object of their existence. I could name many other theories and definitions, but you can trace them out and analyze them for yourself.

Now since, from the mind's constitution, it is certain that each nature will act logically from its own temperaments, it becomes of the utmost importance that its convictions of life's object be of the firmest and truest character, well founded in science, in thought, in love, and in wisdom. Let us, therefore, proceed to ask and answer this question from our own standpoint :

First, Look at the lessons spread out in Nature's fields. What do you feel and see and hear? Do you not both feel and see that there is a *plan*, and a unitary flow and effort, marked out and imaged forth in all visible things? The true inductive philosopher traces " design" backward through the apparent to its central source. The earnest effort of each true investigator is to trace, through the different series of material organizations, the *thought* of God inwardly to the center, which is the heart of the eternal and infinite. When he finds the central Cause, he shouts, "Eureka, Eureka!" More wonderful than Aladdin's lamp is the magical power of this truth. It kindles up all the central fires of creation, fills individual life full of unutterable beauty, and clothes all forms of matter and animation with an undying significance. The moral world, a subterranean sphere to which we seldom go, is divided and subdivided into beautiful series of groups or compounds. It would be useful to describe to you the divine wonders of that dark and mysterious chemical world. You would become delighted and gloriously at home among the elements and their combinations. You should learn how beautifully, how entirely in accordance with the great principle of harmony, the elements and their compounds are arranged in the laboratories of matter. Series give rise to groups, groups develop combinations expressing wholeness, and that "wholeness" constituting the entire mineral kingdom. All this arrangement of matter means something. The materialist asks, " Cui bono ?" Wants to know " what for and what good ?" He asks this wondrous world beneath the soil, and it points him in silence to the revelations of the wonderful worlds above.

Come to the vegetable and floral worlds. Ask our horticulturists, and our pomologists, and our botanists ; ask those who daily and yearly associate with the varieties of beautiful plants and trees and flowers, who cultivate berries—ask them, for they are always enthusiastic and glad to be questioned concerning their pets. You never knew a man, a woman, or a child that had come in pure and full contact with the spirit of Deity in the flower-kingdom, but would speak of it with enkindling enthusiasm, (which means, " God in the heart,") speaking to and warming the loving and beloved flower, the two kissing and embracing, as life meets life in the angel world. But when the hard materialist looks upon all this beautiful kingdom spread out in the world, he asks, " Cui bono ?" " what good ?" Every intelligent human being should ask this question about the glorious physical world, but not without a profound and reverent desire to obtain the true answer.

Next we come to the organic world; out of the simple into the compound, and animated. Look at the finely shaded gradations in this beautiful animal world. Look at the fishes and reptiles, the families of birds, the varieties of marsupials, the many branches of the mammalia, the different tribes of quadrumana, the strange half-human form and features of bi-mana, and lastly the different races of man. What does all this mean? It means that Jacob's ladder had an origin long before the advent of human organization. Its lowest round began way down in the rude fish-world, on which the angels of progress both descended and ascended through all the higher forms of matter. I do not wonder that true philosophers are enthusiasts. I wonder not that Professor Youmans, and Agassiz of Cambridge, and such men as Liebig, look as though they had roses blossoming in their cheeks when they tell the people about these beautiful manifestations of the Divine. Professor Mitchell, who has attained a higher observatory than when he lived in Cincinnati, who laid down his body while working for the grand old flag in South Carolina, can now look out into the pure blue and contemplate the stars. He now sees farther, deeper, and with infinitely more intellectual and spiritual satisfaction. And what does he see? What do the astronomers, Galilleo, Newton, Humboldt, and all such who have eternal homes in the Summer-Land, see? They see unutterably more than mankind can find in the mineral and vegetable and animal. They enjoy the

life of the mathematical, geometrical, organizational
and harmonious. Look at the planets. They are sown
in space, and they seem to grow broadcast over the
sky. The series are not sharply defined and definite.
The varieties of planets are not perfectly visible, nor
do they seem to be entirely mathematical in their
arrangement. But the higher astronomers see better.
The planets are capable of divergence. They have
deliberations and aberrations. The series are, nevertheless, perfectly geometrical and mathematical. Ascend
to the sublime palace of the upper universe, in which
blazing planets, night and day, more "glorify God"
than can all the prayers of innumerable millions. They
are rigidly and immutably mathematical, geometrical,
and perfect in the arrangement of groups and series,
which in the combination constitutes a planetary system. This perfect system never varies from its vitalic
laws. It never has a tangential development; there is
never an accident in it; atoms never get up a fortuitous
manifestation; all roll and unfold together in a glorious
harmony, and in strictest accordance with the divine
heart of the indestructible universe. Do you ask the
question, "Cui buno?" What *good?* and what *for?*

Now comes the personal importance of the question.
Here we are, in this world, standing before ourselves.
What does it mean? It means that man is still man's
unsolved problem. I think I need not assure you that I
have with as much self-forgetful devotion as ever Hindoo
bowed to his idol, with as much sincerity as an orthodox minister addresses the throne of the three deities,
turned my faculties day after day, and year after year,
to the answer of the question, "Why do I exist?"

Why, and for what object or end, does my brother and my sister, *live?*

Daily I see about me the phenomena of marriage and the phenomena of prolification. Here are the facts of marriage and parentage, and the facts of bodily disease and death and disappearance. These phenomena are conspicuous and come before the world every day. Now do you not want to know what lies behind and underneath all these phenomena? Then trace the stream of divine thought back to its fountain. Let us go through the fields of thought and traverse mountains of mystery to their very summits. As fearless explorers work among the bleak and snowy hights of the physical planet, making paths for others to tread, so let us walk upon the beautiful and fertile hights of these mountains of contemplation. Let us scale them. Sleep out every night in your doubts if you choose, or journey forward with the bare-skin of skepticism, exposed to truth's sun, but in the midst of it all hold fast to the healthy idea of the largest integrity and magnanimity in your motives. To *know,* and then to put his best knowledge into harness and to make it draw, is the grand coronation which accompanies and succeeds the good man's search after truth. With a full-hearted and holy devotion, I have pursued this question, and I shall this morning give you what, to me, is the briefest and largest answer. If I ever see more with reference to it, and can then speak to you as I now do, I shall be ready to tell it; but if I do not yield a better answer, I know that each of you will; for what is possible to me *now,* is a prophecy of realization for every other one in the progress of life.

Leaving the kingdoms of the earth and the mighty
questions which they suggest, and retiring from the
starry firmaments and from all the holy questions which
they awaken, I ask your attention to YOURSELF, because
in yourself alone you will find the explanation of "Why
do you exist?" Analyzing the individual externally,
you find a beginning and an end to the career of being.
With the planet it is just the same. All things and
bodies begin with the round 0, what is called "zero"
in numerals. Man begun thus—*no* intellect, *no* industry, *no* science, *no* art; innocence equaled. only by
ignorance, which, under the highest moral standard, is
no excellence at all. It is the absence of both vice and
virtue; a condition equally exposed and assailable. We
began with the negation, 0. But the moment the intellect awakened out of the impulses, (for everything has
love-roots,) that moment an effort was made to expel
and exclude ignorance, to widen the boundary of knowledge. All the first steps of the race were full of
stumblings. But through each "fall" mankind arrived
at much more than they knew before the mistake. Consider now that the race was thus started and educated.
What are the results? Make one straight mark at the
left of the 0, and you will have added 10 to the sum of
benefits. Everything valuable that men do, adds another mark to the left of the 0. The race has added
many figures to the left, while the idiot "makes his
marks" at the right of the 0. What does the ignorant
one get? Nothing, because his marks to the right of
the cypher kills its value. Such is the idiotic plan of
old theology. The progressive plan, on the contrary,
makes its reports at the left of the zero. We are getting

used to great figures in the finances of this country. These great responsibilities will help to develop the better character of the people. Once people would open their eyes to see a man worth two millions. Now it will do to talk about no less than $3,000,000. Persons who plod along through trade and arithmetic, who look daily up and down their ledgers, can see nothing higher than that which is before them. They say, "figures won't lie." So say I. Figures will teach mankind everything. They will bring men's characters up to their standard, because they will not "lie." There is that in marks made to the left of zero which enlarges and expands and makes men magnanimous, even when the "sum" drives them into driveling and shriveling bankruptcy. People never before knew what it was that enabled them to rise above great obstacles and outswim the Gulf Stream of adversity.

Figures, in the progressive history of the race, are made at the left side of the round 0. What does it mean? It means that mankind have been multiplying and enhancing the inherent value of their relations to a diviner life. This has been done for you and for me. It has come out of numbers and out of the teeming centuries. What is man's organization? He has a body, with a sphere of soul-life between the outmost and the spirit, which is deepest within. The greatest external success occurs in the middle region; as between the two extremes on the planet is the greatest fertility, the greatest industry, and the greatest development of wealth. The soul, which is not as high as spirit in refinement and function, is in contact with this world. It is the source and the play-ground of

14*

passions and appetites. It is the fulcrum on which all
passion and force-levers are placed; the bridge over
which all animal emotions, impulses and energies travel
between the body (outmost) and the spirit (inmost).
Only now and then do we perceive glimmerings of
pure spirit in man.

Men and women sing about being angels in this
world. It is difficult to become angels in the cellar-
kitchen of life; but it is possible. You can live a
sweetly ordered life, and can use your will-power to
regulate your thoughts and keep discord away. Genuine
angels know nothing about being " tempted" to do anything that is wrong. If you can be tempted, you are not
yet above the conditions from which temptation ema-
nates. Pure spirit is above the reach of temptation.
Moral strength to overcome or to resist evil, is the
promise of the future angel. It is, in fact, the *basis* on
which the angel-character is finally erected; yet if you
are tempted at all, you have not ascended above the
soul-plane. You do not yet live in the Spirit. You
will, therefore, be tempted to do various things—little
things, great things, bad things, indifferent things—
sometimes, perhaps, good things may be done unwisely,
or overdone, or done to excess. I know persons who
do some good things until they get in everybody's way—
until a very excellent thing in itself becomes a stumbling-block; like the expression of divine music, continued for hours instead of moments, becomes tedious,
because too exquisite, and ultimately the best strains
would be irksome to the highest master of the holy art.

I said that pure SPIRIT is seldom manifested in this
world. Why? Because eighty per cent. of life here is

body and soul. Hence men say, " Well, there are only two parts of us; one is inside, soul; the other outside, body." Some insist that there is nothing but matter about and within man. Col. Colt, the man who invented the pistol bearing his name, a great, splendid looking man, once said, "Mr. Davis, I don't understand your doctrine. You say that I have an immortal soul. If you will trot it out, so I can see it, I will give you five hundred dollars." Wanted me to " trot out" the evidence that he would live after death. A soul! he did not believe in it as an eternal verity. Said he, " Here I am, so much bone and muscle and blood and brain—is there anything else? I am perfectly willing," he continued, " to help with money to support a good thing. I go to the Catholic Church, and to other meetings where I can hear fine singing and eloquent speaking, no matter where or who, and I am willing to pay for it; but I would give most to *know* that I shall always continue." He expressed the skepticism of vast numbers.

Body and soul, not SPIRIT, are most manifested during this life. Body is uppermost sixty-five per cent. of the time, and only the rest of the hours is given to soul, which includes passion, appetite, impulse, and indifferent emotions. All the energies that make soul are displayed in the heat of the blood, the electricity of the nerves, the will-forces of the brain—all enter into the composition of the soul. Now, this fact in life means something. I know that men in the churches say, "It is because individual man is fallen; this is why men have more body than *spirit*. The life of your heart is blackened by the Adamic curse; so you are working along and struggling through materiality."

But look deeper and see if there be not a beautiful meaning in it all. We are not authorized to contend with facts; we are here rather to comprehend and make use of them. The age of flagellation, of sacrificial offerings, of self-excoriation, of unworthy and imbecile adoration, is past. The cosmotheosis is begun. Those who linger in the rear of the vanguard will continue to fall in the ashes, and to roll and crawl like worms in the miserable muck of ignorance and theological superstition. Well, why is materiality uppermost?

The meaning of it all is, THE BODY IS A FACTORY.

Suppose an Indian should enter a factory at Lowell, Mass. Suppose the factory is not at work; that it is being repaired, as he enters for the first observation. Suppose the wheels are still, the shafts down on the floor and piled up in confusion, the belts lying here and there, fire out of the furnace, and that no machinery is in action anywhere. He departs without any definite impression of its utility. In a few weeks he is again shown into that factory; he looks at the buzzing cogwheels, at the swift spindles, he sees the tremendous shafts in the act of revolution, the large leather belts running with still power, and he looks upon it with the same consternation, or with the same stupid expression, as many people look upon the object of their existence in this world. The foreman asks the Indian, "What do you suppose is the object of these wheels and shafts and belts?" "Me don't know." He shakes his head; he is almost dumb. The master-machinist then says, "Red man, let me tell you. The wheels and all the machinery that you see here, are but parts of *one* design, and *one* result will come out of it all." The savage, just like a skeptic, knowing nothing of the end, is confounded. Now, what is that one result? Do you see that *cloth* piled upon those shelves? What! it is *all* designed to make cloth? How is it made? and from what? The savage is now taken down into the lower stories where the stock is received. There he sees coarse and dirty looking stuff—cotton. "Do you tell me," exclaims the Indian to the foreman, "that such stuff is made into that beautiful material I saw on the shelves?" The one perfect result, accomplished through (to him) countless intricacies and most inconsistent parts, was impressed upon his savage mind.

Now, are we not all savages on this problem of life's central object? What means this world so filled with confusion? Behold fishes and birds and reptiles and plants and trees and stars scattered and sown about everywhere. Is it all a system of accidents; all a fortuitous concourse of atoms? What means all this to man? Are not the brightest intellects confounded by the wonderful complexity of the system? Let us stand on the summits of the mountains, in the presence of this grand machinery of the universe, and learn to comprehend the magnitude of its meaning. The human body is a factory full of wheels. The stock to be manufactured into a beautiful fabric, is taken in between the lips. Look at the miserable stuff that is prepared in the world's kitchens! What does it mean? It means that one result is to be accomplished by the wheels. What wheels? The heart, the lungs, the pancreas, the liver, the stomach, the gall-ducts, and kidneys. The soul and body, after taking in stock, wants an easy chair. The brain, the seat of government, has closed doors for a secret session. The wheels are set in motion, for the engine has received energy from the heated fiber. You know enough of physiology not to need any specifications of the digestive process. Material is being manufactured up into the so-called immaterial. The spiritual meaning of life answers the question of the object of man's existence in this world. The passions and appetites may be put to high and grand uses; for all things we eat and drink, and all the elements we breathe, are converted into a garment, which, after death, gives personality and form and immortal beauty to the SPIRIT. You are here just as the silkworm is in the cocoon, winding fine thread into the formation of your spirit's body, so that the essence of the spirit itself can have personality and be protected forever from diffusion. At last the soul predominates and becomes the crowning work; all the rest is subordinate and co-ordinate and auxiliary. Marriage and parentage and homes, and the various arts and sciences, are so many intermediates and accessories and tributaries and streamlets flowing into the one central object of being in this world.

Whatever we eat and whatever we drink is more or less represented in the article manufactured. Hence you may have a soul prepared for the Summer-Land, streaked with tobacco. Or, it may be very odoriferous after death with alcohol. Of course, the fluid alcohol will be left just where you left your money and your clothes, but the effect of it remains, because you have wrought and sprinkled it into your spirit's body. Suppose a paper-maker says, " It is no matter what I put into the composition before the article is manufactured. I can put in cotton and old rags, old boots, some beefsteak, some old beans, and I will make paper as good and white as any other maker." Do you believe that? Ask the artist. Can he put any kind and admixture of colors in his piece? No—a beautiful painting requires a careful arrangement of properly mixed colors. So with man's foods and beverages. He is making a spiritual body from all he eats and drinks and breathes, and to accomplish this result, in the best and highest style, is to fulfill the organic object of the present life.

EXPENSIVENESS OF ERROR IN RELIGION.

"When from the lips of truth one mighty breath
Shall, like a whirlwind, scatter in its breeze
The whole dark pile of human mockeries,
Then shall the RACE OF MIND commence on earth,
And, starting fresh, as from the second birth,
MAN, in the sunshine of the world's new spring,
Shall walk transparent, like some holy thing."

Innovators and reformers are called iconoclasts, or idol-and-church-destroyers, and so they are; because most of them have arisen to a plane of comprehensive thought and of holier inspiration, from which it is easy to see that the time will surely come when whatsoever is fleeting and evanescent in the idol-temples, pagodas, and churches of the world—their forms, their ceremonies, their rituals, liturgies, and whatever you choose to name that, in them, which causes one sect to differ from and hate its neighbor—is destined to be known only in the historic monuments of the world, having passed utterly out of all human confidence, and thus out of existence.

We, therefore, have the reputation of being opposed to churches, which many deem equivalent to being opposed to "religion." I have no acquaintance with any sincere spiritual-minded man or woman who wishes to destroy pure and undefiled religion. Excepting those who make a great mistake in their conceptions of the ordinary meaning of words, I know not one individual in spirituality, who supposes that when he is opposing the mythological theology of the churches, he is necessarily thereby opposing religion. Negationists, or the anti-spiritual skeptics, seem to think and write as if anything that bears the impress or label of religion is worthy of their severest invectives and unqualified condemnation. This is not our mental condition; neither is it the condition of many skeptics. Sift the actuating motives of these minds—trace their thoughts down to the very germs; and you will discover that they oppose, and desire to oppose, only what they conceive to be "pious frauds," and hurtful "errors" in the moral and spiritual sentiments of mankind. They are no more opposed to true spiritual religion, which is immanently fixed in the constitution of the human soul, than they are opposed to the fragrance of flowers.

The universe, as I have before said, is filled with DESIGNS. Reason very simply and logically follows the lead of these designs into very profound depths, and unto far-reaching hights of thought, partly by inductive research, by the hints of its intuitions, and by means of analogy. The existence of *light*, for illustration, presupposes and guarantees the existence of *eyes ;* the existence of *sound* guarantees, presupposes, and fixes as a matter of mathematical necessity, the existence of *ears*. If the fishes in the Kentucky cave have no eyes, it is presumptive evidence—in fact, it is demonstrative— that there is therein no light for them. Apply this method of reasoning to the structure of the human mind, nearest its moral and spiritual apex or summits. We find there the existence of superior faculties which take hold upon truths, ideas and principles—faculties, with hearts and tongues, which give off unutterable yearnings and utter holiest prayers to know *more* concerning human life beyond the grave. Shall we not say that these faculties presuppose and demonstrate the existence of the truths, ideas, and principles, for which they seek and thirst and hunger? Not only so, but also that the Summer-Land life to which they aspire, and after which they perpetually inquire, and into which they lovingly plunge and bathe whenever the cloud of doubt is enough removed to admit of an eternal right, is a reality not made with hands, eternal in the heavens.

These spiritual faculties are dwelling in the summits of the human structure. They, consequently, are the first to catch heaven's light when it streams over the horizon of faithful thought concerning immortality. The superior faculties, being stationed in the superior part of the human structure, are also and necessarily the first to yearn for what is called "religion." They yearn like angelic-children for knowledge of whatsoever is spiritual and celestial, pertaining to eternal life, its beatitudes and its happiness. These faculties do not grow under insincerity and persecution. They are in themselves wise. They are also filled with love. From the center they grow and put forth the purest and most enthusiastic aspirations. These aspirations spring out of divine warmth, which multiplies and fertilizes them, and gives them fruitage and happiness. The perceptive part of mind apprehends, applies checks and modifica-

tions, gives symmetry of manifestation, and perfection
of expression.   Persons who are wise in their religious
emotions, are symmetrical in their manifestations.   Those
who have only love in their spiritual faculties, and not
wisdom, are full of idolatry and impulsiveness—are
given to extremes, excesses, infatuations, and fanaticisms
—which you can read in the private and earliest history
of every religion.   Now, it is not what these spiritual
faculties love that we oppose ; but the *forms* which they
have gathered about them, and through which they have
necessitated the world to express itself.   If the kingdom
of heaven should " come on the earth" week after next,
do you suppose it would indorse the different evangelical forms of expressing religion ?   Do you suppose that
an approval would come from the courts of infinitude,
adopting as essential the various exercises and consequent antagonisms which have grown up full of thorns
in these churches?   Subdue and paint them as much as
you choose, you will still find that the antagonism of
the creeds is anti-kingdom-of-heaven ; it is, rather,
propandemonium, human in origin, and is marked for
an early consignment to the pit of oblivion.

We reformers come, therefore, to announce and to
work for the extinction of these differences. ·Not that
all men will or can think alike, but that they can and
will raise above creedal differences and reject mythological interpretations of interior truths.   On the mere
controversy as to what is meant in the Bible by the
word " baptism," millions of bigots and thousands of
dollars have been added to churches throughout the
country.   That controversy, by making different forms
of faith, has. built church after church ; one to gratify

the Calvinistic faith, another to gratify the Free Will
Baptists, and a third to gratify the Close Communion
Baptists. Do you suppose that, in the good time coming,
alias the kingdom of heaven, these shallow-brained
interpretations will be perpetuated? We do not oppose
" religion," nor what is true *spirituality* in the human
soul; but we oppose the misapprehension and creeds
which have clustered about it in the development of the
religious faculties. The controversy as to whether the
grace of God was, from the foundation of the world,
prepared for and meted out to all persons before their
birth, and thus would foreordain and govern their individual destinies through the eternal ages, or whether
the grace of God was a free gift to all who would accept,
has built all these immense piles of property called the
" Houses of God," or churches and tabernacles. They
loom up before you in magnificent stupidity. These
buildings are confessedly coronating the diabolical controversies that have grown from the foolish interpretations of a few unimportant words which somebody, in a
religious state of mind, uttered twenty centuries ago.
Do you suppose the kingdom of heaven, *alias* " the good
time coming," will approve of such a condition of
things? If you do, pray for the advent of that kingdom; then, (oh, fearful thought!) you *really* pray for
just such *reformers* and for such *iconoclasts* and for such
opponents of the creeds that built the churches, as exist
and speak and write and work for progress in the nineteenth century!

The spiritual faculties, on the summit of the mind,
exist because there are ideas, principles, truths, and
eternal Summer-Lands answering to them. These facul-

ties yearn for these realities in the universe as naturally as one's appetite yearns for food, or the thirsting mouth for drink. Thirst presupposes the existence of water, and hunger indicates the existence of food. You have yearnings to know what is beyond, to appreciate, to realize and to enjoy what is ideal and beautiful and sweet; and these inborn yearnings are infallible demonstrations of the positive existence of all that for which they hunger and thirst, and to promote which they devote property, yield great industry, and pledge so much of time, friendship, love, and worship.

Can you wonder that the soul delights to sit and dream in this beautiful mellow light of the Infinite Spirit? The Lazzaroni of Italy, so poor and so infirm that they cannot obtain wood to keep their bodies warm in the winter, can go out on the southern side of the rocks and cliffs and groves, and absorb the warm sunny influences that emanate from the physical orb in the blue heavens, a beautiful substitute for the heat of the wood that would keep them comfortable. It is thus with every human soul at times. You may be a spiritual mendicant. You may go about asking heart-charities and wisdom-alms of your spiritual brothers or sisters. All persons in the churches on Sunday are really asking alms of heaven through the pulpit, even when the minister himself is miserably "poor in spirit." But almost every soul enters the "interior" at times. This deepening of the mind may come from the reading of ideas, or through contemplation of holy principles, or from a sacred enthusiasm, or it may be awakened by some external cause like the whisperings of an angel. At such a moment the soul will come into a new relation to the

infinite sun. It instantly warms and fertilizes the
affections, gives unity and joy and beautiful happiness
for the moment, and the spirit is lifted beyond utterance. It is a thrill that goes like lightning throughout
the spirit, awakening its gratitude and filling its loves
with inward songs of celestial harmony. Such experiences invariably come through the inward faculties,
which, for the moment, are lifted and gratified by contact with the wise and loving life of the Infinite Father
and Mother.

But start with *an error*, make a radical *mistake*,
through want of wisdom in opening your account in the
day-book and the ledger of theology, and it will run
throughout all your growth in "religion." From the
moment it enters into the compilation, your whole record
is vitiated. Sometimes, in our large banks and in our
commercial institutions, an error creeps stealthily into
the ledger. At first, perhaps, it is but a vulgar frac-
tion. In a few months it increases rapidly; in a few
years it is large and important. In a quarter of a century, when the great day of settlement has come, when
the stockholders apply to know definitely all their
resources and liabilities, then comes an investigation,
and a ponderous and expensive error is found running
through all the books of the institution. Then they
send for the best known accountant to review and analyze the books. Days and weeks, and perhaps months,
are given to the tedious labor of ferreting out the error
and expelling it from the books of the institution. It
requires a good deal of money to compensate the investigator, and a great deal of fine insight is expended in
seeing exactly how that little blunder originated. How

enormously it grew in twenty-five years! sweeping
away much capital and the reputation of honest clerks,
and how anxious all stockholders were to get the wrong
righted, the error expelled, and the reform established.

Now suppose you apply this to the errors of religion.
But just here let us remember it is not claimed that the
business of the mercantile, banking, or commercial institution was in itself *spurious*, but that there was a vicious,
and expensive, and demoralizing *error* introduced ; but
not necessarily by any evil intent on the part of the
persons who opened the account. Of religious error we
say the same. The word "religion" I now use to
express the *spirit of truth* in the human soul, which
includes goodness and virtue and all the higher attributes and beauties of the Infinite. Truth, and a love
for truth, seems to be the finest embodiment and exem-
plification of what is called "God." The faculties
group themselves in worshipful love about that conception. That conception is, in itself, a treasure of infinite
value to the spirit. It gives joy and holy peace. But
in gratifying these faculties, which see truth, and entertain the love of truth, mankind frequently commit mistakes and originate expensive errors. The greatest and
heaviest error is what men call "theology." We discriminate with great tenacity, and forever insist upon
our definition, between the "religion" and "theology"
which has crept into religion. The error of the theology
runs throughout the world, and is threatening the
so-styled civilized portion of mankind with political as
well as religious bankruptcy. To-day it is necessary
that our best spiritual accountants should enter into an

investigation, and ferret out the error, and leave the pure spirit of religion an opportunity to flourish as the white rose of heaven.

Reformers, intellectually, socially, and spiritually, are, like other men and women, more or less imperfect; some are very good, but very peculiar; some talk and write and work with a great deal of discord; some are exceedingly antagonistic and disagreeable to encounter; but with all their eccentricities and sledge-hammer roughness, with all their excoriating adjectives and unrestrained expletives, they are the necessary agents of Justice, the vicegerents of eternal truth, working in the midst of idols and forms and ceremonies, and relieving the world of expensive errors in its theologies. Theology is the systematic form in which the spirit of religion is clothed. Theology I do not at all believe in; while I believe profoundly in religion. That is, I believe in whatsoever my spirit sees and feels is spiritual and interior and eternal. No deep nature can have faith in that which is evanescent, fleeting, formal, ceremonial, and suited only to gratify, for the time, those persons who suppose that " theology" should give shape and expression to pure and undefiled religion. Pure and undefiled truth is simple and easily comprehended. Every one has faith in it from the source of intuition. Did you ever hear any one speak of old theology— the legitimate child of an ignorant priesthood—as being " pure and undefiled" ?

Polytheism, the doctrine of a great many Gods; or Pantheism, in which all being is God; Dualism—meaning a God and a Devil; or Deism, which is Unitarianism, teaching the one God—these all enter into the catalogue of the world's theologies. Anthropomorph-

ism, that is, attributing to God the form and character of man, is sacred to many civilized people. They
will receive no revelations or inspirations which tend
to dissipate the notion that God is a great man. If it
be affirmed that " God is a spirit," and that spirit is
diffused throughout the universe, the statement is label-
ed " pantheism." And yet this is the doctrine of the
New Testament. (See John, chapter iv., 24th verse.)
In the Old Testament, on the other hand, you will find
the doctrine of anthropomorphism, the man-God, or
deism—Jehovah, the concentration of almightiness, the
focalization of all stout convictions concerning the attribute of omnipotence—Jehovah, the Jewish God of infinite, desperate, and destructive attributes, with nothing
for the heart, and generally repulsive to everything
human.

When the heart grows warmer and larger, it sees,
or thinks it sees, a Father in the maker, and calls him
by that endearing name. Such hearts pray to the
" Father" instead of to Jehovah, whose omnipotence
and implacable justice overwhelm the mind. The human
soul is filled with conceptions of pure tenderness, which
call for tender eternal relations. These spiritual faculties require tender relations in every stage of their
development. Hence the Father was revealed, prayed
to, besought, invoked, and teased too much by the childhood stage of the race. It makes children fretful,
peevish, and small-minded to cry all their wants and
troubles and sorrows into the ears of the Infinite Spirit.
But this absurdity is a part of theology, and here is an
error, and yet it is a spontaneous, though unwise,
expression of the spirit of love and worship by the reli-

15

gious faculties. Many souls affect to be severely shocked, and their children in Sunday-schools are really shocked, because their theology says the all-beautiful, all-loving, all-embracing Father is *particeps criminis* to the eternal damnation of nine persons in every ten! There are civilized ministers in the city of New York to-day, who are (I trust) ashamed to the very heart for ever having believed and taught any such error in religion. And yet there are some persons who affect to believe this stupid error with all their heart—of course that organ cannot be very spacious; and there are ministers who yet preach it with all their heads—the capacity whereof does not excite anybody's astonishment. But, unhappily, they have the power to make mothers believe, and the innocent children whom such mothers send to the Sunday-schools also believe, that God is a great Baptist, instead of a Presbyterian sprinkler, or that God is a red-hot Methodist instead of an easy-going Quaker, or polite Unitarian. These are the errors that creep into religion. Whether God be a Quaker, or a Sprinkler, or a Plunger, it is of little consequence in the great future of true religion. God is infinite, a spirit, a man, or a tyrant—just what you choose to make him in your seven-by-nine creeds and dogmas. If the whole isle of New York was soft, malleable, and golden clay—if you could move it and shape it into anything that suited your fancy by your hand, you would doubtless undertake to do it, and all the children would follow your example, and thus you and they would begin to make various forms of thought and countless toys out of the universal plastic substance. Your conception of the spirit of God is like that clay. You make all kinds of idols, creeds, and theologies out of the universal plastic substance. The spirit of God, however, being the same everywhere and at all times, is not thrown from its equilibrium by these childish forms and toys made by learned theologians. The tangible and intangible Gods and Jesuses, which are made by the cartload out of theology, do not disturb the Infinite heart, Mother, neither the Infinite mind, Father. In this light, therefore, theology is an innocent error. And yet the men of the city of New York have spent money enough, to gratify these foolish idolatries, to give ninety-seven thousand families a comfortable home worth five thousand dollars each!

The early Jews, who were in many respects, by far the most intelligent people, maintained a distant allegiance to common sense. They believed in a Jehovah; in one God, in no devil, and in a new Jerusalem. They did not exactly know whether the new Jerusalem would be in this world or in the next. And generally there was a difference of opinion upon these points. The Rabbis differed widely on many religious questions, but they never concocted any of the monstrous errors of theology which have built modern churches. They had their synagogues. Their temples of religion were devoted to the gathering together of the people, so that they might sing and give full expression to their convictions of supernaturalism. They had their shekinahs, their image temples, and their decorated tabernacles; but their forms were all symbolic and brim-full of spiritual meanings. They enjoyed their festivals and glorifications; it was a pleasant way to pass the time. The same old forms are observed by Jews at this late age of the world.

The tinsel and paraphernalia of the New York synagogues would suit thirty-five hundred years ago. The
plan was at first a simple organization of persons,
believers in theocracy, for the enjoyment of religion,
and not to teach a mythical theology. The first conception that formed the basic error in theology, was that
man, by an incomprehensible fall, had lost all connection
with the Infinite Spirit. Theologians have never tried
to reconcile this doctrine with common sense, because it
is never necessary in theology to have things reconciled.
It is a proud peculiarity of the system to be supernatural, which is the name for what is absurd and impossible.

Theology began with the assumption that the human
race was out of joint with God's will. God is represented as being just as anxious as man was to get out
of this state of eternal difference and conflict. It was
necessary to turn a fable inside out, and wrong side
foremost, in order to fix an explanation of the great
quarrel between God and his only two children, which
happened in a very small place called Eden. They had
willfully diverged from the Infinite Love! Theologians
say that God could not help it! He must be excused
for the straying of his two children! He was all
benevolence and all wise. He concocted the atonement
long before the sin was committed, knowing from the
first that Adam and Eve would cut up just the caper
they did in the fable. Preparations were accordingly
made from the foundations of the world. The remedy
was ready to be administered to all who would shut
their eyes, open their mouths, ask no questions, and
swallow. This is what theologians call the atonement.

That is a desperate and most expensive *error*. It is based on the doctrine that you are totally sinful, or that you are sufficiently sinful to deserve an eternal existence in cheap brimstone. To recover you from that dilemma, the atonement was prepared. By its provisions you are to be accepted in the kingdom of heaven, and esteemed worthy of that state of existence, on the merits of an innocent man who was made to suffer for sinners.

Such is the machinery of error in theology. There is nothing of the kingdom of God in it; there is no religion in it. Many excellent persons suppose that their hope of happiness in the future is annihilated with the overthrow of the atonement. Thousands cling to a shallow error, and suppose that by faith in it, they will be prepared after death to enter upon the joys of the kingdom of peace. But thousands come back from the other life to tell us a very different story. What is necessary to make this atonement universally accepted and efficacious? There is but one-third of the population of this globe that has any confidence in or any knowledge whatever of such a supernatural institution as the death of Jesus. Only one person in three of the earth's population—about 370,000,000 out of 1000,-000,000—know anything about this error of theology. Some have heard it; some see it in the newspapers. Away off in China the missionaries preach this absurdity of superstition. They do what Bishop Colenso did, teach the theories of theology; religion, pure and undefiled, they do not often explain to the heathen. What, we again ask, would make this atonement universal and efficacious? Reason will have nothing to do with such a theory. "*Faith!*" Here is the third error which follows of necessity the first, which is the " fall," and the second, which is the " atonement." Look at these churches, and look at their ministers. They are, doubtless, just as earnest in their labors and just as faithful to their convictions as are they who work in a better cause. I am satisfied that, for earnestness and honesty, there is nothing to choose between a Catholic, a Protestant, my brother Beecher, or my brother Tyng. They are as honest in their calling, and· as faithful to their internal convictions as are less or more civilized minds. Toward the individuals of the different forms of faith I do not feel any uncharitableness. I do not believe that they are hypocrites and deceivers. Disreputable as the fact may be to their intelligence, they do believe earnestly in the errors of " theology" as well as in the truths of " religion." But theology, and not religion, is the origin of their churches. Their religious hatreds and creedal antagonisms arise from theology. Hence we are " in duty bound" to oppose the diversal systems of theology as the first step toward the development of true religion.

Christians, impelled by their theology, and moved by their benevolence and charity, which are the best elements of religion, send off millions of money and hundreds of missionaries to carry a knowledge of " faith" as well as of " sin," and of the " atonement," to the heathen. As the person of African descent said: " It is an ill wind that blows nowhar." So this missionary movement: By necessity it carries some items of useful education, somewhat of the impulses of civilization, more advanced habits of social life, a few notions about cultivating the soil, new patterns for garments, and several plans for building houses and churches. It carries "glory" and "grog" to the heathen. The missionary work is, therefore, associated, for the most part, with what is good. For these reasons men willingly subscribe their dollars to help the solemn-hearted missionary on his perilous way. Although his theology is of no consequence, you think that possibly there may be something connected with the minister's family which may be useful and ennobling to the savages. But it will not do to say a great deal in that direction. We do not get encouraging reports from travelers. The flattering reports of great works among the heathen come through the religious papers, written by the missionaries themselves. Of course, they give a ministerial report of the missionary work in which they are involved, and to which they have, with great self-sacrifice, consecrated themselves to carry the "efficacious" errors in religion to the savages of the forest wild.

What follows faith? "Regeneration." This is the climax of the theological structure. Look about you in society and see the original characters who have been born nearly two thousand years after this saving (?) theology was started. Who are your chief men at Washington? Who are they who occupy your highest places to-day? Are they Spiritualists, Reformers, Progressionists—persons who are wholly and unqualifiedly, publicly and privately, opposed to the absurdities of old theology—who have no faith in creeds and ceremonies? No. They are men who are known to be publicly allied to the sectarian churches and to the follies of theology ; but they are not as fully known to be allied to pure and undefiled religion. These public

men at Washington are, many of them, much advanced
in years. Some of them are dead—have you not read
their obituaries in the papers?—in trespasses and sins.
The Republicans and Democrats to-day correspond to
the publicans and sinners of the olden time. The
American government is engineered by persons who
openly and shamelessly profess to have adopted all the
four errors of theology: "sin," the "atonement,"
"faith," and "regeneration." Somebody has been
unkind enough to say that I am *opposed* to "religion."
Does it necessarily follow, because a person is opposed
to the forms of error in theology, that he is therefore
opposed to pure spirituality, and opposed to what is
good and true in religion? Let us discriminate carefully, lest we be stranded upon this rock of illogical
reasoning and wicked prejudice. It is like the passage
between Scylla and Charybdis—ignorance on one side,
theology on the other. Man must steer his bark, his
reason, his intuition, and his character between these
.dangerous obstructions on either side of the channel, or
he will be dashed to pieces.

Religion, without wisdom, is fanatical. It is a cru-
sade of the sepulcher—it worships and fights for a little
piece of ground; it sacrifices everything to an idol.
The simple-minded and loving-hearted nature loves to
appeal to the Infinite Spirit. No person thinks of any
form of faith while under the experience of devotional
prayer. The spirit enjoys the luxury of contact, as the
sense of smell enjoys the special fragrance of a beloved
flower. There is little difference between the rapport
and the spiritual gratification. When you truly approach
the Infinite, you sensibly become part of it. The theory

of the contact is theology; the experience of the contact is religion. Theology stands off and builds up a system. But when your spirit comes in contact with the spirit of truth, which is the spirit of fraternity and unity, you then know nothing of theological notions. A grand joy and a loving happiness thrills and fills the whole temple of your spirit. Then you are divinely warm and tender; you feel kindly and sweetly toward all members of the human family. You were vindictive, but you are now forgiving; you were angular, but you have become harmonious. That is the blessing of God; the fragrance of the Infinite Flower. You now feel that there is nothing in the world as important as pure spirituality. One more step and you become fanatical. You believe devoutly that religion is the chief concern of mortals here below. From this abnormal state it will take but a very slight alteration in your mind to make a religious twaddler or fanatic.

Because man's spiritual faculties are not the whole, but only a part of his mental structure. Look at these faculties throughout the other parts and windows of the temple. Examine them with your reason. They mean something, do they not? They have a high work to do, else why are they such a superior power? Go into these upper chambers of your spirit, and dwell there for a time. Nothing is more important than the just and complete gratification of the desires of your spiritual faculties. But a religious "revival" is mostly abnormal. Methodists frequently experience the fascination and fanaticism thereof. The new convert is too happy to sleep quietly; she gets out of bed, kneels, and prays; but she cannot attend to getting the next morning's

15*

meal. John, who is not converted, wants to go out early on his farm to work ; but Jane, his wife, has just "got religion," and cannot attend tố such labors. Of course the potatoes in the pan are burned, and generally things have grown "irreligious" in the house. But John goes out to his work, and Jane goes into her bed. She prays long and devoutly ; then lies down with great exhaustion, and sleeps. Presently she awakes and turns ˙over the leaves of her Bible. She remembers the minister's last text. It is the first sentence that meets her eye! It seems as though God himself had spoken it to her. It goes right to her heart. Then she remembers the last song that made her heart so joyous, and immediately she sets up to sing the heavenly hymn. By this time her excited feelings have made her very weary. John has just come home for supper, and there is the same difficulty. This folly continues about ten days. Thus some families get religion very bad. Now and then these "revivals" are attended with violent symptoms which subside into imbecility. There is a vast space between pure religion and religious excitement.

We come now to consider the expensiveness of error in religion. We will confine our remarks to this city, saying nothing about the other great cities of superstitious Christendom. In the city of New York alone theological error has erected 33 Baptist churches, 4 Congregational, 22 Dutch Reformed, 18 Jewish Synagogues, 7 Lutheran, 35 Methodist Episcopal churches, 5 African Episcopal churches, 1 Methodist Protestant, 46 Presbyterian, 6 United Presbyterians, 56 Protestant Episcopal churches, (the latter being the *genteelest* of all), 31 Roman Catholic—mother and daughter you see close together—miscellaneous additional 20, and among the whole of them we find but *three* Quaker meeting-houses, two Unitarian, and four Universalist churches.

Therefore we find 284 temples consecrated to error in religion, in New York alone; not counting any of the churches just over in Williamsburg, Brooklyn and Jersey City. These expensive buildings indicate what theology, or religious error, has erected on the island of Manhattan! These temples and pagodas must have talented and expensive ministers, and in -addition they have sextons, and they must, (thank heaven!) they *must* also have choirs. By calculation you will find that the cost of the gas per annum—and there is a great deal of this article used—together with the heat, and sexton's hire, and the excellent music for the churches, amounts yearly to about $500; the average amount of all expenses, in all the churches for ministers, &c. is a little over $2000, for each church per year. Now suppose we add up the original cost of all these churches, and combine the interest on this sum with the annual expenses, for thirty years, or a generation. Salaries, gas, fire, sexton, and music, with interest on the first cost, amounts to not less than one million of dollars per annum; making the aggregate expense of religious error for thirty years in the city of New York more than thirty millions! Now ask Dr. Spring, or any orthodox gentleman, how many souls have been probably saved in the city of New York during thirty years, and he will shudder. For his theology says that only *one* soul in ten ever gets within sight of the kingdom of heaven!

If homes at the rate of $5000 a piece were purchased for the poor of this continent, and given to them out and out, they would amount to just what New York sectarianism costs once in every thirty years. Thousands of worthy fathers and mothers with their families might thus become proprietors of homes worth each $5000, and virtue and happiness would increase in proportion to such benevolence. Various excesses, intemperance, despair, recklessness, and the thousands of influences that go to make up the vagrants and the criminals of the world, would be utterly prevented by the increase of the benevolence of pure and undefiled religion—leading to physical, spiritual, moral, and intellectual education, and to universal democracy and enrichment. Crime diminishes in proportion as people are lifted above the oppressive forms of poverty. Churches absorb immense amounts of money merely to give shape and form to religious errors, which the believers worship as truths. You know that under such perversities and misappropriations, crime must stalk through New York society, and your police system must be doubled and trebled as the population increases.

Mankind must be brought to see that theology is error, and that Religion is "pure and undefiled" and inexpensive; and that to *be more,* and to profess less, is fulfilling life's grand objects, and taking a diviner position in the universe.

WINTER-LAND AND SUMMER-LAND.

"Open thy soul to God, O Man, and talk
Through thine unfolded faculties with Him
Who never, save through faculties of mind,
Spake to the Fathers."

Portions of the New Testament are opulent with hints of eternal truths. They are parts of the unspeakable harmonies of God and Nature. In the writings of John (chap. xix., v. 2,) there is a beautiful, social, spiritual affirmation, which begins, "In my Father's house." Like a child he speaks of his father's possessions in a pleasant and grateful spirit. "In my Father's house there is one immense room—no separate chambers and no compartments—adapted to only one family of one mind and one faith." Does it read so? No; but it would suit the orthodox sectarians if the verse were so written. The passage reads thus: "In my Father's house there are *many mansions;* if it were not so, I would have told you."

Yes, if there were not "many mansions" in the house of God, the intuitive Nazarene would have known the fact. Multitudinous human hopes and tender aspirations have sailed over the river on that beautiful barge—on that mystic affirmation—which, floating on

the flowing sea of the olden time, comes very near to
our hearts to-day, not valuable because it is laden with
priestly authority, but because it comes indorsed by
the spiritual discoveries and positive facts of the last
fifteen years.

"In my Father's house there are many mansions; if
it were not so, I would have told you." How tender
and beautiful, how simple and true, how childlike and
sublime! The earth is the Land of Winter, of storms
and sorrows; but the second sphere is the Summer-
Land of repose and infinite blossoming. Many apartments in the Summer-Land for different peoples and
races of men. Various localities and spheres for different inclinations. Provision is made for the complete gratification of the diversities of spiritual desires
in human character, so that all races and all states of.
mind will be "at home" in the Father's house which is
eternal in the heavens—friendly brotherhoods all,
though billions, trillions of leagues apart!

Whose heart does not beat in melodious harmony
with that beautiful sentiment from the Intuitions of long
ago—with that ever dear and lovingly sweet affirmation
from the source of positive revelation? It comes clad
with the majestic authority in which all truth travels to
mankind. It stamps the spirit with an inward conviction of "eternal reality."

On this globe there are high mountains yet utter
strangers to human footsteps. Those grand old monuments of matter, with their tops perpetually cloud-
vailed, have been for centuries innumerable unknown to
human intelligence and contemplation. Storms are
beneath their lofty summits. No man's foot has pressed

their dizzy hights. The tempests are lower down. So
our mariners report of storms on the vast oceans. But
down deep in the waters all is still; high enough in the
air, all is calm. The middle ground is where the fierce
battles of the elements are fought. The conflicting
powers meet and pass each other, never to meet again.
Sometimes they meet and fight with such terrible energy
as, for the moment, to shake the neighboring earth and
cause the bending heavens to tremble as though they
were to be rolled together as a scroll. And yet deep
enough in the inanimate apartments of the physical
world all is still and peaceful; high enough in the ethereal space all is equally silent and without commotion.
Indeed, so perfectly still is the air above at a certain
hight, that the stroke of a hammer on a log's end could
be heard from New York to California. The slightest
accent of the human voice could be there heard for
hundreds of miles. Persons might converse with the
Atlantic between them, in a voice not louder than is
usual, if they were high enough up in this ethereal
realm. The sun that shines with such glory and splendor,
distributing warmth and fertilization over the earth's
bosom, playing so sweetly and tenderly with the flowers and laughing with the rivers that come flowing
down from the mountains, exerts no influence upon this
upper sky-region. Go up fifteen to twenty miles, and
you find utter night, notwithstanding the noontide glory
and blaze of the sun's rays on the face of the earth.
The effect of the sun's rays is altogether terrestrial, not
atmospherical; that is, the manifestation of its light
and warmth is attributable more to mundane than to
solar causes.

The wonders of the physical atmosphere, within the fifty miles, would be a tax upon any one's faith. And yet I ask you to ascend in your thoughts millions and billions of miles beyond our earth's atmosphere. In the physical world you find works and wonders inexpressible. How expressive of the spiritual grandeur and omnipotence of the Infinite Soul! How can you but be filled with adoration and most glorious contemplations when the celestial truth is brought to your mind, that "in the Father's house are many mansions." If it were *not* so, the seers and mediums would have told you.

Let us think of the physical aspect of the Summer-Land. Many persons have understood me to have said that it is a globe. I do not mean to be so understood. The beautiful Land, as I have frequently seen it, and as many have testified concerning it, is a solid *belt of land*, or zone, round in form like the tire of a wheel, but it is not a globe—is not spherical nor inhabitable in all directions. Imagine a belt extending above the earth two-thirds of the distance from the sun, and say seventy millions of miles wide. Imagine that belt to be immeasurably larger than the sun's path around Alcyone in the deep of immensity. Suppose this belt to be open at the sides, and filled with worlds and crowned with stars and suns, and overhead and all around a firmament just like these heavens above the earth. Look in that direction and you will see just what you see on earth, only everything further unfolded and more perfect. There is exhibited the perfections of the plans of the infinite temple which here is only fractional and fragmentary. Thus you may somewhat imagine the appearance and shape of the Summer-Land.

What is called the "Milky Way" is really a belt of suns, and planets, and satellites. There seems also to be branch-fields of stars, setting off sidewise from the body of the belt. Then when the telescope is pointed in certain directions, where the unaided human eye can see nothing, there are developed, first nebulæ-cloudy regions; next, if the telescope be strong enough, like Lord Ross's, it reveals the fact that what were supposed to be only star-clouds, are immense fields of stars, suns, and lesser bodies. Those star-fields open here and there and make a vista, and, looking through, there is revealed a black space which no telescope has yet been able to dissolve; but clairvoyance has made the promise that when the telescopic power is adequate, what now appear to be only empty portions of immensity will turn out to be as full of those orbs as the great meadow is full of spears of grass. There are large islands of atmosphere between the planets. These air-islands serve as silken cushions (so to say) to keep the rolling planets supplied with electricity and also to prevent the friction which would exist were all the spaces occupied with worlds. So that there are really "atmospheric islands" (as I am impressed to term them) as well as immeasurable star-systems, in the far-off immensity.

Now the Summer-Land is in harmony with this physical circle of planets called the "Milky Way." It is a belt, a zone, or girdle, of real, substantial matter. It is beyond the Milky Way only in the sense of its being far-off according to our habits of using language. When liberated at death, we do not move on toward the sun, nor drop downwards into some dreary depth of darkness; we embark on a sidewise voyage, directly above the southern extremity of our planet, and thence onward until we reach the Summer-Land! What shore do we gain? We gain the shore of a land just like this earth, if this earth were a stratified belt composed of the *finest* possible particles that you can imagine thrown from all the orbs composing the Milky Way. Pulverize and attenuate the finest particles of matter on this earth; then bring them together in chemical relations; make them coalesce and form into an immeasurable golden belt with all the visible suns and stars, and you have the Second Sphere in its substance, position, and formation.

Do you not comprehend that that Land is as substantial to those who live there as this earth is to its inhabitants? The proportions and the adaptations are the same. The Summer-Land, so far as the surrounding immensity is concerned, is bounded on all sides by aerial seas. Suppose you should go down to any of those high points of land along the coast, and look off on the watery expanse of the Atlantic ocean. What would you see? No islands are visible; only an atmosphere overhead; clouds are floating in the blue sky, and all the rest is water. Now suppose you had never seen, or read, or heard of such a spectacle. What would be your first impression? Your first sensuous impression would be that all the immensity beyond was water, as all above is sky, and that, if you should sail off on that dreary waste, you would be lost utterly to land and to human society. Such, I say, would be your impression or apprehension on the supposition that you had no previous knowledge of any such spectacle in Nature.

Now imagine yourself standing on one of those

shining shores on the margin of the Summer-Land. Looking toward the Earth, and Sun, and Mercury, and Venus, what would you see? If you were not a far-seeing clairvoyant, but was contemplating with the first opening of your spiritual eyes, you would see an illimitable ocean of twinkling stars overhead and zones of golden suns shining, and you would realize a holy, celestial atmosphere, bounding your existence on all sides, and from your feet the departure of an ocean without shore or island, without form, and void of all relations. If, however, your clairvoyant sight was opened—if your spiritual eyes had the light of far-penetrating clairvoyance in them—you would instantly perceive that the aerial ocean, which flows out into infinity from your feet, ripples off and divides into beautiful ethereal rivers, and that those rapidly flowing rivers lead away to the planets, even to this Earth, whence you departed, while another river flows onward to Mars, another to Jupiter, another to Saturn, and other celestial streams to other more distant planets belonging to other systems of suns; and so on, and on, throughout the star-paved regions of the firmament, you would behold, in every imaginable direction, streams running musically down these gentle atmospheric declivities, just as tangibly as the rivers that run down the mountains and flow through the spaces in the rough landscapes of this more material world.

I wish! oh how I wish! that I could picture to you the reality of these musical rivers of the heavenly spaces. They are musical to the ear that can hear them flowing between the constellations. Pythagoras and his school believed in the deathless "music of the spheres." Did not the students of Pythagoras listen to catch that compound symphony? And was it not this very star-melody which caused them to be such enthusiasts in Music? Did not some of them in the far-off olden time have clairaudience enough to *hear through the physical,* and also clairvoyance sufficient to see that "in the Father's house there are *many* mansions"—many happy and beautiful places—many apartments or spheres of human life—and that these different apartments in the celestial temple were so many local scenes and land-scapes, belonging to the Summer-Land, which breathe eternal harmony throughout infinitude—" the music of the spheres"?

Now suppose you were this moment standing on the shining shore of the Summer-Land and looking this way, the out-flowing sea would appear about the same to your sight, without the light of clairvoyance, as would the Atlantic Ocean to the natural eye from the promonto-ries of Nahant. It would, perhaps, at first, be no more of a startling spectacle of incomprehensible sublimity. Very many persons depart every day from this Land of Winter for the Summer-Land. When they are led through the celestial gardens and down by the shining shores, and when they begin to hear the lapping of musical waves as they ripple in from the very remote planets, bringing upon their throbbing, undulating bosoms, new persons who had but just died (left their gross bodies) on those planets—the scene operates upon them (because yet uninitiated) just as though you were to see spirits with beautiful forms suddenly coming from off the water by the seaside, or persons walking and riding upon the surface of the waters at Nahant, or down

here on the ocean near the rocky shores of Long Island.
I say the first exhibition astonishes them as much as
such a novel scene would surprise you of this world.

I will now relate a true story: A little girl, who
had lost her darling playmate, dreamed about the
Summer-Land. This sweet little weeping dreamer lived
in Boston. I knew her well. Death had taken her
beautiful mate away. The funeral procession went by
the door of her father's house. Her mother owned a
cushioned seat in a fashionable church, and of course
the little daughter had a fashionable, religious direction
given to her thoughts. What were her thoughts on
death? She thought all of her little mate was put
"into the ground"—laid low in the cold, loveless earth;
and that when the insensate gravel, stones, and chilly
soil, were thrown from the spades upon the coffin, they
covered all that there was of her, and all there would
be of her, until that mysterious "trump" would sound
in the "resurrection morn," when Jehovah would call
those long-sleeping "jewels" that were particularly his
own, to himself.

Well, little Mattie stood weeping by the front-
window as the pageantry went solemnly through the
street toward the green retreats of Mount Auburn. She
asked her mother what it all meant. Over and over
again the mother answered that they were going to bury
the little girl "in the ground"! This seemed to strike
Mattie, for the first time, as something horrible to think
of. She had, perhaps, never thought seriously of it
before; the dread reality of this false view of death
never touched her affections till now. She had seen
funeral processions; but this particular funeral went

out of her saddened heart to the silent cemetery. Her mother said that God always did so; it was his own mysterious way. When people die they are put into the ground, then the ground is thrown over them, and the grass and the ages grow over them; when the time comes, they arise from their long sleep and hasten to God, if they are called; if not—you know the rest of the story.

Mattie sadly swallowed all this religious error, and shuddered. She was a beautiful girl then—a young lady now.

Two weeks after that funeral there was a fashionable party in Boston. Mattie received an invitation. Her parents were very rich, and she had gold rings and chains, and many beautiful dresses; but she now wanted another and a more attractive ring, which she had accidentally seen down in Washington street. It was a splendid ornament. She wanted it in time for the party. Her parents shook their heads and opposed her wishes. They said she had so many ornaments, was always so beautifully dressed, and so elegantly and expensively arranged in her person, she ought not to ask for anything more. It was difficult for parental love to deny her, an only child; but they did, nevertheless, refuse to purchase the ring.

Disappointed and grieved, Mattie hastened to her room and thought it over; and on the second day in the afternoon, as her mother chanced to be looking out of the rear window into the garden, she saw the child working away with a little flower-spade, digging a small, deep hole in the ground. The mother watched for a while, and then went down to her and said,

"Mattie, my child, what are you doing?" Mattie blushed. Already she had deposited in the ground a letter, and was throwing the fresh dirt upon it. She was embarrassed at her mother's question. She feared that she could not quite explain herself. In explanation she at length confessed that she wanted that "letter to go to God." She had secretly written, praying and entreating her heavenly Father to influence her father and mother so that they would consent to buy that beautiful ring for her. Her plan was, to send a letter "through the grave to God."

Now Mattie got the splendid ring; but I think she was never quite certain whether it came in consequence of having "buried" the letter or not. She did not then see why a letter could not go to God through the earth. But in the course of the same year little Mattie had impressed upon her mind a beautiful dream. She told it next morning with a full rose in her cheeks and a new light in her eyes. *She saw her playmate!* She was in a beautiful place, standing by the side of a great silvery sea. The water was shining and twinkling in every part like a lake of white light. She said it seemed that the sun was sending a golden shimmer through the vast space of glittering waters. Mattie described the scene very finely, and said that her playmate was standing up there and sending kisses to her way down that silvery river. She declared that she felt every kiss as it fell upon her lips! And then she added, "She told me that I need not bury anything to go up there, and that I would myself come there and play with her in that beautiful place."

Now this little girl knew nothing whatever of the

Summer-Land. I was at that time a great many leagues away; and her mother, whom I knew, was very cautious to never so much as "whisper" the slightest word favorable to truths of the Harmonial dispensation.

Visions like Mattie's have been duplicated and triplicated over and over throughout this new country. Of course they have been modified and varied in a large variety of ways, but the testimony from different minds is invariably the same—viz.: that there are up there lands, rivers, mansions in the Father's house, temples of beauty in the home of the living God; that countless people live there as naturally as they do here—with the difference that up there are not the earthly customs, nor this routine of daily fret and fight for physical necessities, neither a continuation of the vexations consequent upon men's spurious desires and appetites. Yes, kisses have been sent down the shining rivers to the lips of many human hearts.

A little girl in Bridgeport, in 1853 was moved to utter words of wisdom which only an archangel could authorize. She spoke under a celestial afflatus from the Summer-Land. "Fools confound the wise," when the former are under the inspiration of heavenly minds. Thus, sometimes, the most ignorant grow wise in ten brief minutes. All such mediums and spontaneous "sensitives" describe *rivers of light !* This is supposed by materialists to be poetry. They are right. It is poetry. In essence all poetry is immutable truth, and essentially false imagination is a philosophical impossibility. Take the crudest and most grotesque superstitions of the past, and at their deepest heart you will find, if your own ability to discern is deep enough, revelations "pure and undefiled" of the realities and inhabitants of the Beyond.

I have frequently called your attention to the naturalness of the Summer-Land. Its reality is among the philosophical discoveries of the present out-folding century. The most ancient Spiritualists, in the very earliest centuries, be it ever remembered, gave inspired sentences, and made intuitive statements, and wrote fine revelations of these same celestial wonders and postmundane verities.

Let us now contemplate some of the "Scenes" in the Beautiful Land. Approaching the shining shore upon one of these silvery *rivers*, that sets out from the southern extremity of this globe, you behold thousands of " Piradela," or grottoes and natural temples of clustering foliage, vines, and flowers, closely resembling laceworked chapels. In these peculiar pagodas, or family prayer-grottoes, you behold persons who still believe in Ammon Ra, the original Egyptian name and conception of the Supreme Being. I have already mentioned that the Egyptians had chosen a star," Guptarion," and that they have long seasons of worship, of joy and festivity, equal to an hundred years of restful Sabbaths, or as long as the star of their choice, *Guptarion*, shines over that particular portion of the Summer-Land. When the great star (sun) of their destiny sinks out of their sight, they cease their worshipings and festivities and return to other and less religious interests. They are about the same people they were while living in the valley of the Nile; only they are now in a higher Egypt, clothed in spiritual bodies. Many of them con-

16

tinue their old-time worship just as though they would always remain Egyptians.

It is marvelous how immobile and persistent are some of the human temperaments! In some races they yield almost nothing in the course of a thousand years. The prevalence of other opinions, other thoughts, and other conceptions, exert no remodeling effect in some minds.

Now many persons think this statement is unreal. Well, look at the Jews of this generation. Are they not still the Jews that they were eighteen hundred years ago? The variations and improvements are very slight. The Rabbinites and the Talmudians are the same. Look at their physiognomy, too, and look at the combinations of their characteristics, their inclinations in religion and in trade, and you will find them the same unaltered people. Or, look at the Roman Catholics. You may think that they are greatly modified. No, they are not. There has scarcely been an alteration in them from the first days of their faith. Those who come to this country, are occasionally modified by Protestant influences. But the great Catholic establishment is characterized by a constitutional immobility. It is based in the fixed temperaments of those peculiar minds who belong to it. Protestants still revert to the Catholic Church. Such minds belong to the sphere of authority. They believe in religious system, and they seek and find it in the original establishment. They believe that Protestantism is all afloat; that there must be some "tying-up place," or there will come chaos and destruction in morals and religion. Such persons need some place of discipline and worship where they can "hire their thinking done for them," according to authority extending backward over centuries to holy Saints and holy Fathers whom no Protestant ever undertakes to impeach. In this way this state of mind becomes fixed and immobile.

Now suppose such a person should die: what is the next step? Are such minds instantly changed? Are they ever suddenly re-molded from within? True, they are changed from a natural body into a spiritual body in "the twinkling of an eye." But are they not the same persons, with the same education, and influenced by their long-accustomed thoughts? Many such after death still believe that somewhere, beyond the bright fields of beauty, and even beyond the trials of purgatory, they will find the burning pit. They frequently think that if they should walk off but a few hundred leagues, they would find something worse than purgatory. They naturally enough understand that they are *in* purgatory, and thus the fact dawns slowly upon them, that they are in their appropriate private places, and are receiving the just discipline of Progress in the moral government of God.

So these ancient Egyptians, born in the valley of the Nile—strange children of a strange, sandy, symbolic country—erect countless little "pyramidalia," or temples of festivity and worship, dedicated to their long-chosen planet Sirius—sometimes called the dog-star; but up there they name it "Guptarion"—a large sun in the distant heavens, which our astronomers call a "star of the first magnitude." It rises and sets in the firmament over the Summer-Land once in twenty-seven of our centuries! Suppose a bright orb about one-tenth

of the apparent size of our sun, rising and shedding its
rays over a particular portion of the Beautiful World,
and you get a conception of the star of destiny in the
Egyptian Brotherhood. The pyramidalia are natural
vine-draped grottoes grouped along the shore of a deep
river that branches from the one which flows thither
from our globe.

You will keep in memory how this earth of ours
sends off its main celestial river which flows off south-
wardly in the upper air, and which, being a magnetic
combination of imponderable elements, ascends very
gracefully in the channel of its flight, terminating and
mingling with the silvery sea that bounds the Summer-
Land. The planet-rivers flow through the vast expanse
of sea as the Gulf Stream flows through the Atlantic
Ocean. Thus through this vast celestial sea of magnetic atmosphere the planetary streams flow directly to
the shining shores of the Summer-Land; but nearest to
that shore which is nearest the earth, and along the
inland lake called "Mornia," which is filled with
attractive islands, you will find these embowered chapels and prayer-grottoes of the Egyptians.

In 1853 I was enabled for the first time to see
them. I continued to investigate and to make inquiries
until I got at the motive for the cultivation and continuation of these pyramidalia. They said that those
fragrant floral structures are little statuettes, or minia-
ture pyramids, dedicated to the celebrated dog-star,
Sirius, or "Guptarion," being the accredited home of
Ammon Ra.

I seem to be impressed with the desire to urge upon
your understanding the entire *naturalness* of the next

state of human existence.   It seems desirable that you should see that the inhabitants there live in harmonious accord with each other, because of the omniscient system which is adapted to the infinite varieties of human character and consequent diversities of destiny.   When you arrive there—and you may embark thither before the end of this year—you will not be a stranger, for you will have cultivated some prescience of the "house" constructed with different "mansions."

Have you not had fore-gleams and intuitions of what I now relate? Have you never had thoughts or impressions—in your dreams and visions of the night—of floating or flying through the air? If the thousands of seeresses and clairvoyants and true dreamers could rise up to-day and relate their "experiences," I should have unimpeachable accumulative testimony, sufficient to overwhelm all the skeptical clergymen and logical lawyers in the wide world.

You occasionally read the New Testament, do you not?   I suppose that you believe somewhat in the Pentecostal experience which is therein recorded.   It seemed that, in that joyful day, they all arose from their seats—and then what? They spoke in "unknown tongues"! Of course *unknown* tongues were tongues not understood. The manifestation must have been gibberish and fanatical to those who witnessed and recorded the circumstances.

Suppose that in these days there should be a public *repetition* of that ancient spiritual "experience." Instantly some mediums would begin to discourse in Persian, others in Indian, others in Chinese, others in Japanese, others in Latin, others in Greek—would it

not be "all Greek" to the most of us, and more especially to spectators and non-sympathizing minds? What
would we say? And what would the people say? This:
"Give us something that we can all understand." Yes,
that would be the popular demand. But just step back
into the New Testament and read the statement over
again. In Pentecostal times or seasons there was a
general uprising or condescension of the celestial spirit.
"The spirit of the Lord" was poured out without stint.
Of course you know that every sweet or powerful influence from the firmament was called the "spirit of the
Lord." Influences from the concentrated minds of
millions in the Summer-Land could cause the largest
human audience to rise to their feet in an instant. Then
would occur manifestations according to individual gifts.
Some would exercise the magnetic power and make
passes over the sick; others would hasten off on sweet
missions of mercy; some would declaim in unknown
tongues; while others would fall prostrate and swoon
into a trance, and physicians would say, "Oh, that is
only excitement and hysteria." And all this would be
analogous—*identical*—with what you so reverently read
in your Testament. Now if this Bible statement be
true, it is interesting and applicable to us only just so
far as it is known and corroborated by spiritual experience in the manifestations of these days.

If modern minds were consulted, many would say,
"we have *seen* something of what you relate." "In the
visions of the night, when deep sleep cometh upon men,"
many a sensitive soul would say, "I have seen beautiful landscapes." These visions come and depart suddenly. Sometimes, indeed, they are nothing but the

play of a fertile ideality; but in most instances they are *real* glimpses of scenes in the Summer-Land. True, you might imagine a tree to be where there is no tree; but your ideality obtained its first lesson from seeing a tree which was *real*. One man may be able to imagine in his dreams just what another man cannot imagine without first seeing. So that the one man would have an actual objective experience, and the other only an ideal subjective experience. And it is philosophical that there should first be an *object* outside to impress the surfaces of the mind with a correct notion of its existence.

Certain constituted minds go into the "superior state" in the natural slumber of the night, and never during their ordinary and waking condition. Never, during the day, can such minds be quiet enough. But at night, when all is very still, then the sensitive mind and soul for the first time have an opportunity to realize a sort of independence of material surroundings, then the person's spirit rises up from beneath and attains to a finer state of thought and feeling. This higher conception of spirit-life comes through a vision. But when morning comes, and the business of the world is resumed, the dream may not remain to cheer the weary heart. But if the same person should enter a corresponding state, even if it be after the lapse of weeks or months, the mind will instantly revert to and go on with the corresponding previous experience. The long time which may have elapsed between the two experiences, does not break the chain. To the spirit, years seem like fleeting moments; for spirit, you will remember,

"Lives in *deeds*, not years;
In *feelings*, not in figures on a dial."

The spirit realizes *no time* between an experience of ten years ago and a corresponding experience of last night or to-day.

Once I stood, while in the clairvoyant state, by the overwhelmed brain of a large man in an apoplectic fit. I examined him both physically and spiritually. I watched by his bedside until he recovered from the apoplexy. Being in clairvoyance, I saw the working of his spirit, and could easily understand the state of his mind. He had, in the midst of his sufferings, a clear and truthful vision of the Summer-Land! When he recovered from the fit and came out of " the state," he knew nothing of what had happened. And I too, at that time, when I came out of the magnetic state, did not recollect what I had seen. (I remember everything now.) In the clairvoyant state, subsequently, I examined him a second time. He was then in a deep coma. I plainly saw what he was seeing, and might have felt what he was feeling. His mind was connecting the experience of six months previous with his present vision. He saw his heart's own happy companion—the loved wife who had gone before him—coming to welcome his spirit up the shining way. *He* saw the beauty of her coming, and *I* saw the beauty of her coming. The doctor put his ear down to the sick man's mouth to catch his whisperings. A joyful thought tried to gain utterance through his paralyzed physical organs. He wanted to tell his vision. But in a few moments he passed into the Summer-Land. Before he went he did not realize the six months which had intervened between his first and second vision of the silvery rivers and the scenes of immortal beauty.

A traveler may suddenly turn a corner in a new road and see a house and bridge before him, a few trees, a stream pouring through the grassy meadow, and some farm-houses in the distance, and, though the road and the country are really new to him, somehow the whole scene is familiar to his eyes. He knows that he never saw it with his physical eyes before, and yet he is not surprised. He is surprised only when he realizes that he was never in that region before. Now I find that the picture of that scene was perfectly transferred to the sensitive canvas of his faculties while his body was in a deep sleep in the night-time. While in *your* "superior state," your spirit takes on its impressions of distant objects and scenery. This experience has misled many into the hypothesis of pre-existence.

So the life of the spirit is natural. Your spirit does not realize any difference in feeling, whether you are dreaming or in a state of wakefulness. You travel about in the sleep-state just the same as though you were awake and in open day. You visit people, you go into houses, you cross rivers, or take a long voyage, just as satisfactorily as though you had your physical body around you. Now this experience arises from a projection of your consciousness into the open world about you. This will explain the wondrous phenomena of the whole interior life. It may not explain the private double-consciousness of some persons. One mind may see a real tree, another mind may imagine a tree to be where no tree is; but the latter is a subject of impression in which a tree is involved.

Some peculiarly organized minds have the most horrible dreams. Such dreams are reflections from the
16*

structure and state of their minds. And there are persons who live rightly and abstemiously, who also have
horrible dreams. Why is this? Because they have not
yet outgrown or overcome the influences from the temperaments of their ancestors. They are representatives
of branches of temperamental roots, which go far back
and down in the ancestral soil. They still vibrate and
pulsate in the living generations. This fully accounts
for the "night thoughts" of many who are pure and
beautiful, and who think beautiful thoughts during the
daytime. These same persons sometimes dream the
most repulsive dreams. Ancestors predominate in their
personal consciousness, and they have not will-power
sufficient to keep down the rising hereditary impressions,
especially during the less guarded hours of slumber.

·Already I have said something concerning the
"battle between the spirit and its circumstances,"
showing how all may acquire the power of conquering
the unpleasant inheritance from their ancestors. I have
somewhat conquered the discordant temperaments of
my ancestors. (I do not know who they remotely
were, and I am not anxious to know.) I have a fair-
minded, honorable father yet in this world, and I know
that I had a true, and sweet, and beautiful, and saintly
mother, who now resides in a celestial community. But
there were certain hereditary influences and predispositions which I found absolutely in my spirit's way.
Those inheritances stood sternly up in my presence sometimes when I wished most to be utterly quiet. When
I would gather spiritual strength and restore my
exhausted physical powers, then up would come some
hereditary "imp of darkness," who would propose to

carry me into discordant thoughts and scenes. At such times I would dream that I was where strange, murderous-looking people were secreting themselves in dark passages, or some other equally unpleasant dreaming. It has been so with some of you. You need not claim that you have always had harmonious, splendid, and attractive dreams. Human nature is organized on identical principles. And the action of the human faculties, under a given set of circumstances, is the same, and the experiences arising from such action is the same in all structures of mind.

Some men think there is essential truth in astrology. Well, I once visited an astrologer, with a desire to test the possibilities of destiny. A distinguished professor described to me the influences of the several stars. He drew my horoscope, according to the day and hour of my birth, and then went on to tell when I was sick, or when I should have been; that certain planets were my ruling stars, both for weal and for woe; and that when certain planets came into conjunction with the body of Mars, &c., that certain things would be likely to happen to me—whereupon I concluded that I would *not* be steered in my individual career by the stars, and I have not been. The very star that was astrologically fixed to rule my private destiny I forthwith put out of my house. I would not have a star intercepting the orbit of my individuality. Therefore the events that astrologically were to happen to me, have not occurred in the slightest degree.

Thus I teach you self-possession, although I believe that every great soul will best succeed by steering and steadying himself by the stars. Keep down the disa-

MORNING LECTURES.

greeable which you have received from your ancestors.
Prune away among your roots and branches. Expel
old discords from your minds, and you will then have
the satisfaction of knowing that your dreams are at
least your *own*. And from this starting-point you can
go right onward to solid facts in your mental operations.

What is important to the speedy accomplishment of
this result? First of all, physiology: correct habits of
eating, drinking, working, and resting. If you eat
this, that, and the other thing, it will, to some extent,
appear in your nervous force. Wrong conditions in
your nervo-vital energies will induce your faculties to
produce unpleasant dreams. As soon as you know what
is obstructional, you can and ought to remove it. My
investigations are all between six o'clock in the morning and twelve o'clock of the day. At night I do not
dream. I sleep then. If there are any persons present,
who, as witnesses, heard the lectures given in "Nature's
Divine Revelations," they will remember that though
three or four days might have intervened between two
discourses, yet sometimes the first words would finish a
sentence which perhaps was left incomplete at the end
of the previous lecture, and the thought would be thus
fully expressed—showing that the spirit keeps no
account of *time*, but takes cognizance only of events,
feelings, thoughts, ideas, and principles.

Many have seen the places and the scenes which I
have been describing. I hear mediums mention spiritual
things and describe scenery, and I recognize them as
things and scenes which I have seen. If a man tells
you that he saw Central Park, and that he entered at a

certain gate, which he truthfully describes, then you say, "That is true, for I have seen it myself." In like manner I have had convincing testimony that others have seen the Summer-Land.

Auloania is the name of the island which was ages ago dedicated to those Greeks who steadfastly believe in many Gods—the polytheists. Auloania is still devoted to poetry, rhetoric, history, the ode, and to music. The winding, dancing, silvery river, which flows around this island, is named *Sil-Miral*, meaning a hymn, or an anthem. It sings songs like pine trees. In certain seasons, or under the influence of certain breezes, it gives off hymnal melody—rich, varied harmonies, and æolian, mournful symphonies. Myriads of song-birds live and sing in that region, as the birds live and sing on earth when the warm days of spring come o'er mountain and plain. The birds, of highest beauty, by thousands enter into the æolian symphonies and mournful melodies of the beautiful Sil-Miral.

Vivium is the name of a golden, fountainous spring, on the island of Auloania. I have seen it many times. You will see it in some of your spiritual dreams. Put down the errors in the temperaments inherited from your ancestors. Become natural, and substantial, and wholly yourself. You cannot enter the "superior state" by any way less straight. Become healthy in your inmost; *then* you will see the Summer-Land in visions of the night. You read in your religious book about "the Dayspring from on high," and you think it is a beautiful figure of speech. But I find that there is something corresponding to it in the fields and islands surrounding the house with many mansions. Suppose

I should say that " Innocence is represented by a lamb."
Now you read about the " Lamb of God ;" but is there
not also an animal known as a lamb?   And in like
manner may not the fountainous Vivium,—the dayspring
on high—be something more than a mere figure of
speech ?   Has not every figurative expression a corresponding literal side?

The scenes of the Second Sphere are reflected upon
the human mind whenever it is accessible and impressible.   It is accomplished either by our own clairvoyant
powers to rise into sight and sympathy with them, or
else by the artistic pencilings upon our faculties by
those who are our invisible guardians.   They either do
it for us, or else they kindly clear the celestial way, so
that our own impressibility may invite and secure the
picture.

I would now like to tell you about the *Elgario*, as
they call the plant of sorrow.   In the Summer-Land
there are melancholy characters, who seem disposed to
remember and dwell upon the exceedingly hard times
they experienced on the earth.   They look like very
badly abused people ;   were not appreciated before
death, and are not happy.   They are downcast and sad
for a while, being indulgent of feelings of melancholy,
like certain unfortunates in our lunatic asylums.   But
this wondrous celestial plant, which the botanists of
that region call *Elgario*, is their sweet medicine and
perfect antidote.   The sad ones are led to it.   They
soon begin to inhale its fragrance.   They breathe its
atmosphere.   They chew it a little every day.   They
soon know this flower is for the healing of God's heart-
stricken children.   They carry its petals and are

influenced by them. The plant exerts a mystic charm. They make bouquets of it, and it relieves them of their earthborn mishaps and long-cherished sorrows.

Is not this revelation also natural, beautiful, and simple? Your gifted guardian will bring the Elgario to you and say: "Take this, my beloved; smell of its holy breath; its odor will quickly relieve your aching heart." Why, a homeopathic physician, when treating a patient for a disease in the throat or lungs, may, perhaps, wish to administer phosphorus. He knows that the *odor* of phosphorus will sometimes relieve a severe stricture. Thus the higher physicians hand forth this beautiful plant to spirits depressed with earth-born errors and misfortune. They give it to their patients, and lo! its *odor* heals and translates them into a healthy, happy, and comparatively superior state.

Thus sometimes beautiful "births" take place—births out of states of confirmed despondency. A mother, for example, in order to feed and clothe her children, has been overworked. She has literally worked herself to death for the sake of her dependent family. She at last died from excessive bodily fatigue and heart-broken weariness. She is borne away on the silvery river to the Summer-Land; but she is still weary! This beautiful plant is brought to her, or she is conducted to the garden that is filled with it. Gradually it lifts her into her "superior state." After a time she realizes somewhat of heavenly comfort, sweet and pure; and in the flow of the ensuing seasons, she begins to believe that

"There is a land of pure delight,
    Where saints immortal reign;
Eternal day excludes the night,
    And pleasures banish pain."

From her refreshened memory she says, " I used to sing that song, when I was a girl, in the Methodist Sunday-school, and in our Bible-class meetings. Then it was only words; now it is all so real." She looks about and sees her old neighborhood acquaintances and loved friends. She finds them in the " Father's house," where there are " many mansions." If it were *not* so, the seers would have told you.

LANGUAGE AND LIFE IN THE SUMMER-LAND.

"Get but the TRUTH once uttered, and 'tis like
A new-born star, that drops into its place,
And which once circling in its placid round,
Not all the tumult of the earth can shake."

The sevèral languages called "dead" in this world,
have certain roots which push themselves vigorously up
through the memory-soils of the human mind and continue to bear fruit after death. Thus the Hebrews,
Arabians, Assyrians, Chaldeans, Persians, Grecians,
Romans, Celts, even the Scots and Picts, and various
other smaller tribes and semi-nations, continue for a
long time to to speak the educational language of their
earth-life, and to cherish thoughts that flow through
such verbiage; and often when such spirits have sought
to communicate with impressible or congenial persons
on the earth, they have succeeded in controlling mediums, so that the communication would be imparted in
their native tongue. The celebrated Professor Buchanan,
of Cincinnati, testifies that he heard in the City of
Cleveland, ten years ago, an uneducated American
lady discourse finely in French. And it was reported
that Mr. Selden J. Finney, in the same city, and, I

believe, on the same occasion, uttered a glorious poem in the Indian language, which, it was said, was perfectly well understood by an Indian who chanced to be present.

I know how most people feel and think with reference to these trans-terrestrial questions—that after death "all is different with the individual." There never was a greater mistake. You might as well suppose that Mother-nature, and God-nature, and Man-nature undergo radical transmigrations and reconstructions. Quite otherwise. There are no essential changes in the plan of ultimates. The *final* type of organization, remember, is the spiritual interior of Man and Woman. Both reason and intuition sustain the doctrine of no central change after death. The Bible says: "As a tree falleth, so it lieth." That is, an oak tree does not become a peach, a birch, or a mahogany, the moment it falls. It is an *oak* tree still. Even so if man's body falls, in sympathy with the chemistry and gravitation of the physical word, the spiritual man does not fall with it. Only the external casing is peeled off and rejected, while the personal-inmost, who thought and spoke and acted before, goes onward, unchanged and individualized, to the Summer-Land.

It is the lesson of the *naturalness* of the After-life, which the mind must fully conceive in order to *realize* that the other world is really a " home in the heavens." Earthlings will not be orphans or strangers there. I must know and recognize my acquaintances, and they must know and recognize me, a hundred, a thousand, a million years from this, yea, an eternity hence, or immortality is nothing. The cessation of leading personal peculiarities and the reconstruction or abolishment of the essential traits of the individual organization—the mergement of the person at death from substantiality into a vapory, gauzy, ghostly inhabitant of the kingdom of heaven, there to dwell and sing and adore forever in the presence of the wifeless Trinity—is a supposition too absurd to occupy intelligent minds, being a conception eminently suited to the brainless cranium of old-time orthodoxy. And yet there are ministers who seem to pride themselves upon their profound ignorance on this subject, saying: "It is an unlawful mystery; it is supernatural." In other things those same pulpitarians are just as sensible as fellow-sinners in general. But come to this subject, and forthwith, with a slam, the gate of investigation is shut, and you are driven to the authoritarian's "faith," which they invariably present as the best antidote for heart-bereavements and spiritual prostrations.

Now the after-existence opens before us as a continuation of individual progression. Instead of being a "discrete degree," as Swedenborg describes it, it is seen to be another mansion, another story, in the same house "eternal in the heavens." The heavens are not remote. The earth itself is situated and rolling noiselessly "in the heavens." Do you not know that it travels from January to July about ninety-seven millions of miles, and directly *through* "the heavens"? Else how could the earth move in its path around the sun? You see, therefore, that the earth itself is "in the heavens"; and, reversely, that "the heavens" are about the earth. We float at the rate of sixty-four thousand miles an hour round the sun, which is not more really in "the heavens." Now, I affirm that the Summer-Land is no more "in the heavens" than is our sun or this earth on which we at present reside.

The mind of man is stationed over his visceral organs, which are immersed in darkness within the physical body. But there is a constant communication kept up between all parts of his body and his sensorium. Consequently the mental person who resides in the upper parts of the brain is omnipresent through the physical organs and sensations. In like manner, the Second Sphere is so situated with reference to this earth, that we, its inhabitants, float under the constant inspection of its population. This earth is analogous to a ponderous organ in the perfect and symmetrical anatomy of the stars. I think you will agree that this planet of ours may be, in general analogy, an "organ" in the physiology of the sidereal system; and that the celestial brain, which is the Summer-Land, caps and coronates all these different planets, just as the mind of man covers and crowns the different organs within the trunk.

Earthly languages, perfected, carried out to their ultimates, and simplified to a fine, beautiful orthography, become the language of the other Sphere. But, education still sways the mind and thoughts. Suppose your affections are wrapped up with expressions peculiar to the German language, then, on reaching the higher Land, your memory (which is a spiritual organ,) holds not the English language, nor have you attachments for any other save that in which you were primarily educated. So true is this, that persons who had been in the habit of using "profane language," as it is called, find themselves over-accustomed to expressing their thoughts and emotions through those worthless viaducts and conveyances; and such habits become serious impediments and obstructions to progress, just as in this world, when the coarse, vulgar-word speakers would enter refined society, they meet embarrassment because they cannot use profane language with their customary freedom.   If they use it constantly among ignorant men, they find themselves, when among educated persons, in a state of nervous trepidation lest the next moment they may stumble into the use of an oath.   When thrown a little off their balance, they will involuntarily show that they are accustomed to very improper and very disagreeable words.   This you know is true in this world.

Now look into·the Summer-Land, and you will find that the memory of many is checked when they come into the presence of finer and more educated organizations.   There is a tendency, even after death, to indulge in those mental habits in which the individual has been most strongly educated.   Thus, the first form of speech is that which the person most used on earth.   A friend, who recently died in the Union Army, took the first opportunity to make himself manifest, and expressed his thoughts in the peculiar language which he had been accustomed to use all the years before he went. Although he was situated in finer circumstances, and influenced by the example of finer associates, still his thoughts flowed along in their accustomed channels of conversation.   His thoughts were finer and higher; but they came down through the old verbiage.

The second language used in the higher world is the language of Music.   The spirit of this language is separated from the educational tendencies of the different races. The language of Music is employed in the teaching of what we call "Science." The truths of science, the beauties of science, and very high and glorious lessons in celestial principles, are communicated by means of symphonies, melodies, songs, hymns, anthems, and chants. Hence the impression that heaven is a place of eternal song! This wondrous music fills the whole heavens and awakens echoes among the distant planets; so that, when the stars are touched and summoned to enter the orchestra and make the magnificent chorus full, then the very earth itself seems to vibrate responsively to that grand harmonious beat, which converts the universe into a harp of infinite perfection!

The third language used in the higher world is what we here call "the language of the Heart." It is, more properly speaking, the language of emanation. Every private affection throws out an atmosphere. Whatever your predominating love may be, it emits an atmosphere which winds itself about your person. And when the temperament is fine, sensitive, and susceptible, the odor and influence will correspond. If the individual is the victim of an inverted love—a love turned out of its pure, native channel—he throws out upon you a coarse, vicious atmosphere, which in these days is called a "magnetic influence." Mediums, sensitives, and clairvoyants *see* it, and many persons not so gifted, *feel* it, and they know not whence or why. "That person gives off a peculiar influence," you say; "I feel it." It depresses you; or, it makes you angry. Another person makes you feel "cheerful" and "happy" and "joyous;" and you are physically quieted or spiritually

aroused by mere contact with these more exalted characters.

In the Summer-Land this "language of the heart"
is carried to an inconceivable degree of perfection. For
instance, suppose you and your brother, or you and
your sister, should meet—you who have not met for
long, lonely years. If you have outgrown the necessity
of external speech, and if you have been taught through
the mysterious suggestiveness of pure Music, you then
deepen into the language of impersonal and perfect
LOVE! In the higher Spheres such language is alone the
medium of communication. It is the language of absolute contact of personal love-atmospheres; by which is
meant that two persons, meeting face to face, meet also
heart to heart, and are forever friends. On earth it is
but the hands, or eyes, or lips, that touch and speak.
There, it is the indescribably sweet and perfect meeting
of soul with soul. They thus inhale and thoroughly
understand each other. For the first time there sweeps
through the gladdened heart the eminent satisfaction
of receiving perfect *appreciation* through the deathless
wisdom of a brother, a sister, or a companion. Your
most secret history is wordlessly told and forever
known; the details of your earth-life appreciated, and
with all their innumerable bearings upon the shape of
your character; and so, too, are comprehended all the
steps that have brought you to that position in the upper
existence; so that the "communion" which takes place
at that time extends through all the years, days, hours,
events, and moments of your terrestrial pilgrimage.
The delightfulness of this conjunction constitutes the
beautiful, glorious happiness which diversifies, gladdens,
and exalts the inhabitants of the Spheres.

This interior, unspeakable language, is sometimes called "the language of Communion"—the unutterable speech of the immortals—which poets try in vain to reach and express; which Music, with its unsearchable attributes and great powers, very nearly approaches. When your love is warmest and deepest, when you meet it in another, or when it meets you, then you catch the rudiments of this infinitely finer, this inexpressibly beautiful, this trans-mundane, this celestial, this heart-emanational conversation, which is so divinely-blissful, so spiritually-refreshing, and so exalting to all who dwell under its blessings in the Summer-Land. Let it be once more affirmed that words are not the most eloquent expressions of the Soul. There is no joy so intense as that which sparkles in the eye and crimsons the cheek, yet refuses the aid of the voice; there is also " no grief like that which does not speak." Where the heart has a tale to tell, how poor are the utterances of the lips! Need we these ever to tell us that we are loved? Is there not something in arbitrary signs that breaks the spell of our sweetest feelings? There is a mental electricity more mysterious far than the subtile fluid that thrills through material substances. Its conductors are the soft light of the human eye, the smile of the human lip, the tone of a subdued and earnest voice. Pleasant, indeed, is the solitude that is broken only by this silent speech.

Concerning *Traveling* in the Summer-Land. Traveling there is, at first, just what it is here. Arrived, we use our legs and feet; we see with our eyes; hear with our ears; and we also touch, and smell, and taste things, just as the very young child does on being introduced into this world.   The mind of every one is interested at first in what is most external, and yet, what is called "external" there, is here even too deep for mankind's comprehension at the present time.   When arrived there, you find yourself in possession of higher senses, in every respect similar to these, and with the same attributes and faculties, only more susceptible, and with the essential habits and inclinations of your character even more active.   These all begin to call for their complete gratification.   They lead you along the vernal margins of musical waters, or you traverse different beautiful fields, or away you go on attractive excursions—all in accordance with the most powerful necessities of the ever-active, never-dying, always youthful spirit.   Now and then you meet persons who are still laboring with the effects of an earthly sadness.   These undeveloped souls remain with organizations, or become members of Brotherhoods who have not yet arisen out of the depressions of terrestrial mishaps and imperfections. Every one goes to appropriate and congenial places.

Let your mind be duly impressed with the fact that "great minds," so called while on earth, often lose what was considered the properties of their great "reputation."   It is instantly stripped off from some of them, and they are not known, named, nor bowed to as "distinguished persons."   Great men, so styled on earth, are of no consequence in the Summer-Land; neither king nor queen, nor prince nor princess, are known as such; for all go there clad in their true peri-spherical garments, and not in the costly habiliments you procure at Stewart's.   When arrived, you will appear dressed and adorned, plainly or otherwise,

17

in rigid accordance with your *internal* nature and status. Thus Henry Clay, when he reported himself in the city of New York more than ten years ago, said that his "great earthly (political) attainments had not availed him much." This distinguished American gave a message to a number of personal friends. His communication, which was perfectly verified at the time, shows the mental condition in which the statesman found himself soon after his arrival.

HENRY CLAY'S MESSAGE TO A NUMBER OF FRIENDS.

In July, 1852, the following, with much more of high significance, was delivered: "My worldly wisdom availed me not when my new life commenced. It is very beautiful to become a little child again; and now I understand the meaning of the words: 'Ye must be born again;' and in true sincerity and gratefulness I feel that I am born again—in a life where the vanities of earth have faded from my view, and the bright glories of heaven are opening upon my soul.

"O soul made pure, be thankful for thy high estate, and adore thy God who hath endowed thine eyes with light, and thy soul with the ability to enjoy the pure beauties which crowd upon thy new existence! And yet how I am overwhelmed with the foreshadowing of the glory which is yet in wait for me! But now a form of brightness appears, and saith unto me: 'As thy day is, so shall thy strength increase; and thou shalt grow and wax stronger in the stature of wisdom and the might of love.'

"I am surrounded by those who are, like myself, exploring the wonders of this heavenly land. The realities become more and more transcendently sublime as we proceed. And the beauties of knowledge are increasingly unfolded; more vast and commanding becomes the wide-spread plain of glory, as we travel on in our heavenly path, guided by wisdom supreme and love unbounded."

The mind is "overwhelmed," as Henry Clay expresses it, with the unexpected *naturalness* of the *post-mortem* existence. Persons who read this, I think, will not be as much astonished as was the "Sage of Ashland," who ascended from the Old Kentucky State. He was not "astonished" in the Halls of Congress at Washington—he could easily grasp the great rising propositions before the Government of his country—but when he entered another mansion in the Father's house "not made with hands," then he became as "a little child, guided by wisdom and love."

Persons sometimes change their views rapidly, and they hasten to return, saying that they have experienced a "change" in their convictions. Dr. Emmons, who was a preacher of the old-school doctrine of eternal punishment, comes back after having thoroughly investigated the geography and government of the Summer-Land, saying that there is no place hot enough to suit his sermons.

A MESSAGE FROM DR. EMMONS, IN BOSTON, 1851.

"You of the earth may pretend and think you believe ever so strongly in eternal punishment; but when you bring it home to your own hearts, and those you love, the strongest terms you dare to use are: ' We leave them in God's hands. He doeth all things well!' Yea, verily, I respond to that with all my spirit powers—' God doeth all things well!' Amen and amen forever! saith the spirit of Dr. Emmons. Does not that very remark imply a doubt in the minds of those that thus speak? You could not better express your doubts, if you would;' your firmest, strongest believer in eternal punishment, dare not say of the one he loved: He or she hath gone to *hell !* In plain words let us speak; for you that believe it may not shrink from speaking it. I was one of the old-school, a strong, bold preacher of the *doctrine of eternal punishment ;* would that those sermons were buried in oblivion! They are a curse to the world, a dishonor to the memory of him who could believe or utter such sentiments, a libel on the character of a just and holy God. And yet, as my spirit returns to the friends and scenes of my earthly days, often do I hear the words I uttered in life brought forth as the faith of a good old man ; and by those, too, who cherish my name and memory with almost holy reverence. I long to make my voice heard in tones of thunder, that they may know the truth, and not grope in darkness longer."

Again, the celebrated American author, J. FENNI-MORE COOPER, in the year 1850, gained access to an elderly gentleman in Western New York, and reported in brief as follows :

"I little thought, when, a few months ago, I was investigating the developments that were interesting some of my acquaintances, that I should so soon be seeking an opportunity to make my identity manifest. I was astonished at what I then witnessed, and was afraid to investigate, lest I should find true what others said, and what had been so marvelous to me, because I dreaded the scorn of those whose good opinion I valued. Hence, you see, I was not well prepared for a high mansion in the spirit-life; for I felt ashamed to seek the truth wherever it might be found, and such cowards are not fitted for high enjoyments in the Spirit-World. Yet I was introduced into a state far better than I deserved, for which I feel thankful ; and that feeling of gratitude, as it is cultivated, I feel advances me."

Some spirits report themselves as they were, or as they appeared just before death, in order to satisfy their remaining relatives that they are still in existence, and that death was not the extinguishment of their personality. A remarkable case is reported by Professor Brittan, eleven years ago, showing how entirely simple, yet terribly impressive, is the method which some departed ones adopt, to cause their identity to be fully known to acquaintances who yet live in the body.

CASE OF IDENTIFICATION.

Mr. S. B. Brittan, in the year 1852, put on record the following:

" Last winter, while spending a few days at the house of Mr. Rufus Elmer, Springfield, Mass., I became acquainted with Mr. H.——, a medium. One evening H——, Mr. and Mrs. Elmer, and myself, were engaged in general conversation, when—in a moment and most unexpectedly to us all—H—— was deeply entranced. A momentary silence ensued, when the medium said: 'Hannah B—— is here.' I was surprised at the announcement; for I had not even thought of the person indicated for many days, perhaps weeks or months, and we parted for all time when I was but a little child. I remained silent; but mentally inquired how I might be assured of the actual presence. Immediately the medium began to exhibit signs of the deepest anguish. Rising from his seat, he walked to and fro in the apartment, wringing his hands, and exhibiting a wild and frantic manner and expression. He groaned in spirit, and audibly, and often smote his forehead and uttered incoherent words of prayer. He addressed men in terms of tenderness, and sighed, and uttered bitter lamentations. Ever and anon he gave utterance to expressions like the following:

" ' Oh, how dark! What dismal clouds! What a frightful chasm! Deep—down—far down—I see the fiery flood! Hold! Stay!—Save them from the pit! I'm in a terrible labyrinth! I see no way out! There's no light! How wild!—gloomy! The clouds roll in upon me! The darkness deepens! My head is whirling! Where am I?'

"During this exciting scene, which lasted perhaps half an hour, I remained a silent spectator, the medium was unconscious, and the whole was inexplicable to Mr. and Mrs. Elmer. *The circumstances occurred some twelve years before the birth of the medium.* No person in all that region knew aught of the history of Hannah B——, or that such a person ever existed. But to me the scene was one of peculiar and painful significance. The person referred to was highly gifted by Nature, and endowed with the tenderest sensibilities. She became *insane* from believing in the doctrine of endless punishment, and when I last saw her, the terrible reality, so graphically depicted in the scene I have attempted to describe, was present, in all its mournful details before me."

Now, the testimony of Professor Brittan would probably be taken as unquestionable and trustworthy on any other subject, and perhaps at this late day his word will also be accepted in this direction. In the whole realm of psychology, or of sympathy of mind with mind, there is no known law that will explain the effects he delineates. But those who have held communication with the Summer-Land, find that those who still earnestly desire to communicate, take the first opportunities to stamp the impression which would produce the strongest conviction of personal identity upon the remaining relative or friend. I suppose there are two thousand instances, all of them substantiated so far as human testimony can go, showing that spirit-communications are "literal facts" recorded in history beyond the possibility of refutation.

Some minds who on earth were intellectually inter-

ested in "Ideas," on entering the Second Sphere, begin
to communicate, as soon as possible, to impressible persons remaining, the fact that, in their cogitations, they
had conceived of something like what they now behold,
and that they are *so* glad to find that the realities of
the higher life are even more gratifying than they had
dared to expect.   To illustrate this point, I refer you
to the testimony of Margaret Fuller, given in 1852—a
year remarkable for the outpouring of this peculiar
description of communications :

TESTIMONY OF MARGARET FULLER, OTHERWISE
COUNTESS OSSOLI, DEC. 5, 1852.

"My sojourn on earth seems now as an indistinct
dream, in comparison with the *real* life which I now
enjoy.   And I regard the raging of the elements which
freed my dearest kindred and myself from our earthly
bodies, as the means of opening to us the portals of
immortality.   And we behold that we were born
again—born out of the flesh into the spirit.   How surprised and overjoyed was I when I saw my new condition!   The change was so sudden—so glorious—from
mortality to immortality—that at first I was unable to
comprehend it.   From the dark waves of the ocean—
cold, and overcome with fatigue and terror—I emerged
into a sphere of beauty and loveliness.   How differently
everything appeared!   What an air of calmness and
repose surrounded me!   How transparent and pure
seemed the sky of living blue!   And how delightfully
I inhaled the pure, life-giving atmosphere!   A dim-
ming mist seemed to have fallen from my eyes—so calm
and so beautiful in their perfection were all things
which met my view.   And then kind and loving friends
approached me, with gentle words and sweet affection;
and oh, I said within my soul, surely heaven is more
truly the reality of loveliness than it was ever conceived
to be by the most loving hearts!   Already are my

highest earthly impressions of beauty and happiness *more than realized.*"

Here you remark a vivid contrast between this communication of Margaret Ossoli's and that reported by Professor Brittan. In Margaret you see a mind retaining its characteristics in the transcendentally ideal. She reports the intense gratification which came over her idealizing faculties immediately on her introduction to the Better Land. But the other lady came back purposely to impress upon Mr. Brittan's thoughts and feelings the fact of her presence—not through ideality, but through the frightful gesticulations and paroxysms of a painfully-remembered insanity.

TRAVELING in the *post-mortem* Sphere is at first just like pilgrimizing on earth. But the higher inhabitants have acquired what we shall never be able perfectly to imitate in this world. They have the power, without wings, to rise up and put themselves in harmony with the currents that sweep through the atmospheric spaces. With the spread of light they ride on those currents millions and trillions of miles. It is accomplished by the marvelous power of inherent Will. The ability of the will to check the pulse is a promise of ultimate achievements. It is possible to develop and educate this inherent power of Will. By it, in this world, we lift our heavy bodies from beds or chairs, and cause them to move on the ground through low space. It is a mental power holding insensate muscles to its rule. This executive energy of the arisen human spirit, instead of wings, is the secret of its lightning flight. I do not say that spirits travel by a continuous exertion of the will. They seek the upper currents by will, somewhat like the balloon excursion which occurred some few years since between St. Louis and the northern part of this State. Professor Wise speaks positively of the existence of an unvariable current, and thinks that if the venturesome aeronaut could strike it, he would be rapidly and safely carried from west to east. His first experiment was a failure, as all *first* experiments usually are; but it sufficiently illustrates what is *the universal method* of traveling in the Summer-Land, when they depart on their far-away excursions. They gain that particular current which sweeps away through the spaces between the orbits of the planets, and which takes them " with the celerity of thought" to the destination which they desire to reach, however remote it may be from their point of departure.

We shall not obtain that method in this life, save by uncertain balloons. We see the lesson and the example in birds. But that is done by a direct exertion of the will, and by sympathetic contact of their swift-moving wings with the electricity of the air—part *float* developed by friction, and part *momentum* developed by Will. Just as a message of intelligence can be sent through space by vibrating the telegraphic current over thousands of miles, so the spirit-body and Will can, by the vibration of the celestial rivers which flow between the Summer-Land and the different planets, mount and float and ride upon them with inconceivable speed, and gain any desired destination. Traveling there is social.

In the New Testament you read with wonderment and with longing the report of the Pentecostal experiences. How could such things be unless there were spirits invisible, who gathered as in convention, and,

17*

by one united effort, baptized with sublime zeal whole
congregations of Spiritualists in Syria, in Palestine, in
Rome, or wherever the upper Pentecostalians happened
to be in contact with the lower assemblages of sympathizing and impressible minds.   The spiritualistic congregations of the old time were supposed to be baptized
by the outpouring of the Holy Spirit from the great
Jehovah himself.   That was the shortest explanation
furnished by the converted Pharisees.   They always
furnished the most literal explanation of spiritual phenomena.   Thus Moses imagined that he never could
be visited by any power less exalted than the great
Creator himself. That was the Hebrew mistake. Many
of them have not yet unlearned the error in this world;
and some in the Summer-Land have not changed their
sentiments.   But the truth is, that a combination of
minds, just like ourselves, coming in contact with earthly
congregations, pour out the spirit of real love, uplifting,
elevating, giving inward gladness and unity of feeling
" in the bonds of peace."

By permanent magnets I sometimes illustrate the
law that spirits impart communications with whom they
can enter into direct contact, and with none others.
Hence some have passed all the way through life without receiving a single evidence that any such thing as
a spirit exists; while others have *felt* it and known it
from their earliest recollections. I well know that there
are minds who have not felt the blissful influence of
such spiritual contact, and of course, have no evidence
whatever of the truth of these things.   And yet such
persons are many times helped and saved by proxies.
Guardians cannot reach them, save through the agency

of other parties—a succession of intermediates—the way a great variety of special providences come to pass. As an example, I give the case of an African woman, to show that the benevolent in the beautiful Brotherhoods of heaven still watch over the lowly and unhappy of earth:

HOW A FAMISHING AFRICAN WOMAN AND CHILD WERE SAVED BY THEIR GUARDIANS.

The case is cited from the *Moral Instructor* of 1850. It exhibits interposition, sympathy, and calculation, to a remarkable extent: " A lady medium in this city, whose name we are not at liberty to pronounce, while walking in the streets, in her usual physical and mental mood, was approached and controlled by a spirit, caused to enter a bakery and purchase some victuals, thence led out of the city by a circuitous route into the suburbs, where she met a colored woman sitting by the roadside, weeping, with a small child by her side. She was traveling to find friends, and, destitute and exhausted, she had sunk despondingly down to bewail her condition. Using the organ of the medium, the spirit said to the sufferer: 'Sister, why weepest thou?' The reply, in substance, was, that she was away from friends, and had no means of procuring food for her famishing child —making no mention of her own privations. She said she had knocked at the doors of those who appeared abundantly able to bless, but had been refused even the morsels that fell from their tables, and now despaired of succor. The spirit then gave her the bread, telling her that her afflictions were known, and that he was an angel sent to minister to her wants. Overjoyed, the poor woman fell upon her knees, essaying to offer the spirit a prayer of thanksgiving. But he said: 'Thank not me, but God that sent me.'

"The medium was then conducted home, having been unconscious during most of the transaction, and retaining only an indistinct recollection of the bakery, one or two points in her road, and the meeting with the woman."

Many a man has been saved from committing suicide, by his guardians, by the intermediate method of approach. Why are not *all* men saved from their temptations and indiscretions? Because they can be neither directly nor intermediately reached. Of necessity all such must walk through great agony to a higher intellectual and moral condition. It is the impulse of their inward being. Guardian angels see that it is better for some children to fall down a whole flight of stairs than to be rescued; for the one sad accident or stumble may save them from the misfortune of forty other *worse* falls and blunders in the course of their lives. The saving and protecting arms are not thrown around some gentle natures simply because there is no contact. But what a beautiful law and system of providences are sometimes displayed! Here is an example:

A MAN SAVED FROM SUICIDE BY THE INTERPOSITION OF HIS GUARDIANS.

The following authentic case was reported by a New Haven gentleman, in 1852: "Many years ago a couple of gentlemen, who were room-mates, graduated at Yale College, and became ministers of the gospel. At an after period they settled in the ministry in different States, and carried on a friendly epistolary correspondence during a large portion of their lives. One of them was in the habit of receiving impressions upon his mind of that vivid character which usually constrained him to comply with the dictate of the moment, or suffer loss touching his wonted peace. And though he was seldom able to divine in advance what the result of his compliance would be, he was always obedient to the dictate, and afterward saw clearly that he had only done what duty or interest would have demanded.

"Among the many occasions upon which he was called to act in obedience to this higher power, the following is singular and instructive, and shows, in the language of Cowper, after he had been foiled twice on the same day in his attempts at self-destruction, that 'God moves in a mysterious way his wonders to perform'—that he accomplishes his purposes by ways and means unthought of by man. A vivid impression came over his mind that he must, without delay, get upon the back of his horse, and with all possible speed reach New Haven, a place which he had not seen since he left college, and one that was many miles distant. As had been his custom, he was obedient to the impulse, and reached the place at the midnight hour of a dark night; and finding it greatly altered from what he had ever before seen it, and not descrying any suitable place to stop at, he was induced to ride to the door of a small house, in which he discovered a dim light at the attic window. After knocking and waiting a considerable length of time, he heard footsteps upon the stairway advancing slowly; soon it opened, and a man with a lamp in his hand, and with a stern countenance, and corresponding voice, demanded: 'What do you want here at this unseasonable hour of the night?' The messenger of life, as he proved to be, replied: 'I can scarcely inform you what I came for; I am a stranger here;' after which a short pause ensued, and the man with the lamp, in low and quivering accents, said: 'I will tell you what you came for—it was to prevent me from committing the atrocious act of suicide! When you knocked at this door, I was putting a rope around my neck to hang myself! Your knock broke the spell, and I have now neither desire nor power to destroy my life.' "

Do you not read in the Testament that Saul, mounted on his horse and at the head of a vast army, was bent

upon persecuting the Spiritualists of that day? He was
determined to ride them down and then exterminate
them. When he had very nearly reached the point
where the desperate conflict was to occur, the "scales"
began falling from his eyes, and he tumbled from his
horse to the ground. He was taken away by some friends,
and remained in an unconscious condition for some
time. When he came to "himself," he was a convert
to Spiritualism. He felt ashamed, and said he had
been entirely in the wrong—a short-sighted old sinner.
Now what is the difference between a modern Spiritual
case, put in modern language, and this ancient case
related in the New Testament? The law is identical.
A combination of truth-lovers in the Spirit-Land, who
are loyal to the Divine principles that regulate the universe, directly accomplish these results which men call
"special providences:" The facts of the overthrow and
rapid conversion of Paul are no more "mysterious,"
when analyzed in the light of modern Spiritualism, than
was the modern transaction of saving the lone man from
suicide. Neither can you say that the New Testament
facts are better substantiated by witnesses than are the
analogous facts of to-day. Here is another instance of
special impression:

AN ENGINEER IMPRESSED BY HIS GUARDIANS.

The following statement was published in the *Cale-
donian*, January, 1853, and is, therefore, testimony from
an editor not committed to Spiritualism: "Mr. Butter-
field, who was killed by the late unfortunate accident
upon the Passumpsic Railroad, for a week or two before
it occurred seemed impressed with the idea of some
impending evil. He mentioned his impression to his
friends, appeared downcast, and did not wish to run an

engine any more. Indeed, he had gone so far as to say that after that week he should leave the place he occupied on the road. He was ready to do anything else but, to act as an engineer. In passing up a few days previous to that on which the accident took place, before it was daylight, he whistled for the train to 'break up,' insisting that the fireman should go forward and examine the track; for he plainly saw the figure of a man moving slowly along. He also stopped at another, and about the same time, believing there was a man on the track. It turned out in both cases to be an illusion. If Mr. B. had been a timid and nervous man, these impressions would readily be accounted for, perhaps; but he was just the contrary—cheerful, cool, deliberate, and fearless—so far even as to be remarkable for these qualities. His impressions, viewed in connection with his well-known character and melancholy end, are certainly mysterious, and we do not know how they are to be accounted for, unless it be that evil is sometimes portended to man by a superior intelligence."

Spiritualists, instead of rejecting the Bible, find in its pages experiences that are identical with what in these days has become well-nigh universal. In the Apocalypse of John you read marvelous descriptions of events and awful things which would happen if there was a fair chance for such occurrences. Instead, why not take up some of the equally wonderful visions of Judge Edmonds? Why not read them and believe in them with the same unprejudiced eye and heart? If you look believingly back to Daniel or to Ezekiel to find prophecies, and if you next search the New Testament to find their fulfillments, why not also go faithfully back eight or ten years ago and find whether it be not true that Judge Edmonds had a vision in which the present American Rebellion was predicted and depicted with

wonderful clearness and exactness? He gave it out
with the conviction that it was simply a picturesque
representation of the great battle between Error and
Truth. But when it is read in connection with the
current political history and experiences of to-day, it
will appear as literal a prophecy of what has occurred,
and is occurring in this country, as anything prophetic-
al within the lids of Testaments:

THE AMERICAN REBELLION FORETOLD IN A VISION
BY JUDGE EDMONDS.

In the New York *Harmonial Advocate*, published
ten years ago, vol. 1., we find the following: " A
vast plain is spread out before me, and far in the distance a crowd of human beings. Above them is a vast
banner, outspread all over them. Its groundwork is
black, and its letters still blacker— the extract of blackness itself. The words inscribed upon it are : ' *Superstition, Slavery, Crime,*' forming, as it were, a half-
circle. Many of those beings have smaller banners of
the same material and device, which they hug closely to
their bosoms, as if part of their very life. All have
dark shades over their eyes. It is a sad picture—dark
and melancholy !

" A broad battle-field is being spread. And dark
beings, with their black banners, are coming out, arrayed
for battle with brighter ones. The contest will be fearful.
Those dark ones are confident in their numbers; for
they are as a thousand to one.

" But see! there comes from that bright mountain a
herald of light, and he cries aloud through all the
nations, ' Which shall conquer—Truth, Liberty, and
Progression, or Superstition, Slavery, and Crime? His
words are heralded in the air. How beautiful are his
looks! He is a spirit of light. His thrilling tones
infuse new light into the brighter ones, and they rise
with renewed energy, determined at last to conquer.

" It is a mighty contest, and is to determine the fate of nations.   All the base passions that have degraded humanity are awakening in their might, and rush on in their fury, battling for their very existence.

" A more brilliant beam of light shines from the faces of the progressed ones, showing the light and the life that are within them, and that are cheering them to the contest.

" Now, lo ! the view opens beyond the dark mountains, and behold there a glorious scene, where Love, Truth, and Wisdom are enthroned.   I see the beautiful landscapes, dewy lawns, winding rivers, and rich pastures, and an atmosphere so sweet and balmy, that the spirit might dissolve itself in its loveliness.   A race of spiritual beings inhabit there.   An unearthly radiance flows from the brain of each, and is wafted up by unseen zephyrs to make the glorious light which shines from behind the dark mountains.

" It is the home of Liberty, Truth, and Progression, and has sent forth its spirits, holding up that glorious banner.   It is upheld by their unseen hands, and it is their brilliancy which casts the radiance on the inhabitants below.   From that beautiful place they send forth spirits that whisper, in voiceless tones, encouragement and hope to those who battle in that strife."

You will find nothing in the pages of Scripture, I repeat, more exactly descriptive of events which have occurred years after the vision was given to the world. But this is only one of five hundred prophecies, many of which are in my possession, sent for publication from Wisconsin, Indiana, and Illinois, and from different parts of New England.   I know a gentleman who had rejected Spiritualism *in toto*—over five years ago—in consequence of these extravagant prophecies that there would be " a great war in this country," that " blood would flow," that the people " would have diseases," and that the " Government was to be broken," &c., &c. Prophetic communications of this strange character came to him very frequently. But the gentleman could not believe that we were to have "a war," in this peaceful country. He denounced the communications as unprofitable, and he would not further receive them. I met that gentleman not long since in this city, and he said : " I have repented. Those extravagant spiritual communications have all been literally fulfilled. There was no exaggeration in them."

A MOTHER IN THE SUMMER-LAND.

The gifted poetess, Mrs. Hemans, communicated, December 25, 1852, a picturesque account of scenes in the social life of the angels. The following is a brief extract concerning a mother and her child : " How lovely she seems ! As she glides along, she holds in her arms an innocent babe. What holy affection and chastened love is expressed in her countenance ! She pauses and speaks, and caresses her babe, and says : ' O spirit, I have left my home on earth, and I have met my beloved babe already, and how joyful I am. But will you not send back to earth and tell my dearly loved friends how happy I am, and how useless is all their weeping for me ? Oh, tell them I am learning the ways of peace and happiness ; that I am preparing to receive and instruct them when they shall arrive here ; that, although a mother's form has left the earth, a mother's love still shares all their hopes and joys. And oh ! bid them be hopeful and seek to have the love of God shed abroad in their hearts on earth, that I may be able to approach them on their entrance into the Spirit-World.' Happy, happy mother ! bearing her babe in her arms, who had been brought to meet and comfort her on her upward journey. But mark how she pauses to send back a word of encouragement and hope to those who are left behind."

On another point she says: "The spirit, on entering its next state, only becomes more awake—more sensitive to the realities which lie beyond its view; it but steps on another round of the ladder, which leads upward and onward to spheres of eternal love and unfolding wisdom.   And by thy life here, O man, dost thou make thy heaven fair and lovely, or thy existence dark and gloomy, until thou hast overcome thy errors by earnest labor."

In conclusion, I wish to call your attention to persons in the Spirit-World who take great interest in exciting the hopes of humanity, and in holding up the banner of Progress and Reform.   I have already given accounts of these public-spirited societies.   I will give one out of hundreds of instances, of a communication to minds on earth, who were at the time somewhat despairing:

TESTIMONY IN FAVOR OF FREEDOM.

In November, 1852, Judge Edmonds reported the following from the Summer-Land: "This is the day when Freedom shall be known among the sons of humanity.   This is the day when the chains shall fall from the oppressed spirit.   This is the day when the pulse of humanity shall quicken with an inward life. And now shall the arm of man be made strong.   Now shall the stream of truth brighten and deepen in its flow.   Now shall the light of heaven grow clearer and brighter amid this glorious dawning.   Prepare ye for the resurrection of humanity.   Stand ye up in the strength and majesty of spiritual manhood.   Let the scenes of earth no longer enthrall your senses and deaden the soul.   A voice calls you to a higher destiny.   It is the voice of Freedom breaking from the skies.   Listen! not with your ears only, but with your souls.   Listen!   And in the deep silence of your inner being may ye find its earnest whisperings to lead you up beyond the vale of darkness, beyond the tumults of this lower sphere—to lead you up—up—far up in the pathway of unfolded angels, and give you strength to mount on high, as the eagle soars, to breathe the air of Freedom forever and ever."

MATERIAL WORK FOR SPIRITUAL WORKERS.

" This world is not a fleeting show,
For man's illusion given ;
He that hath soothed a widow's woe,
Or wiped an orphau's tear, doth know
There's something here of heaven."

In relation to this subject it is deemed necessary to set forth three propositions :

First, that the material and spiritual universes are regulated by immutable laws. Law is the external manifestation of principle; a principle is the external manifestation of an idea; an idea is the thoughtful, loveful life of Deity.

Second, that man is endowed with a self-conscious power called Reason ; Reason is the harmony of all his faculties, including the elements of affection and intuition; by the exercise of this power he discovers the laws by which those universes are kept in unvarying order and irreversible harmony.

Third, that he is endowed with abilities and attributes to apply his discoveries to all the common conditions from which he proceeds, and of which he naturally is the governor and supreme head.

The Infinite fountain is composed of ideas. Nothing could be more abstruse, more metaphysical and abstract, than the truth which is hidden within this statement.

Most persons use the word "idea" according to the dictionary sense. An idea, in popular definition, is the form or conception or image in the mind of anything which you read about, or which you are thinking, or of something which is being related to you. To catch "an idea" is to get a definition of whatever may be presented for your reflection. That is not the sense in which the term is used in this discourse. The common definition is applicable to "thought." A thought in the mind is derived from a description, or by means of an object, a sound, a flavor, an odor; in short, whatever may address you, through your senses, will evolve a thought among your faculties, and if that thought is coincident with and exactly representative of that which excited it, the result is a truth, or else a fact. From an accumulation of such facts and truths all positive sciences are developed and established.

But such truths and such facts are not Ideas. If you have an idea, you have the essential life out of which all things and thoughts spring. Clairvoyance is the ability to discern things afar off by coming in contact with the *life* of things, realizing their inherent essences, becoming instantly acquainted with the intelligent principles by which things roll out from unfathomable depths into the phenomenal universe. An idea within vegetation causes all this variety, not only of the form and growth, but also of the distribution of the colors and of the arrangement of the atoms which are insepa- rable from and coincident with those colors, and of the odors also which come with the colors and out of such an atomic arrangement.

There is in the fields no chaos; nothing is left to

chance; all is system—harmony. Man's function is to
learn the principles and ideas contained in the source ;
to ascertain the scientific laws by which atoms, visible
and indivisible, come into their present arrangements;
and thence obtain the secret of the harmonies which
pervade all the ways and works of Wisdom. Having
made discoveries his next business is to reduce them to
what is called "science." Science regulates the perceptive
and intellectual parts of his mind—gives system, proportion, and regularity of action—by means of which
system of thought and precision of procession he makes
all his progress and expands his civilization.

But the restless, progressive mind soon exhausts his
discovery. He must go higher in the same direction,
make further discoveries, and thence more beautiful
expansions in Art, and more complete applications in
common things. Having applied his new facts to things,
he exhausts them, or loses interest in them, and thus
it becomes necessary that he should sow a new crop of
discoveries. So he charges the soil with new fertilizing
thoughts, and puts the old land to other uses. His
restless, progressive mind, needs it; for he is endowed
with a wondrous variety of powers and functions and
attributes, which must be gratified.

The consequence of such awakening is that his mind
is more than ever anxious for advancement. Humboldt
could not rest in his study after having investigated the
physical facts of a quarter of the globe. His discoveries were accurate, so far as they went; but they were
only doors to greater and grander things. Humboldt's
mind is not at rest to-day ; he is still traveling and dis-
covering sections in the " house not made with hands."

His immortal feet press other hills and mountains; his
new-lit eyes see other landscapes; and his large mind
is measuring new scenes of imperishable beauty and significance. Astronomers, too, do not soon rest. Having
discovered one planet, they must discover another. The
discovery of a hundred planets makes it necessary (for
the feeding of such hungry minds) that two hundred
shall be discovered.

The time comes for the application. Then millions
invest in one discovery. All men buy and read almanacs, because the discoveries of a few earnest, truthful,
scientific men have fixed the facts that regulate the
seasons. Suns and moons and stars rise and set so
mathematically and unmistakably accurate, that millions
of people, without a thought of skepticism, purchase
almanacs, regulate their business in-doors and out, and
conduct nearly all their agricultural and commercial
affairs, by means of the application of the discoveries
of a few able, earnest friends of science.

Men must go forward in their work of progressive
civilization; they have the grand example of the
expanded universe ever before them. The physical and
spiritual universes never fail in any of their functions,
because they are regulated by laws that never fail to
carry out the designs with which they were freighted
from the heart. Principles are the *life* of laws; ideas
are the *life* of principles; and GOD IS THE LIFE OF IDEAS.
No man or woman is spiritually-minded until he or she
has arrived at spirit. To be a spiritualist, is to nomi-
nate yourself by a mere term; to be *spiritual*, is to
possess a great soul-stirring and progressing Idea. A
spiritual worker is one who works from the essential

center—from Ideas, through the leverage of laws, using principles as the fulcrum over which the lever acts on any solid substance with which it comes in contact. Standing with the long end of the lever (a knowledge of natural law) in their hands, such workers can "move the mountains" which stand between them and the attractions and benefits of the future. Faith and works are inseparable. No soul is wholly destitute of faith in God. Truth and Love and Wisdom and immutable principles—these millions believe in even when they have no conception of a super-personal consciousness, God, or of an inter-personal love-essence called Nature. No man is destitute of faith in principles. Virtue and goodness and philanthropy, and whatever is high and noble, command the reverent love and respect of all mankind.

Those who possess Ideas are truly spiritual and progressive people. When they work, they work as flowers grow, from centers through their own organizations. Organizations come up here and there around them; they spring up and bring forth like harvests in the fields. Thousands, yea millions, are this hour waiting for such center-born organizations. The world's busy millions do not get at Ideas; they need temporary organizations and supporting substances. When a building is in process of construction, a scaffolding is a necessary part of the work. The carpenter calculates for a scaffold just as carefully as for the various materials out of which the building is to be made. When the structure is perfected, the scaffolding is removed. Even so when progressionists elaborate an idea and get it into the world, let them take down the

18

no longer 'needed scaffolding—the organization by which the idea was attained. Let the temple of Truth stand white and immortally beautiful before the eyes of all men. Let it be based upon the solid rock of scientific knowledge; let it be seen and felt by all; let it be inhabited by every one who feels the essential attraction. Must a man wear the clothes of his youth forever because they fitted him once? Or, must men always cling to their creeds and doctrines because by means of them they attained newer ideas in religion and a few finer habits in civilization? Let creeds, doctrines, definitions cease, as, indeed, they finally do with men and women of ideas. Distinctions vanish like the mists of morning in the presence of ideas that burn with such unutterable, glorious effulgence. But before you get to Ideas, such scaffolding as forms definitions, doctrines, thoughts, creeds, theories, systems, are necessary.

I never stop to battle with the size of the clothes that children must wear. Little patterns are natural to little folks. But I will remonstrate, and pronounce an injunction in the holy authority of Ideas, when I see grown-up persons still trying to keep in the garments of their childhood. Behold sectarians! See the little garments with which they swathe themselves, in which they are bound and cribbed and cabined and confined, and dare not move—miserable, fashionable mummies, grown up apparently as big feeling as anybody with brains—great, handsome looking ladies, and great, beautiful men, going into the churches and taking on the old garments and sitting in sackcloth without ashes —all of it a part of the machinery of childhood in old-time religion! It is plainly a demonstration that they

have not ideas. They are not free. The children of
light are free, because light is truth. Truth gives freedom, not only to your judgments, but also to your
affections—just as true and as free in your externals as
in your inmost. Freedom and purity are commensurate
and inseparable. Pure freedom comes from pure spirit.
License and unrestrained indulgence are the impulsive
freebootery of the impassioned soul toward that to
which it is directed. You can see lustfulness and
licentiousness in their disguises all through the world
—in politics, in society, and in the social relations.
Democratic notions of freedom are but the uncouth
prophecies of what one day will be the common experience of the people, accepted as divine, without any
thought of impurity, and incorporated in the unwritten
statutes of the universal heart.

But there are persons who, destitute of ideas, see
merely the forms which restrain and circumscribe them.
Such externalists think that the world is wrong, and
must be brought to their standard of right. That is
bigotry. Must I hate my brother because he enters the
Calvinistic church, and shun my sister in the Church of
Rome, because she does not think as I do? Ideas lift
us out of thoughts, above forms, above creeds, above
doctrines and systems, and breathe the spirit of
unbounded charity and good will.

Man's power is to discover—not to create. Man
can "create" nothing; he can only discover and apply.
Now man is destined to discover the laws by which the
Infinite has expressed imperishable harmony throughout
the material and spiritual universes—the discovery of
the laws by which all eternal harmony is established.

Succeeding this discovery will come the power to apply. This application will bring in new social, political, and religious relations, like that higher harmony which he beholds and worships in the physical universe. Thus man is endowed with a very vast mission of eternal uses to him. If men were destitute of ideas, they would be animals. If men were animals, they would be regulated by the harmonious laws of life and instinct which regulate animals. But mankind have ideas; therefore we are what animals can never be—capable of winging our way through the empyrean of light, through the universe of boundless freedom. I do not mean that we are free in any absolute physical sense. No man can fly outside of matter. No man can reverse or violate a principle; no man can mortally offend an idea; no man can disturb God. But man can by discovery bring himself into relation with ideas and principles and laws, and become physically healthy like the material universe, and spiritually healthy like the spiritual universe. Then, like them and with them, he is in harmony. Then he can bestow happiness, goodness, and divine strength on those about him. This seems to me to be as simple as any sum in the rudiments of arithmetic. No creations are made in music. Sounds exist through all the temple of Nature. Man can merely discover the laws of the Omnipotent by which sounds may be made to harmonize in different combinations. "Music" is the name given to the science thus discovered, and to the application of the science. But there is a central keynote by which all notes and chords are arranged and attuned.

Man's position with relation to all the kingdoms

beneath is the master chord, and the central key-note. If he is not attuned, his discords shiver through all the subordinate kingdoms. If he is in harmony, all the kingdoms of the earth feel, enjoy, participate, reciprocate, and justice reigns. Reciprocation is an expression of Justice. Distributive justice is seen in the equal expansion of natural reciprocation. From your own system outwardly into society send forth a good and just condition, and you thence and thereby expand into a state by which you can be fed and built up stronger and better.

It is necessary that many should be together in one place in order that all may be fed and nourished and made to grow by spiritual things. All persons testify against and naturally shrink from isolation, desolation, loneliness. They testify against those conditions because Nature, the Spirit-Mother of all intelligences, has determined that society shall be the form, the menstruum, the universal ocean in which all are molded, fashioned, and dissolved.

There is a social sovereignty which is just as obligatory as individual sovereignty. Some accept the doctrine that "individual sovereignty" covers and comprehends all—that a man is allowed by Nature to practice and carry out his individual preferences and decisions "at his own cost." But this doctrine is but *half* the story of man's relation to society. It is logical and true; but true only just so far as the half of anything is true. Social sovereignty is larger and grander, more perfect, more binding, and more divine; just as the ocean is larger, grander, more perfect and more divine, than the spring on the mountain's side or the

rivulet that starts from the quiet valley.   The life of
the individual is the stream that flows down through
the valley.   The ocean is made of all springs and all
streams, and all the rivulets that flow down from the
millions of hills hasten to seek their common social
level.   The ocean is the grand symbol of the Infinite
Spirit in which all minds dwell, and out of which all
things spring into manifestation and animation.
Geologists tell you that all things came from the sea.
First, the water was universal; then came the dry
land.   The first is society.   Society is universal; then
came institutions, organizations, dry land, solid places;
but the individual life is inseparable from the universal
society of mankind.   ·

The spiritual worker is one who sees the *idea*, who
catches the spirit within a *principle*, who works for the
harmonious molding of whatever is about him, and not
selfishly for personal advancement.   For example, look at
the question of "intemperance."   The Maine liquor law,
a matter of so much controversy some years ago, was
passed to legislate alcohol out of existence.   But the
moment you ascend to the presence of an idea, you discover that men are not constituted to be driven into or
out of existence.   Their appetites and passions cannot
be easily destroyed by legislation.   It is true that good
laws may hamper and destroy, to a great extent, the
vices of society.   But how do most of our best laws
originate?   They originate with legislators and gov-
ernors who have Ideas.   A few good men first proclaim the principle; then the office-seeking politicians
grasp it and say: "There is success in that creed," and
they take hold of it, and carry into politics what was

at first a glorious effort with a few philanthropic minds. In ten years the good thought, the good idea that was first promulgated, is degraded or obliterated. Then come organizations, scheming, wire-pulling, log-rolling, all these desperate and diabolical plans which selfish men without principle have instituted, in order to carry out what they supposed would be successful.

Then what is to be done? Why, the Moral Police, composed of men and women, must continue the work. They must go interior—close to the *life* of the law—to the Idea! They must stand upon platforms in public and in private places, and utter those divine thoughts which go deeper than the plans and policies of the world. They are commissioned to act just where and in proportion as they comprehend the idea of justice.

The spiritually-minded person is inspired. Justice is not a word; it is the name of a sacred principle. It does not mean that you must do what *I* think is right. It means that you must be *just ;* first of all to and within yourself. Your justice to me will be like your habitual justice to yourself. Suppose you meet a man who has indulged largely in intoxication. It is useless to appeal to him with " What will people say ?" He don't care what they say ; he is, perhaps, lost to that kind of respect; he does not seek it ; he has been too many times deceived and debauched. The sailor lies down in the hold of his ship, drunken as a beast. And the deserted, abandoned woman cannot be successfully appealed to from the social side of life. There is only one thoroughly practical way to reach those who have got so low in the bed of sorrow. It is by affectionately inspiring the hearts of such persons with the idea that they are immortal, and not only so, but that they have in them the resources of sweet happiness, and that those resources can be opened, and that you will faithfully aid them in such opening and to their consequent happiness. First assure the person that no reliance can be placed upon such help from you, or from God's angels, or from spirits in the flesh or out, until there is basis in the soul's will and aspirations. You reach the heart the moment you ascend to this point of wisdom. It is bringing justice to the person. The sad soul feels it. "Bathe your body, my friend; you have a beautiful body. You have feet and can walk; you have hands and can use your arms; you have eyes and can see; you have ears and can hear; and a tongue with which to speak the words of truth. Do you disregard these parts? Can you carry them day after day and respect them not?"

To such teaching the soul will listen. I knew a person who at once abandoned the use of tobacco when he discovered that his fine teeth were being spoiled. You might have preached to him the "Sermon on the Mount," or any other sermon, but nothing would reach and reform so soon as the appeal personal. The selfish are touched when you appeal to that which is in harmony with their mental conditions. Plenty of persons are lifted out of the mud and despair, not by an idea, but by a pair of comfortable shoes. It is so much better to begin with people where you find them. Show that you are a genuine brother or sister, that your interest is not selfish, but of divine ideas, and the heart. You work from the life of God that is within, from the idea of fraternal affection and resurrection. Preach resurrection to the dead, and tell them that the trump must sound. I believe that the trump is now sounding in the ear of every person in this wide world. The gospel of progress is the trump of the resurrection. The dead are all around you, and sometimes within yourself; that is, dead faculties, or thoughts "dead in trespasses and sins." If you are anywhere inert, you are to the same extent dead, and involved in this question of the resurrection. What portion of you do you feel to-day to be of no service to yourself or to mankind? That portion calls for the influence of some resurrecting mind. We should be to each other a thousand times more precious than we are; each should go out of self, and enter upon a broader and more glorious field of work. Do you wish to promote your own personal development? Then work for the personal development and happiness of others. Only on these terms will you advance. It is like the blacksmith unthinkingly developing his right arm. Does he swing the hammer with the intention of expanding and hardening his muscular power? He stands by his anvil, and you say "What a strong, brawny arm that working man has! What a deep, large chest! What great muscles about his shoulders!" "Yes," he replies; "I have continued at my daily work." He is healthily, muscularly, beautifully developed, because he has wrought with the iron for *others*, and not for the personal purpose of building upon his body.

Thus, if you work and pray for your own private spiritual development, you will not be developed very soon. If I unfold this lecture in your presence for any personal gratification, of the selfish kind, I shall be

neither gratified nor improved by what is uttered.   Do
a benevolent act for the express purpose of being publicly applauded for your organ of benevolence, and the
result will do you no good.   The motive would be selfish, and the action could not bring a blessing.   If your
existence needs expansion and your mind culture, then
promote benevolence and culture in others.   Go out of
your selfish circles into the society of the poor.   Never
think that because you go to the bedside of the sick,
you will yourself be cured.   If you bestow healthful
influences upon the sick, without undue exhaustion, you
are sure to be personally benefited.   Do good from a
selfish motive, and you will find a chemical poison at
the very heart, which will leave your nature as poor as
a miser is with his full coffers.

   The spiritual worker is one who, impressed with the
idea of fraternal love, and feeling its holy warmth in
the soul, goes right out into society with healing in his
wings.   Such a person goes and comes as a peace-
maker.   Natures of this stamp are commissioned from
the heaven of heavens to do unto others as they would
have others do unto them, and that, too, without a
thought of the golden rule.   They obey it because they
are as good as it.   They who so live and so act, are
constantly dwelling in that state to which they would
elevate all mankind.

   Man is destined to bring about in society the harmony of all the passions which are demons, and of the
appetites, too, which are unclean spirits, and the balance
of all the various discords of his mind, which are his
ever-present satans. Demons and unclean spirits are to
be vanquished, but only by the power of spiritual work-

ers who start from the throne of IDEAS.   No man can conquer a passion for tobacco, or destroy the force of any appetite, by merely acting upon it from his will. The soul and body are raised by means of an inspiration, toward health and purity, which reaches and buoys up the mind until the physical passion subsides and the besetting appetite departs.   Some minds attain this state by a sort of change in their physical or chemical growth; others reach it by means of what they call religious revivalism, or conversion.   But the cultured way to it is through the comprehension and application of Ideas.   The principal idea which exalts and equalizes mankind, without filling the individual with egotism, is that each is supreme head of all the kingdoms beneath; that the high function of each is to discover the unchangeable laws which give harmony and perfection to the universe; and finally to apply the teachings of those laws to all the kingdoms, powers, functions about him not only, but also to all the passions, organs, demons, satans, or appetites and discords within the temple of private being.   Mankind are destined to be "lords of creation," both materially and spiritually. What is possible to all, is possible to each, and *vice versa*.   All may become gentle, and useful, and beautiful, loving their neighbors as themselves.   None can live and work in this way, save the truly spiritual.   I know that such souls are in the churches, at the bottom of all religious organizations.   They are the *spiritual* men who first realized IDEAS.   John Wesley, John Murray, John Calvin—these, and many who are visible all the way down the steeps of time, wrought from the life of Ideas.

Let us, therefore, concern ourselves not deeply with organizations and instruments of labor; for, with true Ideas, helpful organizations will inevitably come. Thus every wholesome organization comes up. An idea starts the principle; the principle divulges the law; the law dictates the method. An organization, consequently, is inevitable. Individual labors for mankind will bear "good fruit" when governed by the inspirations of Ideas. Such labors may be distributed and imitated throughout parts of civilization. Great philanthropists slumber here and there waiting for some occasion to resurrect them. Act well the part of a spiritual being; be faithful to what is true and good; the future will take loving care of both itself and you. This is the heavenly rest that comes from true inspiration of ideas. Think not of to-morrow, or next year; work *now*, living nobly in your day and hour. Be true to the life of truth. The life of truth is God. Be faithful ever, and true-hearted to all who love you. Years ago men used to say to me, " Well, Mr. Davis, if God is in this work, it will succeed, and if he is not, it will come to naught." Assuredly; nothing is more certain. It is the good, wholesome, old-fashioned notion about special providences in man's life. I like it. Yes, God is always in everything, and more especially *in the idea* of everything. You and your God may walk together. The Divine is not afar off, looking with a great eye to see whether you are doing the fair thing or not. An IDEA is from God. Work from its inspirations, and you and your God are ONE. Thus the inheritance of life becomes a perpetual blessing.

ULTIMATES IN THE SUMMER-LAND.

"There are some qualities—some incorporate things,
That have a double life, which thus is made
A type of that twin entity which springs
From matter and light, evinced in solid and soul."

By the term Summer-Land is meant a sphere of perpetual youth, where physical disease, which is discord, does not, because it cannot, prevail; where the effects of moral imperfections and evils continue; where the consequences of bodily and mental infirmities are visible, not in the constitution and appearance of that existence, but wholly in the constitution and appearance of those who possess those infirmities when they go from the earth to that land. This lecture is concerning the existence and appearance of "ultimates" in the Summer-Land. In a future volume I hope to be enabled, by means of new astronomical and picturesque diagrams, to illustrate what I cannot impart through language. There are yet very important lessons to be conveyed in connection with this glorious question of man's immortal existence. Word-painting cannot adequately impart to the mind what a few illustrations would beautifully and permanently impress. This question of "ultimates" in the Summer-Land, in con-

tradistinction to primates and proximates, may be very
plainly and briefly stated. In this discourse, however,
I can do little more than lay out the work.

To properly prepare your minds to see the ultimates,
it may be necessary first to speak of primates and
proximates.   Let us endeavor to strike the key-note to
which the music of the world is set, so that every ear
may hear and every heart understand the glorious
truths of eternal existence. We must search the volume
of Nature, because in its pages we find the gospel of
death and of eternal life. "The firmament," which is
overhead in the temple of Nature, "showeth handiwork." The firmament, therefore, is the open scroll of
the infinite volume. Its contents are the true "scriptures" for mankind "to search." Everything in artificial bibles which corresponds to the teachings of the
Scriptures in this expanded universe, is eternal truth.
Everything, on the other hand, which conflicts with
these natural scriptures, must fall among the tares and
errors, and be swept away by the billows of the rolling
years, with every other thing erroneous and outgrown
by man in his onward march.   Men never shrink from
errors that are burnt up and gone.   They only shrink
from the mortification and "the pain" caused at the
moment of their destruction. A new truth, like a dentist,
puts his iron grasp upon the old-time and loved error,
and pulls it out "by the roots" from its deep socket in
the brain.   Sometimes, indeed, the root of the error is
deeper—in very sincere and delicate affections.   Not
many pains suffered by human souls can be more intense
than the extraction of worshiped and costly errors
made sacred by time and important by the pomp of

circumstance and occasion. I know tender souls who shrink from the pain and mortification inseparable from such reformation, somewhat as cowardly men dread the tender caressing of the professional dentist.

But the trial must come sooner or later. Errors, however beautiful and gold-enameled by time, must be extracted from the human mind by the archangel of eternal truth. Search the scriptures of Nature—the handiwork of the firmament—for in them you will find the holy truths of eternal life. To understand the apocalyptic glories of the universe, study the Genesis of this God-inspired volume. The Genesis and the Exodus of the book are the Primates and the Proximates. The Ultimates you cannot see in this world except logically from the force of philosophical principles. In this lecture I may not speak of the Ultimates as I have seen them, and as you will see them one of these days, because time will not permit, and justice to the question admonishes me to present only the fundamental lessons for consideration. Humanity is now divided, by scientific men, into distinct races. Whether such division be correct or incorrect, we need not now stop to consider. They commence with their classifications —down or up, as the case may be—first, the Caucasian; second, the Mongolian; third, the Indian; fourth, the Malay; fifth and lastly, the Negro. This order is tracing mankind from what might be termed Ultimates, down to their rudiments, or Primates. Let us commence with the roots—with the Negro—and come up through the Malay, the Indian race, the Mongolian, and halt at the Caucasian, which civilizees have both the honor and the dishonor to represent. We leave this classification for the present, lodged in the mind.

Scientific men, whether correctly or not, have also classified the organic world into regularly ascending stages. No intelligent mind can long think chaotically. An intelligent mind, to make intellectual progress, must think as Nature compels him to think—from primates, on and up through infinite complications and endlessly successive combinations, to ultimates. Thus he makes progress both by the reflex action of education and by the legitimate and natural exercise of his faculties. Truly scientific men are constrained by Nature to think progressively up from the mollusk to full-blossomed humanity. They arrange the scale musically if they are inclined to music, or arbitrarily, if they are inclined to follow the routine of scholastic learning. They arrange it naturally and deductively if they have spiritual illumination. It is very much like the botany that is taught in the schools; there is the natural analysis of plants, and there is also the artificial method. Some commence naturally with the roots and go on upward, following the chronological order of its growth. The artificial analysis commences with the surfaces and works toward the basis. Nature compels man to investigate with system, because all is a perfect system. Whoso questions Nature aright, truly reads the scriptures which teach of God and eternity.

Nature, by scientific men, is studied and classified in her organic relations progressively. Commence with the lowest form of fish life; work up through the age of serpents; come to birds; study the marsupials; then the mammalia: then the quadrumanals, troglodytes, and the gorillas; then stop at home and investigate Man. I think the scientific world has not yet

taken its own position into the account; it has not
yet ascertained its own relation and importance to the
onward progress of the race. Not having done this, it
is overlooking the very key-note to which all the music
of the world's intellectual growth is set. I suppose
that this blindness is right, because Nature makes
science masculine, superficial, proud, exclusive, exact,
always on the surface, yet necessary to the world's
growth. But there is something more inspiring than
science, *i. e.*—Art. Art is but Nature in her "superior
state." Science is Nature reporting herself with material eyes and in "a common state"—always positive,
never designing to confuse chalk with cheese, never
intentionally calling a thing black when it is white.
Granite is always granite in the eyes of science. It
is natural, therefore, that science should decide that
man's life goes out like his breath when he dies.
Science very honestly, stoutly, sternly, godlessly says
that man does not survive the decay of his organs. The
religious world takes up the evidence not seen by
science. So far as it goes, however, science is the
world's grandest archangel—without wings, without a
heart for humanity, with only a front brain, having no
affections for theories, creeds, or philosophy.

But-Art comes to our relief. She comes from the
woman side of Nature. Art reports the most interior,
and unfolds the ultimates of the life of things. Music
can never be separated from art. Poetry and music
have pure affections. Painting is but another expression
of universal art. Science commences at the right side
and works leftward; art commences in the left side
and works rightward; thus they meet, and interlock,

and silver-chain together in their marchings. Art rises spirally toward heaven, but science continues horizontally with the earth; with its eyes upon the stars it rises not; for it sees only solid bodies reflecting light. Art alone interprets the light of the stars and gives the music to which all bodies are wedded. The magnificent beauty of the physical world is unfolded through art. Science respects art only so far as it will illustrate and develop the exactitudes of science.

Nature works in this wise and beautiful way. She starts her men, the masculine power, from the right, and her feminine elements from the left, and thence they work in opposite directions. Art moves upward until it reaches a certain elevation, and then it begins to draw its credentials from science. Then it lets down its buckets in the deep wells of exact discoveries, and draws up thence its best and most enduring lessons.

As spiritualists, as searchers for eternal life, we should become acquainted with both the right and the left hands of Nature. Let us contemplate nature in man and nature in woman; nature in God, and therefore God in nature. God commences with the right, and thence works leftward round and round, and circles over and over throughout infinitude. Nature commences with the left, and thence works rightward and reaches the ultimate center, and unites with the soul and mind in the fountain of all supreme excellence and glory. The two meet and flow through each other, returning and circling to and fro perpetually, the one being represented by Science and the other by Art.

The negro may be said to represent the left side of humanity. This statement certainly puts a new complexion on the subject. The negro starts from the left side, the Caucasian from the right, and the opposite races work leftward and rightward in all countries and in all history. The negro is artful and emotional. He represents nature in her senses; the Caucasian is nature in her brains and organs. The first manifestation of taste in the female nature is surface ornaments, display, colors, gems, eyes, teeth, personal presentation. This is the feminine power in the senses: the first manifestation of the left side attractions. The masculine commences with the brain and works into the senses, and scarcely ever gets out of them. If more men were out of their senses—in their superior condition—and had arrived at Art, "the world would be the better for it." Woman commences leftward and works rightward. She begins in the heart of things and expands and reaches to the surface-plane from which man started.

The middle or neutral ground is occupied by the transition races—say the Malays, the Indians, and the Mongolians. The middle ground, therefore, is occupied by these bridges, which connect the two sides of humanity. These three types in the organic world, I repeat, bridge over between the feminine and the masculine in ethnology, and in the interior attributes of opposite races. You have often seen the beautiful concentric lines of work in the shells on the sea-shore. All sea-shells are made with spiral lines; they can be constructed in no other way. What does it mean? It means that they are illustrations of Art, which commences from Nature's left side and works artistically. All the shells in the depths, caves, and grottoes of the sea are adorned with her glorious artistic impress and handiwork. But Man's art is not like the art of Nature. His art is science, a thoughtful child of the brain. He studies and works to find out how Nature made her shell, and fish, and birds, and stars. His aim is to imitate such labors. An egg is one of the most simple, wonderful, and beautiful works of Mother Nature. By the fullness and undulations of the large end, and by the spiral crinkles at the small end, an experienced eye can tell which is feminine and which masculine.

All forces meet and conspire in the human organization. You will find that all powers of mind come out in the highest types of the human race. But in the negro' you find what men call the sentiments and emotions. He fully enjoys his senses. Loving simple pleasure, he seeks it on the surface, but readily deepens by education. The Malay is very different. It is the Rhodent. It is the class of mind that seeks to live on others. It chooses a dark abode and burrows in the ground. The Indian, whether he be North American or Oriental, is very different. The squirrel and the raccoon, and the animals that live like them in the forests, represent the Indian, and they will live and they will die together. When Nature gets old enough to destroy all of the animals that live on nuts and acorns and berries and fruits of the field and the forest, and when she also destroys all that live upon the flesh of other animals, then will she be also old enough to seal the destiny of the Oriental as well as the western tribes of the streams and wildernesses.

But the system works onward. She next gets into the Mongolian. The Mongolian is represented by the quadrumanal. Horses, cows, dogs, wolves, and the domestic mammalia, correspond to this branch of the human family. The Caucasian world is represented by the European and the American. This portion of mankind pursues all parts of nature by science, and lays all existence under heavy tribute. The Caucasian subjects the world to himself. No representative of any other race has such pre-eminence. He eats freely of everything, breathes all atmospheres, enjoys all possible shades of pleasures. He pursues happiness through progression. The negro pursues simple life and pleasure through the senses. The Caucasian aspires after happiness, which includes all pleasure and is the white flower of every kind of obedience. Nature contributes freely from all her departments, and constantly yields to his persistent encroachments and innumerable discoveries. The Caucasian seems to be representative of the higher race to come. He expands into the universal Yankee, which is a newspaper epithet of much significance, because he is destined to become the climacteric development of the antecedent races, to expand by means of his energy and encroachments and infringements, all over the inhabitable globe.

The American does not become Europeanized. The negro does not cause the white man to be Africanized, except so far as imitation and temporary association go, and the upshot of it all is, that the African becomes Caucasianized in his habits, tendencies, and aspirations. The African is a simple child of Nature, filled with the sentimentalities of Art. The Caucasian holds up to him the banners of industry, of science, philosophy, nvestigation—opens his eyes to behold the temples of

learning and of universal progress. When a man sits
down to a table and partakes of beef, he does not
become beef, but beef becomes him. That is true of
the Caucasian world. The Negro, the Malayan, the
Indian and the Mongolian are walking and working
together—as none of them could walk and work singly.
The Caucasian shakes hands with them all. Bayard
Taylor is cosmopolitan, so also are other travelers who
feel the blood of America fully developed in their veins.
They go anywhere on the face of this planet, shake
hands with the people, and affiliate with them all as
brother associates with brother. The Negro cannot do
this ; the Malay cannot do it ; no Indian can do it ; only
the Caucasian goes all over the world and makes it contribute its riches to his science. He travels by the map
and the compass ; he steers by the north star ; and he
makes friends with science and philosophy. He subjects
all things around him in order to make of them so many
new instrumentalities of his greater expansion.

What does all this mean ? It means that the human
family ascends, through the gradual development of the
races, to the Caucasian world. It does not, however,
mean that other races are cast down into the earth's
chemistry, and thus lose their immortality at death. It
would be as reasonable to teach that the superior faculties of the mind live forever, while the social and perceptive faculties, which ally him to the interests of
creation, do not survive death. Man goes to the Second
Sphere with the ultimates of all his parts, portions, and
functions. So the Caucasian race goes into the future,
not as the only regal and royal product of the organic
world, but as a member of the family of races. The

ultimates of every race in the Summer-Land establish a community or a world of their own. So long as the individuality of a race can be extended through its organization, so long will that race continue to project itself into the history and experience of coming ages. The Caucasian man and woman can visit all the brotherhoods and mingle with all classes and families there.

Principles incorporated in his mind begin to develope themselves, and to link him sympathetically with all other races and brotherhoods. Thus extremes meet. The negro and the white man—that is to say, the African and the Caucasian, as left hand and right— are coming eventually together, and will friendly face like palm to palm. The star of empire goeth westward; will it not cross the Pacific, and connect itself with that eastern world whence civilization sprung? If the circuit is made and the connection perfect, it will be like a magnetic circle.

When civilization crosses from our Western borders and marches to the steppes of Asia, what then will happen? Europe will follow in the train, leaving the very place whence civilization started, to see where the Yankee is going to; but the old race never can catch him!

When this world is unfolded with a state of civilization all around it, it will then represent what is practically known to be the highest source of joy in the Summer-Land. Extremes and ultimates meet in the sphere to which we go at death. The left hand and the right—the male and the female elements of nature —are certain to meet there, if they do not meet before. Here they meet only on the surface; there they meet

from the interior. The Negro will never fully understand the Caucasian in this world; because the Caucasian will never fully understand the Negro; while the
races that come between these extremes will be neither
understood nor tolerated. Two races will have in this
world a long parallel career—the left and the right,
or the Negro and the Caucasian.

Nature insists upon having both left and right fully
balanced in one body. No Indian prospers on this continent, neither does the Malayan, nor the Mongolian.
Only the Negro can prosper in copartnership with the
Caucasian. I do not mean to teach that the races will
become affiliated and amalgamated each with the other.
The moment the opposite races touch perfectly, that
moment they take separate rooms in the Father's house.
They work for each other and through each other
without affiliation or loss of individuality. The Indian
is nearly related to neither race, and because he does
not affiliate with them as closely as others do, he drops
outward and goes away from among the races.

The two opposite races meet again in the Summer-
Land. Does not the Bible say that the "least shall be
greatest in the kingdom of heaven"? There are
Christians who sincerely believe that the person who
is here the most thoroughly "poor in spirit," will be
the richest and greatest there. You will find that
there is a deep meaning in this sentence. Does it not
mean that the left-race will be equal to the race of the
right-side? The greatest here will be the least there.
They that superficially exalt themselves, are naturally
abased, because the next step they take from a false
exaltation, is certain to plant them upon a lower position.

The Negro, starting from this left side of nature, and the Caucasian from the right, will in the Summer-Land represent two great opposite races. Men do not take their complexions with them. They take only the facts, which are indestructible—the consequences, the ultimates, the realities—not the primates, the fictions and the falsehoods. Ultimates are fully developed after death, and they are so developed that what here corresponds to Indians, Mongolians, and Malays, are there visible and distinguishable by many radical characteristics. •

In the Father's house there are "many mansions," because there are essentially different modifications of the human family. Each wants a comfortable, happy place in the Second Sphere. In the Summer-Land there are localities for all divisions and shades of the human race. There are always wings to great palaces. Middle places too, but grand side-positions invariably. The Caucasian world moves all through one wing, and the African world is free to move all through the opposite wing of the infinite palace. Nature is just as powerful and beautiful and eternal as God. God and nature work together; so Science and Art work together. The male and the female go on through all eternity. Intermediates also long continue. The principles that are at work artistically making the tiny shells upon the sea-shore, are eternal principles. They are working as faithfully in the higher spheres as within and upon the earth. They round out globes and make roads throughout the universe.

On some future occasion it may be shown what has ultimated and blossomed-out in the Second Sphere from

19

the various kingdoms organized on the face of the earth. How natural and beautiful is what men call "spirit!" How rational and philosophical is all that. men term "supernatural!" How entirely "at home," and not as strangers, will we all be when each has ascended to the Summer-Land!